DETOUR

RANDOM HOUSE WORLDS

NEW YORK

JEFF RAKE

D
E
T
O
U
R

a novel

ROB HART

Random House Worlds
An imprint of Random House
A division of Penguin Random House LLC
1745 Broadway, New York, NY 10019
randomhousebooks.com
penguinrandomhouse.com

LIBRARY OF CONGRESS CATALOGING-IN-PUBLICATION DATA
Names: Rake, Jeff author | Hart, Rob (Fiction writer) author
Title: Detour / Jeff Rake, Rob Hart.
Description: First edition. | New York: Random House Worlds, 2026. | Series: Detour series; 1
Identifiers: LCCN 2025020160 (print) | LCCN 2025020161 (ebook) |
ISBN 9780593871379 hardcover acid-free paper | ISBN 9780593871386 ebook
Subjects: LCGFT: Science fiction | Thrillers (Fiction) | Novels
Classification: LCC PS3618.A4346 D48 2026 (print) | LCC PS3618.A4346 (ebook) |
DDC 813/.6—dc23/eng/20250429
LC record available at https://lccn.loc.gov/2025020160
LC ebook record available at https://lccn.loc.gov/2025020161

International edition ISBN 979-8-217-30101-0

Printed in the United States of America

1st Printing

First Edition

BOOK TEAM: Production editor: Jocelyn Kiker • Managing editor: Susan Seeman •
Production manager: Samuel Wetzler • Copy editor: Laura Dragonette •
Proofreaders: Debbie Anderson, Emily Cutler, Alissa Fitzgerald

Book design by Debbie Glasserman

The authorized representative in the EU for product safety and compliance is
Penguin Random House Ireland, Morrison Chambers, 32 Nassau Street, Dublin D02 YH68,
Ireland. https://eu-contact.penguin.ie

To my family, who signed off on the pitch in the hot tub.
And especially to Joey, who gave it a name.
—JEFF

To Mrs. Noll, my seventh-grade teacher, and the first of
my teachers to tell me I might have a future at this writing thing.
—ROB

Two roads diverged in a wood, and I—
I took the one less traveled by,
And that has made all the difference.

—Robert Frost, "The Road Not Taken"

1

THWAITES

LOUISE DEARBORNE
NEWS1 BREAKING NEWS REPORT

"Scientists have confirmed that a massive piece of Antarctica's Thwaites Glacier has collapsed. The Thwaites has long been referred to as the 'Doomsday Glacier,' because its total collapse could cause a catastrophic rise in sea levels.

"Roughly the size of Florida, scientists first discovered it was losing ice at an accelerating rate in the 1970s. Each year, it contributes to four percent of sea level rise as it sheds billions of tons of ice into the ocean. Its complete collapse could elevate sea levels by two feet, which has the potential to put more than ninety-seven million people in the path of expanding flood areas.

"But the Thwaites also plays a vital role in the stability of the surrounding ice sheets. According to the University of Oregon's Glacier Lab, a complete collapse could destabilize the surrounding sheets, which has the potential to raise sea levels by ten feet, causing catastrophic global flooding.

"The piece that broke off is roughly the size of Rhode Island and is enough to set off alarm bells in the scientific community that a total collapse could happen in our lifetime.

"And now, as we approach the fall, denim jackets are back in vogue! Here's fashion correspondent Heather Kane with a special report on the best deals for every style . . ."

EMAIL
FROM JOHN WARD ·

Here we find ourselves. Ready to embark on a mission that will change the course of history. Not just human history, but our fundamental understanding of the universe. It should come as little surprise that I'm going to be the one to do it.

Which is funny, when you think about it.

Everything on my end is set. I would imagine it is on your end, too. I can say that because there's only one person in this entire world who I trust.

I've been thinking a lot about how this whole thing started.

Before the money, before the contracts, before the spaceships.

I mean the very beginning. Sitting in my bedroom as a child. Lonely, scared. Staring out my window, at the vastness of space. I needed to know what was out there. I needed to know how much bigger things were. It made me who I am. That desire to reach, to seek, to discover—it laid the groundwork for Horizons. For everything I've done with my life.

I knew there was so much more beyond what I could see.

We're ready to go, here. The press conference is tomorrow. Hopefully you see this beforehand. Good luck on your end.

Here's to changing the world, my friend.

RYAN CRANE
HILL EAST, WASHINGTON, D.C.

"FUUUUUUUUUUUUUUUUCK!"

Ryan Crane snapped awake. Purely on instinct, he fumbled for the bedside nightstand, trying to get to the biometric gun safe inside. But as he pulled the drawer open and glanced over his shoulder, the only thing he saw was Nina, on the other side of the bed, curled into herself so tightly she was shaking.

He hit the lamp, casting light into the dim space. Nina's face was twisted into a rictus of pain. Her skin covered in sweat, her strawberry-blond hair plastered to her head. Ryan reached over and put his hand on her shoulder. She was burning up.

Before he could even ask the question, she groaned and spoke through gritted teeth.

"Stomach . . ."

Earlier tonight, after dinner. Tummy troubles, she'd said. She thought it was gas pains, so she took some Tums. They put the kids to bed, and Ryan left her on the couch with a peck on the forehead so she could catch up on episodes of *The Great British Baking Show* and he could get enough sleep for tomorrow's early shift.

She'd looked uncomfortable, but she shrugged it off as something she ate.

This wasn't something she ate. She was gripping the lower right side of her abdomen.

Appendix, Ryan thought.

"Mommy?"

Scarlett was standing in the bedroom doorway, her hair hanging in wild tangles, wearing her *Frozen* nightgown. She was half-awake and looked more confused than scared.

"Honey, go to Teddy's room," Ryan told her. "Stay with him there. Mommy's tummy hurts real bad, but I'm going to take her to a doctor."

Ryan hopped off the bed and grabbed a robe to throw over Nina's shoulders, then slipped a pair of jeans over his boxer shorts.

"Mommy said a bad word," Scarlett said.

"I'm sorry, love," Nina said, straining to get the words out in a coherent and calming flow. "Please go to Teddy's room, okay?"

The little girl shrugged, muttered "Okay," and padded down the hallway. Ryan couldn't help but laugh.

That kid. Unflappable.

Nina yelled out again, grabbing a pillow and jamming it into her face to muffle the sound. Ryan pulled his phone from the charger and dialed

911. The call connected, and before the operator could say anything, he blurted out, "This is Ryan Crane, MPD, badge four six nine six. My wife is having severe stomach pain. Most likely appendicitis. We need an ambulance."

"Okay, I have your address here on Massachusetts Avenue southeast. We've had two major emergencies tonight, so it's going to take about fifteen minutes to get someone out there."

Ryan sighed. He could get her to the hospital twice in that time.

"Forget it, just notify Carter Memorial we're coming," he said, and hung up.

He attempted to guide Nina to her feet, but she could barely move, so he picked her up in his arms, maneuvering toward the door. She felt like a furnace. "C'mon, babe, we're going for a ride. You love it when I drive fast, don't you?"

She grunted in response.

At the stairs, he put her on the chair lift—he could dash down, get his shoes on, find his car fob, and be ready to go by the time she got to the bottom . . .

But when he hit the button, the damn thing whirred for a second and then didn't move.

Great.

"C'mon, sweets, I need you to stand," Ryan said, easing Nina to her feet and placing her hand on the banister.

"OkaaaaaayyyyyyyyyYYYYY," Nina said, the word morphing into a scream. She gripped the railing like a vise, and Ryan helped her with one hand, using the other to dial his next-door neighbor, Darnell, who answered with a groggy jumble of letters on the third ring.

"I have to get Nina to the hospital. Can you come over and stay with the kids?"

The call disconnected. By the time Ryan opened the front door, Darnell was bounding onto the porch in red flannel pants and a white tank top, nearly every inch of skin on his bulging arms covered in tattoos.

"C'mon, man, out here making me feel bad for not hitting the gym," Ryan said.

"Told you I'd train you. I think you're just lazy," Darnell said. "She okay?"

"Noooooo!" Nina screamed.

"You heard her," Ryan said. "Check on the kids and I'll call you in a bit. You good?"

"Whatever you need," Darnell said. "I'm working remote tomorrow anyway."

Ryan got Nina down to the curb, and for once, luck was on their side; when he'd come home from the grocery store earlier, he'd found a spot right in front of the townhouse, rather than down the block and around the corner. He opened the passenger-side door and gently lowered Nina into a sitting position, then slid over the hood and hopped into the driver's seat.

"Always . . ." she said, breathing through the pain, ". . . a show-off."

Ryan got the car started, made sure the street was clear, and swung into the road, cutting a hard U-turn.

"C'mon, that's why you married me," he said.

This late, there wouldn't be too much traffic; it'd be a quick shot down Potomac, onto 695, straight to Carter Memorial. Five, six minutes tops.

The only challenge would be if another cop saw him. Which reminded Ryan—he clicked on the police radio as he raced down the empty streets. He was met with a burst of chatter; there was a four-car pileup on 295 and a three-alarm fire in Columbia Heights.

That explains that. Busy night for the Metropolitan Police Department.

As Ryan tore through a red light, Nina leaned forward and screamed.

"It's gonna be okay, sweetheart," Ryan said. "You're a goddamn warrior queen. You gave birth to two whole kids. Remember Teddy?" Sixteen hours of labor—how could she not? "You handled that like a pro."

"Certainly didn't . . . feel that way . . ."

"Well, I was impressed."

"Yeah, I did all the work."

"I provided moral support."

"You did . . ."

Ryan reached over and grabbed Nina's hand.

"Hey, I love you," he said.

"Even more . . . than pizza?" she asked.

"Even more than pizza, babe," he said.

He looked across at her, at the woman he loved with everything he had. And it tore his heart in half to see her in this much pain. He wished he could take it from her. Carry it for her until they got to the hospital . . .

And then a horn blasted from somewhere to the left, an instant before headlights lit up the interior of the car.

He was approaching the quagmire of Pennsylvania Avenue, where he'd have to cut across a slight curve and two lanes of traffic—and saw a car barreling toward him.

And he didn't have the light.

The other driver managed to slam on their brakes as Ryan yanked the wheel to the right. There was a terrible screech, and even with the windows closed, he could smell the burnt rubber.

It wasn't close, but it could have been.

He needed to pay attention. As he approached the entrance ramp for 695, his heart racing in his chest, he whispered an apology to the other driver and then grabbed Nina's hand again. But he kept his eyes on the road.

"Almost there, sweetheart," he said. "Almost there."

PADMA SINGH
CAPITOL HILL, WASHINGTON, D.C.

Padma slammed on the brakes, narrowly avoiding the dark-colored sedan that barreled into the intersection in front of her.

The air in her lungs froze as she waited for the impact, but then it didn't come—the car turned hard, then sped away, and it was just her and the quiet street, her own car poking awkwardly into the cross street.

She reminded herself to breathe, taking a deep inhale, letting her head drop to the steering wheel as Taylor Swift sang about shaking it off.

Easier said than done, Taylor, she thought.

She looked back at the road. The light was green.

"Asshole," she muttered, before easing off the brake, letting the car roll forward.

Padma was glad she'd had that third cup of coffee after dinner. It meant she wasn't going to sleep for a little while longer, but at least she'd been alert.

She drove the final few blocks to her apartment building with her hands tightly gripped at ten and two, then guided the car down the ramp, where the license plate scanner registered her car and the garage door slowly lifted. She drove to her reserved spot, as always marveling at the gleaming luxury cars surrounding her—and a little embarrassed for how her decade-old Civic looked in comparison.

It took a moment to assemble the flurry of papers she'd unceremoniously dumped onto the passenger seat, some of them scattered into the footwell from when she'd slammed on the brakes. Once everything was secured in her bag, she headed out, stopping halfway to the elevator to click the fob on her key chain, unlocking the door and locking it again, just to make sure it was really and truly locked.

Inside the elevator she said, "Hi, it's Padma."

"Good evening, Padma," the AI assistant responded, in the same British accent that always slightly confounded her—why did the designer choose that for an elevator system in D.C.? Because British people sound smarter?

The doors closed, and the elevator began its gentle ascent, the glass walls offering an expansive view of the city.

She'd been hesitant about leaving her home and her family, all the way back in Brooklyn. But Ward really had spared no expense in terms of making her feel comfortable, putting her up in a luxury penthouse in the heart of Capitol Hill.

D.C. wasn't much to look at during the day, almost a little drab, but those government buildings looked beautiful lit up against the night sky.

At her last apartment, in Crown Heights, parking was a full-contact sport, and the front door was frequently broken. Then she had to climb six flights to get to her apartment. The food was better in New York, but she much preferred this.

As the elevator approached the top floor, she felt a little clicking at the back of her brain. She'd forgotten something. She didn't know what. A quick glimpse at her bag confirmed she had the essentials: laptop, paperwork, phone, key fobs, her limited-edition sparkling rainbow tumbler from Starbucks . . .

That feeling, though, just wouldn't go away.

Maybe it wasn't an item; maybe it was something she was supposed to do?

No matter. Nothing mattered right now.

Tomorrow was going to be a big day.

The elevator doors opened, and she stepped off. The camera above her door scanned her face, and the soft light around the handle turned from white to green. She pushed through, vaguely wondering if Brett was awake or asleep.

They'd met at NASA's D.C. headquarters the first week she started. A friendly lunch in the commissary followed by a few dates quickly turned into a relationship. Padma was pretty sure he said he was coming over tonight, and he was well aware that sometimes her work took her into the late hours. He didn't always have it in him to wait up, because as a statistician he was an early riser—typically in by eight and out by six—while Padma's research for Ward . . . well, the hours were basically unending.

Brett at times seemed to resent the fact that his newbie NASA girlfriend had somehow leapfrogged over him at the agency in terms of the import and secrecy of her position, but he never made an issue of it—which Padma appreciated.

She didn't see his shoes by the door. Maybe he wasn't coming over tonight. She dropped her bag and made her way to the kitchen, glancing at her plant collection as she went, which lined the walls and the shelves and nearly every free spot by the windows—the philodendron, the snake plants and elephant ear, the succulents and cacti. She loved her plants. She acknowledged it could be her imagination, but the air in her apartment felt cleaner.

She decided to scrounge up a snack, then maybe watch a little TV. Something to help her decompress and, if she was lucky, lull her into a few hours of sleep before her alarm went off.

The kitchen was all white tile and dark cabinets and gleaming surfaces. She kept telling herself she'd cook in there. Until then, she was happy to let Brett do it. He was so much better at that anyway. Cooking was something Padma had never really taken to; she preferred the ease and assurance of takeout.

And, as usual, the kitchen was spotless—except for a piece of paper on the counter.

Brett's handwriting: DINNER IN THE FRIDGE.

So he did come over. Maybe he wanted to hit the gym in the morning and decided it would be best to go home. He'd probably texted her with his plans. She hadn't taken her phone off "do not disturb" when she left.

That must be what she forgot.

Padma opened the fridge and her stomach dropped.

Nestled on the empty shelves was a tray of lasagna, covered in plastic wrap, with a small piece taken out.

That's what she forgot.

Brett's birthday dinner.

Which he said he'd make himself, he was just excited to cook in her kitchen, and all he wanted was to spend some quality time with her before the big day.

And she'd even worked extra hard this week to clear her schedule, but then the presentation for tomorrow, the slides, the color of it seemed . . . off to her. It was too bright, too feminine, and she knew that winning over a roomful of government officials was going to take something serious, so she'd spent hours futzing, changing the color scheme from deep purple to regular old purple to a royal blue.

In the process, she forgot about the birthday dinner.

Which, big picture, might have been for the best. She had meant to pick him up a present on the way home, too. Which, thinking about it now, didn't make sense; it was after midnight. What could she have bought? A Slurpee at 7-Eleven?

She picked up her phone and took it off "do not disturb," only to find a single text from Brett.

Good luck tomorrow.

Like the twist of a knife.

Brett was normally loquacious, especially in text—updating her on his day, his plans, how long he had to wait for a treadmill at the gym. That the only waiting text was three simple words spoke volumes about his feelings.

She considered calling him but knew her reasoning sounded ridiculous. Brett generally understood, but this one was hard to explain. *I needed to fix the colors.*

Every detail mattered. This wasn't just about a presentation. It wasn't only about the project she'd been working on for the last six years.

It was about the future of the human race.

It was about taking the next big step in the history of their species.

He might not think the color mattered, but it did.

It did to her, at least.

And it would to Ward.

How could she explain that?

And anyway, he'd be sleeping by this point.

Padma considered carving off a hunk of the lasagna but ultimately felt she didn't deserve it. So she pulled the bag of goldfish crackers out of the pantry and stuck a handful in her mouth.

And she thought about it a little more.

Royal blue. She'd initially rejected it because it felt too formal. Like every other presentation this group of people had ever seen. The deep purple felt different. It played well against the deep blacks of outer space. And Ward had already signed off on it; would he be upset to find that the entire thing was a different color now? Maybe.

She sighed and poured herself a glass of seltzer. She ensured the handouts of her white paper—some of the journalist dinosaurs still preferred hard copies—were stacked, ready, and stapled for tomorrow, carefully arranged on the counter, and then pulled out her laptop, ready to revert the slides from royal blue back to dark purple.

But burnt orange could be nice, too . . .

THE CASE FOR TITAN
BY PADMA SINGH

EXECUTIVE SUMMARY

For decades, humanity has looked to Mars as our next stop in the solar system. Over the last several years, technology in ion propulsion drives has increased exponentially, shortening a potential trip from years to months. As such, politicians and the general public alike have been asking: When will we finally step foot on the Red Planet, made famous in these circles by scientists like Carl Sagan and writers like Ray Bradbury and Andy Weir?

But as the scientific community is widely aware, Mars is an inhospitable, barren desert. While we know the planet has ice, and therefore water, the effort of accessing that resource remains monumental. Not to mention the planet's thin atmosphere, which would not protect humanity from cosmic radiation.

To survive, humans would need to wear shielded, pressurized suits. And to thrive, we would have to spend billions just on mining equipment to dig up resources and construct underground habitats.

We're looking in the wrong place.

We should instead be looking past Mars, to Saturn's moon Titan.

Titan is roughly half the size of Earth, and it's so far out that a year on Titan would be roughly twenty-nine years on Earth. But it has a nitrogen-rich atmosphere, 50 percent thicker than Earth's. The surface may seem inhospitable: covered in ice as hard as granite and sand dunes made of plastics, with lakes of ethane and methane. The atmosphere is hazy, limiting visibility, and the amount of sunlight that reaches the surface is lower, creating a perpetual orange twilight.

But humans wouldn't need pressurized suits; they'd need only temperature-controlled suits to combat the freezing cold. The atmosphere would provide ample protection from cosmic rays, meaning habitats could be built on the surface.

Those plastic dunes could be used to construct surface-level habitats, and the ethane and methane lakes could power them. Because of the weaker gravity, a rocket launching from the surface of Titan would take far less fuel than it does on Earth—and fuel is already in ample supply there.

In order to settle a new world, we need accessible resources, and we need to protect the first humans to take that step. We can do both of those things on Titan. I believe, over time, smaller settlements can be linked together, and in the space of a few decades, we could have a thriving colony living and flourishing on Titan's surface.

Thanks to Horizons' newly developed ion thrust engines and *Starblazer,* the ship John Ward has been constructing in low-Earth orbit, we could be there in a year—as compared to seven under previously available technology.

In the following paper, I will make the case that Titan, not Mars, should be humanity's focus as we look beyond Earth . . .

JOHN WARD
NASA HEADQUARTERS CONFERENCE ROOM,
WASHINGTON, D.C.

John Ward let the air out of his lungs in a long, controlled exhale. It served to slow his heartbeat a bit. A tiny moment of meditation before the show started. That he was surrounded by not only Padma but also two of his handlers and three security guards distracted him not in the slightest. White noise, after all these years.

He turned to Padma, who looked like she hadn't slept in days. Which was probably true. The girl was a mess—her raven hair looked like it had been half combed, and her pink blouse was buttoned wrong.

But she was brilliant. That's all that mattered.

"Missed a button there," Ward said.

She looked down, gave a tiny yelp, and turned to reconfigure her top. When she turned back, she looked on the verge of tears, so Ward did what he always did in these situations. He put his hands on her shoulders, looked her deep in the eyes, and said, "You've got this. I believe in you."

Truth was, he could foresee a scenario where this didn't work out the way he'd hoped it would, but he wasn't about to tell her that.

Instead, he added, "You are literally the world's foremost expert on this subject. No one on the planet is more deserving to be in this room—or on this journey—than you."

The affirmation worked. As soon as the words left his mouth, she stood a little straighter. A little more steel in her spine.

"Do we really have to do this?" she asked.

Clearly, not enough steel.

"We've been selling this to senators and subcommittees for months," Ward said. "The president or Congress could always pull funding at the last minute. The point now is to go out and sell it to the public. Tell the story. Get them on our side. None of these goons ever lifted a finger on anything unless they thought it'd get them some votes. So let's go get them some votes."

Which was partly true. If Congress pulled funding, he'd have to put up more of his own money and it would set them back by at least a year. But the partnership with NASA meant access to a lot of the equipment he needed.

And the potential that it could earn *him* some votes didn't hurt.

Padma nodded, determined now. "Okay. We can do this."

"That's the spirit," he said. "Let's go save the world."

With that, Ward nodded to a handler, who promptly pulled aside the curtain to a packed conference room.

To the left was a massive table, every seat taken—reporters with notepads and tape recorders at the ready. The back wall was lined with cameras and television news correspondents.

To the right was a small dais, a lectern, a screen, and Henry Owens, administrator of NASA, wearing the same sort of ill-fitting government-issue gray suit that was popular with the older white male demographic of politician in this town.

Ward was happy about his sartorial choice—a deep purple wool canvas suit with a matching shirt underneath and brown loafers. No-show dress socks—purple, too, because it mattered to *him*. The color of the suit matched the color in the slides Padma had sent over, which he hoped some of the style blogs would pick up on. It was always nice to diversify coverage sources. Get the fashionistas on board, too.

Henry Owens clapped like a seal as Ward made his way to the lectern, where he accepted a handshake and a pat on the back as his security guys efficiently spread throughout the room. Ward was used to applause, but instead the room was filled with the sound of clicking cameras and shouted questions. He put his hands up and then lowered them in a "calm down" gesture.

"We'll get to all your questions, don't worry," he said. "Now, some of you may know me, but just in case, I'm John Ward, CEO of Horizons . . ." That drew a few chuckles from the audience. "And I'm here today with an exciting new plan that, frankly, I'm not smart enough to explain to you, so I'm going to let this young lady take the wheel. Padma Singh is a brilliant astrophysicist and the world's leading expert on the Titan colonization plan."

Damn it, meant to say "settlement," not "colonization"; "colonization" has negative undertones, he thought. *Okay, carry on . . .*

"So," he said, waving his hand like a magician, "I'll let Padma talk to you for a bit and show you some pretty slides, then I'm going to come save her from you lot of vultures. Whaddaya say?"

Again, no applause.

It's okay, not the audience for it.

He stepped aside from the lectern and let Padma get settled behind it. The lights dimmed, and the screen sprung to life, showing a glowing brown orb speckled with yellow.

Saturn's moon Titan.

And the slides were burnt orange now. Damn it. She must have changed them . . .

"Ladies and gentlemen, we're here today to talk about establishing the first human colony outside Earth," Padma said, her voice cracking only slightly.

But after that, she seemed to find her center, and she dug in.

Ward was happy to step back into the shadows and let her work.

And he had to hand it to Padma. Once she locked in, she was spectacular, selling the plan with an incredible amount of passion and confidence. To think, all those years he wasted researching Mars, and then he stumbled across one profoundly insightful paper she wrote, and here they were . . .

"So, to sum up, the purpose of the mission," Padma said, "is proof of concept. We're going to show that the transit time is not only achievable but safe. I'll be able to take readings on the moon once we're there, but we'll also leave behind a satellite that will collect data for us. The mission will take two years, round trip. But another two years after that, we should be prepared to launch a supply shuttle to Titan, and within a few months after that, the first manned mission to the surface."

Padma looked over to Ward, who nodded and stepped to the lectern.

His time to shine.

"Look, it's 2031 and the Earth isn't getting any cleaner," he said. "We all saw what happened with the Thwaites Glacier. The climate has officially reached one point five degrees Celsius above preindustrial levels. Current models show that in another ten years, many parts of the planet could be uninhabitable. Mass migrations out of coastal zones are already destabilizing governments. No matter what we do to reverse the effects of climate change, we have to accept that we turned the knob on the thermostat and then broke it off. Sooner or later we're going to have to look beyond our planet. This is the first step to doing that. This is about taking the next great leap for mankind." Ward eyed the assembly, hoping for at least some recognition of the Armstrong reference. Crickets.

Tough room. He clapped his hands and then raised them to the crowd. "Okay, questions?"

He was met with a cacophony of shouts.

"Since you're not going to behave, I'm going to call on you one at a time," he said, then pointed to a young man with a mop of brown hair. "Yessir, with the hair."

"Queally, *LA Times*. Are you really expecting us to buy this, like it's not some kind of publicity stunt for your presidential run?"

Ward forced a smile. "Coming in hot there. Yes, I'm running for president, and yes, this may win me a couple of votes among the *Star Trek* fans, but that's not the point. The point is scientific exploration and American greatness." Ward went fishing for a slightly friendlier face and found Susanne Matthews from *The Washington Post*. "Hey there, Suzy?"

She stood and arched a harsh blond eyebrow. Right, she didn't like to be called Suzy. "This is a question for Mr. Owens. How much money is NASA investing in this mission, exactly?"

Owens stepped to the lectern with a look on his face like a dog who'd made a mess on the lawn. "Look, we've always valued the options and flexibility that our public-private endeavors have afforded us. It's hard to put a number on it, especially when you look down the stream and consider the return on investment, in terms of new technologies and access to alternative energy sources. But . . . probably in the range of three billion dollars."

Ward rolled his eyes as the room exploded. Owens tried to yell over the din: "Which Mr. Ward is matching dollar for dollar!" But it seemed to be lost.

After a moment the *Post* reporter got control of the room. "So you're investing three billion dollars of taxpayer money into a vanity project for a billionaire who's running for president? And you're basing this on a paper written by . . ." The reporter glanced down at her notes. ". . . I'm sorry, Ms. Singh, what and where did you study?"

Padma swallowed nervously and stepped up to the microphone. "Astronomy and astrophysics at Columbia. I'm starting my fourth year in the PhD pro—"

The *Post* reporter interrupted: "You don't even have a doctorate?" He turned to Ward. "You can't be serious."

Ward was about to speak when Padma put her hand on the mic, a look of grim determination on her face. "Whether I have the word 'doctor' in front of my name is irrelevant. Ward saw something in me, and that's why I'm up here. Because I believe in this project. And you can call this whatever you want, if you think it's going to mean a good headline. But the reality is, we need this mission. Humanity needs this mission. Besides needing to find new habitable homes, some of the greatest technological innovations of our time came from space travel. Water purification systems. Artificial limbs. Baby formula. Smoke detectors. All sprung from research related to space travel. We took our eyes off space, and we've stagnated. If one single invention comes out of it that matches the usefulness of any of those things, this will have been worth it." She paused, then with grave sincerity said, "But beyond all that, what we learn from this mission might just save our children, and their children."

The room seemed to settle a little after that. Part of it may have been Padma's conviction. Part of it might be the fact that the press felt better beating up on Ward than it did on her.

Either way, a win is a win, Ward thought.

He went searching for a friendly face. Paul Simonson, from CNN. He was always good for a softball. "Paulie, what have you got?"

"I've got sources telling me about a report that appeared and suddenly vanished regarding the viability of this mission," he said. "Care to comment?"

Well, that was a swing and a miss. Ward considered his words carefully, poker-faced, as the legion of journalists and even Padma looked on in curious anticipation.

"I've pored over thousands of reports related to this mission," Ward said. "Tens of thousands. If I were still printing on paper, it'd have taken down an entire forest. Stuff gets lost in the shuffle, so I'll tell you what: If you can tell me specifically what you're asking about, give me a ring, okay? Until then, I can't even begin to speculate."

That was followed by another volley of shouted questions. Ward smiled and put his hands up. "All the time we've got for today. Thanks so much for coming out."

With handlers and security promptly on the move, Ward hustled Padma back out of the room, then down a corridor and into the unmarked conference space they'd used as a greenroom. He took another long breath, tried to let it out slowly.

It did nothing to slow his heart.

"How'd we do?" Padma asked.

"Honestly?" Ward said. "Could have gone better."

STYLESHARK.COM
WARD'S TITANIC FACE-PLANT IN EGGPLANT

Wannabe presidential candidate John Ward should invest some of his money in a fashion consultant—the expense of his suit was rivaled only by its garishness, sort of like he wrapped himself in an old eggplant.

The look wasn't helped along by the fact that it clashed with a ridiculous slideshow—burnt orange, yuck—about spending billions of dollars—specifically ours—to go to one of Saturn's moons.

Giving the presentation alongside a woman who looked like she dressed herself in the dark (she's an astrophysicist, so we'll cut her some slack by not plastering her name all over the internet), Ward got a chilly reception from the press and walked out with his face nearly the same color as his suit.

Wethinks he ought to worry a little less about moons and a little more about how he leaves the house in the morning. Seriously, is anyone else as exhausted by this man as we are? When is he going to realize that we're not laughing with him . . .

RYAN CRANE
CARTER MEMORIAL HOSPITAL, WASHINGTON, D.C.

"Mr. Crane?"

Ryan jerked awake from where he'd been dozing in the waiting room. It was a wonder he'd even fallen into that twilight space, given the harshness of the fluorescent lights and the chair that seemed to be designed to inflict pain.

He looked up to find a tall, absurdly handsome man in a white lab coat—square jaw and salt-and-pepper hair, with a twinkle in his blues.

"I'm Dr. Antonio Segura," he said, smiling and extending his hand. "I performed the surgery on your wife."

"I hope she was under the whole time," Ryan said. "You look like one of those TV show doctors. Last thing I need is my wife waking up and running off with you."

Segura smiled in a way that made Ryan think people often commented on his appearance.

"I'm sure your wife is quite taken with you," he said. "She's doing fine, by the way."

"Kinda figured. You didn't have a bad-news face on."

Segura took a breath. He was probably tired. So was Ryan, and he dealt with difficult emotions by plastering them over with humor. Which not everyone liked, but it worked for him. And the truth was, he'd spent the night absolutely terrified. Appendectomies were routine, Carter Memorial was a good hospital—but sometimes things went wrong.

"How'd the surgery go?" Ryan asked, trying to be a bit more serious.

Segura sat on the chair next to him and folded his hands. "Very well. Our preference is to do it laparoscopically, which means smaller incisions. Given the advanced stage, we were worried about a rupture, so we had to do an open surgery. The only difference is a slightly bigger scar, and we may want to keep her one more night, just to keep an eye on things." Then the doctor laughed. "I have to tell you, your wife has a high tolerance for pain. Most people come in well before that."

"She's a hell of a woman, and she can put up with a lot," Ryan said. Then he smiled. "After all, she married me."

Segura laughed again. "I can see how that might take some degree of patience."

"So can I go in and see her?"

"She's sleeping right now, and she will be for a little while longer."

"Okay then," Ryan said, trying to rub the sleep from his face. "Where can I get a good cup of coffee around here?"

"Not in the cafeteria, that's for sure," Segura said. "There's a place down the block. TradeRoast. They're usually a little busy around this time, but it's worth it. Good food, too."

Ryan felt a grumble in his stomach at the mention of something to eat. Coffee and a muffin sounded really good right about now.

"Okay, doc," he said, shaking the man's hand again. "Love of my life in there. Thanks for taking care of her."

"She did great," Segura said. "When you come back, if I'm not here, the nurse will go over the aftercare. But just remember, plenty of rest and fluids, and easy on the canoodling for a bit."

With a smile, the doctor hustled off. Ryan headed for the front doors of the hospital and stepped into the blazing sunlight. It was the start of September. He remembered when September brought the promise of temperate days and cool nights; now they were lucky if the mercury dipped below 90 before October.

In the morning heat, he felt crusty—unshowered, unshaven, wearing a pair of jeans that may have been dirty, a T-shirt, and the closest pair of boots he could find. He scratched his face and considered driving home to check on the kids, but he didn't feel good about leaving Nina. He wanted to be there when she woke up.

As he strolled down the block, hoping it was the right direction, he called Darnell, who answered on the second ring.

"How's she doing?" he asked.

"All good," Ryan said. "She's sleeping now. How are the kids?"

"Teddy ate. Got him downstairs just fine. He's doing some cool drawing. Scarlett has me watching *Frozen 3*. Man, this movie is good."

"I prefer the second one, but hey, there's much crappier fare she could be subjecting you to," Ryan said. "Listen, Nina's still out, and . . . ."

"Dude, we good," Darnell said. "It's a quiet day for me, you know I don't mind hanging with the kids."

"And they're okay?"

"They get it," Darnell said. "I told them their mom was fine and you were with her and she was with the best doctors in the world. Man, you got some good kids right here."

"They're just good to you because you know where we keep the real snacks."

"Whatever works."

"Exactly. I owe you, bud."

"You always get my back, I always get yours. Do your thing and let me know how it goes."

"Okay, can I talk to Scarlett?" Ryan asked.

There was a shuffling sound, and then Scarlett's tiny voice sounded through the phone.

"Hey, Daddy," she said. "Mommy is okay, right?"

"She's fine. She's sleeping now. More important, are you taking good care of Darnell?"

"I'm mad at him," she said.

"Why?"

"Because he said I could have some candy but I wanted more candy and then he said no." Ryan could hear the pout on her face.

"Well, kiddo, the way you eat candy, you're literally going to turn into candy, so I think he made the right call. Listen, I love you, tell Teddy I love him, and I'll let you two know what's going on soon, okay?"

"Okay, Daddy."

Ryan waited a moment, thinking Scarlett might pass the phone back to Darnell, but she just ended the call. He laughed and stuck the phone into his pocket, in time to look up and see a gaggle of reporters outside NASA headquarters, the massive concrete-and-glass behemoth across the street. Must be some kind of event or something. The reporters were surrounding someone who seemed to be trying to get to a black SUV parked at the curb. A very expensive luxury SUV, so probably not a politician.

But then his attention was diverted to a beat-up white delivery van slowly coasting to a stop across the street.

Twelve years on the job, and Ryan had developed a pretty good sense of when something bad might be about to happen.

The sounds of the street—the traffic, the shouting reporters—all of it faded as his focus narrowed on the van. From where he was standing, he couldn't make out the driver. The window was tinted.

It sat there, idling. Not putting on its flashers. No one hopped from the back to deliver something. It wasn't branded. The paint was scratched, and the engine was heaving; it was old, in disrepair. Weren't a lot of old vans in a state of disrepair cruising around this neighborhood.

He glanced over at the scrum across the street and caught a glimpse of a tall, handsome man in the middle of the crowd, wearing a purple suit.

John Ward.

Things were starting to add up.

Ryan didn't have his service weapon on him, and his personal gun was stashed in the bedside drawer at home. He hadn't thought to bring it, and he suddenly wished he had it. Not that he liked carrying a gun around with him—the burden of it always felt a bit too heavy—but better to have it and not need it.

As he glanced around for some kind of makeshift weapon, the side door of the van slid open.

A man stepped out wearing a black ski mask, toting an assault rifle.

Ryan immediately darted to the right, behind a parked car and outside the gunman's field of view. No one seemed to have noticed yet. The man was carrying the gun close to his side. Even the cars screeching to a stop in the street to keep from hitting him—no one seemed to notice the depth of the danger yet.

The man drew closer to the crowd and raised the gun, taking aim. Being careful. He wasn't planning to fire indiscriminately.

It was a gamble, but Ryan could work with it: he needed to create some confusion. He put his hands around his mouth and screamed at the top of his lungs, "GUN!"

That did it.

The gunman paused, wondering where the shout had come from. Ryan had ducked behind a stopped car and was slowly working his way over, getting closer while staying out of sight.

But the screams now cutting the air told him people had seen, so hopefully Ward would duck for cover. Ryan made his way around until he was situated behind the gunman, who was whipping his head around in confusion.

Ryan went in low, from behind, stepping forward so his foot was between the gunman's legs. Then he leaned down, grabbed the man's ankles, and yanked up. The man went airborne before coming down face-first on the pavement with a sickening *crack*.

Ryan grabbed the assault rifle and whipped back toward the van. There was another person climbing out now, also carrying a rifle, but she was fumbling with it, like she didn't understand how to use it.

"MPD, get down on the ground *now*," Ryan shouted.

The woman's eyes went wide behind the ski mask. She tossed down the assault rifle, hurled herself back into the van, and pulled the door closed. Within seconds the van roared to life, and it tore down the street, weaving between stopped cars until it struck a streetlight, the engine still gunning with the car at a full stop.

Ryan turned back to the gunman, who was lying on the ground and groaning, cradling his face, blood seeping between his fingers. The scene was under control. Ryan immediately threw the gun down and put his hands up; he wasn't in uniform and didn't want any first responders approaching the scene to mistake him for the shooter.

Within moments, two cops were coming toward him, guns drawn.

"Get down, get down!" they screamed in unison.

"Ryan Crane, MPD! I'm a cop!" Ryan shouted back, and he slowly lowered himself to his knees, hands up.

The cops got closer, and Ryan recognized one of them: Dan Parish, one of the younger department hotshots who would do or say anything to make a name for himself and climb the ranks.

Parish stopped, pointing his gun down at the ground.

"Crane," he said, barely hiding his disdain.

"Yeah," Ryan said. "Nice to see you, too. You're welcome, by the way."

JANET WILLIAMS
CNN BREAKING NEWS REPORT

"Two days ago, a potential bloodbath was averted outside NASA headquarters in downtown D.C., and tonight, we have exclusive information on the motives behind this terrifying incident.

"Mason and Ivy Cavendish, twins from Butte, Montana, drove to D.C. with the intent of killing billionaire Horizons CEO John Ward. The normally secretive Ward doesn't often appear in public, and authorities believe the perpetrators were using this as an opportunity to catch him out in the open and unaware.

"Police recovered a manifesto from the Cavendishes, explaining that Ward's plan to devote resources to space exploration ignores and exacerbates the impact of global climate change here on Earth. They charge that Horizons is covering up information that, we quote, 'puts the fate of the planet at stake.'

"CNN has reviewed this document and made it available on our website. We have spoken to several independent experts and have not been able to verify any of the assailants' claims. Police sources are also exploring their connection to a dark web conspiracy forum.

"The Cavendish siblings were stopped by police officer Ryan Crane, a twelve-year veteran of the MPD. He was off duty but near the scene when the incident occurred and was able to subdue Mason while Ivy attempted to flee.

"Crane, a married father of two from Hill East, has thus far declined to speak to reporters.

"Ward, meanwhile, has experienced a surge in public opinion, with new light and interest brought to his Titan settlement project, which could launch within a year and explore the possibility of establishing a human colony there.

"A recent Quinnipiac poll shows that, while still considered an underdog in the presidential race, Ward has experienced a bump of four percentage points."

JOHN WARD
PENTHOUSE SUITE, DUPONT CIRCLE HOTEL,
WASHINGTON, D.C.

The glass coffee table shattered.

Ward winced. He hadn't meant to break it, only put his feet up on it, but he should have taken his black Ferragamo boots off before he did so.

And calmed the fuck down.

He'd made eye contact with the shooter for only a split second. But in that instant—the assault rifle aimed between his eyes—Ward felt fear, for the first time in his life.

Camila Reyes came hustling into the room, a look of bewildered shock on her face. Then she smirked when she saw the sound was just a result of his clumsiness and nerves.

She pointed up at the television. "Thought you'd be happy with those numbers."

"It was an accident," he said self-consciously, muting the TV. He looked around the opulent suite, last occupied by a Saudi prince—it took up the entire floor of the hotel and boasted four bedrooms, two full bathrooms, a private terrace, and a small eat-in kitchen. "Have them add it to my bill."

"Right," Camila said, doing a bad job at hiding the eye roll, but he forgave her for it. She was the only one he would forgive for such a clear sign of disrespect.

Born in the Bronx, lacking even a college degree, she'd been working in the cafeteria of his New York office when he met her. He'd recently banned the use of personal phones at work, requiring employees to lock them in cubbies on the way in and pick them up on the way out. He knew it would be unpopular but thought it would make them more focused while in the office.

Camila stopped him in the food line and tore him a new asshole about how her mother was sick and she needed a way to stay in contact with her, on top of all the other employees who had families, and that all this new policy would do was cause resentment.

Then she took out her phone and waved it in his face.

He was immediately intrigued. No one talked to him like that. No one. He could see her point, had even considered it, but when he ran the idea past his advisors, they did what they always did: told him it was a brilliant idea and followed in lockstep.

It was in that moment he realized having a team of yes-men made his job easier, but it didn't make him better at it.

He had lunch with Camila that day. Talked to her, learned about her. He found that what she lacked in formal education she made up for in tenacity, cleverness, a keen understanding of people, and a willingness to learn. She spoke her mind, and she didn't fear him, maybe because she was nearly old enough to be his mother. Plus, she was a rule breaker, and he appreciated rule breakers.

By the end of lunch he had hired her as his assistant, and it was the best decision he'd ever made. Soon he transformed her from a cafeteria worker into the most brutally efficient assistant a CEO had ever seen.

If there were bodies, not only would she know where they were buried, she would have personally overseen the interments.

Ward looked down at the mess on the carpet. He couldn't even take his boots off now, with all the broken glass. "Can you get in touch with housekeeping?" he asked.

Camila was typing furiously on her phone. "Already on it."

"So how do we look?" Ward asked.

Camila sighed. "Four percentage points is great. You need forty."

"Twenty-five," Ward said.

"Forty. You're mounting a third-party candidacy. Against an incumbent who is also a war hero, and a senator people actually seem to like.

They're going to siphon votes off each other, which will get you within spitting distance, but to really make an impact, you need something big."

"And how do we get something big?"

"Cure cancer."

Ward sighed. "How else do we get something big?"

"Well, first, you can drop this insane plan to join the *Starblazer* crew and campaign from space."

Now it was Ward with the eye roll. "We've discussed this to the end of time and back, Camila," he said. "The Constitution doesn't say I have to be on Earth to run. I can patch in by video wherever and however I need."

"And the farther out you get, the more of a delay there'll be," Camila said. "No one's going to sit through a debate where you need ten minutes to hear a question and then ten minutes to answer it."

"The press will be enormous," Ward said. "Everywhere you look, there I'll be."

"No," Camila said. "People will see your picture and they'll see you on a screen, but they won't see you as a genuine candidate. You'll be millions of miles out in space. With no way to address things as they come up. You need to appoint a replacement and commit yourself to the race."

"If I step down now, people will think I'm a coward," he said.

"No, they'll think you're less crazy."

"Am I not already getting some of that everyman attention, with the lottery?" Ward asked.

"That didn't turn out the way we'd hoped," Camila said.

No, Ward thought. *No, it did not.*

"I know you know all of this," Camila added in mild exasperation. "You're too smart not to. So can we stop arguing and come up with a realistic alternative?"

Ward sighed. Watched the muted TV screen. The anchor was saying something, and Crane's picture appeared again.

The hero cop. He hadn't even done an interview yet and he was getting more press than Ward.

"Hey, Camila, how am I doing on public safety? Law-and-order types."

Camila put down her phone. "Well, you don't have a single police union endorsing you, and that's after we spent millions on donations to gun buybacks and after-school programs. You have no public record to speak of, so no one has anything to judge you on or credit you for. Again, you're running against a war hero and a man who wants to bring back the death penalty. There's too much noise. You're crowded out of the conversation."

Ward nodded slowly. "I have an idea. You're going to think it's nuts . . ."

VER1TY
DARK WEB FORUM

Mink688574: Is anyone surprised about the attack on Ward? This trip to Titan is a smoke screen for something bigger, and you can only put the planet at risk for so long before someone goes all schizo about it. This is billions of dollars that could be invested in solar screens, or carbon scrubbers, or a better infrastructure for electric vehicles. Instead he's building a giant toy for him and his friends to ride around in. Probably just wants to build hotels on Titan.

StatusOverr1de: I think he's just doing the smart thing: getting the fuck out of dodge before the planet is a smoldering husk. He probably has access to all kinds of reports that can tell you exactly how fucked the world is.

Anonymous: I was poking about in NASA's servers (don't ask how) and found something referred to as the Lerner report. But it was scrubbed. Totally gone. I think that's where we should focus our efforts.

TAUR0S: Fuck that. Ward is a genius. Dude is going to save the world.

Renegade483034: Dude is an asshole and a narcissist.

NotActuallyJohnWard: The Lerner report is probably a myth.

RYAN CRANE
HILL EAST, WASHINGTON, D.C.

"Do you want one sugar or two?" Scarlett asked.

Ryan leaned forward over the small plastic table, stretching his aching back. "Two, please."

Scarlett took an empty bowl with a spoon in it and put two imaginary scoops of sugar into his teacup. Ryan took an excited sip. "Mmmm. Earl Grey? Hints of chamomile?"

"It's soda tea," Scarlett said.

"Like, tea made out of soda?"

Scarlett nodded, and Ryan laughed as she poured some make-believe brew for the stuffed bunny sitting to her right. "And where did you get soda tea?"

"I made it," Scarlett said.

"Out of what?"

"Soda."

"Makes sense."

The doorbell rang, followed by an insistent knock. Ryan was half tempted to tell whoever it was that he would arrest them for trespassing. Instead, he chose to ignore it. The constant barrage of reporters was trying his patience.

He didn't want to talk to the press. He didn't want to be on TV. He was doing his job. That's all. The point of the job wasn't to get things in return.

He knew that better than most.

In fact, he wished *more* people knew that . . .

It was doubly frustrating because Nina was upstairs sleeping, and he was afraid the noise might wake her up. Not that Scarlett was making it any easier, now singing along loudly to a movie he didn't recognize. Teddy, at least, was quiet, sitting in his wheelchair at the dining room table, absorbed in his latest piece of artwork.

Ryan excused himself from Scarlett—as much as he loved tea-party time, his back could take it for only so long—and stood, stretching long and deep before he wandered over to see what Teddy was working on.

It was an intricate drawing of a superhero wearing armor that resembled a policeman's uniform. It was an amazing thing to look at—he could have sworn it'd been ripped out of a comic book. Not bad for a fourteen-year-old. Upon closer inspection, Ryan realized the superhero was him.

His heart constricted inside his chest, and he leaned down to kiss the top of Teddy's shaggy head.

"You need to get a haircut, hippie," Ryan said.

"And you need to get with the times, old man," Teddy shot back immediately, then threw a little grin at him.

The doorbell rang three times in succession, followed by another insistent knock. "Sorry about this, kiddo," Ryan said.

"Why don't you just go talk to them, Dad?" Teddy asked. "Get it over with. Once someone gets the interview, won't it quiet down?"

"Probably not," Ryan said. "And anyway, no one wants to see this mug on television again."

Ryan's phone rang. He pulled it out of his pocket and found it was from a number he didn't recognize. He resisted the urge to toss the phone into the sink and run the garbage disposal. He wasn't willing to open the door and have a camera shoved in his face, but this, in the privacy of his own home, he could handle.

He answered: "Look, I don't know how you got this number, but I have nothing to say. Stop calling me, and stop bothering my fam—"

"Mr. Crane, it's John Ward. I'm at your door. Will you please let me in?"

Ryan was momentarily struck dumb.

Then he asked, "How did you get this number?"

"I'm the richest man in the world. There's not a lot I can't do."

Humble, too.

Ryan hung up the phone and stared at it a moment, wondering whether this was a prank. But when he crossed the room, glanced through the peephole, then opened the door, he found John Ward, in the flesh, wearing a black blazer and jeans and a white T-shirt, smiling. No reporters, no staffers, nothing. A lone black town car hovered quietly across the street.

He wasn't as tall as he seemed on television.

Ryan went for something to say, to snap himself out of his surprise, and settled on, "Figured a guy like you would travel with bodyguards."

Ward smiled. "They're in the car. You already saved my life once, so

I didn't consider you a threat." Ward paused, like he was expecting Ryan to say something, then added, "Now, this is the part where you invite me in, before someone sees us."

Fair enough. Ryan moved aside and allowed Ward to enter.

The man stepped inside and looked around. Ryan felt embarrassed. He believed there should be a détente among adults—particularly parents—about the state of their homes. Having kids meant you were living in a constant state of entropy. You could not have nice things. So the toys scattered across the living room, the empty cereal bowls on the kitchen table, the overflowing laundry basket by the door leading to the basement—if it were anyone else, he would shrug it off.

"Sorry about the state of things . . ." Ryan started.

"Please," Ward said. "You should have seen my dorm room in college."

He strode through the house like he owned it. Scarlett was oblivious to their guest, drinking tea and chatting with her stuffies, whereas Teddy was staring, mouth agape. Ward, seeming to notice this, beelined over to him.

"What have you got there, pal?" he asked, leaning down to look at the drawing. Then his face broke into a smile. "Hey, that's pretty good. You keep it up, maybe I'll give you a job in our design department. What do you think about that?"

"Uh, yes, sir, Mr. Ward, sir . . ." Teddy stammered.

Ward turned back to Ryan. "Can I bend your ear for a minute?"

"Sure," Ryan said. "Coffee?"

"Always."

Ryan turned to his kids. "Hey, you two, don't burn down the house. We're gonna go talk grown-up stuff." He then led Ward into the cramped kitchen, briefly embarrassed, again, by the pile of unwashed dishes in the sink, but there wasn't much to be done at this point. He rooted around in the cupboard for the cleanest mug he could find, filled it from the half-empty carafe, and handed the cup over.

Ward sniffed it, took a sip, and clearly didn't like it but did his best to pretend that wasn't the case. Then he proffered his hand. "Thank you."

"It's just Folgers," Ryan said.

"For saving my life," Ward said. "I haven't properly thanked you. So I'm here to say, thank you."

Ryan took his hand and shook. "Like I've been saying to anyone who will listen, I was just doing my job. It's just lucky I was there."

"Why *were* you there?"

"My wife. Appendicitis. Woke up screaming in the middle of the night. She was out of surgery, and I went looking for a cup of coffee. Just . . . chance."

"You didn't just save me. You saved a lot of lives. You must be the talk of the department."

Ryan grimaced. "Maybe."

Ward picked up the cup of coffee again, considered it, and put it back down. "Look, this is going to sound a little crazy, but I'm just going to get down to it. How would you like to go to Titan?"

"The . . ." That's all that Ryan could get out. He barely understood the question.

"You know I'm sending a ship to Titan, right? Saturn's moon?" Ward asked. "Going to save the human race?"

"Right, but . . ."

"Look, I was going to go myself, but I've got too much on my plate here. I've got to fill that seat, and I could pick another astronaut, sure, but then I think to myself, I'd love to get a guy up there who knows how to react during a crisis."

"That's . . ."

"I know what you're thinking. We'll get you the training you need. You'll be an even bigger hero, which is never a bad thing. Not just to the world, but to that handsome kid out there. And you'll be one of the first humans to travel that far in space . . ."

"Mr. Ward," Ryan said, putting up his hand. "That's incredibly kind of you to think of me. But I have a job. A family. More responsibilities than I care to think about in a given moment. I read an article about that. It's a two-year trip. I can't just leave for two years."

Ward nodded. "I get it. That's why I'm going to pay you fifteen million dollars for your time. In installments, of course. A quarter now, a quarter when you board the shuttle, and so on."

That snatched the breath from Ryan's lungs.

The number was so big it was impossible to envision.

He thought about all the good that money could do, for him and his family. But it was quickly overshadowed by the thought of two whole years without his kids. Nina was one thing. They loved each other, they could get through a little distance.

The kids needed him.

That was two years of birthdays, recitals, graduations . . .

"I'm sorry, Mr. Ward," Ryan said. "That's incredibly generous of you, but I don't think I can be away that long."

"You drive a hard bargain," Ward said. "Twenty. And I'll tell you what. Take a few days to think about it. Talk to your wife. If at the end you really believe this is something you don't want to do"—he wiped his hands together like he was cleaning them—"no harm, no foul. But I think an offer like this ought to be worth a little consideration."

Yeah, Ryan thought. It warranted a conversation with Nina. That much was fair. He couldn't make this decision without her.

"Sure, I'll think about it," Ryan said.

"Great," Ward said, reaching over and patting him on the shoulder. "I've got your number. Or you've got mine now, too. Either way, let's talk soon. But if I don't hear from you in three days, I'm going to ring you up."

"Okay," Ryan said.

He walked Ward to the door in a haze, almost dizzy. Before he could say anything, Ward leaned into him and said, "Hey, what's your boy's name?"

"Teddy."

Ward called across the room, "You keep drawing, Teddy. I know talent when I see it!"

And without waiting for a response, Ward turned and left.

Ryan stood there for a long time, holding the doorknob.

Nina appeared at his shoulder, half-asleep, in her bathrobe, her hair frazzled, her eyes swimming a little from the painkillers, eyeing Ward through the window blinds as he headed back to his waiting vehicle.

"What the hell was that about?" she asked.

PADMA SINGH
CAPITOL HILL, WASHINGTON, D.C.

Padma stared at the gray text bubble on her phone, trying to figure out what Ward was thinking.

Stepping down from the flight. The hero cop will take my place. Crane. He hasn't said yes, but he will.

Padma knew better than to write back and ask him to explain that, or to call him so they could talk it through. Ward didn't respond to texts. He spoke in declarative statements that didn't welcome rebuttal or discussion. Whatever he wrote would be whatever random thought or question he had, and even if Padma did ask, he would ignore it.

This was a wrinkle.

So far the flight was her, three NASA astronauts, and the winner of Ward's lottery—a publicity stunt meant to drum up interest in the project.

Now this. There was already one civilian on board. Technically two; she didn't have any space training. Now there'd be a third. Which meant less science, more distraction. She wondered if Henry Owens had signed off on this. Probably. Owens did whatever Ward asked . . .

"Are you serious?" Brett asked.

Padma looked up from her phone. "I'm sorry, it was work-related."

Brett sat on the couch across from her, the look on his face somewhere between annoyance and frustrated acceptance. The living room had two couches, one facing the other. The TV was mounted on the wall behind her. The apartment had come furnished, and Padma thought it was weird. She got that it was so people could have conversations with one another, but she didn't like staring at an empty couch while she watched TV.

It's not like she entertained. The only person who ever came over was Brett. And she suspected he wouldn't be coming over much more after today.

Padma put her phone face down on the heavy wooden coffee table. "I'm sorry, it was important."

"This is important," Brett said.

"I know," she said.

And she did. She knew she'd dropped the ball, big-time. She'd waited until after the press conference to text Brett—she knew it was best to give him space when he was processing emotions. She asked if he'd watched, and he wrote back immediately that he had, and that she did amazing, and he was glad she was safe.

She asked him to come over that night so they could talk, and he said he had plans.

She doubted he had plans.

After several days of silence, she reached out again, and he'd finally agreed to come. But the moment he stepped through the door, she knew it wasn't going to be a good conversation. Brett usually walked with a perpetual bounce in his step, and his smooth, handsome face was permanently etched with a smile.

But today, his shoulders were slumped, and he wasn't exactly scowling, but he certainly was not smiling.

"I get what you're doing is important," he said, running his hands through his curly, sandy hair. "And I get that being with you means being patient. I'm not asking you to . . . not do what you do. I love what we do. But I *am* asking you to meet me not even halfway, a quarter of the way. All I wanted for my birthday was a night at home with you. No phones, just us. I even offered to cook. All you had to do was show up."

Padma sighed. "I can make excuses, but I won't. I lost track of time. You know I have ADHD, you know I have issues with time-blindness . . ."

"We've talked about this. You could have set a timer."

"I don't need you to run my life for me."

"I'm not trying to. I'm offering a suggestion. Something to help you keep track of time."

Padma felt a defensive rush of blood to her face. He wasn't wrong, *per se,* she just didn't like her struggles with executive function to be thrown in her face. Especially by Brett. Perpetually punctual Brett. He didn't understand what it was like, when everything else fell away and there was nothing else in the world, just the work.

He's not throwing it in your face, she thought. *He's just upset, and he has the right to be.*

"So where does this leave us?" Padma asked.

Brett put his head in his hands, then he looked up at her, his eyes teetering on the edge of tears. "I have a strong suspicion we're not going to see each other much between now and when you leave. And then you'll be gone for two years. And you're going to be consumed with your work. Maybe . . . this isn't going to work out."

"We talked about this," Padma said, her voice cracking. "We said we could try. I'm . . ." Her voice dropped to a whisper. "I'm sorry about your birthday."

There was a long pause, the two of them looking at each other expectantly.

And in that moment Padma realized: she still hadn't gotten him a gift.

She couldn't be sure, but she saw something click in his eyes. The realization of that. Even after forgetting, she still couldn't make it a priority.

"You're right," Padma said.

Another click. Brett shook his head a little, almost surprised, as if expecting her to argue or fight back more. But seeing she wasn't, he simply shrugged and stood. She sat on the opposite couch, not sure what to do.

She'd never been broken up with before. Shouldn't she be more sad? Or was the fact that she wasn't proof enough that this was the right decision?

Should she hug him, give him a goodbye kiss?

Or would that just make things worse?

"I'm proud of you, Padma," Brett said. "What you're doing is amazing. And I wish you the best of luck."

"I just . . ." Padma started.

Brett lingered.

"You said you'd water my plants while I was gone."

Brett sighed, like he'd expected to hear something else. Then, reciting from memory: "The watering bulbs need to be refilled every three weeks." He paused, before adding, "A promise is a promise. I'll set a reminder so I don't forget."

The way he said it felt a little like a knife twisting in her stomach.

He paused again, like he might add something, but then just nodded and left the apartment.

Padma sat there in silence a long time, cycling through a cavalcade of emotions. The anger, the grief, the sadness, the loneliness. But it didn't take long for her to get to the acceptance phase. Not that she fully accepted it, but she could at least understand it, and by focusing on that, she could pave over those other feelings.

Brett was a great guy. He deserved a girlfriend who remembered his birthday.

And she wasn't a bad person because she was dedicated to her job.

Those would be her mantras, for as long as it took the stew of the other emotions to dissipate.

Switching gears on a dime—she'd mastered that over the years—Padma pulled her laptop over and balanced it on her knees. She opened several windows, went to Google, Reddit, and one of the newer AI search engines, and in each typed "secret Titan report." It had been scratching at the back of her brain since that reporter brought it up. She had meant to ask Ward about it after, and then things went sideways with the shooters.

Her searches brought back a mess of results, mostly related to the press conference.

But she set about, clicking link after link.

Because she couldn't shake the question.

RYAN CRANE
HILL EAST, WASHINGTON, D.C.

Ryan stared at the fuzzy round stain marring the paint of the bedroom ceiling, from a freak blizzard two winters ago. Melting snow had leaked through the roof. He had patched the outside but hadn't gotten to the stain yet.

It meant repainting. It meant buying supplies. It wasn't terribly expensive, but it was expensive enough that he didn't think it was worth the money. There were things his family needed more than he needed an unblemished view of the ceiling as he fell asleep.

"Earth to Ryan," Nina said.

Ryan repositioned himself on the bed so he could look at Nina, who was propped up on some pillows, lying on her back in her fuzzy lavender bathrobe. She looked more rested, her eyes a little brighter.

"I'm sorry," Ryan said. "What were you saying?"

"That it's okay to be thinking about this," Nina said. "It's a lot of money." Then, chuckling at the absurdity: "It's a *shit ton* of money."

"And it's seven hundred and something days away from you and the kids," Ryan said.

Nina leaned back and looked at the ceiling. Was she looking at the stain, too? Thinking the same thing as him? That it would be nice to live in a house with enough space for the four of them? To get Teddy a stair lift that worked and a chair that wasn't in a constant state of disrepair?

"It is a lot of days," she said quietly. "But you have to wonder, with everything going on in the world, how many days do we have left? Don't you want Teddy and Scarlett to have as many as you can give them?"

And of course he did.

More than anything in the world.

"How are you going to manage those two on your own?" Ryan asked.

Nina smiled. "I already spoke to my sister. She said she'd move here for a while. She's tired of Cincinnati. She has nothing else tying her down."

Ryan laughed. "So this is a conspiracy now."

Nina tried to shimmy her body closer to Ryan but winced in pain, so Ryan moved closer to her. He instinctively reached his arm out to put it across her waist, then thought again and rested it on her thigh.

"I don't want to sleep in this bed alone for two years," Nina said. "I don't want to communicate by video. I don't want to have to explain to Scarlett why her dad can't come right home if she has a nightmare. All of that sucks. But it's not just about the money. Think of what an incredible opportunity this is."

Ryan sighed. "I have a job."

"Would you really be so upset about having to leave it? Who knows, maybe you can take a leave, and when you come back it'll still be there."

Nina paused, shifting gears, her tone suggesting an arena they typically left alone. "But do you think you'd even want to go back? I know you love what you do, but that much money? We can invest most of it and still cover day-to-day expenses. And you can ride on parade floats and have your face on a cereal box."

Only a little bit amused, Ryan slumped back onto the pillow. "Starting to feel like you've got this all planned out . . ."

"It's not like that," Nina said. "Hey, look at me." When Ryan continued to resolutely stare at the ceiling, Nina reached over and put her hand on his chin, tilting his face toward her. Their eyes met, and immediately he melted a little.

She had that effect on him.

"You deserve better," she said. "You deserve better than the way they treat you there. This would be great for our family, this would be great for humanity. But more than that, I think it would be great for you. Your kids already think you hung the stars. Why not go out and do it for real?"

"I'm not an astronaut," Ryan said.

"You're a fast learner."

"What if something goes wrong in space? It's not exactly a forgiving environment. Like, when you consider all the factors, it's enormously terrifying."

Nina laughed. "You could get hit by a bus tomorrow."

"Thanks."

She turned serious, utterly sincere. "Hey. I'm not trying to push you away . . ."

"I know, I know," Ryan said, rolling over and running his hand across her thigh again before slipping it under the folds of the bathrobe to feel the smoothness of her skin. "I appreciate that you believe in me. I do."

"You've always made the decision you thought was best," Nina said. "I've always respected it. I've always loved you for it. I just want you to know that whatever you decide, we will make it work."

Ryan pushed the robe aside. On any other night she'd be wearing a cute little silk number under the bathrobe, but tonight she was in a threadbare T-shirt and fuzzy shorts. And on any other night Ryan would have gotten up, made sure the kids were asleep, and then locked the door before removing that cute little silk number.

But Nina was still healing. Instead, he gently lifted the T-shirt to reveal the bandage over her surgical incision. He leaned over and kissed it. "I'm going to sleep on it. Tomorrow, I'll decide."

Then he crawled up and kissed her on the lips, deeply, breathing in the scent of her skin, wondering how he would make it two whole years without this.

Any other cop would have gotten a hero's welcome, Ryan thought as he stood in the bullpen of the District of Columbia's Sixteenth Precinct, watching all his colleagues throw him furtive glances before going back to whatever it was they were doing.

He cut through the maze of desks toward the back of the room, where he knocked on the glass door of Captain Hanover's office.

Hanover looked like he was grown in a lab to be a cop—square jaw, wide shoulders, neat haircut, and a face that read instantly as authoritative and disagreeable. He was on the phone, but he looked up and nodded at Ryan to come in.

Ryan stood at ease, hands behind his back, spine straight, chin out, while Hanover finished the phone call.

"Yeah . . . I understand . . . thank you." He hung up the phone and asked, "How's Nina?"

"She's a champ," Ryan said.

Hanover nodded. "I got your report, had the chance to review it. Nice work, as always. Don't have any questions or concerns. But both the Secret Service and the FBI are currently crawling up my ass on this, so until their investigations are concluded, you'll be on desk duty."

"Captain . . ." Ryan started, thrown at being so casually downgraded.

Hanover put up his hand. "Can't be helped. Now, if you'll excuse me, I've got some more calls to make."

Ryan stood there for a moment, wondering if the guy was going to ask how *he* was doing, or if he even cared, and then finally just shrugged and said, "Yes, sir, thank you, sir."

He did his best to keep the disdain out of his voice, but enough trickled in that the captain noticed. Hanover raised an eyebrow, stared for a moment, and then turned his back and picked up the phone.

Ryan went to his desk and found it already covered with paperwork. Word must have gotten around, and patrol cops were dropping their forms off for him to complete and file, no doubt with smug satisfaction.

As he sat and tried to get it organized, a voice said, "There's the hero."

He looked up to see Detective Wilkinson staring down at him, a smirk on his face. He was a tall man—so tall that from this angle he towered over Ryan, which was probably exactly how Wilkinson liked it.

"Right place, right time," Ryan said.

"Funny how that works," he said, holding up a thick stack of papers.

"Heard about the desk duty. That's a bad beat. But I guess it gives you an opportunity to be a team player. Something you need to brush up on anyway."

Wilkinson held out the stack of papers and dropped them on top of the pile. Half of them slid off the desk and fell onto the floor. The detective didn't even wait to watch them land; he just walked away, softly laughing.

Ryan stooped to pick up the papers, noting that nobody near him bothered to help, then sat back, sighed, and got up, heading through the hallway and down the stairs.

Simon was sitting behind his desk in the cramped space in front of the locked cage to the armory. And, as per usual, he was futzing with the glass funnel of his Japanese pour-over coffee set.

Simon. His only real friend in this place. The man was in his thirties but looked like he was in his twenties, despite his bald head. His glasses and nervous demeanor made him appear more suited for a Dungeons & Dragons party than a police force.

"Got one of those for me?" Ryan asked.

Simon looked up and smiled. "Always."

He put an already steaming mug in front of Ryan, who picked it up and took a sip.

"Let me guess, you're being hailed as a conquering hero, as you should be in a kind and just universe," Simon said.

"Desk duty."

"Jeeeesus," Simon said. "Anyone else, they'd be marching them right to city hall to have the mayor pin a medal on them."

"The prices we pay," Ryan said, holding up his mug and gesturing to Simon's little cubby corner.

"Exactly," Simon said, finally grabbing his own cup, taking a luxurious sip, and then leaning back so far in his roller chair he spilled a little of the coffee down the front of his shirt. On another day, Ryan might teasingly call out the flub, but he had more on his mind today.

"Got something I want to run by you."

Simon put down the coffee, brushing at the wet spot on his shirt. "Shoot."

And Ryan told Simon about Ward's offer.

When he was finished, Simon sat silent for a few breaths before he said, "Don't do it."

"Why?" Ryan asked. Simon stared his friend down, deadpan.

"You ever see a movie where people went to space and things went well?"

Ryan laughed. "I appreciate and value your insight, as always."

Simon smiled, then shifted—always one to honor a weighty question with a thoughtful answer. "No, seriously, man, I get it. Lots of pros and cons. Tell me this though. Take everything else off the table. Every question, every concern, everything. Really think on this. What do *you* want to do?"

Ryan contemplated the coffee in his mug, swirling it a little before taking another sip.

"I don't know," he said.

"Yeah, you do," Simon said, lowering his voice. "You did the right thing once, and it held you back. You've got a chance to do the right thing now to help you and your family. Truth is"—Simon leaned forward and clinked his mug against Ryan's—"I think you already decided. I'm going to miss you, pal."

Ryan smiled and took another sip of his coffee.

EMAIL
FROM JOHN WARD

I checked, and Ryan does qualify. Just to verify, here's the manifest, as it currently stands:

MIKE SEAVER
DELLA JAMESON
ALONSO CARDONA
COURTNEY SMITH
PADMA SINGH
RYAN CRANE

I'll get to work on my end . . .

2

STARBLAZER

MIKE SEAVER
FISHTOWN, PHILADELPHIA, PA

Mike Seaver stared at the cascade of missed calls and texts from Helen. He considered calling back, but first, he plunged his face into the large bowl of ice water he'd prepared on the counter.

The second his skin made contact with the freezing water, he felt a surge through his system, clearing away some of the lingering effects of last night's whiskey. Coupled with the ibuprofen and the coffee, he hoped it would make a dent in his hangover.

He held his face in the water until it felt like his lungs would burst, then stood up, sputtering the cold water from his mouth before drying his face with a hand towel that smelled like it needed to be washed.

He looked around the apartment—the secondhand couch, the beat-up coffee table, the kitchen that was empty save for the takeout containers, the dirty laundry strewn outside the bathroom door. How far he'd fallen—it was almost too much to comprehend.

Dumbshit.

He sighed and picked up the phone, tapped to call Helen, set the phone to speaker, and placed it on the counter.

"Are you okay?" she asked immediately upon answering.

"Couldn't sleep last night," he said. "Just nervous, is all. Big day today."

"Mike . . ." Helen said, and even through the phone's tinny speaker, he could hear the disappointment and exasperation in her voice. "You were supposed to come by and see the kids this morning."

Shit. Mike rubbed his face, trying to warm it back up. "How are they?"

"Emma didn't have her hopes up," she said. "Jack did. Stella's too young to tell the difference."

"I'll make it up to them, I'll—"

"Mike." Helen's voice was sharp now, before trailing off. "You're going to be gone for two years."

"I promise, Helen, I'll see them before I go. After we get through the rest of training."

There was silence from the other end, to the point where Mike thought maybe the call got disconnected. He leaned over to look at the phone and saw that it was still on.

"How much did you have to drink last night?" Helen asked, her voice flat.

Mike glanced at the bottle of whiskey on the counter. He'd opened it shortly after dinner, and there was maybe a mouthful left. He would have finished it, but he'd passed out on the couch before he had the chance.

"I told you," he said. "Just nerves. Couldn't sleep."

"You're making this really hard," she said. "Because I know, just like the entire world knows, that three years ago you single-handedly saved eight people on a lunar excursion because of how well you keep your head together in a stressful situation. So please don't tell me it was nerves."

"Doing the job and being paraded around on television like a dancing monkey are two entirely different things," Mike said.

"Did you look at the pamphlets I sent you?" she asked.

Alcoholics Anonymous. They were at the bottom of the trash can, underneath a pile of takeout containers. "Been busy."

Helen's voice grew cold. "Okay, Mike. I'm trying, but . . . just have a safe flight today, okay? We need to prioritize some time with the kids before you go. And when you get back, I guess there'll be a lot we need to talk about. I just got to the office, and I have a meeting in five minutes. I need to go."

"I love you," Mike said.

He looked down at the phone, but it was already disconnected.

He wondered if she heard that last bit.

And if she had, if it would have made any kind of difference.

He picked up the bottle of whiskey, eyed the final mouthful, shrugged, and downed it. Hair of the dog. The ice water had done only so much, the ibuprofen and coffee were still working their way into his system, and he needed that last little boost to get him ready for the day. The sting of it in his throat distracted him from the sinking feeling in his gut.

There'll be a lot we need to talk about.

Mike put the bottle on the counter and headed into his bedroom, where his empty suitcase was sitting open on the unmade bed. His flight left in a few hours, and he knew he needed to get to work packing, but instead he sat heavily on the mattress and put his head in his hands.

Helen didn't understand. The nerves were ever present. Always there. He drank to quiet them. He drank to clear his head. He drank so he could face the world without fear.

He needed it to be the hero everyone thought he was.

How could he explain that to her? He'd tried so many times . . .

His phone buzzed. He picked it up, hoping it was Helen, but it was Della.

DELLA:

You packed yet?

                                MIKE:

                                Almost done.

DELLA:

I don't believe you. Get in gear.

Mike smiled. It would be nice to see Della. It'd been too long. Alonso, too—they'd never flown a mission together, but they'd met a few times, and he always respected the younger astronaut's knowledge and enthusiasm.

It was the civilians he was most worried about. The ones that were, in fact, making it hard for him to sleep. Especially that one lottery-winning jackass. If not for the nature of the mission, Mike might have begged off just for that.

But he longed to have his name spoken in the same hushed tones as Armstrong and Aldrin, and that would never happen if he was just flying to the moon over and over.

A manned flight to Titan would put him in the history books.

The hangover was finally dulled enough that he felt like he could function, so he dragged himself to his feet and sorted through his clothes, separating what was clean from what wasn't, so that he could get his bag packed and get to the airport.

DELLA JAMESON
CAROL STREAM, CHICAGO, IL

Della pocketed her phone, glad that at least Mike was awake. It had been a fifty-fifty chance he'd make his scheduled flight, but hearing back from him right away, she optimistically upped the odds to 75 percent.

The guy knew how to party—as Della had become keenly aware after multiple shared missions over two decades—but sometimes he had trouble knowing when *not* to party.

No, not sometimes. Oftentimes.

And by any measure, the party days should have come to an end years ago. It had become quite clear to her this was no longer a party. It was a debilitating crutch.

She called up the stairs. "Mila! Nora! Nana is here! Get your little butts moving!"

Frenzied footsteps pattered across the floor upstairs. Della made her way through the house to the kitchen, where her mother, Cosette, was mixing pancakes for the kids. Despite her making the batter from scratch, the kitchen was immaculate, which Della could never understand. If she were making them, it would have looked like someone planted a bomb inside a sack of flour.

Cosette looked up from the bowl of batter and said, "I've got the girls, sweetheart. Why don't you go get ready."

"I'm good," Della said, glancing at the front door, where her luggage was packed and waiting. The first Black female astronaut to have completed more than five missions to space, and a household name throughout the country, Della certainly knew the drill by now. And yet she never got used to leaving her daughters behind.

She checked her phone to confirm that the car was due to arrive in ten minutes, then regarded her ever reliable mom. "Thank you so much for doing this."

Cosette shrugged. "What else would I do with my time?"

"You have your garden."

"I'd rather spend my time tending to the girls," she said, nodding toward the second floor of the house. "Especially considering you won't let their father around . . ."

Della rolled her eyes—a habit she was getting far too used to—and glanced toward the doorway to make sure the kids hadn't made their way down yet. "Sean is not a good man."

"He never raised his hands to you, or to them," she said, lowering her voice. "Never yelled, never hurt anyone. I get that you're angry with him, but those girls need their dad."

"He's got to earn his way back in," Della said, matching her mother's tone.

"Which means you have to give him a chance to do it," Cosette said.

Della wished her mother would drop this argument. Of course she'd take Sean's side on this. He'd "only cheated," she would say. And compared to the things Della's own father had done to them . . .

She pushed the memories away. Her mother was right, Sean wasn't in the same ballpark. But that didn't mean she would tolerate his actions. If anything, it just meant her standards were higher.

And she understood that, in the two years she'd be gone for Titan, Sean would get his supervised visits, and no doubt Cosette would call on him if there was an emergency.

It wasn't that he was a bad dad. He just wasn't a good man.

She'd given up trying to explain that to her mother.

Before the conversation could continue, much to Della's relief, Nora and Mila bound into the kitchen. The twins were still in their princess pajamas, their hair askew like they'd just gotten out of bed.

Della dropped to her knees and pulled them both in for a deep hug. "Be good for Nana, okay?"

"Yes, Mom," they said in unison.

Della was always amazed at how they could do that—they did it all the time, speaking together like they practiced it beforehand. Probably a twin thing.

"Pancakes will be ready in a bit," Cosette said. "Why don't you girls go play in the living room."

The two of them bolted out of the kitchen. Cosette walked to Della and put her hands on her daughter's shoulders. "I'm proud of you, my love. One of these days, you're going to have to take me with you. To see the things you've seen . . ."

"I would love to, Mom. But I promise you, nothing out there compares to those two little girls." Della noticed a small smear of pancake batter on the front of Cosette's blouse. Not supermom after all. Smiling ruefully to herself, Della grabbed a tea towel off the counter and dabbed at it. "There's a part of me that doesn't want to go."

"I know," Cosette said, taking the towel and wiping at the stain herself. "But you will, because it's where you belong. Always knew you were going to do great things. Sean and I will take care of the kids and you'll be back in no time."

"Two years isn't *no time*, but . . ."

Her phone buzzed. The car was here. She kissed her mom on the forehead and went to the living room, giving each of the girls a peck on the cheek. They were absorbed in *Bluey*, which made the process of saying goodbye a little easier.

As she made her way to the front door and picked up her bags, her phone buzzed again.

ALONSO:
See you in a bit?

> **DELLA:**
> Excited to get back to work.
> You?

ALONSO:
Oh yeah, morning runs and
endless pushups? The best.

> **DELLA:**
> Young buck like you shouldn't
> be complaining about a little PT.

Della smiled and stuck the phone into her pocket, making her way to the waiting car.

ALONSO CARDONA
ALLANDALE, AUSTIN, TX

"You didn't have to come with me," Alonso said as Maddie took his hand, nestling it in her lap.

"You're leaving for *two years*," she said. "I know we'll get some time before you take off. But until then, I'll take every second I can get."

The cab creeped slowly down I-35 toward the turnoff onto Route 71, which would take them to Austin-Bergstrom. They were cutting it a little close for the flight, but there was still enough time.

This was maybe not the best setting for saying goodbye.

Part of him would have preferred leaving her nestled in bed with a cup of coffee on the nightstand while the morning sun filtered through the window. He could push her curly hair out of her eyes and give her a lingering kiss. Instead, they had the interior of the cab, with its ripped cushions, smell of musty mystery, and unwitting third wheel. The driver didn't seem to be eavesdropping, but it still made conversation awkward.

Plus, Maddie would just have to take the cab right back around.

Still, another part of him was glad to have her here.

It wasn't his first time in space. But thus far he'd been up only in ISS-2, with one quick jaunt to the moon. Flying across half the solar system in an experimental aircraft was a bit more intimidating.

"So explain to me again how it works," Maddie said. "With communication, while you're gone."

"Well, the farther we're out, the longer it's going to take for messages to travel back and forth," he said. "By the time we're settled and on our way, live chats won't be possible. We use relay systems to communicate, but the time it takes for the data to transfer will increase as the distance increases. They're working on some relays to try to cut down the time, but I can't see it being under twenty minutes, one way."

"Wow," she said.

"Yeah, and that's as long as there's no interference, and nothing blocking the transmission. There'll be a period when we're coming around the back of Titan that we'll be completely cut off."

"And how long will that be?"

"No more than a half hour."

He wanted to add *hopefully* but figured it was best not to.

"This stuff is wild," Maddie said. "I'm sorry you have to keep explaining it. I know I'm not . . ."

"Hey," Alonso said, leaning over so he could look her in the eyes. "I love who you are and I love what you do and I love your beautiful mind."

"Right, but, I just feel like . . . wouldn't you be happier with someone who just got what you did?"

Alonso sighed. This was not a new conversation. Maddie was a beautician. And she was a damn good one, with her own salon in Austin that was constantly booked and had a wait-list a mile long.

He loved that about her—that she'd built her own business, that she brought people joy and comfort. And he had explained, in the three years they'd been together, over and again, that he spent enough time dealing with astrophysics at work. Being with someone who wasn't in the same field made him feel like he had a safe space where he could just let go.

He wished she would hear him when he said that.

But it also made him wonder if he gave her signs that the opposite might be true.

"Maddie, you are amazing and I admire you so much," he said. "I am going to miss you like crazy. And the first thing I'm going to need is for you to fix my hair, because I won't have had a proper trim in two years."

Maddie smiled and ruffled his flowing black hair. "It's going to be out of control."

"You're everything I want," Alonso said. "And I can't wait to see you when I get back."

The car pulled toward the drop-off curb at the airport, into the jumble of cars letting people out. Alonso said thanks to the driver, handed him a wad of cash to cover the whole trip, and climbed out, the trunk popping as he did. He grabbed his bags and embraced Maddie, kissing her deeply, knowing that every word he said to her was true.

But there was always more to the truth, too.

His phone buzzed in his pocket as he stepped through the doors of the terminal.

ETHAN:

Hey. Stay safe out there, okay?

Alonso looked at his phone. Thought about responding.

What was there to say?

He put his phone back into his pocket and made his way toward the security line.

STITCH
LaGUARDIA AIRPORT, QUEENS, NY

Stitch watched as the TSA officer ran her gloved fingers over his bag, like he might be carrying some kind of concealed contraband. He checked his watch; the flight would be done boarding in twenty minutes, which meant he'd have to make a run for the gate.

"Is this going to take long?" he asked.

The TSA agent—her name tag read LOCKWOOD—glanced up at him. "It's going to take as long as it needs to take."

Stitch leaned back in the chair and stared at the ceiling. This always happened, whenever he flew anywhere. The worst part was, his mom had told him to dress nice. The tattered jeans and the retro Jordans and the graffitied T-shirt made him "look like a kid who is also a criminal," his mom said, and that's probably why he always got pulled out of line.

But it's the way he wanted to dress, and he saw no reason why he had to button himself up and mute himself to the world just to make other people happy.

He wasn't a kid or a criminal.

He was a man who was about to be launched into space.

"Look," Stitch said, "I don't want to be a jerk about this, and I can't even believe I'm saying this, but . . . do you know who I am?"

Lockwood laughed dismissively and picked up his ID, which was sitting on the table next to his bag. "Courtney Smith, age twenty-seven."

Stitch bristled. He hated his name—yes, Courtney could be a man's name, but it didn't feel that way, and even shortening it to Court felt a little too formal for him.

"First off, I go by Stitch," he said.

"Where'd you get a nickname like that?" she asked.

"From . . . around," he said, realizing this was not the time to reveal it was his graffiti tag name. "Just, I've been on the news. I'm part of that big expedition to Titan. The one that John Ward is doing? I won the lottery."

Lockwood's eyes widened. "Oh, wow. I entered that. How'd you get picked?"

Stitch shrugged, hoping she wouldn't hold it against him. "Luck, I guess. It's a lottery. Anyway, I'm supposed to be down in Houston today for the press conference, and if I miss my flight and I'm late, I feel like that's not going to set a very good tone for things."

Lockwood raised an eyebrow. "I guess that is pretty important."

"All I'm saying is that my flight leaves soon, and this is a big opportunity for me, and if you could just see it in your heart to realize I'm not, like, a terrorist or something? I'd really appreciate it."

"Didn't say you were a terrorist," she said, rifling through his clothes and picking out his vape. "Are you carrying any drugs? Is this a weed thing?"

"I don't do drugs. It's a regular vape. Nicotine."

Another raised eyebrow from Lockwood.

"Just because I'm Black and I dress like this doesn't mean I use drugs," he said. "That's stereotyping."

Lockwood started to speak, but then the door opened, and another TSA agent came in and handed the woman some paperwork before leaving just as abruptly. She scanned it and nodded. "Swabs came back clean. I guess you're free to go."

Stitch jumped to his feet. "Thank you," he said.

He didn't actually want to say "thank you" for being inconvenienced like this, but he also knew he had to go along to get along sometimes. Lockwood watched as he assembled his bag and stuck his ID back into his pocket.

"Have a nice flight . . . Stitch," she said.

He wanted to add, *Which one? I'll wave at you next month from* Starblazer, *biatch.*

But he didn't. Instead, he stepped outside, looking around to orient himself in the frenzy of the airport, then he heard: "Flight 386 to Houston, final boarding call."

Stitch turned and ran in the direction of the gate.

PADMA SINGH
DULLES INTERNATIONAL AIRPORT,
WASHINGTON, D.C.

Padma mindlessly scrolled through TikTok. The algorithm was feeding her videos about floral arrangements today, and it was nice to get lost in the mind-numbing cascade of videos about flowers while she waited for the flight to board, which, according to the gate agent, was going to be any minute.

It was already departing late, and she was feeling a little anxiety about that, but what else was there to do?

She considered getting up to find some food, or maybe hit the bathroom again. The flight to Houston was a little under four hours, but she had a window seat, and if someone was sitting next to her, she didn't want to have to play that awkward game of getting them to move so she could climb out. She wanted to sit in her seat and read until the flight landed.

She'd picked up her phone again—anything to distract her from the melancholy feeling in her gut about Brett—when she noticed the guy sitting across from her. He was tall and handsome, brown hair and blue eyes. More than that, he looked familiar. Really familiar . . .

The hero cop.

"Excuse me," she said to him, and he looked up at her. "Aren't you, uh . . ."

He smiled an uncomfortable smile and nodded. "Just doing my job."

"No, not that, I mean, I think we're going to the same place." She leaned over and offered her hand to him. "Padma Singh. I'm an astrophysicist. I'm working with Ward on the Titan expedition."

"Ryan Crane," he said, returning the shake and immediately brightening. "Yeah, funny we're both on the same flight."

"If we both live in D.C., it makes sense," she said, realizing that it came out a little sharp, like, *Why wouldn't you know that?*

Ryan nodded. "Right, right. So . . ." He looked around and shrugged. "Ever been to space before?"

"First time," Padma said. "You?"

"Mostly weekend trips," he said.

She paused for a second and then nodded. A joke.

Ryan smiled, realizing it went a little over the rocket scientist's head. "No, it's my first time. And I'm terrified. Honestly, I'm not even sure what I'm doing here . . ."

"Let me guess," Padma said. "Ward offered you a boatload of money."

"Three boatloads, I think," Ryan said.

Padma slid her phone into her purse. "That's what he does. Though I suppose if I were a billionaire I would just throw money at things, too. I don't mean any offense by this, but I do think it's interesting that he chose you."

"A cop from D.C.? Yeah, you'd think he would go with someone who knew literally anything at all about space travel."

"Well, the crew we're going with has an incredible amount of experience," Padma said. "They're the best of the best, from what I'm told. And Ward's ship is state of the art, with every amenity we could want. Did you get the manual yet?"

"I did not."

Padma rummaged through her backpack and found the battered printout. "If you want to do a little light reading on the plane, I've already got it memorized."

"Thanks," Ryan said, folding the booklet over in his hands. "I'm glad we'll be comfortable, I guess." He put it into the shoulder bag at his feet, then he looked at Padma, smiled, and sighed. "It's hard leaving my wife and kids for that long, even though the money is going to make a huge difference in our lives. What about you—got anyone special waiting for you? Your folks must be proud."

Padma gave a pained smile and shook her head. "No. Not really."

Ryan's expression changed to one of embarrassment. "I said the wrong thing, didn't I?"

"It wasn't wrong," Padma said. She looked around to make sure no one was listening—not that it mattered. "My boyfriend just broke up with me. And as for my parents, well . . . they passed. And no, my dad was decidedly not proud of me."

"Are you kidding?" Ryan asked. "I watched the YouTube video of your press conference. You were brilliant."

"But I can't make tikka masala."

Ryan cocked his head, curious.

"My mom died when I was young," Padma said. "My dad owned a restaurant in Brooklyn. He expected me to work there and eventually take it over. But I went to college, and he was not happy."

"Usually works the other way around with parents. What happened?"

"My dad? Heart attack, in the restaurant," she said. "A little over a year ago. I wasn't there, because I took the job with Ward and moved to D.C. . . ."

"Hey," Ryan said, and then he said it again a little softer while holding her gaze. "Hey. I know that look. It's not your fault."

Padma blinked a few times to banish the tears that were forming. She was a little taken aback at how much she was opening up to a complete stranger. But there was something comforting about Ryan. He was a dad, but not like her dad. More like a TV dad. Some idealized sitcom version, charming and confident but not domineering. Like he really wanted to hear what she had to say.

She sighed. "Easy enough to say."

"Yeah. I get it." Ryan shook his head. "So now that I've whiffed it on this entire conversation . . ."

"No, no," Padma said. "It's fine. I'm where I'm supposed to be."

Ryan got a funny little look on his face when she said that, but she couldn't decipher the meaning. He just shrugged and said, "Must be a nice feeling. So, what do you think—"

He was cut off by the intercom crackling to life.

"Thank you for your patience, ladies and gentlemen. Flight 9045 to Houston is now boarding."

Ryan and Padma both stood up, getting their luggage together. Ryan asked, "Where are you sitting?"

"Fourteen F," she said.

Ryan nodded. "Thirty-seven A. I'll wave at you from the back."

Padma laughed. He was charming, at least, which was a good sign if they were going to be roommates for two years. They moved toward the scrum of people crowding around the Jetway. She was glad they weren't sitting together—she really wanted to spend the time reading—but she was glad she wasn't alone on the flight either.

STARBLAZER MANUAL
INTRODUCTION

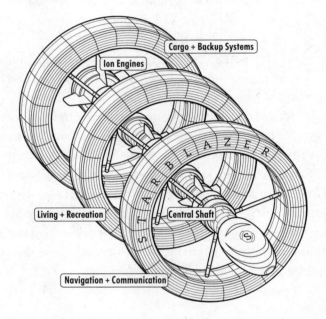

Welcome to *Starblazer*!

This state-of-the-art ship will be your home for the next two years, and we've done everything we can to ensure that you will be safe and comfortable throughout your journey. While the expedition to Titan will include a contingent of six astronauts, the ship is designed to support twelve.

As you can see from the model, the ship is made up of four parts: three wheels (decks), which will turn continuously, creating rotational (aka artificial) gravity, and a gravity-free central spoke, through which you can travel between the three sections.

The first deck includes navigation, communication, and access to life-sustaining systems. The second deck includes living quarters, a cafeteria, a recreation area that includes a gym, and an area for scientific work. The rear deck is for cargo, backup systems, and the satellite that you will launch into Titan's atmosphere.

Located at the back of the central shaft are two pieces of technology that change the game for space travel—an ion engine, which will cut the travel time exponentially, and an electromagnetic shield generator, which will keep you safe from space radiation.

In the following sections, we will go through the specific operational capabilities and amenities of each deck . . .

RYAN CRANE
JOHNSON SPACE CENTER, HOUSTON, TX

Ryan stepped through the heavy blue curtain and toward the long table with a tablecloth the same shade as the curtain, beyond which was a massive crowd of reporters already shouting questions.

The table had eight seats, each one with a microphone and a small bottle of water. Ryan tuned out the reporters and picked a seat on the far end. Padma sat next to him, which was comforting.

The flight delay—both in taking off and then waiting for a free gate upon arrival—meant they had to come straight to the press conference at NASA's Johnson Space Center, where he and the rest of the crew were about to undergo four weeks of intensive training.

His head spun at the prospect.

This was real.

And he wished he had some time to at least talk to Ward before they were hustled onto the stage, but it seemed everyone was running late. It's not like he was having second thoughts, but he would have liked the opportunity to have *some* thoughts before diving into the fray.

He barely had a chance to meet anyone else, and as everyone took their seats, he did his best to assess them. Being a cop made him good at that; a lot of his job, and sometimes his life, depended on his ability to make snap judgments.

Padma, who must be in her late twenties, was clearly brilliant, but her flat affect and blank stare made him wonder if she was on a spectrum of some kind. He couldn't say for sure; he wasn't a psychologist. But he also liked her immediately. She seemed almost as scared about this whole thing as he was.

There was Mike, early fifties: tall, solid, with a buzz cut and a perpetually suspect look on his face, which Ryan recognized from magazine covers over the years. He clearly had some issues with the setup here but was holding it back. He was a good soldier, doing what he was told. There also seemed to be a slight redness to his nose, his eyes the slightest bit bloodshot. He could be tired, but if Ryan had pulled him over while driving, he would feel compelled to conduct a field sobriety test.

Then there was Della. In her forties, a short Black woman with a shaved head, also a familiar face from years of news coverage. Her makeup was subtle but elegant, and she and Mike seemed to gravitate toward each other, whispering in each other's ears and smiling. It wasn't romantic, just the conduct of very old friends who trusted each other.

Next up was Alonso, early thirties. A handsome Hispanic man who seemed a bit out of his depth around Mike and Della. They were old pros, and he was the new hotshot. But they seemed to offer him a good bit of attention and deference. Probably because he was one of them.

No surprise that they were sitting together on one side of the table.

Finally, next to Padma was Courtney, or, as he kept on insisting everyone call him, Stitch. Late twenties, tall and dressed like a teenager. He looked at everything around him like he was a kid in a candy factory— the kind of kid, a jaded cop might think, you had to watch and make sure he wouldn't start grabbing things and knocking stuff over. But there was a sharpness to his eyes, like he was doing the same thing Ryan was: assessing.

And then there was him. Ryan Crane. D.C. cop. Forty-two years old.

All of them, about to be shot into space.

Ward sat at the center of the table next to Henry Owens, the head of NASA. Early sixties, gray suit. A factory-issue bureaucrat. Exactly how you'd expect the head of NASA to look. There was a neediness, almost desperation, in the way Owens was trying to hold Ward's attention as they whispered to each other.

It was obvious Ward was running the show, and Owens just seemed excited to get a little cast-off sliver of the spotlight.

Ward tapped the microphone, which did nothing to dull the cacophony, and said, "It seems like you folks might have a few questions."

An older woman with her hair in a tight bun stood and said, "Is this some kind of joke?"

"I don't see anyone laughing," Ward said, barely masking his immediate annoyance.

Other people tried to join, but the woman put her hand up, yelling over the crowd. "You really think putting three untrained civilians in space is a smart idea?"

Owens leaned over to the microphone. "We have three of the best astronauts ever produced sitting right here. Seaver and Jameson both twenty-plus-year veterans. Cardona, the youngest astronaut ever and already three flights under his belt. They've all been training on this mission for months. And flight director Bill Blanton has overseen more successful missions than anyone else in the history of NASA. Everyone will be required to complete the training. If they don't, they're off the flight."

Ward threw Owens a little glance, like maybe they hadn't talked about that, before leaning into his own microphone.

"And I'm sure that won't happen," Ward said, "because we're working with the best of the best."

Interesting.

A young woman with long blond hair—Ryan recognized her from television, but he wasn't sure which program—waved at him. "Officer Crane, any comment on the events that unfolded that put you here? Your heroic actions that saved Ward's life?"

"I was just doing my job," Ryan said into the mic, his voice crackling and booming as he got too close. He pulled back a little. "I wasn't angling for this. Ward generously offered it to me."

She continued, "And what do you make of the rumors that Ward put you on the flight to curry favor with law enforcement for his presidential run?"

Also interesting. He threw Ward a glance, but the billionaire was just smiling, his slightly narrowed eyes reading as *Answer the question and make it good.*

"I think I've got enough to learn about space travel," Ryan said.

"Politics seems slightly more complicated, and probably more danger-ous."

That drew a few chuckles, and before anyone could ask a follow-up, Ward said, "I'm here to talk about *Starblazer* and our mission to Titan. I won't be taking questions about my presidential bid."

"Mr. Smith, Mr. Smith," another reporter called. "How does it feel to be sitting here right now?"

"First off, call me Stitch," the young man said. "Second off, it's fuck-ing amazing . . . oh wait, shit, can I say 'fucking'? Oh fuck. Look, just, it's awesome, okay?"

This drew some more laughs, but they felt a little more condescend-ing. Whether he was embarrassed, there was no way to tell—Stitch was smiling like he'd just found a hundred-dollar bill on the ground.

Ward was smiling, too—but his was slightly tighter and more re-signed.

"Look," Mike said, his voice immediately commanding the room. "We're not here to play games. We're here to embark on a mission that's going to advance humanity and, frankly, has been a long time coming. So if you've got some serious questions about what we're aiming to do, ask them. If not, we can just get to work."

The chided crowd seemed to quiet a little at that.

Whatever Ryan had assumed about Mike, it was clear the man was a natural leader. He made a mental note that he'd have to navigate that.

The questions got more serious, focusing on the training, the time-lines, what kind of experiments would be conducted. Ryan struggled to keep up; the science of it occasionally outpaced his understanding.

Finally Ward said, "Okay, our intrepid heroes need a break, and we have to get started, so that's enough for today. Thank you all for coming. We'll see you in five weeks at the launch."

The assembled reporters kept yelling questions, but Ward turned off his microphone and leaned closer to Owens, whispering something in his ear. They were cut off mid-conversation by Mike, who leaned down toward Owens with a look on his face like he might hit the man. Mike said something terse and direct, pointing a finger less than an inch from his nose. Owens stared at him for a moment before nodding, and the two of them got up and quickly disappeared behind the curtain.

The rest of the crew followed. Ryan was the last to go. Before he ducked through the curtain, he gave one last look to the reporters and wondered what the hell he was getting himself into.

MIKE SEAVER
OFFICE OF HENRY OWENS, JOHNSON SPACE CENTER,
HOUSTON, TX

"Five weeks," Mike said, sitting heavily in the seat in front of Henry Owens's wide walnut desk. "Five fucking weeks. You told me we were going to launch six months from now."

"There's a perfectly good launch window, and given the length of time and what's at stake, it's in our best interest to move with some purpose," Owens said.

Mike shook his head. "This is a clown show."

"No, this is the mission," Owens said.

"You're sending us out in a privately built ship with three civilians," Mike said. "One of whom looks like he's not qualified to operate a go-kart. And now you're telling me that we're going to, what, give them a quick overview?"

Owens took off his glasses, placed them on the desk, and pinched the bridge of his nose. "You understand how NASA works, correct? I don't need to explain to you the economics of this."

"Yes, the politicians love us until they have to fund us, and we need Ward's money to stay afloat," Mike said. "I get all that. What I don't get is why you're letting him call the shots here."

Owens leaned forward and massaged his temples before falling back into the seat, the chair creaking underneath him. "Look, I'm not gonna deny that Ward has his own reasons for getting this up and running fast. But with the current state of the technology, so much of this is automated that the old days of every person needing to understand every part of the ship are pretty much over," he said. "And you heard what I said out there. Anyone who doesn't pass is off."

"Ward doesn't seem to agree. What happens when things don't go his way?" Mike asked. "Is he going to throw more money at you until you agree to his terms?"

"We are going to continue to—"

There was an insistent knock on the door, cutting off Owens, but before he could say anything, Bill Blanton walked in. The older, heavyset flight director's face was turned down like he was ready for war. Then he saw Mike and brightened a little.

"There you are," Bill said, crossing the room. Mike got up, and the two men embraced before stepping back and shaking hands.

"Figured you could use the backup," Mike said.

"Henry, I'm going to say it again, I have serious misgivings about this," Bill said. "That right there . . ."

He trailed off, like he was thinking for the right words, so Mike offered, "Clown show."

"Exactly. That clown show. I know you think this is what's going to save us, but it's gonna do more harm than good to our reputation in the long run. And that's if nothing goes wrong. If something does go wrong, people will die."

Owens pointed at Blanton. "And it's your responsibility to make sure that doesn't happen. Now, I've got a debrief with the president in five minutes, so why don't you two go get a cup of coffee and do whatever you have to do to make this work." He glanced at Mike. "You look like you could use one."

Mike started to protest but realized he shouldn't. He'd had only two drinks on the flight, just to calm his nerves. He followed Bill out of the room and into the hallway.

Bill glanced around to make sure they were alone. Then he looked at Mike and said, "I can smell it on your breath."

"We're not training today," Mike said.

"But we have a lot more in front of us, and I'm going to need you on this one," Bill said. "As much as I'd like to walk away, they're doing this with or without me—and I'm going to be even angrier at myself if I walk away and something goes wrong."

"How many of these rodeos have we been on together? I'm fine."

"You're fine," Bill said. "And what if I ask Helen how you're doing?"

"I'm *fine,*" Mike said.

Bill shook his head. "You damn well better be. I wish Owens would have gotten his head out of Ward's ass long enough to tell us he was moving up the schedule." He sighed and patted Mike on the shoulder. "Seems this is the hand we've been dealt. Bright and early tomorrow, okay?"

"Bright and early," Mike said.

He watched Bill march off down the hallway, probably to go have a meltdown in his office—there was always at least one piece of freshly patched drywall in there that was waiting to be painted over.

And Mike made himself a promise.

No drinking tonight. He'd go into the next day with a clear head.

DELLA JAMESON
ASTRONAUT QUARTERS, JOHNSON SPACE CENTER, HOUSTON, TX

Della looked around the dinner table at the assembled group: the hero cop, the overeager kid, the socially awkward physicist. Then there was Mike, his usual gruff self, and Alonso, who just seemed happy to be there.

This was going to be a hell of a trip.

The surroundings, at least, were amazing. It was a newly constructed facility—all paid for by Ward—so that all the trainees could stay at the center. It would certainly make things easier, cutting down on commute times had they been sent to a hotel. It came with the bonus of keeping them all in close contact.

Pretty soon they would be stuck on a tin can traveling through space at incomprehensible speed for two years. If this was a powder keg of personalities, better to sort it out soon.

She glanced down at the printed menu in front of her, which was offering three dinner options—a Korean rice bowl with beef, one with chicken, or a vegan version. There was an appetizer course of spring rolls and dumplings.

Another nice thing: while the living quarters included a communal kitchen, Ward had hired a team of private chefs to take care of their meals while they were here. Again, probably so they could concentrate.

A woman came out and took their drink orders. Ryan and Padma opted for Diet Coke, while Stitch went with a Sprite. Alonso stuck to water. Mike ordered a beer. Della gave him a little look, and he mouthed, *Just one.* She'd prefer he didn't drink at all, but she also didn't want to leave him to drink alone, so she ordered a white wine.

As they waited for their drinks, she turned to Ryan, Padma, and Stitch. "So, how are y'all feeling? I can imagine this is a lot."

"It's crazy," Stitch said. "I'm sorry I said so many curse words at the conference . . ."

Della waved her hand. "There are worse fucking things."

That won a little smile from Stitch.

"So, Ryan," she said. "Padma and Stitch have had time to mentally prepare for this, but you just got dropped in. Is there anything you'd like to ask us? I'm sure you have questions."

"Only about a million," Ryan said. "I appreciate and respect the position you and Mike and Alonso are in, trying to get us through this safely. I'm here to listen and learn, and I'll be the first to step aside if you tell me I'm not up to the task."

Good answer.

Della glanced at Mike, who seemed to be pleased with that, too.

"Look, I'm not going to lie," Della said. "This isn't going to be easy. And space is dangerous. Something goes wrong, we'll do the best we can, but help will be a long way away. If we're all going to do this . . ."

The waitress came back in with a tray of drinks. She placed them down and asked if they were ready to order, and Della asked for a moment. The waitress nodded and hustled out of the room, and Della raised her wineglass. The rest of the group followed suit.

"If we're going to do this, we have to trust each other," she said. "We all walked in here with baggage. Let's leave it at the door and focus on the task at hand. How does that sound?"

"Good to me," Ryan said.

"Sure," Mike said, though Della didn't buy it, from the brusque tone of his voice.

"Let's do this," Stitch said. "Let's go to Titan, motherfuckers!"

Even Mike cracked a smile as they all leaned over the table, clinking their glasses together.

Della wasn't naïve. She knew a simple toast wasn't going to lock them all into place and make this whole process go smoothly.

She expected one or two people to drop out along the way.

But this felt like a decent enough start.

ALONSO CARDONA
ASTRONAUT QUARTERS, JOHNSON SPACE CENTER,
HOUSTON, TX

Alonso stood outside in the chilly night air—chilly for Houston; it was probably only in the sixties—and looked out over the jumble of buildings where they'd be training for the next month.

He felt some degree of hope. Della had established a good tone.

He sighed and did the thing he didn't want to do. He looked at his phone. More texts from Ethan.

ETHAN:
You looked great up there at the press conference.

ETHAN:
Gonna miss you.
Maybe we can check in before you launch?

Alonso stared at the keyboard, trying to think of a response, and found he had no idea what to say. Before he could settle on something, he heard a voice behind him. "Hey, man."

He turned to find Stitch, who offered his hand.

"I guess we didn't really get a chance to meet yet," he said. "Like, formally. This whole thing has been such a rush."

"Right." Alonso returned the shake.

Stitch pulled a small pink vape from the pocket of his jeans, taking a long pull before blowing a cloud of fruity-smelling smoke into the air. He offered it, but Alonso waved it off.

"So, how did you get the name Stitch?" Alonso asked.

"It's . . ." Stitch looked around. "It's my tag name. Graffiti. I'm an artist. And I know, I know. It's art, I don't care what anyone says. I don't tag people's houses or anything. But vacant properties? Sure. Bring a little beauty to something that's falling apart."

"I get that. But Stitch . . . what does it *mean*?"

Stitch took another hit and blew out the smoke, thinking about it. "It's one of those things that's kinda hard to explain." He looked down at his hand. "Art is an act of creation, right? It's stitching together something with something else to create something new." He shrugged. "I dunno. Just like the way it sounds inside me, you know? Sometimes it's just hard to express a feeling like that. Something you just *know* is right."

Alonso thought about Ethan—his movie-star grin, the way he arched his left eyebrow when he laughed. He caught himself smiling, and Stitch gave him a curious look.

"Yeah, I get that," Alonso said, scrambling to change the subject. "So, what do you think? Ready to go to space?"

Stitch took a long, thoughtful drag on the vape, not breaking eye contact with Alonso. Clearly he realized there was something Alonso didn't want to talk about, but Stitch was content to let it lie.

"Ready?" he asked. "On the one hand, sure. The name of the game in graffiti is who will last the longest, go the furthest. That's about to be me. On the other hand, absolutely not, but we'll see how it plays out. I mean, I have questions. A ton of questions. Like, I want to have kids one day, and is this electromagnetic shield generator Ward developed really going to keep out space radiation the way it's supposed to? If *Starblazer* is being constructed in space and the overall weight of the ship isn't a big deal, why not just use a low-atomic-mass material, like lithium or boron? I just wish we were using something a little more tested."

Alonso's head spun. He hadn't expected that. "Holy shit. Someone knows their rocket science."

Stitch gave a half smile and a shrug. "Wikipedia, baby."

"Well, look," Alonso said, "the radiation shields have been tested. I'm not too worried about that. Honestly, the scariest part is going around the dark side of Titan. No communication with Earth. Completely out of view. Facing the darkness of space. That's big."

"Yeah," Stitch said, gazing up into the night sky. "Makes you think about just how small we really are."

"Yeah, it does."

Stitch put up his hands. "Sorry, didn't mean to intrude if you were deep in some thoughts. They're about to serve dessert. Some kind of Korean shaved ice thing. This food is dope."

"Why don't you just head in," Alonso said. "I need another minute."

Stitch nodded, pocketed the vape, and disappeared inside.

Alonso looked up at the sky again.

Felt both the smallness and the vastness of the universe.

And he took out his phone.

Ethan wanting to know if they could check in before he left.

ALONSO: Maybe, yeah.

He started to type out *I'm going to miss you, too.* Then he stopped, put his phone away, and went back inside, both hoping and not hoping it would buzz with a response.

JOHN WARD
FOUR SEASONS, HOUSTON, TX

John leaned back into the couch, watching the video feed on his laptop of the *Starblazer* crew sitting around the communal table, enjoying their dessert.

They'd fallen into an easy rapport. Well, everyone except Mike Seaver. He continued to be a hard-ass, addressing mostly Della and Alonso and not really anyone else.

Camila sat down on the chair across from him and kicked off her high heels, leaning down to rub her feet, all business. "What do you think?"

"So far it's going as well as we could have hoped," he said. "Seaver is going to be an issue. As is Blanton. Neither seems thrilled we moved up the launch window."

"Speaking of, you didn't even tell me," she said. "And you tell me everything."

Ward shrugged, peering into the screen, watching Mike order his fourth beer of the night. "Because the timing works better this way. I'd explain it, but . . ."

"But you don't want to."

"Nope," Ward said. He sat back and gestured to the screen. "Seaver and Blanton. Our biggest obstacles. The two of them are old-school, and they're old pals."

"But they're not in charge," Camila said. "Henry Owens is."

"Henry Owens is a sycophant who wants to keep his job when I'm president," Ward said. "If he had something to offer the other candidates, he'd be rolling over for them, too. Lucky for me I'm the only one who cares about NASA. Ultimately it doesn't matter what he thinks. If the two of them make a sufficient amount of noise, it could screw us."

"Then why not try and push them out?"

Ward scratched the back of his head before waving his hand like he was trying to disperse a puff of smoke. "Don't think I haven't thought about it. But if this is going to play, we need the best."

"A grumpy old alcoholic is the best?" Camila asked.

"I think of him more as a seasoned vet with a drinking problem," he said.

Which wasn't the entire truth. There was more to it than that—way more—but he couldn't explain it. It was one thing he had to keep from Camila.

The only thing.

Camila nodded toward the computer. "Sure hope they don't find the cameras."

"They won't," he said. "That's why I oversaw construction."

Camila nodded. "Want some food?"

"I'm going to listen for a little longer. Arm myself with knowledge."

"I'll order something extra for when you smell it and get annoyed at me for not anticipating that you *would* be hungry," she said, disappearing into the hotel suite.

Ward considered saying something back but ultimately shrugged and focused on the screen.

So much was riding on this.

On these six people, specifically.

RYAN CRANE
JOHNSON SPACE CENTER, HOUSTON, TX

Ryan looked around the small, windowless classroom at his fellow astronauts.

Astronauts. Himself included.

He was still trying to wrap his head around it.

It didn't help that his head felt partially shrink-wrapped. He'd had a few too many beers with dinner last night. He wasn't going to drink at all, but once Mike started in, Ryan figured why not. Padma looked to be feeling the effects of the long night, too, though he suspected that was something else; she'd excused herself before the end of the night to go catch up on some paperwork.

Stitch was slumping in his seat, while Mike, Della, and Alonso were sitting up front, ramrod straight and ready to go. He was most surprised to see Mike upright. He'd stopped counting Mike's beers after the third, but the man looked ready to run a marathon.

Maybe he just had more practice.

As Ryan downed the last of his coffee out of his new NASA mug, wondering if he had time to find some ibuprofen, a heavyset man in a rumpled dress shirt came in. His hair was slicked back but slightly unkempt, like he'd done it in a rush.

"Good morning, kids," he said. "For those of you who don't know me, I'm Bill Blanton, your flight director." Bill and Mike exchanged subtle nods, apparently members of the same Old Boys Club.

He was carrying a heavy stack of paperwork under his arm, which he passed to Alonso, who then passed copies out to everyone in the classroom. Ryan accepted his with a "thank you" and dropped the novel-sized printout on the desk in front of him.

"My job is to get you into space, to Titan, and back, alive," Blanton said. "If this were a football team, I would be the coach. But the stakes are a hell of a lot higher. Now, for this to work, I need the six of you . . ."

A small snore erupted from behind Ryan. Blanton's face darkened. Ryan turned around to see Stitch leaning back, asleep. He reached over and knocked on the desk, and Stitch jerked awake, looked around like he had no idea where he was, and then threw two enthusiastic thumbs-ups at Blanton.

Blanton sighed, his shoulders slumping, before he continued. "I need the six of you to work as a team. Something happens up there, you have to be able to rely on each other. Do I want you to memorize all that information I just handed you? Hell yes. But you're going to be backed up by an amazing team of experts. You'll have all the tools you need. Your ability to recall how an oxygen recycler works is slightly less important than your ability to work as a cohesive unit. Understand?"

The three professional astronauts responded with "yes, sir."

Ryan nodded, and Stitch and Padma mumbled in affirmation.

Blanton continued, eyes skeptical: "To be perfectly clear, the only way this mission succeeds is if and only if all six of you pull your weight.

At any given time, two of you could be pulling rotations, two of you could be asleep, and the other two could be alone facing any number of unforeseen crises. If any of you have the bright idea to coast through this training, expecting the others to cover for you when it comes to the heavy lifting, I assure you that's a recipe for disaster."

Stitch scoffed. "Look, I'm just a lottery winner. Here for a good time. When you say disaster—"

Blanton didn't miss a beat. "I mean the squandering of billions, utter humiliation in the eyes of the global population, and almost certain death. Are we clear?"

Stitch, humbled, gave a shrug.

"Understand one more thing," Blanton said. "I have final say on this. The next few weeks are going to be intense. If any one of you doesn't pass muster"—he nodded toward Mike, Della, and Alonso—"yourselves included, I will pull the plug on this so fast that Ward's head will spin. I've never lost an astronaut, and I don't mean to start. Everyone got that?"

Everyone said "yes, sir" this time.

Blanton took one more look over the group, like he was measuring each of them in turn. Ryan wasn't sure if Blanton liked what he saw, but this was what he had to work with.

Ryan, meanwhile, felt his own stomach dropping.

"Now, if you'll open to the first page . . ."

He did, flipping to a page full of text. He flipped through the next couple of pages, too. It was dense. A lot to learn in a short time.

Okay, Ryan thought. *We can do this.*

3

TRAINING

DELLA JAMESON
"STARBLAZER DECK"

The high-pitched whine of the alarm pierced Della's eardrums. She turned to the console to assess the situation, then clicked over to the communication system to give everyone a status report.

"Okay, here's what we got," she said. "As you can tell from the fact that you're floating, we've lost rotational spin, and therefore artificial gravity. In addition, oxygen saturation is dropping, fast, which seems to indicate a leak. We need to find the section it's coming from and seal it off."

Ryan was the first to come over, vaguely disconcerted. "What's the play, boss?"

"Everyone put on an oxygen mask," she said, keeping her voice calm and even—she had to set the right tone, which was *don't panic*. "Then I need you and Alonso to get to engineering. See if you can get us spinning again. Padma and Stitch, await further instructions, but be ready to move. You'll have to manually close off the section of the ship with the leak, and we can figure it out once things are stabilized."

"Got it," Stitch said.

No answer from Padma. Della asked, "You there, Padma?"

"Yeah, sorry, just . . . okay, nervous. I mean, this is bad, right?"

From the look on Padma's face, it seemed like she immediately regretted her insecurity.

Della clenched her teeth and inhaled deeply through her nose. *This shouldn't be so hard,* she thought. "It's only bad if we don't do our jobs. Mike, how you holding up?"

Mike sighed into his communicator. "Don't understand why you're keeping me on the sidelines here."

"Because your leg is broken, you big dope," she said.

"Shouldn't make much difference if we're weightless . . ."

"Stay put," Della said. "Can't risk you getting any more hurt. We've trained for this. The team can handle it."

She wasn't sure if that was the truth, or what she was hoping for.

"All right, approaching engineering," Alonso said. "We'll report back shortly."

Della took a deep breath and surveyed the console in front of her. It was a multiple system failure. Not good. There was some kind of malfunction, but she had no video, which meant she couldn't see what anyone was doing. And while the oxygen was dropping across the ship, she couldn't pinpoint the leak. A broken sensor, on top of everything else.

She had to walk everyone through this, without her equipment to guide her.

She felt blind and useless, and that made her want to leave the bridge, to see who she could assist, but she knew that she was better off where she was, on the off chance the sensors or video came back.

"Hey, any idea of where that leak is coming from?" Stitch asked.

"Just wondering that myself," Della said, surveying the screens.

"If you can't get a specific location, can you at least view oxygen levels by section?" Stitch asked. "See if one of them is losing oxygen any faster than the others."

"I don't think you can do that . . ." Mike started.

"Actually, I think we can," Della said, clicking at the array of buttons in front of her.

Mike offered an annoyed grunt in response.

"Lucky guess," Stitch offered sheepishly.

Alonso jumped in. "There seems to be a malfunction in the rotational thrusters. Which explains why we lost gravity. Since it's all three decks, I'm thinking software, not hardware. If we can get them firing again, we can get rotation restored."

"Software is good," Della said. "Less chance we have to do an EVA."

"I'm going to help them," Mike said.

"Damn it, Mike, no, you're not," Della said. "Your leg is broken. If they get the spin restored while you're floating and you suddenly hit the floor, you're going to be way worse off."

"Hey, did you try the thing?" Stitch asked.

"Stitch, don't jump in like that, and be patient, okay?" Della said. "This is an emergency, but we have time to solve it. Slow is smooth, and smooth is fast."

She checked the screens in front of her, which showed an overall schematic of the ship. Oxygen in the first deck was holding at 78 percent. Same with the second.

But the third was 76. She clicked back to the first, which was still 78.

"Okay, I've isolated the problem to deck three," she said. "Padma and Stitch, get over there now. Alonso, what have you got?"

"We have to manually reset the engines. Get the decks spinning in the right direction. Shouldn't be too hard, it's just going to take some time."

"Okay, you got this, Ryan?"

"I think so," he said, his tone less than sure. "This sound about right to you, Mike?"

"Well, I think . . ."

"Hey," Della said, breaking in. "The captain is incapacitated, making me acting captain. You take my orders, not his, you understand?"

"Yes, Captain," Ryan said. "Sorry, Captain."

Della rolled her eyes. He seemed way more interested in deferring to Mike, which was not sitting well with her. Something they'd need to discuss.

"Padma and Stitch," Della said. "Report."

"Just waiting on you," Stitch said.

Della didn't like that Padma wasn't answering on the comms, but that was something to address later, too. She clicked through the various sections of the third deck—the bunks, the gym, the lounge. It didn't take long to find: the cafeteria, which was down to 71 percent and dropping more steadily than the rest of the deck.

"The leak is coming from the cafeteria," Della said. "Seal off the section, and then get to engineering to see if you can help."

Della heard Stitch talking, but not into the comm. "I've got this, Padma, why don't you head on over?"

"Negative, Stitch," Della said. "It's not your job to give orders. The two of you work together. We don't do that Clint Eastwood shit here."

"Who's Clint Eastwood?" Stitch asked.

"Jesus," Mike muttered.

"Seal off the doors on either side of the mess," Della said. "You remember where the manual door controls are?"

Silence on the other end.

"Padma and Stitch, come back."

"We're here," Stitch said. "I think I see the problem. Why don't I just use the patch kit?"

"You're not qualified to use the patch kit," Della said. "Seal off the section, we'll do an EVA to repair the hull from the outside. It's safer."

"Right, but, why don't I just give it a try," Stitch said. "Gotta learn sometime."

"Damn it, that's your captain," Mike said. "An order is an order."

No response.

"Stitch," Della said.

Still no response.

"Padma?" Della asked.

"Yeah, uh . . . here," Padma said.

"Where's Stitch?"

"He's, uh . . . he's using the patch kit. He's not responding to me either. I think he turned off his comm."

"That little asshole," Mike said. "I'm heading over there."

Della's pulse quickened. She was losing control of the situation, and fast.

"Mike, stay put," Della said. "Alonso, sitrep."

"We're working on the problem," he said, with a slight hint of annoyance in his voice. "We're moving a little slow. There are some manual switches to throw, and Ryan wants to make sure we're doing it right."

"Ryan, what's the problem here?" Della asked. "You two can cover this twice as fast if you come at it from either side. The rotation of the decks helps generate power to the electromagnetic shields. Until we get those moving, we're vulnerable to radiation and debris."

"Right, Captain, just, you know, don't want to do it wrong," Ryan said, his tone lacking his characteristic self-confidence.

"No time to be shy. Get to those switches, and . . ."

"Patch is done!" Stitch said.

"Stitch, I told you to seal off the section," Della said.

"Right, but then we'd have no place to eat," he said.

"I gave you . . ."

The alarm cut in again, but with the sensors down, it took Della a moment to figure out what it was.

And then she saw it: oxygen was dropping precipitously now.

Sixty-two percent.

Fifty-eight percent . . .

There was another hole somewhere on the ship, or else the hole that Stitch tried to patch got bigger. She flicked through the computer screens, trying to find a fix, when suddenly Blanton's voice came crackling into the comm.

"And . . . you're all dead," he said.

Della sighed and pulled off the VR headset. She looked around the large, mostly empty room, where everyone was suspended from animatronic gimbals and harnesses that gave them the sense of weightlessness. It wasn't the same as being in space, of course, because nothing compared to that incredible feeling of your organs floating in your body without the downward pull of the planet. But it was close enough.

Mike stood up from his chair across the room—his "broken leg" part of the simulation, to see how they'd respond with a crew member out of commission. He pulled off his VR set as staffers in navy NASA polos came flooding into the center of the room, helping the crew unfasten themselves from their floating pods. It took a good ten minutes to get everyone down, and they all silently shuffled over to the circle of chairs in the corner of the room. Stitch looked casually defiant, Ryan decidedly glum, and Padma like she'd just spelled her own name wrong on her SAT.

Once they were all seated, Blanton dragged another chair over and fell into it, exhausted by the entire ordeal. He spoke with a heavy resignation, not making eye contact with anyone in the room. "So, what went wrong this time?"

"I'll tell you what went wrong," Mike said. "We pulled three civilians into a mission they weren't qualified for." Stitch discreetly flipped Mike the bird, and Ryan's downcast expression implied that he didn't exactly disagree with the assessment. Padma just sat with her hands folded in her lap.

"What went *wrong*," Della said, looking at Mike, "was a failure in communication." She eyed the crew members in turn. "Ryan, you have to trust your instincts. Me or Mike or Alonso don't have to sign off on every little thing. Stitch, there's a reason I gave you that order. The patch kits take specialized training. That's an Alonso job, but I needed him in engineering. Sealing off the section would have bought us more than enough time. And Padma, if you lock up during a simulation, what's going to happen when a multisystem failure happens for real?"

"I mean, is something like that really going to happen?" Stitch asked.

"Doesn't matter," Della said. "This isn't about those particular fixes. It's about our ability to work as a team. And right now, we're not working as a team."

"Two weeks," Mike said, only barely under his breath. "We should be further along."

"We should," Blanton said. "We're zero for six on today's simulations. This does not bode well."

Della sighed. "This is how we work out the kinks . . ."

But her heart wasn't in the defense. It was clear this wasn't working.

There was a reason astronauts were an elite bunch and went through a rigorous testing and selection process. As much as she wanted to believe that anyone could rise to the challenge, as much as she liked Ryan and Padma, and even, sometimes, Stitch, for his unbridled excitement and enthusiasm—the simple fact was: this wasn't working.

She could tell from the look on Blanton's face that he knew that as well.

Blanton got up, whispered something to Mike, and stalked off down the hall. Della was starting to feel like it was less and less likely they were going to go to Titan at all.

MIKE SEAVER
BILL BLANTON'S OFFICE, JOHNSON SPACE CENTER, HOUSTON, TX

"You wanted to see me?" Mike asked, sticking his head through the open doorway.

Blanton waved Mike over. "Close the door. Sit."

Mike did so, then plopped into the chair across from the flight director. "Feels like I'm getting called to the principal's office," he said, scanning the room—there were two fresh holes in the drywall.

"A little bit, you are," Blanton said. "You have to cool it with the drinking."

Mike's shoulders tightened. "The hell do you mean by that?"

"We've been friends a long time," Blanton said. "Don't treat me like an idiot."

"Look, Bill," Mike said, leaning forward, folding his hands before rubbing them together, "what's the big deal? Things are getting done. On my end, at least."

"This is from higher up," Blanton said. "You know me, this isn't the kind of thing that makes me lose sleep. But one of your piss tests came up hot. We take those in the morning. Which means you either drank enough the night before that you still had it in your system, or you woke up and put vodka in your Wheaties. Owens wants to pull you off."

"What's it even matter," Mike said. "Not like I can drink up there."

"That's the problem," Blanton said. "Last thing we need is you getting the DTs in goddamn outer space. Not to mention, you know anything that brings a whiff of addiction is a big no-no around these parts. So I need you to put down the booze, now. Get it out of your system before we have to strap your ass to a rocket."

"Bill, I . . ."

"Mike, you know as well as I do how fragile all of this is," he said. "The longer the people up top have to think about this stuff, the more likely someone's going to raise an objection that can't be overruled. I don't give a goddamn about your health, and I know you don't. It's the mission that matters."

Mike sighed. "Thanks, friend."

"You know what I mean. I see how bad you want this. So, cut it out with the booze, because they're probably going to start doing random tests, and I won't be able to do anything about that."

Mike nodded, feeling both frustrated and a little ashamed. It really was a call to the principal's office. And as much as he wanted to argue back, to try to make the point that the drinking didn't matter . . . it did.

Something Helen would be happy to confirm.

"Not that this mission is looking like a sure bet," Blanton said. "What do you think?"

"I think we're doing the best we can with what we've got," Mike said. "And if you were smart, you'd bounce out those three civilians."

Blanton laughed. "NASA? Smart? What rock have you been living under?"

Mike nodded. "It's just not gelling. Della is great, Alonso is doing some fine work. But we have to get people on the same page. I don't know that I see it happening."

Blanton sighed. "This is happening, whether we want it to or not." Then he pushed himself to standing, walked around the desk, and sat in the chair directly opposite Mike. "The reason we're having this conversation is because, despite everything, I trust you the same way I trust the sun to go down at night. If we're stuck with these civvies, then I need you at the wheel. I need you to help me bring everyone home. Can you do that for me?"

Mike dropped his chin to his chest. Then he looked back at Blanton. "Yeah. I can do that."

Blanton patted Mike on his knee. "Good man."

"You want to hug it out?" Mike asked.

Blanton laughed. "Get the fuck out of my office."

STITCH
ASTRONAUT QUARTERS, JOHNSON SPACE CENTER, HOUSTON, TX

Stitch looked at himself in the bathroom mirror, raking the stubble on his chin, and sighed.

Just listen and do what you're told, he thought.

He understood, intellectually, everything about what they were doing. He knew there was a chain of command. He knew how everyone else looked at him—like he was some douchebag who didn't deserve to be there. High school dropout, skater, tagger. Little did they know he taught himself to code at thirteen, aced the SAT with zero tutoring, probably could have landed at an Ivy. Developed a generative AI app for creating custom digital art toolboxes, which he could have sold for millions but decided to give away to the public because it fit better with his artistic moral compass.

Maybe if he'd finished college or taken the money or worn khakis every day, people would respect him. But that life wasn't for him. And now he was paying the price in dismissive scowls and disrespect.

Which meant he had to work even harder to prove himself.

But in the heat of the moment, it all went out the window.

It was a personality asset or flaw, depending on the situation. He could move fast, think faster, and come up with clever solutions. Just, sometimes that bit him in the ass, when he moved a little too fast, or got a little too clever.

He needed to slow down.

"Slow is smooth, smooth is fast," he said to himself in the mirror. Then he headed out of the shared men's room and made his way to the entertainment room, which consisted of a table for games, some theater-style seating—big plush seats—and a giant projector hooked to every streaming service imaginable.

Downtime was rare. They'd been training nonstop for two weeks now, but it was nice to have a place like this to unwind. Especially on the harder days. Sitting in a centrifuge trying not to puke, hanging in a VR harness all day—these were not his ideas of a good time.

The television was already on—some cooking competition show. Must be Alonso. That was his thing. As Stitch walked toward the front of the room, he confirmed it was him, curled in one of the big chairs, and offered him a nod.

"Hey," Stitch said.

"Hey," Alonso said back, barely taking his eyes off the screen.

"Cool if I join?" Stitch asked.

Alonso nodded at the seat next to him. Stitch sat and offered Alonso a pack of gum. Alonso waved it off as Stitch popped out a piece and stuck it between his teeth.

"Docs told me I had to stop vaping," he said, noisily chewing.

"Health reasons, sure, but they said no way are they packing vapes for the trip. They think sending a case of smoking devices filled with lithium-ion batteries into space is an unwise decision. Buncha nerds."

"You'll thank them in twenty years when you don't have popcorn lung," Alonso said.

"I will," Stitch said. "Doesn't make them not nerds."

They fell into an easy silence, watching as chefs used an assortment of uncommon ingredients to try to make a meal. As a young woman struggled with cleaning and prepping chicken feet, Stitch popped another piece of gum and said, "I'm sorry."

"For what?" Alonso asked.

"Not listening."

Alonso made an affirmative noise in the back of his throat. After a moment Stitch wondered if that was it, but then Alonso lifted the remote, paused the show, and turned toward him.

"We need you on board here," Alonso said. "You're smart. Maybe no one else sees it, but I do. You have to understand the psychology here for us. Me, Mike, Della . . . we want more than anything to go. This is our names in the history books. This is possibly giving the entire human race a shot at survival. But more than going, we want to come home."

Stitch felt his face flush, and he sat back in the chair. "Man . . . I'm really sorry."

Alonso sighed. "It's not just you. It's all of us."

"That's a fact," Stitch said. "Ryan is too ass-kissy. He's got good instincts, but he's worried that if he takes the alpha role it's gonna offend Mike, which I don't think is true. Mike's not that kind of guy—I think he just wants everyone to do their job. And Padma, she just needs a little of my energy, I think. Just a bit. She's somewhere in A-Ville."

"What's A-Ville?"

"ADHD-Asperger's-autism territory," Stitch said. "It's not my place to diagnose her. Just, you know, neurodivergent. And then there's me, who's a permanent resident of that town as well. I need to focus, Ryan needs to trust himself, and so does Padma. Or I guess, more specifically, they need to trust themselves, and I need to trust myself less and trust the three of you a little more."

Alonso nodded. "That's actually a very concise take on the whole thing."

They sat in silence for a moment before Alonso turned the show back on. They watched for a bit, but Stitch couldn't focus. He was more zoned in on the problem in front of him. They had two weeks to get things straightened out. And he believed Alonso that if they didn't, any one of them would march right into Henry Owens's office and tell him they were out.

"Maybe we should do some trust falls or something," Stitch offered.

Alonso gave him a half smile, then cocked his head, like something had occurred to him, and whipped out his phone.

"I think I have an idea," Alonso said. "Let me poke around a little . . ."

Stitch turned back to the television show, happy to let Alonso fall down whatever rabbit hole he was in. He was just beginning to feel sleep sneaking in at the edge of his brain when Alonso said, "Ha!"

"What?" Stitch asked.

Alonso turned his phone around and showed Stitch what he had found.

And Stitch couldn't help but laugh.

"Seriously?" Stitch asked.

"Seriously. What do you think?"

"I think it's fucking brilliant," Stitch said.

PADMA SINGH
ASTRONAUT QUARTERS, JOHNSON SPACE CENTER, HOUSTON, TX

The screen in front of Padma blurred. She'd been staring at it for too long.

It should have been Titan research. She still had an impossible amount of prep to do. Instead she'd been googling phrases like "how to combat frozen nerves" and "how to be confident" and was finding a ton of results, but mostly for self-help courses, and nothing that was immediately useful.

She knew the things she needed to do.

She just had to *do* them.

The problem was, at every critical juncture, Padma questioned whether it was the right move. She ran the steps over in her head to make sure she was prepared to execute them. She worried that she would do it wrong and what that would mean for the rest of the crew. She considered whether it was worth suggesting other options . . .

And by the time those thought processes were complete, she found that everyone was staring at her, waiting for her to act.

Do it, Padma thought to herself. *Just do it. It'll be fine.*

Easier thought than done.

An incoming video message cut through the fog in her head.

Ward.

She answered the call, and Ward was staring at the screen. It looked like he was on a plane.

Padma held her breath. Maybe this was it. He was going to ream her out and pull her off the mission. Tell her that since she couldn't get her act together, he was going to have to replace her. She wouldn't have blamed him for trying, but more than anything in this world, she wanted to go, so she started to formulate defenses in her head.

"There's my rock star," Ward said. "Henry tells me things are going swimmingly."

That was not what she expected.

Was Owens lying to Ward?

Or was Ward lying to boost her confidence?

Someone was full of shit. That's all she could be sure of.

"It's going," Padma said. "You know, just a lot of material to get familiar with. We're all trying our best."

"I'm sure you're going to pull it off," Ward said, seemingly distracted by something offscreen, which made Padma suspect that Ward was the one who was lying.

"Did you get those questions I sent to you?" Padma asked. "I wanted to go over the probe. Specifically how the collected data is going to be sent back, and how I'm going to access the system to review it. I imagine that—"

Ward waved his hand. "Not important. Once you get back, I'm going to have an office set up for you, near your place in D.C. Twenty-four-hour, seven-day access. With a cot and a kitchenette, because as much as I'll encourage you to go home and get some rest, I doubt you will."

Ward paused for an awkward beat, then proceeded, his typically casual tone oddly stilted.

"I've got something else to ask you. And I need you to be straight with me."

"Sure," Padma said.

"No one else in the room with you?"

Padma glanced around her small, empty bunk, just to be sure, even though the question itself made her stomach drop a little.

"Just me," she said.

Ward nodded slowly. "Has anyone contacted you?"

"Has anyone . . ."

"You know, anything weird, or uncomfortable, or just strange. Anyone asking you about the project, who's involved, what's going on, et cetera et cetera. Phone calls, emails?"

Padma paused for a moment, unsure how to take that one.

"Of course not," she said.

"And you'd tell me if someone did, correct?"

"Immediately, of course," Padma said.

"Excellent, good to know," Ward said, a smile stretching across his face. "Okay, have a great night."

And the video clicked off.

Padma stared at the screen, wondering what the hell that was about. She'd gotten used to Ward's eccentricities, but that was a whole new level of weird. He seemed paranoid about something. But what?

Maybe it had something to do with the people who'd tried to mow them down with assault weapons, something that still had Padma checking over her shoulder and struggling to fall asleep. How close she'd come to getting hurt; it was another reason why she was thankful to have Ryan there.

She felt safer with a cop around.

There was a knock at the door.

"Come in," she said.

Alonso poked his head in. "Hey, need everyone assembled at the van, nine A.M. tomorrow morning."

"Our call time isn't until ten," she said.

Alonso winked. "Change of plans. We're mixing things up. Wear comfortable shoes."

"What the hell are we doing?" she asked, more thrown than amused.

But Alonso had already ducked out of the doorway. Padma wanted to chase him down and ask him what was going on. She didn't do well with surprises. Wondering what he had in store for them would be another thing that would keep her up far longer than she intended, on top of the fact that she now had to wake up earlier.

She turned back to her laptop. With the video-chat screen gone, she was back to staring at the search results for "how not to freeze."

Maybe this was a good first step. Trust the process.

RYAN CRANE
ASTRONAUT QUARTERS, JOHNSON SPACE CENTER, HOUSTON, TX

Nina's face appeared on the screen. She was propped up in bed, hair askew, like maybe she'd been sleeping.

"I'm sorry, sweetheart, did I wake you?" Ryan asked, trying to project a positive attitude.

"You did," she said with a smirk, "but I'll give you a pass because you're cute."

"I accept," he said. "Kids in bed?"

"Yeah, they wanted to stay up, but, school night." She sighed. "You can't get away any earlier?"

"Not really," Ryan said. "They've got us from morning until night. Tomorrow we get a bit of a later start, so maybe I can check in with them before they go to school. How are they holding up?"

"They miss their dad," Nina said. "I miss him, too."

"How are *you* holding up?"

Nina welled up, wiped away a tear, and looked off to the side, like she was considering her answer, which Ryan didn't like. "I'm okay. My sister came by for a bit to help. She's going to move here permanently in a month. It was a little easier with her. I knew this would be hard . . ."

Ryan nodded to himself, then said evenly: "Maybe this wasn't the best idea after all."

"Why do you say that?" she asked quickly, obviously thrown. "What do *you* want?"

Ryan shrugged. "A big part of me wants to go through with this. But it's hard, you know? My instincts don't apply. If we're in space and losing oxygen, that's a lot different from being on the job and assessing a threat."

"Do you want to come home?" she asked.

Ryan took a contemplative beat. "Of course I want to come home," he finally said. "I miss you. I miss the kids. The training is kicking my ass. And there's gonna be a point where it'll be too late to make a different decision. I doubt they'll go for it if I ask them to pop a U-turn at Mars."

Nina chuckled at the joke, but Ryan could sense she wasn't in a joking mood.

He sighed and stretched, his body sore from the morning PT. "But there's still a part of me that's very excited about all of this. The possibility of it."

"Then you should stay," Nina said.

"I don't know," Ryan said. "I think I'm going to give it another day. One more simulation. Then . . . if I'm not feeling more confident . . ." He trailed off, but the implication was clear.

"Okay," Nina said.

Was that a look of disappointment on her face?

"That's it, *okay*?" Ryan asked.

Nina nodded. "Yes, okay. You know I have your back no matter what. Forget the money. You need to be happy, and you don't sound happy. Money doesn't buy happiness."

"It does buy comfort, which is a kind of happiness."

"But not the right kind."

"One more day," Ryan said. "Then I have a feeling I might be seeing you soon."

"Hey," Nina said, putting on a big, wide smile. "Did you know I love you more than pizza?"

"Same, babe. Big-time same."

Ryan hung up the phone and tossed it onto his bed, just as there was a knock on the door. Alonso poked his head into the room.

"Outside, nine A.M.," he said. "By the van."

"Thought we were starting at ten," Ryan said.

Alonso just smiled and ducked out the door.

ALONSO CARDONA
I-610, HOUSTON, TX

Mike sat in the passenger seat, arms folded, a frustrated look on his face.

"Where the hell are you taking us, Cardona?" he asked.

"Be patient," Alonso said. "We're almost there."

"I don't think patience is this man's strong suit," Della said from the seat behind Alonso.

"I heard something about it being a virtue," Stitch said, from the rear of the van.

Mike turned like he wanted to say something, then held his tongue. He muttered something under his breath, but Alonso couldn't catch it over the sounds of the highway roaring around them.

Their exit came up, so he clicked on his blinker and drifted to the right. Should be just off the exit ramp and around the corner. He guided the van by memory—he had looked at a map, and he didn't want the GPS to give it away. It was more fun to make this a surprise, but also less likely that Mike would complain and tell him to turn back.

And as he brought the car to a stop in front of their destination—a large beige building—his fears were confirmed.

"You have to be kidding me," Mike said.

"Dope!" Stitch yelled, catching sight of the large Technicolor sign that read EXTREME ESCAPE ROOMS HOUSTON.

Alonso took a deep breath. He knew it was a gamble, and he knew Mike would object, but it seemed worth the risk.

"Interesting . . ." Della said.

"You said it yourself, we're not working as a team." Alonso turned off the van, twisting in his seat to look back at the crew. "I think this is a great way for us to just relax a little. Outside the pressure of training."

Mike started to say something, but Della jumped in. "I think it's a fantastic idea."

"I've always wanted to do one of these," Ryan said.

"Me, too," Stitch said, sliding open the door of the van and hopping out. "Let's go get our escape on."

Mike was less ready to get his escape on. "And you're telling me Blanton's okay with this?"

Alonso smiled mischievously. "He thinks we're long-distance running. But this is basically the same thing."

With that, Alonso climbed out of the van and led everyone to the door, where a young woman with green hair and a nose ring was waiting. "Alonso?" she asked.

"That's me," he said. "Reservation for nine-thirty."

The woman looked over the assembled group and nodded, then said, "Follow me."

The front lobby of the building was mostly blank, save for a desk and a few television screens that were displaying the business's logo. She gestured to a handful of couches, then started into her remarks, her tone friendly if a bit flat from hundreds of prior recitations. "Welcome, everyone. My name is Ella. We're excited to have you here. Today you'll be doing the Lunar Escape Room, and . . ."

"Jesus," Mike muttered, but then Della reached over and smacked him on the arm. He pursed his lips and fell silent.

Ella continued, "You have one hour, and you picked a good one. It's our most difficult room. There's a live video feed inside so our game master can see everything you're doing. You'll see two panels on the wall next to the door. One has a red panic button, which you can press at any time to end the game and come out. The other has three switches. You can get up to three hints, which will appear on a video screen above it. Use them wisely. Finally, while there are plenty of clues for you to find, nothing is hidden on top of anything, so don't try to climb on anything, and if it feels like you have to force it—don't. It's probably not a clue. Those are the basics. Now, any questions?"

"What do we win if we make it out in time?" Stitch asked.

"Your picture on the wall of fame," Ella said, gesturing to a wall made up entirely of group photographs.

"We're already famous," Stitch muttered, a little disappointed, like there might have been a prize.

"What's the record for the room?" Della asked.

"Fifty-one minutes," Ella said. "It's a tough one, but you all look pretty up to the task."

"Yeah, we'll see about that," Mike said, and Della swatted him in the arm again.

Ella offered a painful smirk at the comment and said, "Okay, if everybody is ready, you can follow me."

She led the group down a long hallway, past a number of big, heavy doors. There were eight other rooms available—including a casino, a beach boardwalk, and an old-timey saloon. But when Alonso had seen that one of them was space-themed, it felt like the right call.

Padma tapped Alonso on the shoulder, and to his surprise, she looked happy and relaxed. "Hey, this is cool. Thanks for arranging it all."

"You are very welcome," Alonso said.

Ella reached a door that was cracked open. She stepped aside and allowed everyone to enter the darkened space and then, without much fanfare, closed the door.

The lights flickered to life, and they found themselves in a room covered in cheap electronic monitors, like they'd been scavenged and cobbled together from the dumpster of a shuttered electronics store. They were housed in large units meant to look like they were metal, but the wear showed they were actually silver-painted plywood.

It was a living space, too, with a bed and a kitchenette, and a smaller, separate room off to the side that looked like a storage area with lockers. Still, the room was barely spacious enough for the six of them.

Mike looked less than enthused. "I'm happy to sit this one out. Pretty sure I saw a Mexican joint down the block."

Alonso immediately blurted back, a bit more seriously than intended, "We're doing this. All of us." He quickly put on a smile, but Mike and the others got the message. This was important to him. Mike stood down.

Alonso glanced at the wall, verifying the location of the panic button and the hint switches with the video screen. His competitive streak hoped they wouldn't have to use the hints, but he was glad they were there.

Because something told him that the real mission hinged on whether they made it out of this escape room in time. If they could do that . . . it wasn't a guarantee that they could handle the rigors of space together, but it would be a win—and one that they desperately needed in this moment.

A radio somewhere squawked to life and a voice said, "Welcome, astronauts. The base's nuclear core has been compromised and requires the access code to trip the fail-safe and prevent a meltdown. You have one hour to find it."

A red LED clock on the wall sprung to life, counting down from one hour.

"Okay," Alonso said. "Let's get to work."

RYAN CRANE
LUNAR ESCAPE ROOM, HOUSTON, TX

Ryan surveyed the room, with no earthly idea where to start. He'd never done one of these before. He'd thought it might be a fun activity with the kids, but Scarlett was still too young and Teddy had mobility issues, so Ryan had held off.

Part of him was excited.

Part of him was nervous, like this was a test.

Not that it mattered. Later today he was going to tell them the news: he was out. This was all too much for him. He missed his family, and he wasn't fitting in. Hopefully they still had time to fill the slot with some-one more qualified. Maybe another astronaut they wouldn't have so much trouble training, and they could still take off on time.

"This doesn't exactly look NASA-approved," Mike said, rapping his knuckles on one of the consoles, which resulted in a hollow, wooden sound.

"That's not the point," Alonso said, a hint of frustration in his voice. "Ryan, what do you think we should do first?"

Ryan glanced at the group, who all looked at him expectantly, except for Mike, who just folded his arms and raised an eyebrow. Ryan took a deep breath and nodded, then pointed to a small card table at the center of the room on which there was a discarded poker game, with stacks of cards and chips.

"Alonso and Padma, this is probably important, so why don't you look at the cards and see what you can figure out there," Ryan said. "Mike and Stitch, take the storage room and see what you can find. Della, want to give me a hand doing a circuit of the room? Let's get a sense of the bigger picture, and then we can tackle things one by one."

Ryan expected some pushback, but it seemed the most sensible combination if they had any chance of achieving some kind of cooperation for the mission at large. Mike clearly detested Stitch, so forcing them into proximity was either going to be a breakthrough or a disaster. Alonso had a gentle way about him, which he suspected would play well with Padma.

And as for himself, he wasn't exactly looking to win over Della, but he did feel like he owed her an apology.

Rather than the protests he expected were coming, everyone nodded and got to work.

Ryan started on one side of the room while Della took the other. There were some locked cabinets and books strewn about. Ryan picked up one of the books and flipped through, finding a bookmarked section. It opened to a page with a series of numbers, with three random digits highlighted: five, six, and two.

"Hey," Ryan asked. "Anybody got anything with a three-number combination?"

"Right here," Della said, walking over with a small metal box with a padlock on it.

"Thanks," Ryan said to her, taking the box, then, discreetly: "And hey . . . I just . . . I'm sorry. For the way I've been acting."

"Like you don't want to take direction from a woman?" Della asked, with a razor-sharp smirk.

"It's not that," he said, placing the box down, lowering his voice further. "I'm a cop. I'm around excessively manly men every day. A lot of toxic masculinity. That's never been my thing, but I learned to navigate it. And I guess with Mike . . ."

Della nodded. "Mike is masculine, though I wouldn't call it toxic. He's not exactly a ray of sunshine either, but if you think you're going to step on his toes, you're not. He just wants to see the job get done. You're playing it wrong—he sees the way you look to him for approval for everything and he considers it a weakness, not deference."

Ryan nodded, picked up the lockbox, and keyed in the three numbers. The latch popped open.

"There we go," Della said, impressed. "For what it's worth," she added, "I think you're smart, and you're a capable leader. You need to trust yourself more."

"Thanks," Ryan said. "I trust you, too, and I respect the hell out of you. I'm sorry for making you think otherwise."

"Good," Della said. "Apology accepted."

Ryan opened the box and found a playing card.

"Huh," he said.

Padma materialized at his side, a look of excitement on her face. "I'll take that," she said before dashing back to the poker table. "I think I'm getting this. It's the even-numbered red cards that make a pattern . . ."

"Okay," Ryan said. "Go, team. Let's do this!"

And he stood back for a moment, watching as everyone scurried around the room. For the first time since he got here, Ryan felt like they were working together.

STITCH
LUNAR ESCAPE ROOM, HOUSTON, TX

There was a bank of stacked metal lockers—four of them, with doors on both the top and the bottom. He yanked them open, one after another, looking for something, but they were all empty, and otherwise the room was too dark to really make anything out.

"We got a plan here or what?" Mike asked.

Stitch stopped. Looked back at the older astronaut, who looked supremely annoyed to be there. Mike was right; Stitch was getting too excited. He stopped and took a breath, tried to slow himself down a little.

Slow is smooth, and smooth is fast, he thought.

Mike seemed like he wasn't engaged with the activity. More like he was just waiting for Stitch to do something. So Stitch looked around the room, wondering what he was missing. It was fairly plain, with the lockers and a coatrack across from them, three haggard jumpsuits hanging from the hooks.

But there was something behind Mike . . .

"Hey, man, can you move?"

Mike looked behind him, shrugged, and got out of the way, revealing a light switch behind a plastic clamshell case, which had a small padlock dangling from the bottom of it.

"That looks important," Stitch said.

"Yeah, it does," Mike conceded, leaning down to inspect it and then giving it a cursory tug. "Need a key for it though."

Stitch walked to the doorway and called out, "Anyone got a key? A really small one."

Padma looked up from a lockbox and said, "Yeah, figured it out, there was a pattern to the playing cards, and it corresponded to this . . ." She held up a small key, then tossed it to Stitch, who gave it to Mike.

"Let's see what it does," Stitch said.

Mike leaned down to fit the key into the lock. He popped it, then opened the clamshell and turned on the light. The room was illuminated in a deep purple.

Black light.

"Looks like a college dorm room," Mike said.

Stitch searched the room, looking for anything that might be glowing. And he was pleasantly surprised to find that Mike was doing the same, suddenly invested in the mystery.

"Well, they wouldn't have it here if it didn't show something," Mike said.

"Right, right," Stitch said.

His frustration grew as he looked around and didn't see an obvious answer. Stitch considered ducking out of the room, finding something else to work on that was a little easier, but he took another deep breath and thought, *No, you're here, figure this one out.*

He took one more look around the room, and . . .

"Ah," he said.

"What?" Mike asked.

Stitch opened one of the lockers, and on the back of it, painted in glowing swirls, was the number 6. He pulled the door aside and showed it to Mike, who smirked.

"Nice work," Mike said, and then stepped forward so the two of them could continue opening the locker doors. By the time they were done, they had six numbers in total: six, two, four, zero, one, and three.

"All right," Mike said, undeniably impressed. "Let's go figure out what this is for," he said, casually offering Stitch a fist bump as they headed out.

It took all of Stitch's effort to mask his glee.

DELLA JAMESON
SYLVIE'S, HOUSTON, TX

Della raised her glass and said, "Forty-six minutes!"

"Forty-six minutes!" the rest of them said in unison, hoisting their glasses and clinking them together over the table, which was covered in plates laden with wings and mozzarella sticks and nachos.

"Can't believe we beat the record," Stitch said.

"It certainly helped that you were able to skip three steps just by figuring out that one combination," Alonso said.

Stitch shrugged. "You could tell which numbers were the most used on that lock by how they were worn down."

"Some good thinking there," Mike said, swigging his beer.

Della tapped her glass with her fork and stood. "Let's all take a second and thank Alonso. That was a great idea. I think we were all feeling a little zoned out. We needed to have some fun. And I'd say we did. To Alonso!"

Everyone hoisted their glasses again, cheering Alonso's name in unison.

Alonso smiled. "Just a thought. Glad it worked out."

"Don't downplay it," Ryan said. "We needed to get out of our heads a little." He turned to Padma. "Am I right?"

"That was perfect," Padma said. "I think I needed to stop looking at this stuff like it's life or death, which, I get that it is, but it's really just about moving from a problem to a solution and taking things in order."

"Exactly," Alonso said. "And now I think we can tackle some more of those multisystem failure drills with a little more confidence."

Della smiled and took a sip of her margarita, then sat back and watched the table. It was like night and day. Everyone was happily chatting away. Even Mike seemed to be warming up, responding in actual sentences that contained words with more than one syllable each.

They'd worked as a team.

And now they were celebrating as a team.

Were they mission-ready? Not nearly. But it was a huge leap in the right direction.

It was exactly what they needed.

The quietest, oddly enough, was Ryan. He was mostly listening, jumping in when asked a question, but otherwise, he seemed like he had something on his mind.

"What do you think, Ryan?" Della asked. "You ready to tackle that drill again?"

Ryan smiled, took a long swig of his beer, and said, "Yeah. Yeah, I think that I am."

RYAN CRANE
ASTRONAUT QUARTERS, JOHNSON SPACE CENTER, HOUSTON, TX

"You're sure?" Nina asked.

"It felt better today than it has the entire time I've been here," Ryan said. "I think we're getting the hang of this. I'm just . . . I'm feeling a little more comfortable than I did last night."

Nina smiled. Ryan peered through the screen of his phone, trying to figure out what kind of smile it was. Happy? Sad? He wasn't sure.

"Tell me what you're thinking, babe," he said.

"I'm thinking . . . I'm happy, mostly," Nina said. "I'm not going to lie, there was a part of me that was glad you were thinking of coming home. But this feels right. I'm still going to support you on this. Please, just . . . let's keep it consistent, okay?"

Ryan nodded. "I'm sorry. I understand. That's got to be hard. I'm in this. And it's going to suck to be away, but when I get back, we're going to take the kids to Disney for, like, a month. Do every single add-on we can."

Nina laughed. "That'll be a good start on winning them over." Then she added candidly, "Meantime, I have to admit it'll be nice when the money comes over."

"Ward hasn't sent it yet?"

"No," Nina said. "I keep checking the bank account. I've been wanting to sign Scarlett up for dance lessons. Get that stair lift fixed . . ."

Ryan sighed. "I'll see if I can find out what's going on with the money."

"That would be great," Nina said. "Now, bright and early tomorrow morning, okay? Seven A.M. You have to be up, because we'll do a check-in before they go to school."

"I promise . . ."

Ryan was cut off by a notification appearing at the top of the screen. A phone call from John Ward.

"Hey, honey, our benefactor is calling, so I should probably take this. I love you, and I'll see you and the kids in the morning, okay?"

"Love you, too," she said.

Ryan clicked over to the call. "Mr. Ward, can I help you?"

"Where are you?"

He looked around. "Inside my room."

"Great, can you come outside to the parking lot? Stay on the phone."

"Sure," Ryan said, though the request was a little strange. He slipped into his shoes and walked down the empty hallway and through the rec room, where Alonso was asleep, a movie playing on the television. Once he got outside, the parking lot was empty, save for a few cars. The Houston night was humid and unpleasant. He stood there, looking out over the barren asphalt, and said, "I'm here."

Across the lot, a bright light popped on. The headlights of a car. It drifted toward him and then pulled up to where he was standing. The window rolled down, revealing Ward in the darkened interior, flashing a grin.

"Okay . . ." Ryan said into the phone.

"You can hang up now," Ward said.

Ryan complied, slipping the phone into his pocket. Ward held up a plain white envelope. "I need you to do me a favor. Take this to Titan with you. When you land back on Earth, I want you to hand it to either me or my assistant, Camila, and no one else. It should probably go without saying, but don't open it."

Ward passed the envelope through the window. Ryan took it, holding it with both hands. Written on the front was simply FOR JOHN WARD. There was something inside. Something small, possibly plastic.

"Okay, this is a little weird . . ."

"Nothing weird about it," Ward said. "Just something I'd rather keep off the books for the trip."

"And why are you giving it to me?" Ryan asked, holding it up with one hand.

"Padma will misplace it, and Stitch will look inside. The astronauts might feel compelled to log it. That leaves you."

Ryan didn't like things that were off the books—it was a huge bundle of red flags. He thought about the process ahead: the way they had to meticulously log all their personal belongings for the trip, to be loaded into the rocket taking them into orbit, so they could dock with *Starblazer*. Weight mattered, because it affected how much fuel they needed.

The envelope was light—it barely weighed anything—but NASA had a process. And that process was important.

"I don't know about this," Ryan said, shaking his head.

Ward rolled his eyes. "What did I say I was going to give you for this gig?"

"Twenty million, in installments," Ryan said.

"Right. Let's forget about that part. I'm going to wire the whole sum to your account now. And I'll sweeten the pot. I don't know who the best spinal surgeon in the world is, off the top of my head, but I'm going to find him"—he paused—"or her, and I'm going to send them to consult with your wife and son. Fully covered. No expense will be spared."

Ryan smiled, near speechless. "That's . . . that's . . . his injury . . ."

"Doesn't hurt to take another look. The way medicine is advancing, maybe there's something to do there."

Ryan's head spun. The very idea of it felt dangerous. Like he didn't want to allow the possibility that it could be real. Because what if he did, and then it didn't work out?

"So you'll do it," Ward said.

It wasn't a question.

Ryan looked out over the parking lot, then behind him, at the entrance to the barracks. He took a deep breath. Something about this wasn't sitting right with him. The cloak-and-dagger of it. If Ward was so intent on keeping it a secret, he had to wonder what he was getting himself into.

But it was an envelope. He could slip it between the pages of one of the books he knew he would bring and probably never get to, and he'd completely forget about it in the time it took them to get back.

It was easy enough.

And it meant a bigger cushion for Nina while he was away. A gigantic cushion.

The dance lessons. The stair lift.

Comfort.

A kind of happiness.

And maybe, just maybe . . .

"I'll do it," Ryan said.

"Good," Ward said. "Now put it somewhere safe."

With that, Ward rolled up his window and pulled away.

Ryan turned the envelope over in his hand, walking slowly back inside. And by the time he made it to his room, his phone vibrated with a text. Nina. It was a picture of their joint checking account, now twenty million dollars richer, followed by two dozen heart-eye emojis.

STITCH
ASTRONAUT QUARTERS, JOHNSON SPACE CENTER, HOUSTON, TX

Stitch took one more deep pull of his vape, but nothing came out. He turned it over and saw the LED light on the bottom flashing; the battery was dead. He was hit by a sudden feeling of disappointment.

He had promised himself this would be the last vape; he just wished he had known which drag would be the last, so he could have enjoyed it more.

He looked up from his little hiding space between a set of tall, thick shrubs as Ward's car exited the parking lot and Ryan walked back into the barracks, turning an envelope over in his hand.

Stitch couldn't hear what they said, but from his vantage point, he could see both their faces, and he knew a conspiracy when he saw one.

He waited a few minutes to let Ryan get inside and settled. Then he went inside, too, tossing the spent vape into the trash can outside the front doors.

NEW YORK POST
PAGE SIX

TITAN MISSION CREW BLASTS OFF AT LOCAL BAR

It seems like John Ward's pet Titan crew is getting along famously. An anonymous tipster sent in these photos of the astronauts, both professional and wannabe, yukking it up at a local Houston watering hole.

Seems they devoured the wings, left the mozzarella sticks untouched, and drank enough that they won't need any extra jet fuel to make the trip to Saturn's moon.

Hopefully they work as hard as they play . . .

MIKE SEAVER
MEDICAL OFFICE, JOHNSON SPACE CENTER,
HOUSTON, TX

Mike stood in the bathroom, arms folded, leaning against the wall, staring at the specimen cup he had placed on the sink.

Willing it to disappear.

But of course it wouldn't.

Yes, Alonso's idea was brilliant—until the *Post* ran pictures of them getting lit up at Sylvie's. Mike had planned to have one beer, with lunch, but then they got the night off unexpectedly because the VR simulation crashed, and he had another beer with dinner, and that turned into three, then four, and finally, half a handle of whiskey that he'd stashed under his sink.

It was like tumbling down a hill. And Mike could tell that the worst of the hangover hadn't come on yet, which meant there was no way he was going to piss into that cup and have it come out clean.

He was such an idiot. Blanton told him exactly what to do, and he still fucked it up.

The worst part was letting down his kids. They saw him for who he was. Imperfect. And he knew that as time went on, they might drift away from him. But his career was the one thing they might be able to hold on to, and in the better moments say: *He was still a hero.*

At least he did something with that mess of a life.

And now he was going to end up getting bounced from one of the biggest missions in the history of the human race, and probably end up drinking himself to death in some sad dive bar.

The door opened, and Stitch walked in, holding his own specimen cup. He gave a little wave, heading for a stall, then stopped.

"You okay?" he asked.

Mike remained silent.

He didn't owe this kid an answer. Even if he was getting less annoying.

Stitch looked at the specimen cup, then back at Mike, and nodded. He went over and picked up Mike's cup and headed toward the stall. "Lucky for you I drank a lot of coffee this morning."

"The hell are you doing?" Mike asked.

Stitch turned and smiled. "Saving your ass. If you hadn't noticed, I don't drink."

Mike was stunned, unsure of what to say.

"I . . ." he started.

"Don't worry about it," Stitch said. "I want to go, you want to go. We're never going to be texting buddies, but we have that in common. Important thing is, I trust you."

Mike dropped his head, felt his throat grow thick. The kid. Mike had been nothing but unkind to him until the escape room, and even then didn't offer him a whole hell of a lot.

He raised his eyes, blinking away tears, and said, "Thank you."

Stitch nodded and disappeared into the stall.

"Hey, can you turn on the faucet or something?" Stitch called. "I'm a nervous pee-er."

Mike walked over to the sink, turned on the faucet as high as it would go, and looked into the mirror, at the stubble and the bags under his eyes.

"Get it together," he whispered. "You can do this."

DELLA JAMESON
"STARBLAZER DECK"

"Nice work, everyone," Blanton's voice called out.

Della ripped off the headset and looked around the room at the other crew members and the team coming in to get them down from the pods. She was smiling so hard it hurt.

Another multisystem failure drill, and this time, they nailed it. Mike wasn't out of commission for this one, and he and Stitch actually worked together, with only minor friction. More important, Stitch listened, Ryan didn't second-guess everything, and Padma didn't freeze up.

They were becoming a team.

Once they were all safely down and in their little circle of chairs in the corner, Blanton stood in the middle of them, smiling for the first time in weeks.

"I guess Alonso was on the money," he said, leaning over and patting the young astronaut on the shoulder. "For the first time, I'm not terrified of sending the six of you up into space, so I'd call this a win."

"You can say that again," Stitch said.

"So we're good?" Mike asked.

Blanton turned and fixed Mike with a long stare—a second longer than was necessary—and Della wondered what that was about. Finally Blanton said, "Yeah, we're good. Now, everyone to the track. Time for your favorite part of the day—more PT."

A good-natured groan erupted from the group as they all climbed to their feet and made their way to the door. Della lingered, watching everyone go.

And she smiled, again.

Because she could feel it.

They were going to Titan.

4

GOODBYES

MIKE SEAVER
RALPH'S, PHILADELPHIA, PA

Mike watched the waiter weave between the tables, holding aloft two pizzas. He rubbed his sweating palms together. It was stuffy inside Ralph's, and the air wasn't on.

It had nothing to do with the glass of water in front of him.

He eyed the group of twenty-somethings hoisting beers at the next table and unconsciously licked his lips. Then he looked across the table at Emma, her dark brown hair hanging in curly tangles, framing her growing face. She stared back down at the screen, one condescending eyebrow raised.

Of course, the one time she looked up from her phone . . .

It was moments like that where Emma looked so much like Helen. And it killed Mike to admit how familiar it was, seeing that expression of disappointment.

"One extra cheese, one pepperoni," the waiter said, struggling to find room among the drinks and mostly finished plates of mozzarella sticks and fried calamari.

"Thank you!" Jack said, beaming. The tray was barely down before he was hungrily grabbing at a slice.

"Be careful," Mike said. "Someone's going to lose a hand."

"Pizzaaa" was all Jack said in response.

Mike picked up a slice and put it on one of the paper plates they'd been provided—part of the reason he loved this place so much, it wasn't fussy—and began cutting up a slice for Stella, who was sitting in her booster seat, studiously coloring in a sheet featuring cute and fuzzy animals.

Mike eyed Emma, who sat unmoving. "You gonna eat?"

She shrugged. "Not hungry."

Mike sighed. How could she not be hungry? She had eaten three pieces of calamari. This was after Helen said she didn't eat breakfast this morning.

It's the other girls at school, Helen had said. Emma was a little heavy—not unhealthy, but she looked younger than fourteen, holding on to a little baby fat still. That was Emma's draw on the genetic lottery. Helen was a curvy woman, and Mike was built like a whiskey barrel. Apparently the other girls at school had been teasing her about her weight.

"You know those other girls are full of shit, and you shouldn't listen to them," Mike said, placing the cut-up pizza in front of Stella. "Bigger girls are beautiful, and . . ."

"Did you just call me *big*?" Emma asked, her eyes widening.

"Well, no, I didn't mean it like that . . ."

"Dad called you faaaat," Jack said under his breath.

"Jack, stop that. I did not say that, all I meant was . . ."

Emma got up from the table. For a moment Mike thought she might be going to the bathroom, but she headed for the front door.

Probably to call Helen.

Great.

Jack munched on his pizza, eyeing Mike.

"Your sister is not fat," Mike said. "I did not say that, and *you* do not say that, understand?"

Jack shrugged, and Stella kept eating her pizza. Mike's phone buzzed, and his heart sank. He picked it up to find a text from Helen.

Are you kidding me?

Mike considered a response, but it didn't seem worth it. First, what would he say? And anyway, Helen was going to be here to pick up the kids in a few minutes. His time with them was done, and in a few days he'd be leaving for two years.

This was a hell of a note to leave things on.

"Hey, Jack, buddy, can you listen to me for a second?"

Jack looked up and nodded, his mouth full.

"While I'm gone, you're the man of the house, okay? I need you to take care of your mom and your sisters. And part of taking care of them is taking care of their hearts. I hurt Emma's feelings right now, and I'm sorry about that. You need to be . . ."

He wanted to say *better than me,* but the words caught in his throat.

What he'd give for a beer.

Why did this have to be so damn hard?

Mike wolfed down a slice of pizza, his stomach suddenly sour but knowing he needed to eat something. He waved to the waiter for the check and pointed to the leftover pizza. The waiter returned shortly with the bill and an empty box. Mike packed up the pizza, left some cash on the table, hefted Stella against him with his free arm, and took the kids outside.

The minivan was already idling at the curb, Emma inside. Helen was leaning against it, arms folded. Mike walked past her and opened the door, putting Stella into her car seat. Emma ignored him. Jack climbed in, and Mike closed the door.

"I ask again, are you kidding me?" Helen asked. "You called her fat?"

"I didn't call her fat, I told her big girls were beautiful, too," he said, knowing there was no winning this one.

Helen closed her eyes and sighed, pinching the bridge of her nose. "Mike, you will never understand the very particular hell of being a teenage girl who does not look like a cheerleader. It's miserable, and I get what you were trying to do, but you need to understand that anything you do or say is just going to be blown out of proportion."

"So I can't speak honestly and openly with my own daughter? What are we going to do, shelter her from the world?"

"It's not about sheltering her, Mike. It's just about being sensitive to where she's at. Which means thinking before you speak."

"Okay. I'm sorry."

Helen nodded, then narrowed her eyes at him.

"I didn't have anything to drink."

She stared at him for another moment before nodding. Whether she believed it was probably immaterial at this point.

"Let me say goodbye," Mike said.

Helen nodded and stepped back. Mike opened the door, and Jack looked up expectantly. "So, we can send videos?"

"Of course, kid, we'll send plenty of videos."

"Can you bring me back a rock from Titan?"

"Again, we're not landing on Titan, we're flying by it, but I'll take some cool photos for you, okay?"

"Are you going to meet any aliens?"

Mike laughed and patted his head. "I sure hope so. I'll tell them you said hi."

Emma continued staring at her phone.

"Hey, Em?" Mike asked.

Emma made a sound in her throat but didn't look up.

"I love you," he said. "And I'm sorry. You're the most beautiful woman in the world. After your mother, of course."

She stopped typing, her fingers hovering over the screen, then glanced at him. "I love you, too, Dad."

Mike hated leaving his kids behind, especially for this long. Especially when he felt like there was an outside chance he might come back to divorce papers.

"Hugs all around," he said, and then he pulled each of his children close to him in turn. He expected Emma to be resistant, but she buried her face into the side of his neck and whispered, "Be safe, okay?"

It took everything Mike had not to break into tears right then and there.

With the goodbyes said, he closed the door again and stood with Helen, the silence between them like a chasm, so deep he couldn't imagine finding a bottom.

"Have fun, stay safe," she said. "Don't do anything stupid."

"You know me," Mike said with a half smile. "I can only promise the first two things."

They embraced, and Mike considered trying to move his head toward hers to kiss her on the lips, but he knew that wouldn't be welcome, so instead he kissed the side of her head, a hair getting caught in his mouth.

"I love you," he said.

"Me, too," she responded.

And it cut a little, that she didn't say the words themselves.

He watched her climb into the minivan and drive away. Once he was sure they were gone, he headed back inside, so he could order himself a beer.

STITCH
FLATBUSH, BROOKLYN, NY

The microwave beeped, and Stitch took the Lean Cuisine out of the microwave. The plastic was hot, and he almost dropped it, but he successfully got it onto a plate, then removed the cellophane top and gave the chicken teriyaki and rice a stir.

He carried it to the living room, where his mom was sitting on the couch, a blanket over her legs, even though it felt warm in the small apartment. He placed the plate on the table next to her, along with a fork. She barely looked up from what she was watching on television—some Korean soap opera, but without the subtitles, which Stitch never understood, because it's not like she spoke Korean.

"Okay, Ma," he said. "Dinner is ready."

"Thank you," she said, without looking up.

He sat on the recliner across from her. The one his dad used to sit in, before a heart attack struck him down in that very chair nearly ten years ago. They'd found him too late to do anything about it. Some days Stitch wanted to get rid of it, but he knew he never could. It was how he remembered his dad, sitting there at night, watching TV with him and Mom.

Sitting in the chair made him feel close to his dad still, despite the sadness that had seeped into the leather upholstery.

"So, tomorrow is the big day," he said. "I'm outta here. Then I'm outta planet Earth. It's pretty cool, right?"

"Hopefully when you come back, you'll get a real job," his mother said, without taking her eyes from the screen, and Stitch felt his heart rip clean in two.

"Aren't you at least a little proud of me?" he asked.

"Courtney, you're leaving me all by myself for the next two years," she said.

"Right, and the money Ward is giving me for this means you can hire a home health aide," he said. "You can fix this place up. You don't have to worry about bills, and . . ."

"All by myself," she said. "Forgive me for not being excited."

"What about the girls down at the senior center?" he asked. "You like hanging out with them, don't you?"

She shrugged before picking up the plate and balancing it on her lap. She started to eat, staring at the screen.

Stitch sighed. He wanted to turn off the television and ask her to have a real conversation with him. He wished it was something else—her failing health, the loss of her husband, being on a fixed income. But he had to admit the truth: she had always been like this, like she could barely tolerate him.

Like he'd been a mistake.

Another thing he missed about his father: the way he seemed to soften that side of her. His dad had been a little stern, a little quiet, but always quick with a witty joke . . . or a reminder that they shouldn't be so hard on their son.

What Stitch would give for his dad to be here.

"Okay, Ma, I'm going out," he said.

"Try not to get into trouble," she said, and while from anyone else that might have been friendly, from her lips it dripped with condemnation.

Stitch considered calling her out but then shrugged and went to the front door. He grabbed his backpack from the floor and hoisted it over his shoulder, then stepped outside into the cool night air.

He walked, not really sure of his destination but letting his feet lead him. He had several regular tagging spots—a fallow train yard, a block of homes that were mostly foreclosed properties, an abandoned factory. After a while he realized he was headed toward the train yard, without even really having picked that location.

It just felt good to walk. To be out of that tiny apartment. It was all his family could afford on his dad's pension as a long-haul trucker. Which wasn't much of a pension to begin with. Once he couldn't drive the big rigs anymore, he settled into that chair and never really got up until the day he died.

Stitch helped where he could, getting odd jobs, but he still carried a lot of disappointment in himself. He knew he could have made a mint off that app. It was a game changer for artists, allowing them to quickly and deeply customize the digital tools available to them. But he knew whoever bought it would just turn it into another program that would create "original" art by scraping the web and stealing stuff from other artists.

So he gave the code away, made it public, so anyone could download it and use it. The algorithm he developed was far less valuable when it couldn't be copyrighted or patented.

He didn't want that life. Didn't want to run a company, didn't want to compromise his artistic sensibilities.

He wanted something bigger.

Titan was bigger.

But to his mom, Titan wasn't a *career*. It was just an excuse for him to get away from her.

And a little bit, it was.

He reached the train yard and found the hole in the fence where he usually slipped through, then wandered a bit until he found an old subway car that was a little tagged up—but one side offered a big, blank canvas to him.

He dropped the backpack and rifled through the spray paint cans, looking for the gloss white, and went to work. It wasn't long before he was in a flow state, letting the gentle hiss of the paint change the car from something ugly into something beautiful.

This trip was going to change his life. He knew it. He was going to come back and people would notice him. They would care about what he had to say. And he would make something. For himself, and for his mom.

Even if she didn't care, he would do it anyway.

Because that was his job. To take care of her. He made a mental note to call that home health organization tomorrow and pay in advance for care, so that someone would be there to watch over her while he was gone.

After a little while—he wasn't sure how long, because time tended to disappear when he was working—he stepped back and looked at the side of the car. It was a constellation of stars, with a big planet in the middle.

Not a planet, really.

A moon.

He signed his name at the bottom of the piece.

"There," he said, surveying the work. "That's better."

And then he packed up the spray cans dotting the asphalt and headed back home, expecting to find his mother asleep on the couch, the half-eaten plate still balanced on her lap, the TV still on. He'd take the plate, clean it, and turn off the TV. Then bed.

Tomorrow was a big day.

He had places to be.

DELLA JAMESON
CAROL STREAM, CHICAGO, IL

Della pulled up to the house and knew something was off. She wasn't sure what, and it took her a moment to realize that the lawn had been mowed.

As she guided the car into the driveway, she saw movement on the porch—someone sitting on the wicker chair, and the glow of a hastily put-out cigarette.

Mila and Nora were passed out in the back, the two of them lying at odd angles in their car seats. Della stopped the engine, and the two of them didn't even stir. She got out of the car quietly, closing the door carefully. They could sleep a little longer. It was already past their bedtime.

And she'd already dealt with a lot.

The girls were seven—young enough to be excited that their mom was flying halfway across the solar system, old enough to understand that two years was a very long time. There had been a lot of laughter, and a lot of tears, on today's "Yes Day."

It was something they'd seen in a movie. Probably one they watched with their grandmother, about a family that creates this tradition where the parents have to say yes to anything the kids ask.

Della set limits, of course, in terms of spending and driving distance, so it didn't get too out of control. But after a trip to the mall, clothes shopping, ice cream for dinner, and then a movie that started slightly too late for Della's comfort—they were zonked out.

And after a day of big feelings, she didn't need to put anything else on them.

She approached the porch, where Sean was sitting in the chair. He got up and then hovered in the space, clearly wanting to embrace her but knowing it would be the wrong move. He'd put on some weight since the last time she saw him, but he was carrying it well, still strong in his shoulders and broad in his chest.

"Where are the girls?" he asked.

Della nodded behind her. "Asleep in the car."

Sean frowned. "You shouldn't leave them alone in the car like that."

Della looked around. "The sun is down. We're in a suburb. We're standing within eyesight of the vehicle. They will be fine."

"I'm just saying . . ."

"Saying what?" Della asked. "Are you trying to say I'm a bad mom?"

"I'm not saying that. I just worry about them. I never get to see them . . ."

"You know the terms," Della said. "You're getting your two weekends a month."

"Just in time for you to leave for two years," he said.

Della took a step forward and lowered her voice. "I am undertaking a mission that is part of my job. There will be support systems set up for them while I am gone. My mother will be with them. Do you want to talk about leaving, Sean? How about when you left me with them for a woman half your age, and you didn't even give me the courtesy of explaining why until three months later?"

Sean dropped his head. "Becoming a father . . . it wasn't what I expected."

"Yes, it takes work," Della said. "Which is something you never seem interested in." She swept her hand around at the lawn. "You think you can come over and mow the lawn and I'm going to forgive you."

"Grass was getting a little long," he said. "I thought if I showed you . . ."

"Showed me what?" she asked. "That you'll come over, lift a finger one single time, and that would be that? You left me alone with those babies for three months. Three *months,* Sean. While you were off fucking some girl who was barely out of college."

"Della, I know I can never make up for what I did, but I recognize that what I did was wrong," he said. "That was three long years ago. I just want to be a part of their lives."

There was something about Sean's tone, the desperate look on his face, that made Della think there was more to it. And then it dawned on her.

"She dumped you, didn't she?"

Sean didn't answer.

Which was all the answer she needed.

"Look, you can hate me for the rest of my damn life, and I probably deserve it," he said. "But your mom is going to need help with the girls."

"My mom raised four kids by herself," Della said. "She's getting a little old, but she can handle two. And no, I'm not agreeing to let you back into their lives. You'll get your supervised visits, that's all."

"They're my kids, too," he said, his voice growing sharp.

"And you dropped them for a hot little piece of ass," she said. "You abandoned us all. You want to know why I don't want you in their lives? Because I'm afraid that the second things get hard again, you'll run, just like you did last time. Except now they're old enough to remember that. They're old enough to be hurt by that in a way that they'll carry with them for the rest of their lives. I'm not going to let you hurt them the way you did me."

Della started to well up, but she choked it back, not wanting to offer him the satisfaction.

"Just give me a chance," Sean asked, his voice pleading.

"Go home, Sean," she said. "Just go home. I don't need this right now."

"Can I at least help carry them ins—"

"I got it," Della interrupted firmly.

Sean puffed up, looked like he was ready to argue. But then he put his hands on his hips and exhaled, shook his head, and walked off down the block, where he probably parked his car around the corner so Della wouldn't see it when she drove up.

She stood there and watched until he was gone, and then, in the quiet of the block, with her kids sleeping safely in the car, she risked a couple of tears.

But just a few.

That's all she would give him.

She scratched a chip of paint off one of the house's lavender shutters— she'd been meaning to repaint them, but she loved the shade and couldn't find the exact right one to match. Something to do when she got back.

Until then, no matter what, she had to protect those girls.

ALONSO CARDONA
LAYLA'S, AUSTIN, TX

Alonso parked outside the bar and sat with the engine running. *Turn around,* he thought. *You don't need to do this.*

But he did. He was going to space. Bad things can happen in space. And he knew that if something bad happened, in his final moments, he'd regret turning around and going home, where Maddie was already passed out, asleep like the dead. There was no way she would notice he was gone.

And it's not like he was doing anything wrong.

He was just meeting Ethan for a drink.

Closure. That's all.

Of course, if he wasn't doing anything wrong, why did he leave Maddie sleeping? Why did he close the door so quietly when he left?

He decided not to worry about that.

After tonight, it was over.

He picked up his phone off the passenger seat and saw he had a missed call from his mother, Liliana. He called back—even though it was nearly eleven, she would be up. She answered on the second ring.

"Mijo," she said. "You can't call your mother before you fly to the outer reaches of the solar system?"

Alonso could see the gentle smirk on her face, and he laughed.

"I was going to FaceTime you in the morning," he said. "And I saw you two days ago."

"You did, you did," she said, her voice taking on a serious tone. "I'm worried about you."

"Mami, it's just nerves."

"It's more than that, I think," she said. "You didn't bring Maddie."

"Maddie was working. It's a long drive to Dallas."

"My love . . ." Liliana trailed off. "I just want you to be happy."

The muscles in Alonso's shoulders bunched. "I am happy."

"Hmm."

This was classic behavior from his mom. Wait until a few days later and have the tough conversation over the phone, rather than do it in person. He was searching for something to say when a group of college kids stumbled out of the front door of the bar, hooting and hollering in drunken revelry.

"Where are you, mijo?" she asked.

"Grabbing a drink with a friend."

"A friend?"

Alonso sighed. All his life she'd been needling him if she caught him in a lie. "Ethan."

"Hmm. Do I know this boy?"

Alonso silently sighed, closed his eyes. "Yes, mami. You've met him many times. Listen, I have to be up early. Let me go in so I can head home and get a decent night's sleep."

There was a pause, long enough that Alonso wondered if the call got dropped. Then Liliana said, "Te quiero mucho."

"Same, mami."

Alonso ended the call and stared at the phone. Not the tone he wanted for going into this conversation. Then he climbed out of the car and stepped inside the bar, where he was hit by a wall of blaring country music. He loved Layla's—with its dirty shag carpet and wood paneling, it reminded him of his grandmother's basement. He looked around to find it mostly empty, save for Ethan, sitting at a booth in the corner, two beers in front of him. Ethan was wearing a tight black T-shirt, his blond hair slicked back.

He looked good.

Alonso sat in the booth across from him, and Ethan slid a beer over. Alonso thanked him and took a sip—a bitter IPA.

"You bastard," Alonso said, smiling.

"You'll come around to them," he said. "You just have to drink them more."

"I will never for the life of me understand beer this bitter," Alonso said, taking another swig, the liquid offensive to his tongue. "Why do you subject yourself to this?"

"It's about the complexity," Ethan said with a wink. "And having the palate of an adult."

"Right."

Alonso took another sip, to fill the silence, and also for the liquid courage. He had to drive home, so this was the only one he would have, but it still felt like it'd be helpful.

"So, how's Maddie?" Ethan asked.

"She's good. Work is going well. It's going to be hard, being away for two years, but she's committed, and so am I."

Alonso didn't mean that last part to sound harsh, but Ethan still bristled at it, like it was a barb.

"Let me ask you something—" Ethan started.

"Ethan . . ."

"Just, let me say my piece, okay? I think you owe me that. I just need to know . . . was there ever a world where you and I could have been together?"

Alonso sighed, took another swig of his beer.

"I love you," Ethan said. "I know you love me. I just . . . I don't know what the problem was."

"Because . . ." Alonso started, then stopped. He'd made this speech so many times in his head, and it always sounded right, but in the light of actually giving it, it suddenly no longer felt sturdy.

He proceeded anyway.

"You know what sucks about being a bisexual man?" Alonso asked. "No one will ever believe you're bisexual. They think you're just gay and too cowardly to admit it. They think any relationship you're in will never be legitimate because you're going to spend all your time looking at the grass on the other side of the fence. And then every story that ever gets written about me is going to be Alonso Cardona, the Bisexual Astronaut. I'll become some kind of sideshow, and that's going to take away from the things I've accomplished."

Ethan just sat for a moment, digesting Alonso's words and drawing a conclusion. "So I take it Maddie still doesn't know."

"It hasn't come up."

"Imagine that," Ethan blurted, a bit more sarcastic than intended. Softening, he continued, "She has to suspect, I mean . . . she's met me. She sees the way we interact."

Alonso dropped his head. "She loves how accepting I am of gay culture."

"You're a part of gay culture."

"I'm not. I'm in this . . . weird nebulous space. I don't know where the hell I stand. I just want to do my job and go home. That's all. I don't want to be a symbol or an icon."

"No one ever said you had to be anything for anyone," Ethan said, dropping his voice. "And I'm not asking you to leave Maddie. I'm not asking you to come out publicly. But you're leaving for two years. When you get back, Maddie's going to want to start a family. Will you please just admit to me that a part of you still loves me?"

"I will always love you . . ." Alonso started.

And he considered cutting the last part off, at the way Ethan smiled and inflated, but he saw how easily that could be misinterpreted, so he finished the thought.

". . . as a friend. And that's all it can be."

Ethan nodded, a look of resignation on his face.

"I'm sorry," he said. "I'm sorry I asked you for this conversation. And the next part of this, I say with love. I'm sorry for the space you're living in. I'm sorry that you've trapped yourself in this cage and decided you need to be what you think the world wants you to be."

Alonso felt a flash of anger. "I am who I am."

"I know," Ethan said. "That's the problem."

He drained the rest of his beer and placed down the empty glass, then looked at Alonso. Alonso's hands were on the table, and for a second it seemed like Ethan might reach over and take one.

And part of Alonso wanted him to do that.

But then Ethan stood up and left.

Alonso sat there and finished his beer, bitter on his tongue.

It felt appropriate for his mood.

PADMA SINGH
CAPITOL HILL, WASHINGTON, D.C.

Padma sat in her apartment, looking over the neat pile of her luggage. Everything was packed. The fridge was cleared out. The watering bulbs were in the plants, and Brett had confirmed he'd be stopping by every few weeks to take care of them. She still felt a little guilty about that, like she should have hired someone to do it, but it seemed like he wanted to, and she trusted him more than she trusted some stranger.

Tomorrow she'd get on a plane to Florida, and then it was off to Titan.

Her life's dream.

She was excited and frightened in equal measure.

She wondered if she should go to bed but knew there was no way she'd fall asleep. So she got up and paced the apartment, making sure she hadn't forgotten anything, that she'd done everything that needed to be done.

The doorbell chimed, which made her stop in her tracks. She checked her watch. It was 11:32. Too late for a delivery. She went to the video console by the front door, hoping to see Brett, even though he would have texted first before coming over.

It wasn't him.

Instead, it was a thin older man with a heavy gray beard, his face tired and haggard. It would be easy enough for Padma to ignore it, and she considered doing just that, but she was curious, too, so she pressed the intercom button and asked, "Yes?"

"Is this Padma Singh?"

Her blood ran a little cold.

"Who are you?"

"I think it's better I don't give you my name," he said. "We need to speak. About Titan. About John Ward. Can I come up?"

Padma laughed. "You're a strange man who won't tell me his name, ringing my doorbell at eleven-thirty. You think I'm just going to invite you up?"

He nodded, looking into the camera. "I understand your reservation. But please." He craned his neck, looking around. "There's a restaurant over on the corner. It's still open. Meet me for a coffee. There'll be people there. It'll be safe."

Padma didn't know what to say to that.

"Just, please," the man said. "This whole mission. Ward isn't telling you the truth. There's something much bigger at play here. I need you to meet me. Please. I'll be there. I'll wait until close. I'll understand if you don't come, but your life may depend on it."

And he disappeared from view.

Well, that was weird.

Padma pulled out her phone and checked the restaurant on the corner. Serafina, a cute little Italian bistro. It was open for another two hours. Which meant she had two hours to decide what the hell she wanted to do.

She pulled up Ward's contact info on her phone and considered calling, but she always felt so weird calling him. Like she was being a bother.

What did the man mean, that her life could depend on it?

It was a scientific research trip. A flyby of a moon. They'd never leave the confines of the ship. This trip was so carefully planned and calculated, what could Ward possibly do that would put their lives in danger?

Unless he was skimping on safety protocols, but even then, the man was running for president. He wouldn't risk blowing up six people on an experimental ship. It'd mean the end of his political career.

Padma sighed, thought about it.

Paced the apartment some more.

Poured a glass of water, which she just stared at, sitting on the counter.

Considered getting into bed.

Then she got dressed.

As she stepped outside the building, she noticed a half dozen cigarette butts on the ground. She wondered if they belonged to this mystery man, and, if so, how long he'd been out there.

She walked the block to the restaurant, every fiber of her being telling her to turn around and run. She entered, expecting to find the man sitting at the bar, but he wasn't there.

Instead, she found Camila, Ward's assistant.

She turned slightly, took a sip from her wine, and said, "Hello, Padma."

Padma's face turned red with embarrassment, as if she'd somehow been caught in the act. She hesitated in the doorway, reluctant to make her way over, but Camila waved at her. "Join me," she said.

Padma went to the bar, pulled out one of the heavy stools, and sat beside Camila. Padma would never admit it, but she was terrified of the woman. Camila was cutthroat, effective . . . the handler of all of Ward's most difficult work and his closest confidant. You don't get a job like that without being a little vicious.

"You have questions," Camila said.

"Many," Padma said.

Camila nodded and waved over the bartender, ordering another glass of whatever she was drinking for Padma. Padma would have preferred a white wine, or at least a rosé, but she was sure whatever it was would probably be expensive, and that was nice.

As the bartender went to fetch the bottle, Camila said, "That man's name was Stephen Lerner. He worked for Ward for many years before he started having . . . mental health issues. Severe paranoia. Maybe it was the pressure he was under. He left under very unfortunate circumstances."

"How did he find me?"

Camila shrugged. "Information is easy to come by in this day and age. The important thing to know is that he's disgruntled, and he has a vendetta against Ward and would probably do anything to hurt the mission. He probably saw you as an easy way to do it."

"And how did you know he was here?"

"We take your safety very seriously," she said. "The building's security system is outfitted with facial recognition software so that it'll alert the authorities if someone comes to the building who you don't want coming to the building. We fed the system his data a while ago."

"Then what are you doing here?"

She shrugged. "I get an alert, too."

Creepy, Padma thought. How much did Ward know about her comings and goings? "And where is he now?"

"Spooked, probably, and ran," she said.

"You could have told me," Padma replied.

"It didn't seem relevant, and we never thought he would try to contact you," Camila said, turning to face Padma fully. "I'm sorry, that must have been unsettling."

"It was, a little," Padma said, then conceded, "more than a little. He said Ward's not telling us the truth. He implied the mission is in danger."

Camila nodded, not at all surprised. "Like I said. He's disgruntled. And mentally ill."

She waved over the bartender, a handsome young guy, and handed him a credit card. "Add a fifty percent tip when she's done." Then she turned to Padma. "I have to go. Feel free to have another drink, or order some food if you'd like. You can put this out of your head. Everything is fine."

But Camila wasn't done. She scrutinized Padma. "One last thing. Next time someone approaches you with unfounded accusations about your benefactor, the man who handed you your career on a silver platter, think twice. No one on this mission is irreplaceable."

Ouch. Padma instinctively nodded, stung by the spanking.

The bartender returned the card with a smile and a wink. Camila scoffed, said a curt goodbye, and left.

Shaken, Padma sipped her wine. She wouldn't have another one. She needed a clear head. Because it did not feel like everything was fine. The prospect of some kind of redacted report had been floating at the back of her mind for weeks, and now she had a name: Stephen Lerner. That could help in her research. Research that she'd have to keep sufficiently encrypted, away from Camila's eyes.

And Ward's.

It was going to be another late night on the computer . . .

VER1TY
DARK WEB FORUM

Anonymous: I found it! Well, not the report itself, just, what I think is proof that it exists. See, the problem was, I was looking through NASA's systems (don't ask how) and I was looking for the report itself, when I should have been looking for the ABSENCE of the report. When a file gets deleted off a computer, it's not really gone. The data lingers until it's overwritten. Doing this remotely and covertly is pretty difficult, but look what I found. This is PROOF that there's a full report out there somewhere . . .

DARK MATTER AND THE ███████████████

A report by Dr. Stephen Lerner

For decades, ██████████████████████████ only recently have we begun to understand what it really is.

████████████████████████████████

that can't be explained by general relativity—essentially, ██████

████████████████████████████████

It is greater than that.

working with proprietary technology developed in tandem with John Ward,

But we have identified a number of

share information and resources.
The possibilities here are limitless.

could help us save our planet.

this stands as one of the greatest discoveries in the history of science and will further expand our understanding of the fundamental building blocks of the universe.

My only concern is the ███████████████████
██
██
██
████████████████████████████████
It will no doubt take decades, ███████████████
██

This, not space travel, is humanity's next great leap.

Bananananana8: Well, isn't that interesting. What could it mean?

YodaGuy45: Aliens. Definitely aliens.

Bananananana8: This could be any number of things, but it's clear that there's some kind of conspiracy afoot.

NotActuallyJohnWard: This is ridiculous. It proves nothing. Reports get scrapped all the time.

Status0verr1de: The fanboy is right. Ward is too much of an idiot to figure out something like this.

NotActuallyJohnWard: Okay, I wouldn't say that . . .

RYAN CRANE
SHENANDOAH VALLEY, VA

Ryan blew out the flaming marshmallow and stuck it between the graham crackers, giving the chocolate a moment to melt. He watched Teddy doing the same, while Scarlett curled in Nina's lap, half-asleep. It was late, much later than the kids were accustomed to being up, but he wanted to spend as much time with them as possible.

The setting couldn't have been more perfect. Nina's grandfather's cabin in Virginia. He'd died years ago and left it to Nina in his will. The place had been a wreck, but they'd spent the last few years cleaning it up. It was in the middle of nowhere. No cell signal. The closest market, at a gas station, was a good forty-minute drive away. It was another hour past that to get into town.

Ryan looked out from the small ring of light cast by the fire; other than that and a soft yellow glow from the kitchen, it was pitch black. There may as well have been nothing else in the world but them.

They loved it.

It felt safe.

Nina stood, hoisting Scarlett. "I'm going to put this one to bed. You boys don't stay up too late," she said.

"Love you, Mom," Teddy said.

"Love you, too, sweetheart," she said, moving up toward the cabin.

Ryan tossed the last scrap of wood into the fire with his free hand, then bit into his s'more. "Is there anything better, kiddo?"

Teddy shook his head, but clearly his mind was elsewhere. "I'm gonna miss you, Dad," Teddy said, sadness creeping into his voice.

"I'm going to miss you, too," Ryan assured his son. "I'm going to miss the three of you like crazy. But listen, I'm so on the fence, you say the word, I might just cancel the whole thing. Screw 'em."

Teddy laughed, then said insistently, "You have to go. This is so cool. You're gonna be a part of history."

"It's still hard to believe it's really happening," Ryan said. "Are you scared?"

Teddy seemed to think about it for a moment. "A little? I mean, it's NASA. They know what they're doing. And Ward is a genius. I'm sure he's thought of every possible scenario." He paused. "Are *you* scared?"

"Of course I'm scared," Ryan said. "They're strapping me to a rocket and shooting me into space."

"I wish *I* could go," Teddy said.

"Who knows, maybe you will someday."

Teddy absentmindedly rubbed his legs. "Probably not though."

Ryan considered telling him about Ward's offer to consult with a spinal surgeon, but he hadn't even discussed it with Nina. And he didn't want to get his boy's hopes up. Instead, Ryan got up from his chair and knelt next to Teddy. "You want to hear something cool?"

Teddy nodded, his eyes downcast.

"I've learned a lot about Titan in the past month," Ryan said. "And one of the things I learned is that the atmosphere is really thick, but the gravity isn't. That means you could attach wings to your arms and fly like a bird. They think we might be able to cover large distances with these hang glider things, and they'll be really easy to steer and land."

"That does sound pretty cool," Teddy said.

"Right? And the point is this. I want to do this for the money, and to save the planet, and for all that fun stuff. But as soon as I heard that, I decided I wanted to do this so one day we can get you up to Titan, flying through the air."

"Dad . . ."

"Nothing's impossible," Ryan said. "Nothing."

"Yeah, but . . ." Teddy said. "There are always things I won't be able to do."

Ryan smiled. "You never know. But no matter what, your life is what you make of it. You can make it look how you want."

"I just wish I was strong like you," he said.

"You're stronger than me," Ryan said. "You got dealt a shitty hand. And you came out of it with a big, open heart. A lot of people in this world would have gotten bitter and angry. You didn't. I love you for that. It's almost like you have an awesome dad or something."

"Well, my mom is pretty great," Teddy said with a sly smile.

"Don't make me ground you for two years."

"But I also have the coolest, bravest dad ever."

Ryan stood and tousled Teddy's mop of brown hair. "Let's get inside. Fire's dying, and I need to sleep at some point."

Teddy lingered in the moment, like he wanted to say something. Then he glanced up at Ryan with a look that nearly broke his heart in two.

"You really think I can fly someday?"

"I know the guy running the show now," Ryan said. "I'm going to pull as many strings as I can."

Teddy smiled and turned toward the cabin while Ryan cleaned up the s'mores supplies and kicked some dirt over the last of the embers, then went inside. Teddy had already made his way up the ramp to his bedroom, so Ryan climbed the stairs to the master bedroom on the second floor, where Nina was lying in bed, a romance novel perched on her chest.

Ryan climbed into bed next to her, regarding her adoringly. "Gonna miss you."

"Gonna miss you, too," she said.

"Second thoughts?" he asked.

Nina smiled. "Never. I trust you. And this is going to make a better life for our family."

"It is," Ryan said, his mind drifting to the envelope sitting inside his luggage. It meant that better life would be even better . . . but what was the cost?

What the hell was in there?

"Okay, out with it," Nina said.

"What?"

"I keep telling you, you'd make the worst poker player in the world," she said. "Something's been on your mind ever since you got here, and I know it's not just us."

Ryan sighed. Then he stood and went to his bag, digging out the envelope. He held it up.

"I'm not supposed to tell anyone, but Ward gave me this," he said. "Told me to bring it with me and hand it back to him when I return."

"That's an odd one," Nina said. "What's in it?"

"No idea," Ryan said. "I mean . . . I'm getting on the ship, staying on, and getting off."

"Why'd you say yes?" she asked.

"He offered me the entire sum of money up front, instead of a fraction now and the rest when I get back. And he said he'd find the top spinal surgeon in the world and get us a consult for Teddy."

Nina frowned. "The doctors have always been pretty adamant about where things stood."

"I know," Ryan said. "But Ward has access to stuff the average person doesn't. We could at least see what they have to say."

Nina shook her head. "I don't want to get his hopes up."

"Again, I know." He turned the envelope over in his hand.

They sat in silence for a few moments before Nina finally said, "Just take it. What can it hurt?"

"Yeah," Ryan said. "Yeah." Then he buried the envelope back in his bag.

"Now, get over here, handsome," Nina said. "I have to get my fill before you abandon your family."

Ryan laughed and jumped onto the bed, crawling up toward her. He lifted her T-shirt and gently kissed the scar on her abdomen. It still had a little healing to do, but the mottled pink skin had almost faded into the same color as the rest of her stomach.

"I love you," he said.

"Even more than pizza?" she asked.

"Way more than pizza," he said, kissing her hard on the mouth.

JANET WILLIAMS
CNN BREAKING NEWS REPORT

"At ten fifty-two Eastern time this morning, the crew bound for Titan launched from Cape Canaveral in an Atlas VII rocket. Around six-thirty this evening, they'll dock with *Starblazer,* the ship developed jointly by NASA and billionaire presidential candidate John Ward. Tomorrow morning, at nine A.M. Eastern, they're scheduled to begin the year-long journey to Saturn's moon.

"Ward has experienced a surge in popularity as the world watches, filled with hope that this could be a first step toward establishing humanity's first off-world settlement. Polling shows his election chances have stunningly climbed by more than thirty points.

"I know I'm speaking for all of us when I say: I wish these six brave men and women the best of luck."

5

TITAN

EMAIL
FROM JOHN WARD

It's almost time. You keep your end of the deal, and I'll keep mine. I think it's best that we maintain radio silence. No contact, just to be safe. This thing with Lerner is a problem. I've done the best I can on my end to keep it under wraps. I think I got every copy of the report. Hopefully you haven't gotten any static on your end.

The closer I get to the White House, the more I imagine foreign countries are going to be looking closely at my communications. And the encryption here is top-notch, but some of the AI technology coming out of China these days makes me a little nervous.

Mostly because I keep trying to buy it off them and they won't let me.

I'm trusting you on this. Which, if there's anyone I can trust, I figure it would be you, right?

RYAN CRANE
STARBLAZER COMMUNICATION SUITE

Ryan watched the fuzzy image on the screen. Teddy had the phone propped on something on the kitchen table. It was dark—he must have filmed it before bedtime. Which was funny to think about: day and night

didn't really exist out here. Sometimes the only way he could tell the difference was the lighting: it had a bluish tint during the "day," but in the
evening, when they were supposed to be winding down, it was a softer
yellow. Blue light messes with circadian rhythms, so it was meant to keep
them on a somewhat Earthlike schedule.

Teddy looked tired, and a little sad, and Ryan told himself it was
because he had a long day at school, not because his dad had been gone
for a year and was currently 900 million miles away.

"So Mom says you look like Grizzly Adams, whoever that is," Teddy
said. "She says you have to shave the beard before you get home, because she doesn't want to get all scratched up. Personally, I think you
should keep growing it. Grow it as long as you can. It looks cool."

Ryan scratched his face. The thing was itchy and sometimes a little
too hot, but it felt good. He'd always wanted to grow out his facial hair,
and Nina was never on board, but there wasn't much she could do about
it now.

And then he noticed Teddy absentmindedly scratching his own face.
Ryan leaned forward in the seat and noticed wisps of hair on his son's
chin.

And he was struck in that moment by a mix of emotions he had trouble sorting out.

Pride, at the way his son was becoming a man.

And deep disappointment, that the boy was old enough to shave and
Ryan wasn't there to show him how to do it. That's how it was supposed
to work.

A little crack opened along the surface of his heart, joining all the others that had formed over the last year every time he thought about his
family.

"Not much else to update you on," Teddy said. "Things have been
quiet here. But we're all really excited. I know there's a delay, but they'll
be doing live news updates when you get to Titan, and we're going to
watch. It's nice 'cause that'll mean after, you'll be on your way home."

Teddy paused, and it sounded like his voice was growing thick, but it
was hard to tell. The picture and video quality weren't great.

"Scarlett misses you a lot," Teddy said. "So do I. I'd love to hear
more about how things have been going out there." Then his eyes widened. "Oh, so we're meeting with Dr. Stegman again. He wants to go

over the latest test results and talk about some potential treatments. I'll keep you updated on that."

Ryan closed his eyes and took a deep breath. Things sounded promising, in that they were still doing the tests and exploring options. That wouldn't be the case if there weren't some glimmer of hope. He wished he could be sitting in the room with them for this.

"Well, good luck, Dad," Teddy said. "We'll be watching. I love you."

He reached forward to hit the button on his phone, ending the call.

Ryan took a moment to collect himself before starting up the recording in response.

"Hey, kiddo," Ryan said, watching himself speak. The beard really was getting long, and a little unkempt, but it was too scraggly to shave, the trimmer they'd brought on board broke, and he couldn't find any scissors. "I'm glad you guys will be able to watch. And I'd love to tell you more, but honestly, the most exciting thing we've done lately is reinstate movie night."

Which had been going great, until Stitch picked a movie called *Aniara,* about a ship headed to Mars that goes off course, doomed to drift in space forever. It hit a little too close to home, and they had to take a break after that—but it was a nice activity to bring back. The agreement was they'd watch only comedies.

"Oh, and we found some more board games that we had forgotten we packed," he said. "We did a big Monopoly game, but that devolved into chaos. Then we set up a chess tournament. I came in third. Padma beat me, and Stitch came in first. But I was thinking maybe we could keep playing when I get back. I really enjoyed it, and I know you'd kick some butt."

Ryan sighed.

"Otherwise, buddy, it's pretty basic. We wake up, we do our jobs, we eat, we work some more, we go back to sleep. I'm mostly doing maintenance stuff and helping keep the place clean. Sometimes Padma explains some of her research to me, which is cool."

Ryan looked around the darkened interior of the communication room—a small, soundproofed space carved out for them to receive and record videos. Out of everyone on the ship, he and Della probably spent the most time in here.

"Other than that, the past year seemed to fly by," he said. "We already started our deceleration, not that you can feel it on the ship. It's exciting, and a little nerve-racking. So now it's going to get real, and I'm sure afterward I'll have some cool stuff to tell you."

Ryan scratched his beard again.

"You tell your mom the beard might have to stay. She can kiss the broom until I get back to get used to it."

Ryan laughed, wondering how the joke would go over.

"I love you, kid. Tell your mom and sister I said hi, and I'll record another video as soon as we're done and safely headed home."

Ryan pressed the red button on the screen to end the recording and sat back, wishing more than anything in this moment that he was back home, sitting on the couch with his family. He'd lied; the past year had dragged. Every day without them felt like a month, and it was hard to think that they were only at the halfway point.

But that was halfway closer to home.

He thought about the envelope Ward had given him. A few times he'd considered opening it, but he didn't. It wasn't worth the risk, if Ward found out and decided to punish him in some way. Especially because with the election coming up next week, it was pretty clear that the man would be president.

They got news updates from a couple of major media sources, which Ryan preferred to sit down with and absorb in big gulps. He had always been a passive reader of the news, but it was something to do to fill the gaping voids of time.

The ship was almost fully automated, and it didn't take a lot of work to keep things running. He really did wish that he had some more exciting stories to tell Teddy, but the truth was the truth. The only thing of any real interest was when the climate control malfunctioned, turning the inside of the ship into a sauna, and he and Alonso had to spend an afternoon crawling around ductwork, trying to fix it based on instructions that were sent over from Earth.

And whenever he had to move among the three decks of the ship, through the central shaft where there was no artificial gravity—that was a thrill. Grabbing one of the stabilizer bars and launching himself forward, it almost felt like flying.

That right there, that was something he still wished he could share with Teddy. And he wished to make good on his hope of one day bringing Teddy to Titan.

Ryan stepped out of the communication room, where Alonso was waiting patiently.

"Sorry, man, didn't know you were waiting to get in there," Ryan said.

"Nah, it's all good," Alonso said. "How's the fam?"

"Good, you know," he said. "They're feeling it just as much as I am."

"I can't imagine how hard this must be when you have kids. But hey, pretty soon you'll be on your way back to them, and to your old job. That must be exciting."

Ryan laughed a little, catching himself, and Alonso furrowed his eyebrows in confusion.

"The kids I miss," Ryan said. "The job, not so much."

"You're the hero cop."

"To the public," Ryan said. "To my colleagues, I'm . . ." He sighed, searching for the words. "You know how cops have a reputation for protecting their own, no matter what?"

Alonso nodded. "Blue wall of silence."

"Yeah, I don't get down with that so much," he said. "I didn't become a cop to make my life easier, I did it to help people. That's put me in . . . conflict with some folks."

Alonso patted him on the shoulder. "You're a rule follower."

Ryan thought, briefly, about the envelope. Then he changed the subject.

"How's your girlfriend?" he asked.

"She is . . ." Alonso smiled and shook his head. "Not thrilled. It's hard, being this far away from someone you love, you know? Of course you know."

"It sucks, big-time," Ryan said. "But hey, almost there, right? How much longer we got?"

"This time tomorrow we'll be on our way back," Alonso replied. "The whole satellite thing will take a few hours, but it should be pretty straightforward."

"Right, right," Ryan said. "And, I'm sorry, I'm not a math guy. How long are we out of contact? And how long will the transmissions take? My son said something about live updates, but they're not exactly live."

"Yeah, so it'll be only seven minutes going around Titan that we'll be completely out of range," Alonso said. "We've also been able to get the relay time down to seven minutes. Which is, frankly, remarkable."

"Still, if something goes wrong, we're on our own, huh?"

"It could be worse. It was supposed to be twenty-four minutes, but apparently there was a decommissioned probe nearby that still had some juice left, and Ward was able to piggyback off it for communication," he said. "But nothing's going to go wrong."

"You sure about that?"

Alonso clapped Ryan on the shoulder. "I gotta be. No sense in worrying about something that hasn't happened yet."

Alonso gave Ryan a casual little salute and popped into the communication room, shutting the door behind him. He seemed confident, and Ryan hoped he wasn't putting on a show.

He checked his watch. Lunchtime. Stretching out his cramped legs, he wandered the narrow, serpentine hallways of *Starblazer* toward the cafeteria, wondering if there were still a few of the prepackaged lasagna meals left. His favorite, which meant of course they were in short supply.

As he went, he ran his hand along the metallic wall, stopping at one of the port windows—a small circle of glass that let them look out into space. Another disappointment: space travel wasn't like it was in the movies. All those beautiful nebulas, the sky dotted with a billion stars.

The truth was, when he looked out the window, all he saw was the black void of space, and he couldn't look at it longer than a minute or so before he felt like he might fall into it.

MIKE SEAVER
STARBLAZER CHEMISTRY LAB

Mike sat back, looking over the contraption he'd just set up. A heating mantle with a round-bottom flask, which was clamped to a ring stand. Next to it was another ring stand, on which he'd placed an Erlenmeyer flask, and a series of tubes and clamps connected them. Chemistry wasn't his forte, but he had a rudimentary understanding of the process, and it looked close enough to what he saw in the YouTube video.

He poured two bottles of mouthwash into the round-bottom flask, then turned on the heating mantle and let it come to a boil. Then he sat back and waited.

He had two more Erlenmeyer flasks standing by. Apparently there were three phases in the distillation process—the head, the heart, and the tails. The head was the immediate runoff, which would include harmful substances like methanol. The tails, at the end, would be less dangerous but could contribute to off flavors.

The goal was the middle part—the hearts. Everyday, safe-to-drink ethanol.

It wouldn't taste good, but it would do the job.

He waited, watching the mouthwash slowly bubble, and tried not to think too much about his shame. Not just over the fact that he felt compelled to cobble together a rudimentary distiller out of things they should be using for legitimate research or hygiene—but how he got here.

He'd convinced himself he'd use the trip to dry out so when he got back to Helen and the kids, maybe he could do things right this time. But then he discovered the crew loading pallets of beer and wine in cans—enough for the whole crew to enjoy every now and again—which NASA had gone back and forth about but rubber-stamped thanks to a push from a subcommittee Mike may have schmoozed with once or twice.

Mike promptly shuffled the pallets to the back of the storage room and erased them from the logs so it'd look like they were never loaded. And despite his best intentions to parse it out over the entire mission, reminding himself daily and nightly, he had of course worked his way through a two-year supply for six people in the last year alone, just by sneaking off when no one was looking.

And now the supply was gone, and they were about to enter the most dangerous portion of the run.

He couldn't have the shakes. Not now.

Twelve more hours. That's all he needed.

He'd torn apart the ship looking for anything he might be able to drink. But everything alcohol-based had too much methanol or isopropyl—not safe for human consumption.

And then he remembered the mouthwash.

He could cut the resulting concoction with water or a mixer like or-ange juice—they had plenty of that—and it might be enough to keep him straight. Once they came around the other side of Titan, he could get sober. He'd packed some Alcoholics Anonymous literature, including the *Big Book*.

And then he'd get home, to Helen and the kids, a new man . . .

"What are you doing?"

Mike turned to find Della, arms folded, her face turned down.

"Just—"

"Mike," Della said, using her mom voice to full effect.

He couldn't come up with a response other than "I'm sorry."

She sat on the empty stool next to him. "Run out of the good stuff?"

Mike looked at her in surprise.

"You think I didn't notice?" she asked, her voice barely above a whisper. "Sneaking off, coming back with beer on your breath? I didn't say anything to the crew because I didn't want to cause any hard feel-ings."

"Why didn't you say anything to *me*?" he asked.

Della shook her head. "Because you have a problem, Mike. Just gonna say it. You have a problem. And if anything had gone sideways—if you'd become a liability—don't get me wrong, I'd have busted your ass in a heartbeat. But things have been smooth, and, honestly, I didn't want to fight you."

Mike wanted to defend himself, to argue, to say anything, but he couldn't. She was right. He did have a problem. Worse, it was the kind of problem that didn't track as one on the surface.

He did his job well. No one got hurt.

It was everyone else in his orbit.

The distillation process had started: the flask was filling up with clear liquid, and he gave it a sniff. Harsh and astringent. He dipped his finger and touched it to his tongue. Medicinal; it nearly made him gag.

Della offered a judgmental headshake. Which instinctively put Mike on the defense.

"This is a onetime thing. Just to keep me steady for the Titan loop."

Della eyed him skeptically. "Better be. We've got a year after this. A year for you to get your shit together. And you're going to do it. I'm going to help you with whatever you need, okay? And it's not for me, and it's not for Helen, and it's not even for you. It's for the kids, Mike."

Mike nodded. "Thank you." He took a deep breath, trying to keep the tears at bay. Della loved him, and he loved her. Not in a romantic way. But no one saw him the way she did. Rather than get maudlin, he changed the subject. "Speaking of, how are the girls?"

"Fine," Della said. "Pretty sure my mom has been letting Sean come by more than he should and not really telling me about it. She knows I won't approve."

"Why not give the guy a break?" Mike asked. "He's trying."

"Of course he's trying," Della said, her voice dripping with disdain. "He's trying after leaving me high and dry for three months to bang a girl young enough to be his daughter. I'm never going to forgive him, but I still need to figure out if I can tolerate him."

Mike again dipped his finger into the slow drip and pressed it to his tongue. This time, it tasted—well, not palatable, but not deadly. Probably in the heart stage. He swapped out one flask for an empty one, then watched as liquid slowly pooled at the bottom.

"Let me ask you this," Mike said. "Is he a good dad?"

"That's beside the point," Della said, holding eye contact. "The man left. He left those girls alone. Doesn't matter how many times he buys them ice cream, I can't ever trust him. How do I know he's not going to walk away from them again? And worse, do it when they're old enough to remember and have their hearts broken? Mine was bad enough."

Mike nodded thoughtfully. "Yeah. Yeah, those are good points."

"I consider the two years we're out here like a probationary period," Della said. "See how he does, without me there to call him on his shit. If I get back and get glowing reports from my mom and the kids, then I'll be open to letting him be more a part of their lives. But he's never going to be a part of mine. One strike, he is out."

"Got it," Mike said.

"You think I'm being too harsh?"

Mike took another taste. It seemed to be turning. Probably the tails. He swapped out the last flask, making sure to put the one with the hearts well away from the others, so he didn't mix them up.

"Look, there's a certain way a man is supposed to act, and no doubt that's not it. But it's hard for me to sit in judgment of anyone at this moment. I let my drinking get in the way of time with the kids and screwed up my relationship with them. Isn't that just as bad?"

Della shrugged. "At least you want to be there. You're just your own worst enemy."

"This is true," Mike said.

He turned off the heating element, picked up the flask with the hearts, and gave it a swirl. It wasn't a lot. A couple of mouthfuls maybe.

"You'd better not go blind," Della said.

"Least of our problems," he said, taking a sip.

It was the harshest thing he'd ever tasted—worse than that time he drank straight Everclear because it was the only thing in the cabinet and he was too tired and drunk to find a mixer—but he immediately felt a flood of relief. His muscles unfurling, his head clearing.

He turned to Della, then looked past her shoulder and ten feet to the right, pretending to make eye contact with her while looking at a cabinet across the room. "See, Della? I'm not blind."

Della leaned forward and slapped him on the chest. "Don't joke."

Mike looked her in the eyes, laughed, and offered her the beaker. Della eyed it suspiciously before shrugging and saying, "What the hell."

She'd barely touched it to her lips when she coughed and sputtered, like she was trying to clear a solid mass from her chest. As her eyes teared up, Mike laughed again, because it was a little funny.

Until it wasn't.

The beaker tumbled from her hand and shattered on the floor.

The two of them watched as glass and liquid spread around their feet. And to Mike's shame, his first thought was to drop to his knees and lick up whatever he could, just so it wouldn't go to waste.

Della put her hand over her mouth. "Mike, I'm so sorry . . ." She looked around and lowered her voice. "Can you make more?"

"Not unless I start taking mouthwash from other people," Mike said.

He wanted to be upset, but he had no right to be. It was insane for him to be doing this. It meant that the next few days were going to be rough—and it was coming at the absolute worst time—but maybe this was the wake-up call he needed.

Della tracked what he was thinking immediately.

"You're going to be fine," she said. "You've got this. And no matter what, I've got *you*."

"Why?"

"Why what?"

"Why do you have my back? Do I deserve it? I literally stole from the crew, I fucked things up with my family, I'm—"

Della leaned forward and put her hand on Mike's knee. "Hey. I've always got your back. Because you've always got mine. And that's all that matters in the end. The rest is just details."

Mike took her hand in both of his.

"Thank you, Della," he said.

"You got it, partner. Now, let's get to work."

STITCH
STARBLAZER BUNKS

"Bored bored bored bored bored bored bored bored," Stitch whispered to himself as he wandered through the bunk area.

Each one of them had their own room, which was nice, except that each room was about the size of the bed that it held, with some shelving and a window that simulated either daylight or twilight. Stitch's room was musty and smelled like it was full of sweat and farts. You'd think NASA could have figured out an antidote for bad odors.

He peeked into the media room, considered watching a movie or something, but couldn't bring himself to. He'd just come off a binge of the TV show *Manifest* and needed a break from screens. He wanted something to interact with. He'd already filled the walls in his bunk with artwork—no one noticed the three cases of paint markers he'd smuggled on board, thankfully—but he was running out of room, and he was going to get in enough trouble for that. Probably best if he didn't start tagging up the hallways.

Then he remembered Ryan's offer to let him borrow a book. It might be nice to read: something to distract him from the coming task, the enormity of which was making him feel jittery and scatterbrained. He went to knock on Ryan's door, but it was sitting wide open, and the bookshelf was in reach, so he looked over the options. All paperbacks, all thrillers. Stitch picked one that looked interesting—*Assassins Anonymous*. The title and the cover—a coffee cup with a knife through it—looked pretty cool. He pulled it off the shelf but found there was something crammed between the pages.

He opened it and found a white envelope, beaten and worn, with something inside.

FOR JOHN WARD.

Huh. The envelope that Ward gave Ryan outside the barracks.

Stitch smiled. His main goal coming over to the bunks was to find something to occupy his time. But he couldn't say he was upset by this turn of events. Because that clandestine exchange had been scratching at the back of his head for the past year. He knew better than to ask Ryan; it was clearly something that wasn't supposed to be public knowledge.

But now that he'd just stumbled across it . . .

He tugged at the corner of the envelope, but it was sealed. Ran his hands over it, and could feel the hard plastic and gentle curves of a thumb drive. Interesting.

He considered picking another book, or taking this one and sticking the envelope into another of Ryan's books.

Instead, he stuck the package into his back pocket.

Stitch promised himself he'd return it.

But curiosity had always been a little gremlin that lived on his shoulder and whispered into his ear. Encouraging him to look at things he shouldn't be looking at.

Because you never knew what kind of cool shit you might find.

ALONSO CARDONA
STARBLAZER GYM

Alonso approached the last mile of his jog. The first four had been gentle, but for the last one he increased the speed and the incline. This would be the last run he'd get in for a couple of days—between the swing around Titan and the safety and maintenance checks for the journey home, it'd be busy, and he wanted to make it count.

That, and he wanted to outrun the feeling in his gut, after watching the last message from Maddie. She looked tired, and she'd clearly been crying before she recorded it.

She missed him, she said. Too much. And she was struggling with the thought of another year without him. She insisted that she was proud of him and she didn't want to end it, but Alonso could tell she was trying to convince herself of that.

They'd talked about opening their relationship while he was gone. He couldn't exactly date around—the pool here was pretty small, and anyway, that would be a whole *thing* on board a tin can hurtling at impossible speeds through space. But he thought that maybe Maddie would have an easier time if she could have some companionship, some physical connection while he was gone.

Too much like cheating, she had said.

Which wasn't how Alonso saw it. The heart was a house with many rooms. You could love more than one person at once. It didn't take away from one, or make another any less special. But he knew that telling her that would start a conversation he wasn't ready to have. That Maddie wasn't ready to hear.

Part of him wished he had broached it with her anyway.

Another part of him missed Ethan. It was unfair to think this, but he figured Ethan wouldn't have had a problem with the distance, with the idea of being open.

Had he chosen wrong?

He pumped his legs harder, sweat coating his skin, making his shirt stick to his back.

It didn't help.

That was the problem with treadmills. You're just running in place; you never actually get anywhere.

He finished, breathing hard, and made his way out of the gym, weaving through the free weights littered around the floor. He wondered who was leaving them out but didn't think it was helpful to speculate. He ducked into the attached locker room, which wasn't much more than a single locker and a stand-up shower he could barely fit inside, but he rinsed the best he could before pulling on a clean jumpsuit.

That was what he missed most: hot showers. The water here barely ever went above lukewarm. But at least it was working.

His legs ached from the run, so he took his time navigating the narrow corridors of the ship toward the hatch that brought him to the ladder, and he enjoyed a leisurely float down the overly lit central shaft. It wasn't a very wide space—you could barely fit two people next to each other—

and the whole thing was cushioned with rubber pads to keep the crew from getting hurt.

It was a bright, sterile space, but sometimes he liked to spend time down here and just drift. Like his problems might float away, too.

They never did.

He climbed the ladder into the main wheel and made his way to the flight deck, which was empty when he arrived. It was cramped like the rest of the space—the six of them could just fit inside with a little room left over, so it was rare that they all assembled in here. It was full of consoles and an array of flashing and blinking buttons. There were only three chairs.

The thing he loved about it was the view. The naked human eye had never been this far out, never seen this. Not that there was much to see. He'd been staring into the dark for months now.

But there, coming up fast . . .

The main console offered a strange little beep. He leaned forward and looked at the screen.

The telemetry data didn't look right.

Their trajectory was suddenly a few degrees off, and the ship was firing thrusters on the port side to compensate. Except, it shouldn't be doing that. The course had been plotted, planned, and plugged in before they left.

He ran a quick check and couldn't find any immediate evidence of someone changing the log entries. Maybe it was just a glitch. But his gut told him it wasn't. It was like a new flight path had been uploaded to the system, and the ship was moving to match it.

Which could be bad.

Like, they were all going to die bad.

PADMA SINGH
STARBLAZER SATELLITE ROOM

Padma examined the satellite for, probably, the seven thousandth time since she'd boarded the ship.

And for the seven thousandth time, she felt like there was something wrong.

The satellite they'd be leaving behind was about the size of a car.

Once the bay doors in the third wheel at the back of the ship opened, a railing system would eject it into space before a set of massive solar panels extended—miles wide, because they were so far from the sun out here and needed extra surface area to collect solar energy—and thrusters would push it into orbit. Everything was preprogrammed. Nothing to do but hit a button on the flight deck.

It would circle Titan, offering them analysis on the weather, the terrain, and the temperature and, more important, helping them start working out the best landing sites for the next phase of the mission down the line—a supply drop that would include a bevy of scientific equipment for even more accurate on-surface readings, which would precede the first manned mission to Titan's surface.

It had been an unspoken thing between Padma and Ward that she would be the first person to step foot on Titan. Padma had always thought Ward would want to be the one to do it, but if he was going to be president, that didn't exactly leave room for a years-long excursion.

Maybe more. Padma imagined touching down on Titan and never leaving. What did she have back home that was so great?

Some plants. An ex-boyfriend.

At least out here she could do something with her life. Pave the way for the future of humanity.

But as she peered into the components of the satellite, she had a funny feeling, like something about the contraption was off.

"Everything okay?"

Padma turned to find Stitch standing in the doorway, chewing on a protein bar.

"I think so," Padma said. She stood up and stretched her aching back—how long had she been bending down there? "Just going over things one last time."

"You've got a look," Stitch said.

"A look?"

"Yeah, the kinda look that says there's a lot more to what you're saying."

Padma sighed, waved over Stitch, and had him look inside the open panel. He stared at it for a few moments before nodding and saying, "Yeah, I have no idea what I'm looking at."

"I'm not sure I do either," Padma said. "There are things in here that I'm not sure why they're there. Like, I helped design this thing. Not the actual satellite itself, but I consulted on the things that go into it. For a satellite like this, you want stuff like an infrared camera and a spectrograph, so we can get accurate readings from the moon. But there's a lot of communication equipment in here that seems way more sophisticated than necessary for just shooting some data back to Earth."

Stitch shrugged. "I mean . . . no disrespect, but are you qualified to make that call? Maybe Ward wanted something heftier. Maybe he wanted some backup systems. This is a big, complicated mission. I know I'd want some redundancies."

"Right, but the added cost . . ."

"From the richest man in the world? What's it matter to him."

Padma paused. That was a good point. Maybe Ward just wanted this thing to be failure-proof. What was the point of worrying now anyway?

The communication speaker crackled to life.

"We're in visual distance of the moon," Alonso said. "Could everyone report to the flight deck?"

Padma and Stitch looked at each other and dashed down the hallway, so they could access the central spoke. They opened the hatch, and Stitch put out his hand, beckoning Padma to go first. She dropped through, the feeling of weightlessness taking over. No matter how many times she did this, it never got old.

She floated down to the main passageway, grabbed a support bar, and launched herself forward, toward the front of the ship. She kept an eye on the walls, occasionally pressing off things to adjust her path.

Stitch floated past her, at a higher rate of speed. "Race you," he said.

She grabbed another support bar and really put her arms into it, throwing herself forward, and then the two of them were floating, aimed for the front. Stitch reached it first, Padma a moment behind.

"How lucky are we?" Stitch asked.

"The luckiest," Padma said, her voice high and light, teetering on the edge of laughter.

The two of them climbed into the front wheel, gravity returning as they reached the hatch, then navigated the hallways, where they ran into Della and Mike. After a moment Ryan was behind them, and they ran with the excitement of schoolchildren onto the deck.

They found Alonso staring through the front windshield. When they came in, he just shook his head and said, "Guys . . ."

Suspended in the darkness of space before them was Titan.

It was beautiful. A burnt-orange marble suspended in the void of space, dark bands and stippling across it, the nitrogen atmosphere a stormy haze.

Padma's eyes welled up. She could barely believe it. After all this time, all this work, all this energy, there it was. The prize she'd been after.

They were the first humans to see it without a telescope.

"Amazing," Ryan said, his voice an awed whisper.

"Goddamn," Mike said, stepping closer to the window and reaching out his hand, like he might be able to touch it.

They all took a moment, letting it sink in.

"Okay," Alonso said. "I thought that deserved a moment before we go into this." He sat at the chair and pulled up a screen of numbers, then turned and met the eyes of each crew member. "We have a problem."

JOHN WARD
NASA MISSION CONTROL, JOHNSON SPACE CENTER, HOUSTON, TX

The room was buzzing with activity, and Ward stood at the center of it all, feeding off the energy. Better than sex, better than any drug—all these people, working for him.

NASA's old Mission Control room had fallen into a state of disrepair: government-issue furniture, worn carpet, out-of-date screens. Thank you, Congress.

So he'd swooped in and updated the décor. Top-of-the-line ergonomic chairs for everyone, state-of-the-art screens—so state of the art they weren't even available on the consumer market. Even an AI-enhanced snack and coffee bar in the corner. If you decided you wanted coffee, you'd find it ready and waiting for you.

His heart raced. Speaking of coffee, that sixth cup was probably a mistake. But he couldn't sleep last night. He'd been up for nearly eighteen hours at this point.

How could he sleep, at a time like this?

"Hell of a thing."

Ward turned to find Owens, in his pressed navy suit that fit slightly off at the shoulders, the cut on the cuff a little too long. The man needed to learn how to dress. Ward looked down at his own burgundy suit and black T-shirt. Crisp, clean, and perfectly tailored. He needed to get this man a stylist if he was going to consider adding him to the administration. Standing next to him at press conferences was already a little embarrassing.

"It's amazing," Ward said. "Your team has really pulled it out. Now we get to the fun part."

"I'm going to have Blanton address the room in a moment, but in the meantime, I still wanted to make sure that, uh . . ."

Ward clapped Owens on the shoulder. "I appreciate a straight shooter. You can come out and say it. You want to stay on board as the director of NASA in my new administration."

"Yes, sir," Owens said. "That would be an incredible honor, sir. I think, after today, there'll be a lot of new opportunities, and I think steady leadership . . ."

"Don't stand on formality," Ward said. "You got my back when I needed it. You made all of this possible. I owe you, big-time. We're going to do some incredible things together."

"Thank you," Owens said before scurrying off.

Sycophant, Ward thought. He would never hire Owens at one of his own companies; the man was a political drone, cut from the same cloth as most of the men in Washington. No vision, no creativity, unable to see anything other than their next opportunity.

But he was loyal, and he did what he was told.

If that changed, Ward had a handful of candidates waiting in the wings.

Camila maneuvered through the desks and seats toward him and said, "A word."

Ward took another look around and, not seeing Blanton, figured they had a few minutes, so he followed Camila to a small conference room on the far side of the floor. She carefully shut the door and took out her phone, which would check for any recording devices. Satisfied there were none, she stashed her phone inside her suit jacket and smiled.

She didn't smile often.

"You're surging," she said. "Latest poll numbers came in a half hour ago. You're ten points ahead. It looks like, at this point, you're winning undecideds, and the other two candidates are just going to have to cannibalize each other among their loyalists."

"For once, the third-party system works," Ward said, peering over Camila's shoulder and through the window, watching the activity of the room increase.

Camila snapped her fingers. "This is good news."

"Sure. But it's not nearly as important as what we're doing here today."

"About that . . . you're sure? I mean, you're going to be president. Isn't that enough?"

"When has enough ever been enough?" Ward asked. "Any schmuck with a hedge fund can be president. I get to be god."

Camila paused, looking around the room, searching for the words she wanted to say. This made Ward nervous; she never hesitated.

"What is it?" he asked.

"Lerner," she said.

"He was a nut job, and he has been dealt with."

"No, he hasn't," Camila said. "If he'd been dealt with, then no one would ever hear from him again. And we know that's not the case. He's out there somewhere."

"And soon I'm going to have access to some of the greatest information and surveillance tools the world has to offer. We're going to find him, and we're going to get it taken care of. I'm not worried. You shouldn't be either."

Camila nodded. "Okay."

"Okay," Ward said, catching movement in the window over Camila's shoulder. Blanton was making his way to the front of the room.

Ward clapped his hands and rubbed them together.

"Showtime!"

He stepped outside the room just in time for Blanton to have someone pass him a microphone. He tapped it a few times to make sure it was working and then said, "Okay, everyone, can I have your attention please."

The whole room stopped and turned to look at Blanton. The man

looked exhausted, disheveled, and equally hopped up on too much caffeine.

"Today we are about to make history," he said. "The farthest
manned flight we've ever achieved. The exploration of a potentially habitable moon. This is our first step into humanity's next phase. So, make
no mistake, this must be perfect. It's not just those six lives up there, it's
every life down here. I want you to know how deeply proud I am, of each
and every one of you. None of this would have been possible. And I want
to thank our friend and partner, John Ward . . ."

Blanton swept his hand toward Ward, which brought a rousing wave
of applause through the room. Ward smiled and waved.

"Without you, sir, we wouldn't be here, so thank you. Now, let's go
bring our team through this safely, and home safer than that."

Another burst of applause, during which Blanton caught Ward's eye
and nodded for him to come over. Ward cut his way through the room,
patting people on the back as he passed, and got close to Blanton.

"We okay?" Ward asked.

Blanton steered Ward away from the assembly, his tone uncomfort-
ably discreet.

"Numbers are a little off. I need to talk to someone on *Starblazer*
IT."

"Why are the numbers off?"

"Not sure. Could be some kind of glitch. But it's like the navigational
data has been . . . overwritten, and the ship is trying to course correct,
but from the wrong direction. We're working on it down here, but with
the delay, that's a lot for the team to have to fix on the fly."

"Maybe it's interference."

Blanton cocked his head, curious. "Not sure what would be interfer-
ing with the signal."

Ward shrugged, catching himself. "Just spitballing. Okay. Let's hud-
dle with the rocket scientists and figure this out."

As he and Blanton made their way over to the *Starblazer* team, which
had their own section of the room, Camila raised an eyebrow at him. She
didn't need to say it.

Told you so.

MIKE SEAVER
STARBLAZER FLIGHT DECK

Mike surveyed the screen, trying to make sense of what he was seeing.

"What's going on?" Della asked.

"No idea," Mike said, struggling to keep up with the cascade of numbers. He'd give anything for a gulp of that distilled mouthwash. Already his palms were sweaty, the muscles in his neck strained. It was like he was holding on to something that didn't want to be held.

Alonso appeared over his shoulder and squinted. "Yeah, like I said, the approach numbers are off."

"Why the hell would the approach numbers be off?" Mike asked.

"No idea," Alonso said. "This shit is all supposed to be automated for us. There might be some kind of glitch in the system and . . . oh fuck."

"What?" Mike asked.

"If the numbers are off, that means the satellite launch will be off. We have a narrow window to get that thing out of the ship so it stays in a sustained orbit."

"What happens if we don't launch at the right time?" Ryan asked.

Everyone turned to Padma. She paused for a second, like she was trying to find the right words, and said, "Too soon, it doesn't get caught in the orbit and floats out into space. Too late, and it crashes on the surface. We can't let either happen."

"But what difference does it make, if it's automated?" Ryan asked.

"If the approach numbers are off, that means *we* run the risk of those things as well," Alonso said.

"Well, just . . . put in the right numbers," Ryan said.

"It's not that simple," Mike said. "We have to recalculate everything based on where we are, and double- and triple-check the work. We also have to stop the glitch from happening, so it doesn't get changed again."

The bridge fell silent, everyone looking at one another, like someone else might have an idea. Mike took a deep breath and closed his eyes, running the options through his head. His brain felt full of wet leaves.

But these were the kinds of moments he lived for.

"Here's what we're going to do," Mike said. "Alonso, take Padma and Ryan to the satellite in case we have to do a manual ejection. Della, you stay here with me, and let's see if we can get everything back where it belongs. Mission critical is we get everyone home alive. If we have to skip the satellite, we skip the satellite."

"We can't . . ." Padma started.

"We can, and we will," Mike snapped. "There are six souls on this ship, and we're getting home with six. The satellite doesn't have one. As mission commander, I'm making an executive decision that we will only eject the payload if we can ensure everyone's safety. Now, everyone, go."

Alonso didn't wait. He bounded out the door, ready to fulfill his orders. Ryan followed closely behind, and after a raised eyebrow from Mike, Padma left, too. Stitch tentatively raised a hand from where he was standing in the corner. "What should I do?"

"Stay out of everyone's way," Mike said, turning back to the terminal.

Stitch started to say something, so Mike put up a hand.

"Shut up, now," he said.

Della said something to Stitch, but Mike missed it—he was too busy looking over the numbers, trying to make sense of it all. Della sat at the terminal next to him.

"I'm on telemetry," he said. "You figure out what caused the problem in the first place."

"Will do, Captain," she said, then lowered her voice. "Lay off the kid, okay? He's just trying to help."

"So you just want me to stand here?" Stitch asked.

Mike sighed. While he had grown to trust Stitch—to a degree—this was life-or-death. Mike wanted to keep him close, rather than send him off somewhere that he couldn't be directly supervised. "You're the utility man, in case we need an extra hand."

"How about I . . ." Stitch started.

But Mike wasn't listening. He was too busy trying to make the numbers stop dancing, as Della talked into the microphone on the console, recording a message that would be beamed to flight control. And appear there, seven minutes from now.

They'd wait another seven minutes for a response . . .

The best minds in the world were in that room, and they were too damn far away.

RYAN CRANE
STARBLAZER CENTRAL SHAFT

Ryan floated alongside Alonso through the ship's main spoke, headed for the release bay on the rear deck of the ship. From somewhere behind them, Padma said, "We have to do whatever we can to salvage this."

"What's the big deal?" Ryan asked. "Don't we get plenty of data just by being here?"

"We get some," Padma said. "We need more. We can only tell so much from so far away. Forty years ago, an unmanned NASA spacecraft flew by, and we got a glimpse of Titan's shoreline and the way it was eroded by waves of liquid methane and ethane. All we've been able to do since then is create computer models, guessing at the mechanics of it."

Ryan and Alonso reached the end of the hallway, aiming for the padded sections to stop their trajectory. Padma came up behind them, and they made space so she could safely land, too.

"There are so many things we need to learn about this place, chief among them, if it truly can support life, and if so, where we need to focus our efforts. If we don't get that satellite out, sure, Ward loses a few billion, which I'm sure is the equivalent of a rounding error in his stock portfolio, but we lose years of research that humanity desperately needs."

Ryan nodded. "If given the choice of saving the future of humanity and seeing my kids . . ."

"You want them to live on a burned-out husk?" Padma asked.

Anger flashed through Ryan. "Then they'll do it with me. I will *walk* back if that's what it takes to see my kids again," he said, his voice rising.

"This is a fascinating debate," Alonso said, "and maybe one we should have later. The focus right now is on getting up there and prepping for the next thing we need to do." He tapped the rung of the ladder in front of him. "Which means climbing this, okay?"

Padma narrowed her eyes, wanting to argue further.

"Okay?" Alonso asked, looking between Ryan and Padma.

"Okay," Padma said.

"I'm sorry," Ryan said. "I didn't mean to snap at you."

Padma nodded, accepting the apology, and they started their climb.

Going up the ladder was easy; it was just a matter of floating in the right direction. Gravity didn't kick in until they reached the top portion, at the hatch. Climbing through it was sometimes a struggle, like one side of him was being pulled while the other was being pushed.

Alonso was the first to the hatch. He opened it up and scuttled through, followed by Ryan. The two of them knelt down to help Padma the rest of the way, and they ran down the corridors to the satellite bay.

Padma dashed to the main control screen and tapped a few buttons on the attached keyboard, to bring up the diagnostics, but the screen flashed. Even on the other side of the room, Ryan could read it: SYSTEM LOCKED.

"What does that mean?" he asked.

Alonso joined Padma at the screen. "The ship's main computer knows there's a problem, so it's locked us out. It won't grant access until it knows everything has been corrected."

"Can you override?" Padma asked, her voice desperate.

"Move over," Alonso said, and pecked at the keys. "I can try."

Ryan started to protest—if the computer didn't think it was safe, maybe they shouldn't be trying to override it—but held his tongue. He'd keep an eye on things. Let them play out.

And if he had to step in to stop this, he would.

JOHN WARD
NASA MISSION CONTROL, JOHNSON SPACE CENTER, HOUSTON, TX

"What the hell is going on up there?" Blanton called out, his voice booming through the space.

"No idea," Ward said, more to himself than to anyone else. He was sitting at a computer terminal looking at the telemetry data. The numbers were all wrong.

Worse, with the time delay between the ship and flight control, they couldn't work in tandem to solve the problem. Both sides had to work independently and hope they were able to get to an answer in time, and if the answer was sorted out down on Earth, there had to be time to get it to *Starblazer* . . .

Camila appeared at Ward's shoulder and leaned into his ear. "Is this because . . ."

"Possibly," Ward allowed after a considered beat.

"Don't you think you should . . ."

Ward looked up at Camila, who tilted her head toward Blanton, who was huddled with a bunch of men and women who all looked like they were about to have a collective aneurysm.

"Not yet," Ward said.

"If they knew what we know?"

"It wouldn't make a goddamn ounce of difference," Ward said. Camila's eyes went wide. He'd said it much more harshly than he intended. Her face dropped, and she was about to say something that one of them would regret, so Ward jumped on the grenade.

"I'm sorry, Cam, I shouldn't have said it like that. But there's still time to fix this. And the ship is designed to abort the satellite drop if it interferes with getting anyone home. Even if we don't launch it, we can still spin this as a success if everyone lives."

Camila nodded. "Apology accepted, on the condition you never use that tone with me again. And is there any kind of override? What do you think Padma is going to do?"

Padma.

Shit.

He'd never told her, or any of the crew, about the abort sequence. Didn't think it was necessary. So it stood to reason that they might think there was an opportunity to salvage the mission . . .

Ward fell back into the seat. Every station was occupied with someone whose hands were furiously typing on a keyboard. Almost double the amount of people seemed to have appeared, hovering on the sidelines, and Blanton was at the center of it all, anxiously moving pieces around like it was a chessboard.

Owens was here, too, waving at Ward to come over.

"This isn't playing out the way we expected," Camila said.

"It's going to be fine," Ward tossed off.

"How can you know that?"

He gave a little smile. "Because it's me. Things always work out in the end."

And he forgave her for rolling her eyes in response to that.

JANET WILLIAMS
CNN BREAKING NEWS REPORT

"According to preliminary reports, the mission to Titan, a joint effort between NASA and billionaire presidential candidate John Ward, appears to be experiencing some sort of communication issue.

"Sources inside NASA headquarters say that the navigational information required to properly send the six astronauts around Saturn's moon and onto a safe journey home has been corrupted, which could have devastating effects for the safety of the flight crew and their multibillion-dollar vessel.

"The Titan mission, the longest and farthest manned flight into our solar system, has captured the attention of the world, and brought Ward's campaign a much-needed boost—his polling numbers skyrocketed in anticipation of today, with his third-party insurgent candidacy considered by many to be a lock for the White House.

"That could change within the hour, depending on what happens next . . ."

NINA CRANE
HILL EAST, WASHINGTON, D.C.

"Mom, is Dad going to be okay?"

Nina leaned forward so she could put an arm around Teddy and pull him as close as she could. "I'm sure it's nothing," she said, watching as the CNN anchor cut to a shot of a crowd in Times Square staring up at a jumbo television screen, which was broadcasting footage of an empty podium.

We expect an official update from NASA at any moment, as the world watches . . .

Scarlett, who had been happily sitting on the floor coloring, was now standing next to them, looking between them and the TV. "Where's Daddy?" she asked.

"Still in space, baby," Nina said, picking the girl up and holding her tight.

Still in space, and he's going to be okay, she thought.

Nina smiled, doing her best to put on an air of confidence, but it was impossible to get anything past Scarlett. She was a tiny little empath, able to pick up on other people's emotions. It was something Nina had never had a knack for herself. She must have gotten that ability from Ryan.

Cynthia came in from the kitchen, hoisting a bowl of popcorn. She paused in the doorway and looked at the three of them huddled on the couch, then glanced at the television.

According to our experts, if the navigational data is indeed incorrect, it could spell havoc . . .

Just as Nina lunged forward to hit the mute button on the remote, Cynthia put down the bowl of popcorn and picked up Scarlett. "Hey, sweetheart, how about we go for a walk. I think it's going to be a long wait watching boring news. That doesn't sound like fun, does it?"

"Noooo!" Scarlett said, immediately keying in to Cynthia's positive energy.

Nina and Cynthia locked eyes, and Nina mouthed, *Thank you.* Having her sister here was a gift from the heavens.

Cynthia nodded and led Scarlett outside, grabbing her shoes on the way out the door. As soon as they were gone, Nina picked up the remote and turned the volume back up. Ward was now standing at the podium. He was smiling, but only with his mouth.

His eyes seemed to be telling a different story.

". . . can assure you that everything is under control. I could sit here and bore you with the science of it, but my abilities are better used in that room, making sure that our brave men and women up there return home. And I promise you, when they do, we're going to throw them one hell of a parade."

The next shot showed crowds of people in Piccadilly Circus in London.

The whole world *was* watching.

"He's scared" was all Teddy could say.

"Yeah," Nina said.

"What if Dad . . ."

Nina stood and hunched over to hug him. "Let's not think like that, okay? They have the best minds in the world working on this. I'm sure it's a hiccup."

She said it.

She didn't believe it.

All she knew for sure was that her stomach was slowly sinking, and she had never felt more helpless in her entire life. She glanced up, like she might catch a glimpse of Ryan, but all she could see was the pockmarked, crumbling paint in the corner of the ceiling. She fought back tears. This was not the moment to cry in front of Teddy.

She had to be strong.

MIKE SEAVER
STARBLAZER FLIGHT DECK

Someone was saying something. Mike couldn't focus. He was sweating and shivering at the same time. The numbers on the screen were moving too fast for him to comprehend. And whatever someone in the room was saying, the words were floating on the air, impossible to pin down.

A hand appeared on his shoulder.

"Mike," Stitch said. "The numbers are backward."

He shook his head. A moment of clarity.

"The hell are you talking about?"

Stitch leaned down and pointed to the screen. "We've been looking at these numbers for months, right? I feel like I've memorized them at this point. On top of which I've been spraying geometric palindromes as long as I can remember. So I can see this, clearly. All the numbers are just reversed."

"That doesn't make any sense . . ."

"But it doesn't make it not true," Stitch said. "Let me take a run at this."

Mike laughed. Even at his worst, there was no way he was letting this lunkhead take over the controls. "Go sit down."

"Mike, if the kid sees something . . ." Della started.

"The kid doesn't see shit," Mike said. "We can't run on a hunch right now."

"It's not a hunch, you cranky bastard," Stitch said. "I'm looking at it, and the numbers are all inverted."

Mike begrudgingly crossed to take a look for himself—but all he saw was a jumble of numbers.

A static-riddled voice came in over the communicator. "Bridge, this is Alonso. We're currently trying to figure out how to manually jettison the satellite. How do things look on your end?"

Stitch dove for the microphone stem and pressed the glowing yellow button on the console to open the channel. "The telemetry numbers are reversed, and Mike is sitting here staring at the screen like he has no idea how to read."

Mike knew the smart thing to do was to sit there and work the problem. But he didn't want to do the smart thing. His patience felt as brittle as cold glass, and he turned in his seat and said, "I swear to god if you don't sit down I'm going to come over there and knock you out."

Stitch turned and puffed out his chest. "Well, I want to get home in one piece, and I'm not going to put my life in the hands of a barely functioning alcoholic."

"Fucking . . ." Mike said, barely able to finish the sentence as he got out of his seat and moved toward Stitch. Della immediately got in the middle, her arms spread to keep distance between them.

"Both of you, shut the hell up," she said. "We have about ten minutes to correct this thing or we're all going to have a very bad day."

Mike reached up his hand and pointed past Della's face. "I'm not letting this little son of a bitch take over."

"Yeah, Mike?" Della asked. "So what else do you propose we do?"

"Yeah, Mike," Stitch said in a singsong mocking tone. "You wouldn't even be here right now if not for me."

Which gave Mike momentary pause, knowing this was true. Della turned to Stitch and snapped back, "You are *not* helping things. I think I've solved the other issue on my end. There was some kind of outside signal screwing with the data. Maybe another satellite or something. I fixed it, but I need to stay on top of it so it doesn't happen again." She turned back to Mike. "C'mon, Commander. *Command.* Which in this case might mean getting off your high horse and giving the kid a shot! What did I tell you about becoming a liability . . . ?"

Mike clenched his fists. This was bullshit. After all these years, after all the work he'd done, being treated like this. He wasn't about to kowtow to some upstart kid, nor was he going to allow Della to treat him like a child.

"Della, I love you, but I'll go through both of you if it means getting us home," Mike said.

ALONSO CARDONA
STARBLAZER SATELLITE BAY

I'll go through both of you if it means getting us home.

"Bridge," Alonso said, leaning into the microphone. "Bridge!"

"That does not sound good," Padma said.

"No, it does not," Alonso said. "Ryan, maybe you should . . ."

But Crane was already making his way toward the door. "On it."

And then he was gone.

Alonso shook his head. "Mike is stubborn."

"Stubborn enough to get us killed?" Padma asked.

"I hope not."

"He didn't look great before," Padma said. "He looked green. I mean, I think we all know . . ."

"Look . . . Mike is Mike," Alonso said. "He's an American hero."

"I know you idolize the guy, and I know you're all on the same team, but if your loyalty right now is the thing that gets us killed . . ."

Alonso sighed. Took a deep breath, trying to reset his nervous system. The truth was, he had seen it, too. Smelled the booze on Mike, and he looked the other way. If there was alcohol on board for the crew and Mike was hoarding it, he didn't really care. It was nice to relax sometimes with a beer or a glass of wine, but he was in work mode. He probably wouldn't have taken it if it were offered to him.

Which was easy to say . . .

"Let's focus on the task at hand," Alonso said. "See if we can't get this damn hunk of junk out into space."

"Yeah," Padma said, retreating to the satellite and pulling up the screen on a computer panel built into the side. "Whatever it is we came here for."

Alonso was working his own computer, combing through menu screens, trying to find a way to override the system. "And what does that mean?"

"It means I'm not sure this satellite is meant to do what Ward says it's meant to do."

"And what gives you that idea?"

"Just a hunch."

"Let's not worry about that now," Alonso said, keeping one ear on the arguments going on over the communication channel. It didn't seem too heated, yet, but certainly seemed like it could move in that direction. It was mostly Della and Mike speaking to each other, but the words were coming in scattered, like there was interference.

And then a high-pitched whine erupted from the speakers, so harsh Alonso had to cover his ears. He turned and found Padma was doing the same. It persisted for nearly thirty seconds before it stopped, replaced by the sound of crashing and grunts.

"Shit . . ." Alonso said. "I should go there."

"Look, if they need to fight this out, let them fight this out," Padma said. "I came here to do something, and even if I'm not sure what that thing is in this moment, I'm not leaving until I get it done. We're just going to get in the way."

Another high-pitched whine, this one shorter. And then Ryan's voice came over clearly. "Mike, step aside, or you and me can have it out."

There was a pause that stretched on for far too long.

And then finally there was a muttered "fine" in response.

"Weird," Alonso said.

"We can figure out 'weird' later," Padma said. "I have work to do."

But even though her words conveyed determination, her voice was riddled with fear.

DELLA JAMESON
STARBLAZER FLIGHT DECK

Mike plopped into a chair in the corner, his body folding in on itself. Stitch hopped into the chair in front of the main control panel and began furiously typing. Ryan stood guard between the two of them, watching Mike.

It broke her heart to see it. There was a moment there where she thought Mike would do something rash, and she cursed herself for not saying something sooner about the drinking. Of course it was a powder keg of a situation. Of course, all the way out here, they'd run out of alcohol and then he'd be drowning in withdrawal symptoms.

And of course it happened at the worst possible moment . . .

"There, I think I got it," Stitch said.

Della looked up from her own terminal and stifled a laugh. "Just like that?"

"Just like that."

Della leaned down to the mic. "Alonso, do you copy?"

"Loud and clear. Everything okay over there? Sounded like a hell of a fight."

Della glanced around the room and met the look of confusion on Ryan's face with one of her own. "No fighting here. All peace and love. How are things on your end?"

"Hold on . . ." There was a long pause. "We're good. The system is back up."

"Excellent. Let's drop the payload and go home. Do whatever you have to do there, and then come back here, okay?"

"Got it," Alonso replied. "Preparing to jettison." He checked the console. "Just under a minute."

The collective tension in the room seemed to dissipate for a moment.

And then everyone turned to Mike, who was sitting with his shoulders hunched and staring at his hands sitting lifelessly in his lap. After a moment he seemed to notice where everyone's attention had gone, and he looked up, starting to speak . . .

Something massive rocked the ship.

Della didn't know if it was an explosion or if they'd suddenly experienced a loss of pressure. All she knew was that she was hurtling toward the wall, and then her head was racked with pain as her vision stuttered and flickered.

Were the lights going out?

Or was she passing out?

PADMA SINGH
STARBLAZER REAR DECK

Padma pressed her fingers to her brow, trying to steady herself. Was there a leak in here somewhere? Something from the ceiling dripping on her head?

She inspected her hand.

Nope, that was blood.

A lot of it, too. The interior lights of the room reflected off it. There was pain, but she couldn't access it. It was there in the room, and it would hurt later. Right now it just felt like a gentle buzz on her scalp. *Human bodies are so strange,* she thought.

Was this shock?

A pair of arms grabbed her from behind, under the armpits, and lifted her up.

"Are you okay?" Alonso asked.

"This is a lot of blood," Padma said, holding up her hand.

"Focus," he said, his voice calm and even. "Are you okay?"

Padma thought about it. Was she? The ship seemed to have been rocked by a massive explosion—or impact? She was bleeding from the head, and the probability of them dying had just gone up a whole lot.

"Ask me again in five minutes," Padma said.

Alonso shook his head like he was frustrated and then turned to the computer screen. They'd just exited the bay holding the satellite and sealed the doors when the explosion hit. Or was it a few moments ago? Was it long enough for the device to make it safely outside?

Or was it the satellite that caused the explosion?

"Did it launch?" Padma asked.

"I don't know," he said. "Hold on . . ."

Padma stared out the nearest window port in search of the satellite but, now presumably well in the midst of Titan's dark side, saw only blackness. Meantime, Alonso tapped at the keyboard and swiped through various screens, mumbling to himself. "Ship doesn't show any damage. We got knocked slightly off course, but the thrusters are correcting, so we should be good there . . . satellite is out, and . . . huh."

"Huh?" Padma asked. "What's huh?"

"Picking up some weird readings, like, the satellite is out there, and the internal navs are online and moving it into place, but it's almost like . . ."

Padma moved closer to the screen, trying to make sense of what it said, but she couldn't tell if the lines were wavy because it was something she didn't understand or because the head injury was messing with her perception.

"It looked like there was something else out there . . . but now it's gone."

"What do you mean, something else?"

That's when the second explosion hit, and Padma blacked out.

NINA CRANE
HILL EAST, WASHINGTON, D.C.

"There seems to have been some kind of explosion aboard the *Starblazer*, and . . ."

A gasp erupted from Nina's throat. She clamped her hand over her mouth, trying to keep it in, but it was too late. Teddy croaked something next to her.

The front door opened, and Cynthia walked in with Scarlett, who was finishing an ice-cream cone, her hand covered in melted chocolate.

"What happened?" Cynthia asked, seeing terror on her sister's face.

Nina could only point at the screen, at the anchor pressing a hand to his earpiece.

". . . currently waiting for word from NASA on the status of the crew . . ."

Cynthia sat heavily next to Nina on the couch, and they embraced. Teddy pushed himself up and threw himself out of his chair, climbing between the two of them for comfort.

Scarlett stood, munching her ice cream, focused more on finishing it before it melted.

"What's going on?" she asked.

JOHN WARD
NASA MISSION CONTROL, JOHNSON SPACE CENTER, HOUSTON, TX

When the second explosion hit, Ward realized it was over.

His campaign, surely.

His career, most likely. His phone was blowing up, the numbers of his various companies. Executives and shareholders frantically texting him.

The room was even more packed, and it descended into further chaos, but he didn't care. He wanted to drop to the floor and crawl out of here before anyone saw. Empty his bank accounts of whatever was liquid, then go disappear to some beach down on the coast in Mexico. Some little town where he could drink margaritas on the beach all day and no one would recognize him and he could just enjoy the solitude and the anonymity.

Because he was about to go down as the biggest failure in history.

Camila must have been thinking the same thing. "There's no coming back from this," she said, her voice a dejected whisper.

"I am aware," Ward said.

"What do you suppose we should do?"

"Run?"

"Might be better to face the music."

"Says who?"

Camila started to say something but then closed her mouth and shook her head.

"I'm not going to say it," she said.

"Stop."

"But you know what I want to say."

I told you so.

"Don't," Ward said. "Not now."

She nodded. "As long as you know it. So I guess I'll start sending out my résumé . . ."

Ward laughed. "You think anyone is going to hire you based off my recommendation?"

"How the hell could you be laughing at a moment like this?"

Ward turned to see Owens towering over him, his face twisted and red. Ward knew why. This wasn't just the end of his career. This was the end of every aspiration Owens had. They were going down together. And at least Ward was rich. Owens had his government paycheck and pension and crappy suit and that was it. There wasn't much he could do but disappear for a while as well.

But a Mexican beach wasn't in his future. He would be lucky to find a shack on the Jersey Shore.

Ward glanced over at Blanton, who was sitting in a chair, his head in his hands. He felt worse for Blanton than for Owens. At least Blanton cared about the people aboard the ship. Owens just cared about his next job.

He thought briefly in that moment about Ryan Crane.

Talking him into the mission.

He had kids . . .

"Wait!"

Every voice in the room fell silent, everyone looking at a tall man in a white polo shirt. He was frantically waving his hands in the air, trying to get everyone's attention. He leaned over his console and tapped a few buttons. There was a burst of static, and then Della Jameson's voice rang through the space.

"Flight, this is Della Jameson, reporting that everyone is safe, and we are on our way home. More soon. Over."

The applause was so loud, it hurt Ward's ears.

He made a big show of standing up, doffing his maroon jacket, smoothing out his dark gray T-shirt, and sitting back down. Then he put his hands behind his head, turned to Camila, and said, "I told you so."

NINA CRANE
HILL EAST, WASHINGTON, D.C.

Flight, this is Della Jameson, reporting that everyone is safe, and we are on our way home. More soon. Over.

Nina could barely believe it. She had been trying to make peace with the fact that her husband was dead, hundreds of millions of miles away from home . . .

And then he wasn't.

There was nothing to do in that moment but sob. A big, racking sob that shook her whole body. She held Cynthia and Teddy close, then pulled Scarlett in, the remainder of the girl's vanilla ice cream smooshing against Nina's shirt.

"Daddy is okay?" Scarlett asked.

Nina watched as on TV the camera cut between the different crowds watching the news: Times Square, Piccadilly Circus, Shibuya Crossing in Tokyo. It looked like New Year's Eve by daylight: uproarious cheers, people hugging one another, holding one another aloft, screaming to the heavens, like the astronauts themselves might hear the cheers of approval.

"Yes," Nina said, kissing the top of the girl's head, tears streaming down her face. "Daddy is just fine."

STITCH
STARBLAZER FLIGHT DECK

"So, it's been a day."

They'd been sitting in silence since Della sent the transmission. It would be another few minutes before they got some kind of response from Earth, and after everything that happened, it seemed like they needed the breather.

Stitch surveyed the room—Della and Ryan seated at the main console, the two of them looking like they just ran a marathon. Alonso patching up a wound on Padma's forehead. She was dazed, but they were all a little dazed.

Mike was still sitting in the dunce seat in the corner.

He finally poked his head up and asked, "What happened?"

Anger shot through Stitch. "What happened was, you should have listened to me."

Mike rolled his eyes. "For all we know, whatever you did was what caused the explosions."

"Mike . . ." Della started.

"If they even were explosions," Alonso chimed in. "Padma saw something external."

All eyes turned to Padma, who quickly vacillated. "I thought I did, but . . ."

Della leaned in, her curiosity piqued. "Like what? A meteor? We would've picked that up ten thousand miles out."

"Hey, whatever happened, we're alive," Stitch said, jumping to his feet. "And why do I feel like if I'd left you sitting there we'd all be dead?"

Mike climbed to his feet and strode toward Stitch until they were nearly nose to nose. The man was a good six inches taller and a hundred pounds heavier. But Stitch had the power of righteous indignation on his side.

"What are you trying to say?" Mike asked.

"That a 'thank you' would be nice."

Mike scoffed.

So Stitch reared back and punched him.

It wasn't a good punch. Stitch was a lover, not a fighter. It barely staggered Mike, and Ryan immediately got between the two of them.

Stitch set himself, expecting Mike to come at him, but the man just cradled his jaw, shook his head, and said, "Didn't think you had it in ya, kid. My daughter hits harder than that, but you know what? Fine. *Thank you.*"

Stitch felt a flood of relief. He hadn't exactly been prepared for where that might go.

"Are we good?" he asked.

Mike nodded. "For now. More important is, what the hell happened?"

"No idea," Della said. "But we've got a year to figure it out. I'm running diagnostics now. I say we look at that, see what Mission Control has to say, then we all take a minute to get some food and some rest. Then we get to work going over all the data."

Ryan said something, and Mike turned to him and asked, "What?"

But Ryan was staring out the front of the view port, out into the void of space, Titan safely behind them and the satellite currently in orbit.

"Home," he said. "We're going home."

"Yeah, we are," Alonso said.

And in that moment, they allowed themselves a celebration—the six of them, even Padma, erupting in cheers and laughter, falling into one another in one massive hug in the middle of the flight deck.

DELLA JAMESON
REPORT TO NASA

We've finished running diagnostics, and we've got some good news and bad news. All life support systems are fine. The hull is intact, and our course is correct, but we're monitoring it to make sure that nothing changes. A water pipe burst in the bunks, which caused a fair bit of damage, but we got the system capped off and working again. The temperature controls are a little wonky—deck two is currently freezing. Padma suffered a minor head wound in the explosions. We're monitoring her for concussion, though at the moment she seems okay.

But that's not the real problem. The reason you're getting this as a message rather than a video, as I'm sure you've surmised, is that our communications have been knocked out. We can barely move enough data to send this, and we've lost access to the relay, which means you probably won't get it for another twenty minutes or so.

We'll send over data as we can, but it's going to take some time. And we're going to analyze what we can on our end. But it looks like the satellite made it into the orbit around Titan, and everyone is alive, so at this point, we can call the mission a success.

We're going to take a few days off. I think we earned it.

Oh, realizing the election is soon . . . tell Ward we all said good luck.

EXCERPT FROM JOHN WARD'S INAUGURATION SPEECH
U.S. CAPITOL, WASHINGTON, D.C.

"My fellow Americans . . . it had to happen sooner or later. You finally elected a third-party candidate!

"I'm here today to tell you that I appreciate every one of you. Even the ones who didn't vote for me. I take this office with the deepest respect, and with an enormous feeling of excitement. For too long, you've been governed by politicians driven by greed, by their own vanity, by the next opportunity they saw to make a buck.

"That ends today. I am going to be honest with you, even when it hurts. I'm going to demand honesty in my administration, and drum out anyone who can't live up to that standard.

"I know we're all disappointed—me more than anyone—that the timeline for our Titan settlement plans is being pushed back. We're still analyzing the data our hero astronauts have enabled us to get, and we want to make sure that we don't put anyone's life at risk as we explore our next step into the solar system. So, for the moment, I will prioritize initiatives that will help heal the planet and ensure future generations are able to call Earth home. We are going to fix the mess that our predecessors made, and we are going to come up with an airtight, rock-solid plan to get us to Titan.

"All I'm asking for is a little patience . . ."

6

HOME

EMAIL
FROM JOHN WARD

I don't even know why I'm still writing at this point.

We had a deal. And clearly something on your end didn't go the way it was supposed to, but that's not my fault. If you would just respond to me, we could figure something out. But instead, no, I get radio silence for an entire year.

I guess I shouldn't be surprised, considering who I'm dealing with. But I'll tell you this much: if I were in your shoes, I would be coming up with a new plan instead of sulking. For what it's worth, the crew arrived safely. I'm supposed to meet with them, but honestly, I'm starting to wonder if you're playing some kind of game with me now . . .

This will be my last message. You're welcome to stop being such a goddamn baby about this and write back.

JANET WILLIAMS
CNN BREAKING NEWS REPORT

"After nearly two years in space, and three days after rendezvousing with the International Space Station, where they boarded their transport shuttle, the *Starblazer* crew has safely returned to Earth. Live footage shows the six astronauts disembarking from transport vehicles after a smooth landing at the Johnson Space Center in Houston and waving to the assembled crowd before being swiftly taken into the facility, where they will undergo a battery of tests to assess their health.

"The entire world is breathing a sigh of relief. The explosions that rocked the ship as they completed their mission at Titan seriously disabled their communication equipment, limiting the crew to rudimentary communications with NASA.

"Experts continue to pore over data, hoping to discover the cause of the two explosions. Sources say a combination of a glitch in navigational data plus a mysterious phenomenon in space may have been the culprit, but they hope that with the ship back largely intact, they'll be able to gather firsthand information.

"As for now, the astronauts are home safely, and the satellite left behind continues to return valuable data about the potentially habitable moon.

"A planned press conference with the returning astronauts has been postponed, pending medical assessments. Meanwhile, President Ward had planned to meet the astronauts but, according to his press team, was stuck in Washington dealing with the impending Amtrak strike . . ."

RYAN CRANE
JOHNSON SPACE CENTER, HOUSTON, TX

The treadmill finally stopped, and Ryan lurched forward, grabbing the support bars. He moved carefully, so as not to disturb or dislodge the various sensors trailing from his body to an array of machines. He took the break to suck air into his emptying lungs.

He glanced through the window to his left, behind which stood a dozen doctors, surveying equipment or staring down and swiping at tablet screens.

"Not exactly the hero's welcome I thought we'd get," he said, raising his voice to be heard. A few of them glanced up at him, then went back to their work as if he hadn't said anything at all.

According to the clock on the wall, he'd been at this for four hours now. He'd given blood and urine, undergone reflex tests, and answered questions about his physical and mental state. It was beyond frustrating. This wasn't how it was supposed to go. The plan had been that Ward would meet them with their families and they'd do a little victory lap for the press.

Instead, the families were told to stay home, and Ryan was immediately separated from the other crew members.

After spending two years cooped up with them, he wanted to say it was a relief—but it wasn't. He'd just traveled halfway across the solar system and back, and he wanted to see his family. Not a bunch of doctors who stared at him through a window with stone faces.

But like everyone kept telling him, no one had ever traveled this far in space before. No one had ever spent two years in artificially generated gravity, or under the protection of the space radiation shields used on *Starblazer*. So they needed to be extra certain that none of them were experiencing any negative health effects from the trip.

Despite the mountains of paperwork that Ryan had to sign—which included liability waivers for death, injury, or long-term ailments—he wondered how much of this protocol was standard and how much of it was meant to protect Ward and NASA in case one of the crew members decided to sue.

Didn't matter. He'd made it two years. He could make it another few hours—despite the fact that for the entire second half of the trip, they were all cut off from their families, thanks to the communication issues caused by the explosions. Communication was limited to "necessary" updates only, which mostly meant stuff coming straight from NASA. They'd gotten vague assurances that flight control would let them know if there were any family emergencies, but none came over.

Which meant Ryan had no idea where things stood with Teddy and the spinal surgeon.

He did feel a little lightheaded when he first stepped off the shuttle into the blazing Houston sun. He'd been in a dark, temperature-controlled environment for so long, it was a shock to the system to be back on Earth, feeling the warmth of the sun, breathing air that wasn't recycled. His limbs felt a little heavier, but within a few minutes it felt like he'd never left.

He kept saying that to the doctors—that he was fine, it was all *fine*—
but they weren't listening.

He'd play along, do what he had to do, and go home to his family,
many millions of dollars richer and ready to build a new, more comfortable life for all of them. The only question was: What would he do for
work? True, he didn't *have* to work anymore. But he wasn't the type of
guy to just sit around for the rest of his life. What kind of example would
that be for the kids?

And yet, what to do? The police department had put him on leave,
but the more time he spent away from it, the better he felt. He wasn't
keen to go back to that environment. Especially when he saw what it was
like to work with people who didn't despise him.

He thought back to the day it all changed.

Three months on the force, and he got drafted into a raid on a drug
dealer's house in Deanwood . . .

"Mr. Crane?"

What if he had said yes to Wilkinson? His family would have been a
little better off, sure, and he wouldn't be a pariah within the department.

But he also wouldn't have been able to live with himself.

"Mr. Crane? Are you okay?"

Ryan looked over to the window, where there was only one doctor
left—an older man, staring expectantly at him.

"I'm fine, yeah," he said. "Distracted. How much longer do I have
to play lab rat?"

"Actually, I think we're all about finished," he said. He nodded toward
the back of the room. "You can remove all those stickers. Through there
is a bathroom with a shower. You can get cleaned up, and then we'll take
you to the car that'll bring you to the airport."

"Finally," Ryan said, a little too sarcastically. Then he added,
"Thanks, Doc. I appreciate it."

The doctor nodded and turned to sit at a computer. Ryan peeled off
the stickers clinging to various parts of his body, then made his way into
the bathroom. He stripped out of the hospital gown, turned on the
shower, and was immediately met with a steaming-hot blast of water. He
turned the temperature down a little and climbed in, then luxuriated in
the feeling of the pressure and the heat.

Oh, how he had missed that.

Once he was done, he toweled off and got dressed—underwear and socks, a T-shirt and jeans, and canvas shoes, all freshly laundered and wrapped in plastic. It was the outfit he'd left behind to go home in. Putting on his old clothes felt good, even though they were a little looser than anticipated. All that prepackaged food, designed more for nutritional balance than taste, had left an impression. Or the lack of one.

He wiped his hand across the steamed mirror over the sink and looked at the beard. He considered shaving it, but that felt like too much work. Maybe Nina would like it. Maybe not. He was curious to find out. Fully dressed, he exited the room to find a woman in a dark gray pantsuit waiting for him.

It took a second, but he recognized her.

Camila. Ward's assistant.

"Mr. Crane," she said.

"Hey, sorry," Ryan said. "Didn't expect anyone to be in here."

Camila nodded and looked around the room, then peered through the glass to make sure they were alone. The last doctor had left. "I believe you have something for the president."

Ryan's heart took a little stutter-beat. He'd been waiting for this moment.

"Yeah, about that," he said. "During the explosions, our bunks got destroyed. A water pipe burst. I looked high and low but never found it."

Camila fixed him with a hard stare. The hair on the back of Ryan's neck stood up.

"It's not like you dropped it on the side of the road," she said.

"I looked for it. Might have gotten pushed under something, fell through a crack, I don't know. But I promise you, I tried my best. Other than taking apart the ship, I didn't know what to do. And I couldn't exactly ask anyone for help."

She nodded, looking around the room, and Ryan suddenly wondered how much trouble he was going to be in. But Ward already sent them the money; it's not like he could take it back.

"I'll inform Ward and see what he says," Camila said.

"It doesn't really matter what he says, it's gone," Ryan blurted out. He didn't intend to be so confrontational, yet why was he being put on the defensive?

Ryan cleared his throat, feeling a little sheepish but not wanting to let the next part go: "Speaking of, we traveled all that way, could have died in the process, and Ward can't be bothered to swing by and see how we're doing?"

Camila stepped forward and lowered her voice. Ryan unconsciously stepped back. "The *president* is trying to avert a strike that would grind our nation's transportation to a halt. He couldn't be here, so he sent me. I've looked at your medical reports, along with the others. You all appear to be in perfect health, and you will continue to be monitored for the next six months to ensure there are no lasting effects."

"Well, when you see the president, tell him hi for me," Ryan said.

Camila smirked. "Obviously the envelope remains our little secret. Finally, and most important, we are doing our best to insulate you, but you will no doubt be contacted by people seeking an interview. You are to refuse them all until Ward speaks with you. You are also to refrain from contacting the other crew members until everyone's had the chance to debrief."

"Are you serious?" Ryan asked. "Debrief what?"

"This is all standard protocol, Mr. Crane. And not your concern at the moment."

"Sounds like you're hiding us from something. Or something from us," Ryan said.

"The pressures of the journey must have been great, and this is a good time to focus on your family. The trip was taxing, and you should do your best to settle into a routine."

"That's a very polished statement that does nothing to answer my question."

Camila shrugged. "You didn't actually ask a question, Mr. Crane."

"This is all starting to sound a little threatening."

Camila got closer still to Ryan and dropped her voice. This time Ryan stood his ground.

"That is the point," she said, her voice somewhere between a whisper and a hiss. "Please understand that Ward was already the most powerful man in the world before he got into the White House. And it's not good to piss off presidents. The best advice I can give you in this moment is to keep your head down."

And with that, she left the room.

Ryan lingered in the space for a moment, wondering what the hell was going on.

An Amtrak strike? Serious, sure, but it seemed a little unbelievable that Ward would skip the opportunity to get his picture taken with the crew, especially now that they were all alive and well. He may be president, but half the job of being president is staying president for a second term.

Plus, why couldn't they give interviews, or even speak to one another?

Ryan put it out of his head. At this moment, he truly didn't care. Only one thing mattered: it was time to go see his family.

MIKE SEAVER
PHILADELPHIA INTERNATIONAL AIRPORT,
PHILADELPHIA, PA

Mike stood on the escalator, slowly descending into the pickup area of the airport. To his left, on the escalator going up, was a young boy traveling with his parents. He saw Mike and his eyes went so wide it looked like they might drop out of his head.

Mike gave the kid a little wink. The boy beamed with excitement, hopping up and down.

It was always nice to be recognized. Astronauts weren't exactly celebrities, but for the next week or so it would probably happen more often; his face was plastered all over televisions, social media feeds, newspapers, and magazines across the country.

Which made him think twice about his plans.

As he'd exited the plane, he told himself he was going to head straight home, get some sleep in his own bed, and then wake up to get the kids and have breakfast. But he couldn't deny how much he wanted to find the closest bar and throw back a few beers.

He sighed, frustrated at himself.

The last year had been a hard one. After the incident at Titan, they really were bone-dry for the rest of the trip. He spent a few days sweating the last of the booze out of his system, which came with some fevers and mild hallucinations. He tried one time to set up another distiller in the lab, ready to break down some harsher chemicals and hope it came out drinkable, but Della stopped him.

He hadn't had a drink since then.

And he hoped this was a new start.

Then the doctors said they found markers in his blood work for heavy alcohol use—which weren't present before he left. Maybe his poor decisions were finally catching up with his body.

Still, he was negotiating with himself. What if he had one beer? Maybe two? That was barely enough for a buzz. The only thing keeping him from doing it in that moment was knowing someone would probably take a photo of him and post it on some site, and then Helen would know he prioritized drinking over seeing his kids.

Plus, there was the unsettled feeling in his gut. He was immediately separated from the rest of the crew, Ward was a no-show, and apparently Mike himself had to go into hiding for a little while, according to Ward's battle-ax of an assistant.

What was that about? He understood the part about not doing interviews, but not being able to speak to one another?

Best considered a few beers deep . . .

Before he could put himself to the test, the wind was suddenly knocked out of him as a tiny body collided with his midsection. For a moment he thought it was the kid from the escalator, but when he looked down, he saw Jack, a humongous smile on his face.

"What?" Mike said, stunned.

Across the baggage claim area was Helen, Stella perched on her shoulders and Emma standing alongside, holding up a handmade sign that said WELCOME HOME, DAD. It was decorated with crudely drawn stars and a rocket ship.

And for the briefest, most beautiful moment, Mike was able to forget about his desire to have a drink.

He hefted his duffel bag onto his shoulder and tried to move toward his family, in an awkward shamble because Jack refused to let go. As he got closer to Helen he asked, "What's this?"

"I know it's late, but I thought we'd surprise you," she said.

There was something different about her.

It was the way she was smiling at him. It was the way she *used* to smile at him.

"Daddy!" Stella yelled, and Mike dropped his bag. Helen passed her over, and he held on to her tight, then felt Emma wrap her arms around him, too.

"I missed you so much, Dad," she said. "I'm glad you're safe."

Mike tried his best to keep from tearing up. He didn't like to cry in front of his kids. Call it old masculine programming. His dad was from the "boys don't cry" school of parenting. And it's not that Mike thought it was wrong to be emotional—he just sometimes felt like, as a dad, he ought to put on a strong front for them. That it would make them feel safe.

He tried, and he failed.

He remembered too well where he had left things, and the sparse videos that had arrived in the first year, followed by the communication blackout in the second. This was not the reception he was expecting to get.

Helen moved into the scrum and pecked him on the lips. "Hey there, handsome," she said. "How about we go home?"

Home.

To their house.

Not to his sad little apartment.

"Are you sure?" he asked.

Helen gave him a funny little look, like he was a moderately confusing puzzle. "I made you some dinner. Mexican rice and chicken. It might be a little cold, but it's in the car, in case you're hungry."

"Thank you" was all Mike could say in response, his throat thick.

Anything more than that, and it'd be all over for him. He'd end up a blubbering mess on the airport floor. He held his children tight, giving them all a squeeze, and then made his way after Helen, beyond thankful to be home.

And deeply proud of himself.

This was his second chance. He wasn't going to waste it.

DELLA JAMESON
CAROL STREAM, CHICAGO, IL

The car pulled up to Della's home. It was close to 11 P.M., and she wondered if the girls would be awake, but the two of them always struggled to stay up past bedtime at nine. They were early risers and early to bed. She thought it best to let them sleep, though there was no way in hell she wasn't going to at least peek into their room to see them.

She was still incredibly frustrated by the barrage of tests they had to endure and the communication blackout they'd been handed. It seemed deeply unfair that the families weren't allowed to be there to pick them up, but that frustration dissipated as the driver wordlessly opened the car door for her.

Della was home.

She pulled her bag out of the trunk, and the driver waited until she made it to the curb before speeding off. She surveyed the house. The lawn was perfectly manicured. And it looked like the shutters on the front of the house had been painted.

The shade matched perfectly. It was exactly what she wanted.

Sean must have been busy, building credit while she was gone.

She hoped that was all it was, and not him trying to make up for another transgression.

She opened the door and stepped inside, and before she could draw a full breath, the girls barreled into her, clutching her midsection, yelling "Mommy!" in unison.

Della dropped to a knee and kissed them—their cheeks, their hair, anything she could reach—and pulled them in tight. They'd grown. How much she'd missed . . .

"They said they were waiting up, no matter how long it took you to get home."

Della froze and turned to see Sean standing in the doorway of the kitchen.

"What the f—" She caught herself. "What are you doing here, Sean?"

Sean squinted, confused. "I made you something to eat. I know I'm not much of a cook . . ."

Della slowly stood, the girls still clinging to her.

"Sean," she said, her voice a mix between angry and scared.

"What?" he asked, shrugging. Oblivious.

Nora tugged at Della's arm. "Mommy, can we sleep in your bed tonight?"

Della pushed a smile onto her face. "Of course you can. In fact, why don't you two get upstairs and get those teeth brushed. Wait for me and I'll be up, and I'll tell you all about how much I missed you."

The girls giggled and bounded up the stairs. As soon as the water was running, Della turned to Sean.

"Did my mom let you in?" Della asked.

Sean shook his head. "What do you mean, did she let me in? Look, it's been two years. I've had a lot of time to think about this, okay? I get where we left things. I deserve that. But I love those girls. And you don't have to take my word. Just ask your mom. I think I did a pretty good job while you were gone."

Della's head spun. She wasn't sure if she was being gaslighted or if Sean was just completely mistaken. She needed to talk to her mother. She'd given explicit instructions, but her mom was always a soft touch when it came to him, and much more willing to forgive.

"I'm just glad you're safe," Sean said. "The girls are, too."

"Where's my mom?" Della asked.

"Sleeping, probably," Sean said with a shrug.

Della turned to the stairs. "I'm going to wake her . . ."

"She's not here."

Della turned. "The hell do you mean, she's not here?"

"She was at the park with us today, but she went home after that," he said.

This was too much. Her mom was supposed to be staying here while Della was gone. And now she'd just completely ceded control to Sean in her absence? Della was furious. She pulled out her cellphone.

"I'm calling her," she said. "I need to know what the hell is going on."

"Della . . ." Sean started, looking down at the floor. "After everything we talked about before you left . . . look, I know I have to wear the mistakes I made around my neck, but what happened to giving me a second chance?"

PADMA SINGH
CAPITOL HILL, WASHINGTON, D.C.

Padma opened the door to her apartment. It smelled stale, like the windows hadn't been opened since she left. She dropped her belongings and moved through the space, the motion-sensor lights coming on as she did.

What had once been a lush, verdant living room was now full of brown, wilted dead things. The floor was littered with fallen leaves. It took her a moment to process.

Brett had promised he was going to water the plants.

Had it been a mistake, trusting him?

She stepped into the kitchen and found the same—the plants along the windowsill, at the back of the counter, all of them were dead. She tried to calculate the time and effort and money it had taken to assemble them all.

Then she gave up.

It was too depressing.

She wandered to the living room and sat heavily on the couch. Should she have been surprised? She forgot his birthday, then she broke up with him right before she left for two years. Maybe he'd stuck with it for a little bit, but two years was a lot to ask from someone whom you'd admitted you didn't want in your life.

Padma looked around the empty apartment, wondering what to do with herself. The trip to Titan and back had given her ample time to further her research, to create endless reading lists and to-do items for when she returned. She had plenty to do.

Hell, she could go to the lab right now. There would be a ton of data to process, and even though she was bone-tired, she knew it was unlikely she'd go to sleep.

Being here didn't feel like home anymore.

Her new home was out there, suspended in space, 700 million miles away. Or at least it would be within the next few years. Which meant she had to work.

And the dead plants surrounding her made it feel like she was being mocked.

She pulled out her phone. There'd been no messages from Brett while she was away, nor did she have any texts upon landing. A heads-up would have been nice. She opened up her texts and fired off a message to him.

You could have told me you were giving up on the plants. I would have hired someone.

She put her phone down, and within a few seconds, it buzzed with a response.

Who is this?

Padma sighed.

Not funny, Brett.

The response came back quickly.

My name is Linda. I'm sorry. You have the wrong number.

Padma shook her head. He changed his number? Had the breakup been that hard on him? Was this his way of getting back at her? She briefly considered going to his apartment to ask him what the hell was going on, but then she tossed the phone onto the couch.

She wouldn't do that. That would be a waste of time and wouldn't result in anything satisfying.

She would go to the lab. It would help get this out of her head.

But first, she needed a shower.

She got up and stretched, then walked over to the window, looking down at the street. It was late, so there was no traffic and no one out, but something caught her eye: a small, glowing ember in a black SUV parked across the street.

Padma watched for a moment, the ember moving and slowly growing brighter before dimming. Someone smoking a cigarette. It made her think of the strange man who'd knocked on her door before she left. Lerner. Could it be him? But wouldn't he have said something to her a few moments ago, while she was fumbling to get into the front door with her luggage?

Did it have anything to do with what Camila had said?

Don't talk to the press, don't talk to one another?

After a moment, the driver's head seemed to turn in her direction—it was hard to tell from this height—and then the vehicle's headlights sprung to life, and it slipped out of the spot and quietly headed off down the street.

Padma watched it disappear.

Wondering.

Maybe they were waiting for someone. Maybe they didn't smoke and drive. It could be anything. There were a million reasons for that.

But as she made her way to the bathroom, she couldn't help but feel like she was being watched.

ALONSO CARDONA
ALLANDALE, AUSTIN, TX

Alonso poured himself a glass of water from the sink, took a big gulp, and put down the glass. He couldn't bring himself to go into the empty bedroom.

It was hard enough getting those emotionally heavy messages from Maddie on the way to Titan. It was ten times worse getting nothing on the way home.

And his fears were borne out when he realized that she had taken most of her belongings with her. The colorful sweaters and wraps she kept hung by the front door were gone, as was her favorite lamp, her pod coffee maker, and the pile of shoes she kept in the corner of the living room.

Shoe Mountain, he called it.

What he would give to see Shoe Mountain.

Maybe this was for the best. The two years apart had revealed the cracks in the foundation of their relationship. It would have been nice to have some closure, maybe a discussion about it. Maybe she planned to have one with him. He could call her tomorrow and see if she wanted to meet for coffee.

But still, the whole thing felt a little cold and abrupt.

He took out his phone, prepared to call Ethan. He needed some comfort, some kind of familiarity, but maybe Ethan was in the same place. Tired of his indecision, ready to move on after two years apart. He sighed and put down his phone on the counter.

Then he considered calling Stitch.

The two of them had bonded during their time in space. They were closest in age—well, Padma was closer, but she acted like a ninety-year-old most of the time—and he and Stitch spent a lot of late nights sitting in the media room, watching movies or playing co-op video games together. They spent most of the way home playing Mario Kart, and Stitch had won 782 races to Alonso's 491.

Sitting there by himself was unsettling. He didn't like the quiet. He'd had enough quiet for a lifetime on that trip to Titan. Not that it was quiet in the ship itself—something was always beeping or humming. But there was an all-encompassing quiet, from the void of space, that seemed to be pressing into the ship.

Alonso made a mental note to follow up with his therapist.

There was currently a lot to process.

Alonso got up and made his way toward the bedroom. A good night's sleep would help. As he passed the front door, there was a soft knock. It was late, after midnight, and his heart jumped. It could be Maddie. Even though they weren't giving interviews, the world knew they were home. He opened the door, expecting to see her, but instead found Ethan.

He was holding a takeout bag and a bottle—Alonso's favorite taco place and a bottle of tequila, respectively. Ethan smiled, his entire body lighting up, and he stepped forward and kissed Alonso. It was a brief, friendly kiss, full of familiarity.

"Hey," he said. "There you are."

STITCH
PARK SLOPE, BROOKLYN, NY

This was wrong.

This was all wrong.

Stitch nearly got into an argument with the driver; they weren't at the right house. He had dozed off in the car, and when he woke up, they were sitting in front of a Park Slope brownstone that probably cost more than he or his parents would make in six lifetimes.

But the driver clearly had places to be, because he put Stitch's stuff on the curb and drove off, leaving him standing there in the middle of the night. He looked up at the building, wondering what the hell he should do, and considered taking out his phone to order a cab to take him back to where he really lived.

He never heard from his mom. Not once, the whole time he was gone. But Ward had promised to pay them ten million dollars to cover costs and expenses while he was gone. Maybe his mom did move to a new house and just didn't tell him. Which was a little shitty, he thought. That was his money, and he would have liked to be consulted about it. He'd sent her a dozen messages, which she never bothered to respond to.

He climbed the stairs and took out his key fobs, realizing it was unlikely they would work, but he noticed that the doorknob had a thumbprint scanner on it, so he pressed his hand to it and heard a click as the lock disengaged.

There was a shelf of expensive sneakers next to the door, and a coatrack filled with bright hoodies—any of which he would happily wear, but which he knew he didn't own. As he moved into the space, he saw pieces of art that he would have picked. Mid-century modern furniture he had loved from afar but knew he could never afford.

Would his mom really do this for him? She barely had the energy to get off the couch most days. Frankly, he'd half wondered if she had died during the trip, and figured maybe NASA didn't tell him so he didn't have to deal with the mental anguish on the journey. But after he finished his battery of tests, after he got that weird passive-aggressive threat from Camila, she told him, "I'm sure your mom will be happy to see you."

He purposely hadn't asked.

And he was glad to hear she was okay.

The lights in the house were out, but as he made it into the spacious kitchen, he found dirty dishes in the sink. He climbed the stairs to the second floor, to a long hallway with a series of doors. One of them was ajar. He pressed it open, but before he could see what was inside, he heard a voice behind him.

"Sweetie?"

He turned to find his mother standing in the doorway of another one of the rooms.

"Ma?"

"Oh, my love," she said, wearing a fuzzy bathrobe, shuffling forward and throwing her arms around Stitch. "I was hoping that was you. I've missed you so much."

Stitch had no idea what to say.

He couldn't remember the last time his mother had said she loved him.

If she'd ever said it at all.

Hearing it out of her mouth should have been comforting. It was not.

It was terrifying.

RYAN CRANE
HILL EAST, WASHINGTON, D.C.

Ryan couldn't tell how long the kiss lasted, just that it wasn't long enough.

When Nina finally pulled back, she tilted her head and inspected the beard. "Okay, it's not as bad as I thought. Maybe it'll grow on me."

"Just give it some time." Ryan winked. "So, where are the kids? Couldn't stay up?"

"Scarlett is unconscious," Nina said. "She tried to stay up but couldn't make it. Teddy is at a sleepover with his friends. I told him you might be upset, that he ought to be here when you got home . . ."

Ryan's face split into a huge smile. Teddy had trouble making friends; he was a sweet kid, but the wheelchair made some activities—sports, amusement parks—a lot more difficult. He'd never been on a sleepover in his life, so the idea that his son was out with friends erased any sadness he could have felt at not seeing him right away.

"Good for him," Ryan said.

Nina squinted, then started to say something, but ultimately shrugged and then pulled him in for another kiss.

Before Ryan could ask how things were going with Teddy's doctor,

Nina put her hands on either side of his face and said, "And with Scarlett asleep, it's time for you to show me *exactly* how much you missed me."

Ryan couldn't argue with that.

He followed her up the stairs, and as soon as they got into the bedroom and locked the door, it turned into a frenzy, the two of them tearing each other's clothes off. He breathed her in, that familiar smell of her favorite body wash—vanilla and roses.

Ryan was so glad to be home. So glad to have this moment.

He pushed her down onto the bed and leapt on top of her, kissing her on the mouth, then trailing down her collarbone to her breasts.

"I love you more than pizza," he said.

Nina laughed. "What does that mean?"

Ryan paused.

That had been their inside joke ever since the first time he'd said it, the two of them out at a local pizza place. It was two months after they'd started dating. They were tearing into some coal-fired pizzas, and Ryan rolled his eyes back and said, *God, I love pizza more than anything.*

Nina put down her slice and smiled. *What about me?*

Fair, he had said. *I love you more than pizza.*

It'd become their shorthand. The secret code of their devotion to each other.

Surely she hadn't forgotten that.

But rather than saying anything, he filed it away and kissed lower, aiming for that appendix scar, which at this point must be fully healed. He wanted to see how it looked—the thing that set this whole crazy trip into motion.

Because if he'd never been at that hospital, he never would have gone to Titan.

Never would have missed her so much it felt like a limb was missing.

But as he reached the spot where her belly met her hip, he found nothing but smooth, unblemished skin. He looked closer, rubbing his hand across it, then pushed himself up to get a better look.

There was no scar.

"Did you forget how this works?" she asked. "We could watch some videos to refresh your memory . . ."

But Ryan couldn't speak. Couldn't think.

Finally he mustered, "Where's your . . ." He stopped, unable to even finish the thought.

Nina's voice grew serious. "Where's my what? . . . Honey? What's wrong?"

Ryan sat back heavily on the bed, bewildered.

"I don't know."

F

F

FRANCISCAN MONASTERY OF THE HOLY LAND, WASHINGTON, D.C.

F felt the ravenous twinge at the back of his skull and unwrapped another foil square of nicotine gum. The fruit chill flavor exploded between his teeth and instantly put him at ease.

He would have preferred a cigarette, but he was getting older, and it was harder to complete his morning six-mile run. Probably better for his health to give it up, but he missed the feeling of breathing smoke into his lungs.

The catacombs were empty—just a few tourists floating through the dimly lit web of passages. It was quiet, and it was private. There were cameras, but the device in his pocket ensured they'd produce nothing but static while he was in the vicinity.

The subterranean complex was housed under the Franciscan Monastery of the Holy Land, built at the turn of the twentieth century to give Americans who couldn't afford a trip overseas a taste of the actual Holy Land.

In the abstract, it was beautiful, peaceful even.

F wouldn't have chosen it as a meeting place.

To him, it felt garish, like trying to learn about America by visiting Disneyland. He had stood in the Holy Land, taken in the majesty and the history of it.

And after twenty years in the Mossad, with his final five leading the Caesarea—special operations and assassinations—he'd gotten his fill of what religion could do to people. The blood and death that came with belief. It was why he went into private intelligence. It all came down to money in the end—may as well be honest, instead of hiding behind a sheen of righteousness.

As he stood before the marble altar, emblazoned with some colorful religious iconography he didn't care to examine, he thought, *This is the play-school version of spirituality.*

"Efraim?"

F turned to find a short, older Hispanic woman in a dark pantsuit—currently the only other person in the room. She'd managed to sneak up on him, and she had a cool stillness and a steel gaze that F had seen only in hardened killers.

Which meant she was making a good first impression.

"I go by F," he said, turning back to the altar. "You must be Camila."

Camila turned again to make sure they were alone, stepped a little closer, and handed him a bulky envelope. "Surveillance on six people. And we need you to find a seventh missing person."

"That's a lot of resources. We aren't cheap."

"I'm sure you know who I work for," Camila said.

"Of course I do. How invisible do you want my men?"

"Not very," Camila said. "We want them to know they're being watched. It'll make them careful, but also keep them docile."

"The missing person. How long have you been looking for him?"

Camila paused, then said, a little embarrassed, "Two years."

"Jesus," F said. "What's the problem? Ex-military?"

"A scientist. He's smart, and he doesn't have a family. So he knows how to stay off the grid, and there's no one else for us to lean on to flush him out."

F shrugged. "That's why you called me. Castle Keep is the best in the business."

"Pull this off," Camila said, "and you can count on regular employment. You have my number, and I'll be the only one you need to liaise with. We have our own security watching them. How soon should we pull them?"

"I'll have my people on them within an hour."

"They're spread out. Brooklyn, Chicago . . ."

"An hour," F said.

Camila nodded, trying to hide the fact that she was impressed and not doing a great job of it.

An older couple came ambling into the altar room, surveying the artwork, babbling about where they should get lunch. F and Camila nodded to each other; the conversation was over. Without another word, Camila turned and left the room.

F took out another square of nicotine gum and popped it into his mouth. It never hurt to have a president in your pocket. In order for Castle Keep to remain competitive on the global stage, it needed some kind of entrée into the Oval Office. And with a regular politician, that was easy enough. F's connections ran deep.

But for an upstart, rogue candidate like Ward, that meant starting from scratch.

And here he was, the connection falling into his lap.

RYAN CRANE
HILL EAST, WASHINGTON, D.C.

Ryan leaned on the kitchen counter, watching the stream of coffee pour into the mug. Nina was still asleep. Scarlett, too. He'd managed to play off that awkward interaction over the scar to exhaustion, and despite her clear desire to have sex, Ryan played that off, too.

Much to his chagrin.

He'd spent two years fantasizing about the next time he'd have the opportunity to be intimate with his wife, but was that even his wife?

Scars don't just disappear.

Ryan picked up the coffee mug and wandered through the house, which looked familiar, and yet not.

The television was a massive OLED flat-screen, easily three or four times what the last one cost. The kitchen was bumped out, bigger and better organized. The furniture in the living room was brand-new, not scavenged from secondhand sources. And it was spotless.

They kept a tidy home, but he also couldn't remember the last time they dusted. Ryan wondered if she was having a cleaner come in to help alleviate the stress of being alone with the kids. Maybe Cynthia was helping out more than he realized, despite not usually being the tidiest person herself.

His house, but not his house.

There was something else, too. Something he couldn't put his finger on. The whole experience was so overwhelming.

He sat on the couch and sipped on his coffee, wondering if he should break the no-contact rule with the other crewmates, then the front door opened.

And in walked Teddy.

Walked. Teddy walked in.

Ryan nearly dropped his coffee mug.

There it was. The thing that was missing: the chair lift on the stairs. How did he miss that?

Teddy paused in the doorway. He looked so different. He was tall—Ryan would never have guessed he could get that tall—and more filled out.

"You made it back," Teddy said, dropping his backpack in the foyer and speaking with the same kind of affect as if he were observing the weather.

Ryan put the mug down and stood. "Yeah, I'm . . . you . . ."

"Dad," Teddy said, slightly exasperated. "What?"

"You're walking?"

He rolled his eyes. "What else would I be doing?"

Ryan crossed the space between them. He threw his arms around his son—who twisted to get away from the embrace. "Dad, c'mon, you're being weird."

Ryan took a step back. "I've been gone for two years. That doesn't warrant a hug?"

"I'm glad you're home, okay?" he said. "I have to get to football practice."

And with that, Teddy bounded up to his bedroom, slamming the door. Ryan's knees buckled, and he sat on the stairs. He'd dreamed of this. That he would come home and find that the surgeon had made some kind of breakthrough.

But this wasn't his son.

His son was kind, and would have been thrilled to see him, and this

Teddy couldn't be bothered, like his dad's presence was an inconvenience. Ryan's head spun. Then he vaulted himself to his feet, climbed the stairs, and cracked Scarlett's door. She was still sleeping, curled up under her *Frozen* blanket. He sat on the edge of her bed and pressed his hand to the top of her head. She stirred, then looked up at him with sleepy eyes and climbed into his lap.

"Daddy, you're home," she said. "I tried to wait up for you."

Ryan kissed the top of her head, trying to hide from her that he was crying. This much, at least, felt familiar. "I missed you so much, sweetheart."

"Me, too, Daddy," she said. "Did you know I can swim now?"

Ryan laughed. "Can you? I'm so proud of you."

"Can I have some breakfast?"

"Yeah," Ryan said. "Let's go get you something."

He led Scarlett downstairs and found Nina standing at the kitchen counter, wearing a floral-print silk bathrobe and puttering with the coffee maker. "You feeling any better?"

No, he thought.

"Yeah," Ryan said. "I saw Teddy. So he's playing football?"

Nina turned and pursed her lips. "He never stopped playing football."

Ryan took a beat, digesting, trying to mask his bewilderment. Then, cautiously: "And Coach Whitmer . . ."

Nina squinted at him. "Ryan? Are you okay?"

"What do you mean?"

"Hold on," Nina said, pulling a Nutella Uncrustables out of the freezer and placing it on a plate with a banana. Scarlett happily accepted the offering and tottered off to the living room, which was quickly followed by the sound of the television turning on. Confident she couldn't hear them, Nina turned to Ryan. "Coach Whitmer died. In that car accident, years ago." Then almost pleadingly: "We all went to his funeral."

Whitmer had been Teddy's peewee football coach. And he had a habit of sneaking beers during practice. Which Ryan didn't know.

Had he known, he never would have consented to letting Whitmer drive Teddy home from practice on a day when he and Nina were both stuck at work.

The accident had killed Whitmer and paralyzed Teddy. Ryan lived with the weight of that decision every day—getting stuck on the night shift at work, a punishment because he hadn't played ball with the other cops on the force. So many things sprung from that one decision, to not take the money that was offered to him, to keep his integrity intact . . .

"I thought Teddy was in the car with him," Ryan blurted, immediately wishing he'd kept the thought to himself.

"Jesus, Ryan, of course Teddy wasn't in the car. You picked him up from practice that day." She put down her mug and walked over to him, placing a hand on his shoulder. "You're scaring me. What's going on?"

"I don't know, I just . . . maybe the trip messed with my head a little."

"You should see a doctor. Or call the doctors who saw you. You've been through a lot, and . . . you're just acting a little off, okay?" She kissed him, carefully, on the cheek. "Listen, I have to take Scarlett to a birthday party. You going to be okay on your own?"

"Yeah," Ryan said. "I just need to get a bit more sleep. The last few days of the trip were pretty restless."

"Okay. And Detective Wilkinson called yesterday. Said he wanted to check in about when you'll be back to work. He said he and the boys miss you. Why don't you give him a call?"

Wilkinson called.

For him?

At this point Ryan knew better than to say anything, but Nina saw the look on his face and said, "Actually, why don't you go upstairs, lie down. I've got the kids."

She got on her toes and pecked him on the lips this time.

Ryan nodded and climbed the stairs. Got into bed and stared at the ceiling. The water spot from the roof leak was gone.

This went beyond exhaustion.

This went beyond being away for two years.

This was not his family. This was not his house. They were, but they weren't. He picked up his phone and considered calling Padma. She was brilliant. She might know what was going on.

But then he remembered Camila's warning and, out of an abundance of caution, went to the window, where he saw a black SUV with tinted glass sitting across the street.

He watched the windows for a few moments and could swear he saw movement.

Tomorrow. They were all due back for a parade to celebrate the safe completion of their mission. Hopefully he'd get some answers tomorrow.

MIKE SEAVER
CHERRY HILL, NJ

Mike sat outside the liquor store and checked his watch. Still an hour to go before it opened.

He'd told Helen he was going to his GP for a quick follow-up—something required by the doctors at NASA to make sure there were no ill effects from the trip.

It was a lie. He could barely stand being in that house sober.

It had nothing to do with his family. This was the dream: his wife and children, one happy family, under one roof.

The problem was his Phillies T-shirt.

It was his good-luck shirt, so old and threadbare that it was nearly see-through. He'd left it in his apartment, and he knew Helen didn't have a key. But there it was, neatly folded and waiting for him when he got home.

It shouldn't be there.

There were things about the house that seemed off, too. His favorite easy chair felt . . . wrong. Like it wasn't him who'd spent years sitting in it. And all the half-drunk flasks of vodka he'd stashed around the house were missing. The one hidden at the back of the garage, the one behind the boxes of baby clothes, the one tucked in the bathroom vent. If Helen had found them, even while he was away, she would have said something about it.

The thing that threw him most was when he turned on the Phillies game last night, wishing he were winding down with a beer but otherwise happy that he'd made it sober that long. He still felt the draw of it—the oblivion it offered, those perfect little moments when his problems just melted away and the harsh edges of the world seemed softer. The general strangeness of things wasn't helping.

And as he watched the game, the ninth inning closed with the Mariners down by two runs.

Then the tenth inning started.

He had considered asking Helen if this was a thing—had the MLB added a tenth inning since he'd been gone? But that, together with all the little differences—with the way his family was receiving him, with the presence of his T-shirt—made him feel like something was deeply, deeply wrong.

And the best way to cope with something deeply wrong was a stiff drink.

He hated that he was here. Hated that he was hoping they'd open a few minutes early. Hated how much he needed that hit of something with a high proof to make him feel settled.

An older Chinese man walked to the front of the store and began to fiddle with the locks. Mike didn't know the man's name but knew he was the owner. That much, at least, was consistent. He sat and watched as the man opened the door and went inside, locking the door behind him. Mike was considering getting out and seeing if he could talk the guy into letting him in early when there was a sharp knock at the window.

He turned to find a man in a black T-shirt and sunglasses staring at him. The man gave off cop energy, but he wasn't wearing a uniform. Mike rolled down the window.

"Yeah?" he asked.

The man didn't respond. He simply handed Mike a phone. Mike held it for a second, not sure what to do, but then pressed it to his ear.

A woman's voice asked, "Mike?"

"Speaking."

"This is Camila. John Ward's assistant. I wouldn't do that if I were you."

Mike froze and looked around, expecting to find her standing there, too. But it was just him and the mystery man in the sunglasses.

"I would strongly advise you to stay away from alcohol for the time being."

"Why?" Mike asked.

Her voice took on a condescending tone. "Mike, please. We know how you can get. You need a clear head right now. Go home. Enjoy the time with your family. We'll see you at the parade. Until then, remember what I told you in Houston. Don't contact your crewmates."

"You know, this is . . ."

Before Mike could finish, the call ended. The man at the window put out his hand expectantly, and Mike returned the phone. The man took it and stepped back, staring expressionlessly, clearly waiting for Mike to drive away.

With a defeated exhale, Mike did.

DELLA JAMESON
CAROL STREAM, CHICAGO, IL

"What the hell do you mean, I gave him a second chance?"

Cosette didn't turn from the pan, where she was frying up strips of bacon. "I was there, honey. I heard it."

Della sat heavily at the kitchen table. Relieved, at least, to have a couple of minutes alone with her mom, after Sean agreed to take the kids to the park. They'd been so excited to see her, and she wanted more than anything to just spend the day on the couch, in their pajamas, watching movies, and pretend the rest of the world didn't exist.

But she was more concerned with figuring out what the hell was going on. Because when she went to bed, walking past the guest room, she saw Sean had clearly made it his own; there were different art prints on the wall, a new bedspread.

"I never would have done that," Della said.

"Well, you did," Cosette said. "And let me tell you, that man has stepped up since you've been gone. Been here nearly every day. And there was no funny business that I could see. Between the hours he was putting in with work and the hours he was putting in with the kids, I don't think he would have had the time to be carrying on with something."

"Walk me through it," Della said. "Walk me through what I said."

With an exasperated eye roll, Cosette turned off the burner and slid over a plate covered with paper towels, using tongs to lay the bacon across the plate. "Well, I was upstairs. But I could hear the two of you pretty clearly. I'm sorry to say I turned off the television so I would know where things stood. He asked for a second chance, and you said you were open to it, that you'd think about things while you were away, and if he was on his best behavior, well, maybe something might work out . . ."

Della didn't know what to say.

She knew that wasn't how the conversation went.

Cosette put the plate of bacon in front of her. "Eat. You look like you could use it."

Della picked up a slice of bacon and stuck it in her mouth. It was burnt—not the way she liked it, but the way her mother liked it. She chewed on it, trying to figure out what this was. Did they come up with this plan while she was away? Her mother had always wanted her to get back together with Sean.

But this was too much, the thought of them conspiring with each other.

She picked up her phone and searched for the last string of text messages between the two of them. She scrolled back, confused by what she saw. An exchange from the morning of the launch.

SEAN:
Good luck out there.

> **DELLA:**
> Thanks. It's going to be tough,
> being away from the girls. Make
> sure they're eating vegetables.
> And don't let them stay up too
> late. They get cranky if they
> don't get enough sleep.

SEAN:
I wrote everything down.

SEAN:
Thank you for this, Della.

> **DELLA:**
> You still have to earn it.

SEAN:
I'm going to do my best.

SEAN:
Would it be inappropriate to tell you
that I love you?

DELLA:

Yes.

DELLA:

But you can say it.

DELLA:

Just don't expect to hear it
back. Not yet.

SEAN:

I love you. And I understand.

Della turned the phone over in her hand. It looked exactly like the phone she'd handed over, along with her personal items, to be held until she returned.

But she never would have said those things.

So who did?

She dialed up Mike. Forget Camila's ridiculous blackout. If someone got mad, they got mad. Della needed to know if things were different for him.

But the call wouldn't connect. She tried it again, and the same thing happened. She checked that she was on the Wi-Fi network and the data was turned on.

When it didn't go through a third time, she slapped the phone onto the table and ate another piece of burnt bacon.

STITCH
PARK SLOPE, BROOKLYN, NY

Stitch slugged another energy drink. He hadn't slept since he'd gotten home.

Home, in theory.

He knew something was wrong from the start. The house he was in wasn't his. It belonged to a richer, more boring version of him. Gone were the spray cans, the sketch pads, everything that made him *him*.

So he needed to do some research.

He sat at his computer, which for some reason had a different password, but it didn't take long to root the terminal and find a back door around it; passwords on most consumer electronics were like deadlocks on doors. Perfectly functional until you delivered a swift kick.

And what he found was incredibly fucked up.

Apparently, he—Stitch, Courtney Smith, *whoever*—had sold off that artificial intelligence art program. And like he suspected, it was turned into an app that scraped the internet for original artwork so people could make their own art, Frankensteined from the efforts of actual artists. It went against everything he believed.

Then he pivoted and started poking around, trying to confirm the things he knew, finding they were no longer true.

Pepsi was more popular than Coke.

The Mets had a dozen World Series wins.

Gore beat Bush.

There were subtle differences and bigger ones, but one thing was clear: this was not the Earth he left. So where the hell was he? There was so much that was familiar. His cellphone recognized his face, though as he went through the photo roll, he couldn't find any pictures of his artwork. His social media posts sounded like they were written by him, but he didn't remember writing them. It was unsettling, in a way that made him feel like a kid—terrified of something he didn't understand.

A knock emanated from the bedroom door. His mother. "Sweetie? I made breakfast. Pancakes."

No, this was definitely not his Earth. He couldn't remember the last time his mom had made him breakfast, and even then, it was never more than cereal.

Another knock at the door. "Honey, are you feeling okay?"

"It's okay, Ma, just wiped from the trip, need to get a little rest. I'll be down in a bit."

"Okay, I'll put them in the oven on low for you to keep them warm."

Footsteps receded and descended the stairs. Stitch went over to the bedroom door and carefully, silently, engaged the lock. He didn't care if she was offering him pancakes, even though he was so hungry his stomach was twisting on itself.

That wasn't his mom.

It was an impostor.

He sat back down at the computer and considered who he should talk to. Maybe Della? She was like the mom of the crew. And she was a mom he could trust, at least. He picked up his phone. It was warm. Warmer than it should be, considering it had been sitting on the desk, untouched, for the last few hours. He opened it up and found the battery was almost dead.

"Shit," he muttered to himself.

Then he opened the screen to show his data usage, and there'd been spikes all night. More than it would take for regular background processes, like email fetching.

He put the phone down.

Camila had given it back to him.

She, or someone else, must have installed some kind of monitoring software.

Which meant they were tracking what he was doing. He glanced up at his computer. Were they tracking that, too? He picked up a Post-it note from the stack next to his desk and placed it over the camera lens on the top of the screen, and then sat back.

He had no idea where he was, or what to do.

ALONSO CARDONA
ALLANDALE, AUSTIN, TX

Alonso read the letter for the fourth time, hoping the words on the page would change. But they didn't. It had been pinned to the fridge with a magnet, with a handwritten note at the bottom—his handwriting, except he didn't remember writing it: DON'T FORGET, in big, bold letters.

"While I'm sure the journey home will be a long one, we are thrilled to welcome you to the Austin LGBT Center to discuss the mission. While we're planning this two years ahead of time, we know that there'll be an incredible crowd of young people excited to hear about your accomplishments. And we expect many of them will be deeply inspired—some of them might even follow in your footsteps. We appreciate your commitment to your community, and we're even more excited that your mom is planning to attend with you."

He was out.

On this world, he was out.

That much he knew—that this wasn't his world. The conversation with Ethan had been long and complicated. Ethan was hurt, at first, as Alonso wondered where Maddie was, if she had moved out.

But apparently, he and Maddie never happened.

At least, not the way he remembered it.

Six years ago, he had been casually dating Ethan when he met Maddie. He told Ethan about Maddie but didn't tell Maddie about Ethan. And Ethan was supportive at first—Ethan wasn't interested in women but was happy for Alonso to stay in connection with that part of his sexuality.

Ethan was happy—until Alonso started spending more time with Maddie and began to think about the optics. That if he were to enter into a full-fledged relationship with Ethan, it would change everything.

Part of his fear was related to his mother. She was a good, kind, accepting woman, but she was also a practicing Catholic, and he had no idea how she would react to knowing that her son was in a relationship with a man. He had stress dreams about telling her, that she would be devastated. That she would disown him.

According to the letter, his mother would be attending.

According to Ethan, his mother had embraced them, and Ethan had spent the two years Alonso was away stopping by to check on her, to have dinner with her, to take her to church when she fell and twisted her ankle and couldn't drive.

She called Ethan "son."

After a long and confusing conversation, which Alonso chalked up to nerves and fatigue, Ethan left, encouraging him to get some sleep.

Alonso tried, but he was in and out for most of the night. He felt a deep well of shame. Like he had lost out on an entire part of his life.

He needed to get out. Needed to go for a ride. He needed some food. He put the letter back on the fridge, went outside into the stifling afternoon heat, and climbed into the car. There was a McDonald's five minutes away, and he wanted to indulge in something junky to get his mind off everything else.

That was always his easiest and best coping mechanism: eating his feelings. He'd pay for it tomorrow, but it'd feel good now.

He waited in line as the cars ahead of him placed their orders. When it was finally his turn, he pulled up to the menu and stopped.

One of the items was the McPizza.

That was discontinued more than thirty years ago. Maybe they brought it back? It was a limited-time thing? He sat there in a daze, until the person behind him began to honk, and he realized the person on the intercom had been asking for his order.

So he ordered the McPizza.

At the window, he paid, and a young Asian woman handed him a cardboard box.

"Hey," he said, "can I ask you a weird question?"

"Uh, sure?" the woman responded, now eyeing him curiously.

"Is this like a promotional item? I thought you stopped serving them."

She looked at him with a mix of confusion and frustration, knowing there was a long line behind him. "We never stopped serving these. Usually they take longer to make, but we had a few ready. They're popular around this time of day." She then blushed, adding, "Welcome home."

Alonso nodded and rolled the car away from the window, pulling into a spot in the parking lot. He opened the box. The pizza didn't look good—like something you'd get in a school cafeteria. It tasted that way, too.

But he needed to know that it was real.

He finished the whole thing in a daze, and it sat in his stomach like a lead balloon. His phone buzzed on the passenger seat. He picked it up and found a text from Maddie.

Hey stranger. Welcome home. I'm glad you made it safe. No pressure but maybe we can get a drink when you're free? Finish that conversation we had at Layla's before you left?

Alonso scrolled up through his messages and found a series of back-and-forth texts that sounded, a little, like the way he used to talk to Ethan.

PADMA SINGH
FAUST TOWERS, WASHINGTON, D.C.

Padma keyed in the code to enter the lab, looking forward to diving into the data from the trip.

It was clear that something was deeply wrong, and she couldn't help but wonder if it had something to do with their hiccup coming around Titan.

Hiccup. It was easy to call it that now, being so far removed from the event, but she remembered, as it was happening, thinking that it was the end for her and she'd die without her dream being realized.

Instead she came back to a nightmare.

A world that was like her own, just slightly different. She'd written off the thing with Brett as an anomaly, until she sat down on the couch and fired up her favorite television show: *Freaks and Geeks.* It was canceled after one season, but she'd loved every episode. It was the show she put on when she wanted to just let her brain unfurl and not focus on anything else.

There were three seasons available on Netflix.

She wondered if maybe the show had been revived, like the cast had all come back as adults, but no, there were Linda Cardellini and Seth Rogen and Jason Segel, as baby-faced as they were back in 1999. The second season picked up right where the first ended, with the crew on their way to a Grateful Dead concert.

She stayed up all night, watching the new seasons. And they were good. Just as good as, if not better than, the original season.

But it was bizarre, too. Impossible. A cursory search around the internet revealed enough differences from the things she knew that there was only one conclusion: this was not the Earth she left.

She needed to work. She needed to figure this out. Ward had rented half a floor in Faust Towers, a coworking space near her apartment. As she entered the lab, she found she wasn't alone. There was a young Asian woman in a white lab coat sitting at a desk, peering at a sleek desktop monitor. She turned and smiled. "Well, hey there."

"Hey . . . uh . . ."

The woman leapt to her feet and crossed the room, hand extended, practically shaking with nervous energy. "I'm Mei, your research assistant. I cannot tell you what an honor it is to meet you, and I'm sure you're still wiped from the trip and you have to go to the parade tomorrow, but I just want you to know that if you need *anything . . .*"

"I'm sorry," Padma said, accepting the handshake with some hesitancy. "Mei. It's nice to meet you. I just need a second. It's been a long night, and . . . Ward never said anything about a research assistant."

Mei pushed up her glasses and grinned. "Well, I was hired while you were up there," she said, pointing at the ceiling, "because President Ward figured you would need a hand and there would be a lot of data to go through. I want you to know that I'm here for whatever you need. If you need me to just fetch you coffee and compile spreadsheets, I'll do that."

Padma smiled. "Actually, coffee would be amazing, thank you. The biggest size they have, with almond creamer and two Splenda."

Mei stood ramrod straight and offered a salute. "Sure thing. There's a coffee setup down the hall."

"Actually, and I'm sorry to do this, but do you think you can go downstairs, to the place on the corner? I'm a little picky about my coffee. And maybe you can grab us something to snack on. Like muffins or something? Here . . ." Padma went searching for her wallet in her shoulder bag, but Mei put up a hand, then reached into her pocket and pulled out a credit card.

"Courtesy of Ward," she said. "For office expenses, and I think caffeine is an important office expense. I'll be right back."

With that, Mei whisked through the door. Padma felt a little bad, sending the girl away so quickly, but she needed a moment to herself.

She took a deep breath, taking in the surroundings.

The lab and offices were spacious, with an incredible view of the city. There were several desks with computers, and through a doorway she could make out massive servers, humming with the computer power they'd need to process the data. They didn't need much otherwise; all the heavy lifting was being done at NASA, and any pertinent data would be funneled over.

There was another room, off to the side; it included a foldout couch, a coffee table, and a mini fridge, which was stocked with water, juice, and energy drinks. As she moved through the space, she felt like she was being watched. She looked in the corners for cameras and didn't see any, but that didn't mean they weren't there.

She did the only thing she knew to do. She sat at a computer terminal and fired it up.

It took her a few minutes to get her account set up, and once she did, she was off. In the shared folder there were already thousands of files: satellite images, information on X-ray and gamma emissions. More than she could have ever hoped for.

But it wasn't what she needed. She clicked over to the ship logs, looking over the reports from the Titan incident. She knew that Mike and Della had both put in reports, and she'd read them at the time, but looking at them now, they seemed . . . shorter. Like data had been stripped out of them. Nothing about the communication issues they had.

There were some follow-up reports from NASA, which attributed the explosion to a faulty coolant valve.

But there were two explosions, not one.

Data was supposed to be infallible. It was the one thing that Padma trusted. And this wasn't the full picture of what happened.

"How's it going?" Mei asked.

Padma jumped, quickly exiting the screen. She turned to Mei, who was holding the coffee in her hand, but her cheery expression had disappeared. Her face was flat, expressionless. Like she had caught Padma doing something she wasn't supposed to do. After a moment, Padma said, "Just clicking around, seeing what we have available thus far."

Mei's smile returned. "Perfect. There's a ton of stuff to go over, and I'm excited to get started. In the meantime, here you go."

Padma took the coffee and muffin bag with a forced smile, and Mei headed to her own computer terminal on the other side of the room.

"Need to make a quick call," Padma said.

"Sure thing," Mei replied.

Padma stepped into the break room and dialed up John Ward's number, hoping to ask him what was going on—she'd never approved having an assistant, and if she were to have one, she'd want to hire the person herself.

There wasn't even a ringtone. Just a beep, and an automated message: *The number you are trying to reach has been disconnected.*

Padma stared at her phone. Well, that made some sense. He was president now. He probably had some fancy security-locked phone. Still, it didn't feel good to be cut off like this. She considered asking Mei for help, but she didn't trust the woman. Not yet.

She could call someone else on the crew—maybe Alonso—but she remembered what Camila had said about them not contacting one another, and if they did, they would risk being bounced from the project. The threat had struck her as odd, but now, the more she thought about it, the more it made sense.

Ward was trying to keep them separated.

Tomorrow couldn't come soon enough.

Tomorrow, at least, they'd have a chance to talk.

8

THEORY

RYAN CRANE
WASHINGTON, D.C.

As the shiny red Cadillac crept down the wide expanse of Constitution Avenue, Ryan waved and smiled at the thousands of people lining the street. A high school marching band led the parade, the sound of their drums and horns sounding through the sunny morning air, and revelers held aloft handmade signs.

WELCOME BACK!!!

THANK YOU, HEROES

MARRY ME, RYAN CRANE

That last one made him blush, but the well-wishes did little to assuage the unsettled feeling in his stomach.

They were all there to welcome him home.

Except, this wasn't home.

Padma was in the car ahead of him, and Stitch in the car behind. Their reunion had been unceremonious—they were shuffled out of chauffeured cars into waiting Cadillac convertibles, all of them kept separate, not able to exchange even a word. It was clear Ward didn't want them talking to one another, which meant he had to have some sense of what was going on.

Every time the cars slowed, Ryan considered jumping out of his and hustling up to Padma's. He wanted to know if he was the only one, but even if he was, she would be the best suited to explain what was happening.

The only thing preventing him from doing it was Camila's threats, which lingered heavily on his conscience.

It's not good to piss off presidents.

So Ryan forced a smile onto his face and waved at the crowds, doing his best to make it seem like everything was normal.

He was further thrown by the cops he saw along the parade route—faces he recognized from the precinct, who normally would have looked at him with scorn and derision, now giving him knowing nods and thumbs-up. They were happy to see him.

What kind of cop was he in this world?

He leaned forward, toward the man driving the car. He had a buzz cut and was wearing sunglasses, and he had a little plastic knob stuck into his ear, which he would touch from time to time, probably receiving updates and instructions. He might be Secret Service; Ryan had immediately clocked the gun concealed under his jacket. "So what's the plan after this? We're doing a press conference?"

"Press conference is canceled," the man called out, not turning back. "Ward got called away."

"Can we talk to Camila then?"

"Ms. Reyes isn't available."

"So who's in charge?"

The man didn't respond. He didn't have to say it: questions were not being encouraged. So Ryan turned back to the crowds, smiled, and waved some more. Playing the role he had to play, keeping his head down.

He had to talk to the others. He needed to do something to get them all together, but it had to be something that appeared accidental.

Then he heard a familiar voice, if unfamiliarly warm in tone.

"There he is. I've been calling."

Ryan turned to find Detective Wilkinson walking alongside the car. He was in his uniform, cap and all, so the driver of the car gave him a harsh look but didn't say anything.

"Haven't seen my wife and kids in two years," Ryan said. "Needed a little time to catch up."

"I bet," Wilkinson said, before he vaulted himself over the side of the car and into the seat next to him.

The driver twisted in his seat. "Hey, you can't . . ."

Wilkinson leaned forward and got close to the driver's ear. "Keep driving. We're old friends. Anyway, you have to be smart enough to know this isn't where you want to make a scene."

The driver turned and exhaled, hard.

"There we go," Wilkinson said, settling into his seat and leaning into Ryan's side, smirking conspiratorially. "We've missed you. Hasn't been the same."

Ryan stared down his old superior, trying to mask his own confusion and disbelief. Wilkinson was the architect of Ryan's ostracizing, his hazing, his being exiled from the metaphorical island that was the District of Columbia's Sixteenth Precinct. And yet here they were, peas in a pod?

Wilkinson spoke under his breath. "Out of respect for all your hard work, we've been putting away half your usual cut. There were some grumbles, but I think everyone recognizes what an asset you are and how we wanted to take care of you and your family while you were away. We've made sure Nina had the access she needed."

Ryan pressed his hands together, trying to process what he was hearing. "Let me ask you a dumb question."

"No dumb questions, only dumb people," Wilkinson said. "Shoot."

Ryan thought back to the moment that everything changed. When they uncovered ten million dollars wrapped in plastic underneath the floorboards of a drug dealer's kitchen. Wilkinson pulled him aside, telling him to voucher eight million with the precinct.

It's the way things are done, Wilkinson had said. *Don't worry. You'll get a taste.*

It was a test, asking Ryan to do it.

And he failed. Because he put in paperwork counting the whole ten mil.

"That raid, in Deanwood, all those years ago . . ." Ryan started.

Wilkinson looked at him and squinted. "You okay there? All those space rays mess with your head? That's not something we talk about."

"Sorry, I just . . ."

Ryan didn't know how to ask it, but he was beginning to suspect that the Ryan who should have been sitting here, the Ryan that Wilkinson knew, had taken the money instead of refusing it, and proceeded to slide down the slippery slope of graft and corruption.

It was enough to twist his stomach, but it also wasn't helpful to dwell on in this moment. Because as Wilkinson waved to the other cops stand-ing along the route, Ryan got an idea.

"Listen," Ryan said, leaning into Wilkinson's ear and whispering, so as not to be overheard by the driver. "I need a favor."

PADMA SINGH
WASHINGTON, D.C.

At the end of the route, the driver—a woman with her hair in a bun al-most as severe as her demeanor—opened the door and nodded toward a waiting town car. "We'll take you back to the office now."

"But I thought there was going to be a press conference . . ."

"Rescheduled," the woman said, and she was about to say some-thing else when a voice boomed out.

"Hold up!"

Padma turned to find a cop walking toward them, with the kind of smile that made it clear that he was in charge, at all times, and would brook no argument.

"Can I help you?" Padma's driver asked.

"Wilkinson, MPD. I'm an old friend of Crane's. I think it'd be nice to get a photo of everyone together, don't you think?"

"We need to clear the area . . ."

Wilkinson tapped his badge. "Well, again, I'm MPD, and I'm in charge of the parade route, so I think we can hold everyone for just a couple of minutes." Wilkinson reached out and took the driver's hand, to shake, but pulled her forward, getting close to her ear. "It'll only take a second."

The driver stammered something, but Wilkinson was already wav-ing everyone over. "C'mon, Crane, I know you're shy, but I think the people here deserve a couple of photos of all of you together. C'mon, ev-eryone, real quick."

Padma looked at Ryan, who winked at her. Stitch and Mike and Della and Alonso came over, everyone looking a little dazed. They slowly formed into a group. All of the drivers, in their suits and sunglasses, looked confused and furious, inching closer to them, presumably to listen to what they were saying, but Wilkinson waved over a couple of beat cops to get between them. "Let's give them some space, okay? Let the folks here get a couple of pictures of them all together."

One of the drivers broke off and got into a heated discussion with Wilkinson.

"Everyone smile and wave," Ryan said, keeping his voice down. "This won't last long. We need to find a way to talk to each other . . ."

"Our phones are tapped," Stitch said, waving at the crowd. "Everyone needs to get to a computer. One you don't own. Go to a library or something. Go to Gmail. Username stitchrocks, one word, password is tequila666."

"The hell are you talking about?" Mike asked.

"Trust me," Stitch said. "Just . . ."

But before he could say anything, a few of the drivers had pushed through the wall of cops and were now within earshot. One of them raised his hand to get their attention. "Everyone, now, let's go."

Padma looked at the rest of them, wishing desperately she could just whisk away to a room somewhere and talk. But that didn't seem possible. So she followed her driver over to her car, where she climbed into the back seat. The car door slammed closed, and the driver got in the front, then started the engine.

"What did they say?" she asked.

"What do you mean?"

"What did the other members of the team say to you?"

"They asked how I was feeling."

"What, specifically, did they say? What words?"

It made Padma wonder if they were all being quizzed, and if their answers would be compared, so she kept it as vague as possible. "I don't know. I don't remember. It was a few seconds. There was a lot of noise." Off the driver's lingering stare, Padma added, "And, forgive me, but it's none of your goddamn business."

Padma couldn't believe those aggressive words came out of her typically timid mouth. But, liking the sound of them, she crossed her arms and waited for a response.

The driver sat there, gripping the steering wheel. It unnerved Padma, but she knew that if she started talking it would just confuse things, or potentially give something away, so she sat and held her breath before the driver finally clicked the blinker and pulled away from the curb.

"Back to the office?" she asked.

"Home," she said. "I'm tired. Need a rest."

The driver didn't respond. But within a few moments they were free of the parade route and headed back toward her apartment. As they drove, she formulated a plan in her head, so by the time the driver dropped her at the front, she knew exactly what to do.

First, she went up to her apartment and dropped her stuff. If Stitch was right and her phone was tapped, it probably meant her location could be tracked, too.

With her phone safely on the counter, she exited the apartment and took the elevator down. But rather than leave through the front, figuring she was being watched, she moved toward the back of the building, to the garbage area. There was a small loading bay where garbage trucks could pull up, alongside a row of multicolored cans to denote regular trash versus recycling. The smell was overpowering, but there was a clear path down a short staircase to the sidewalk.

She hit the bottom and looked around. There didn't seem to be anyone watching, so she hustled down to the corner and around to the next block, where she knew there was a hotel. It was early in the day, after checkout but before people would start checking in. She acted like she knew where she was going, walking past the front desk and then roaming the hallways until she found what she needed: the business center.

It was a small room with four computer terminals. A young man in a button-down shirt and slacks was sitting at one of the computers. Padma knocked and waved. He looked up and made a face, then rolled his eyes. But he got up and opened the door for her.

"Yeah?" he asked.

"Left my key card in my room," she said. "Sorry, need to send a document."

The man shrugged and held the door open. Padma crossed over to the computer farthest from the man, where she was sure he couldn't see her screen, called up Gmail, then typed in the username and password that Stitch had rattled off. The inbox was empty. Padma stared at it for a moment, wondering what she should do next, then she saw an item in the drafts folder.

EMAIL DRAFT
FROM STITCH

Yo!

I'm writing this before the parade. I'm gonna do my best to get the log-in information to each of you, but I'm not sure if we're going to have the opportunity. And it may take some time for you to find a safe computer to log in from—I really hope you're not using your phone or home desktop for this. If that's the case, come on, people, delete this message immediately and clear the trash bin.

But in case I'm able to get you the log-in, and you're able to find a safe computer, you should know a fun fact about emails: *they can't really be tracked and read until they're sent.* So we can use this as a way to communicate. Just write your messages in draft form. It'll be a little confusing to sort out the order, but we're doing the best we can with what we got.

Now, let's start this off with: What in the *fucking fuck* is going on?!

I'm going to review how things look on my end, and we can take it from there, because I can't be the only one . . .

Anyway, Camila made it pretty clear not to contact you guys. And I discovered that my phone is running some backgrounded processes that indicate there's tracking software installed on it. (Which, hey, if you went to the library or something, good job, but if you still have your phone with you, maybe leave RIGHT NOW and go dump it somewhere and find another one . . .)

But that's not the really weird thing.

The really weird thing is that I get home and it's not my home. It looks like my home, what *could* be my home. How I would have deco-rated it. But a really boring, really rich version of me. My mom was there, and she's suddenly all lovey-dovey with me. Bizarre, as when we took off I was pretty sure she didn't care whether I lived or died.

So what is this? Parallel world? Mass delusion? Invasion of some body snatchers?

It seems like most things are the same for me, except, there's one big thing: as I told a few of you at some point, years ago I was playing around with some software and was going to make an app for artists, which I could have made a mint on and ended up giving away for free.

But the version of me that lived in that boring-ass house *didn't* have the same high ethical standards as I do, and went ahead and made the stupid app, and then sold it off for twelve million dollars.

So what the fuck, right?

I haven't really slept, and I've got enough caffeine in my system that I can hear colors (red is like a harsh buzz, blue like ocean waves, if you're curious), and I think something happened when we went around Titan. I'm really hoping Padma weighs in soon with a little bit of reason here. Okay, I have to leave to go to this dumb parade. But something is happening, and it's not good.

I hope this works.

EMAIL DRAFT
FROM RYAN CRANE

This all sounds nuts, but for what it's worth: I got the same threat from Camila. Here's my end, and I'll try to keep this brief. Years ago I was offered the opportunity to participate in some very illegal activities with some of the other cops on the force. I refused, and I've been on the outs ever since. I ended up on the night shift, couldn't pick up my son from football practice, and he was paralyzed in a car accident. Then right before we left, my wife had an appendectomy.

But now I come home, and my wife has no surgery scar. My son is walking. He was never in the accident. And it seems like I went all in with the other cops, took the money, and kept on taking money. Now I'm part of some kind of team of dirty cops, and it seems like so many things that are different from me and my life can be traced back to that one decision.

I took the money, and after that, everything was different. I don't think the appendectomy has anything to do with it, but, butterfly effect? I say that having seen *Jurassic Park,* and that is the entirety of my understanding of the butterfly effect, that small changes can create larger ones.

I have no idea what to do. These threats from Camila and Ward make me nervous. There's something very, very wrong here—something they're trying very hard to keep quiet. I have people sitting outside my house. So I think the safest thing for us to do is to just assemble whatever information we can and do our best to play along until we can figure out what to do.

Good job by the way, Stitch. I logged in at one of the terminals at the precinct, and I won't save the log-in info on the computer. Hopefully they're not tracking all the computers here; that seems like it might be a bit beyond their power, and it's okay that my phone is here anyway.

That's all I've got for now. Oh, also, Ward had given me an envelope with something small in it to carry with me and give to him when we landed. Which, I'm sorry for keeping a secret, but in any event, strikes me as incredibly weird, right? Anyone have any thoughts on that? Not that it's much use. It got lost when the bunks flooded.

I can't believe we've waited two years to see our actual families and now this. I think I'm some combination of depressed and outraged and losing my mind.

EMAIL DRAFT
FROM PADMA SINGH

This is a lot to take in. Let's start off with the problematic reality.

Multiverse theory is exactly that: theory. So there's unfortunately no rule book for whatever's happening to us.

But let's back up and acknowledge what we know.

I'm going to assume you all have a rough sense of what the Big Bang was. Created the universe. That was a whole thing. Not going to get into specifics on that. The rest I'm basing on what I remember from things I've read, so this isn't super scientific, but stick with me.

There have been experiments done over the years that scientists have thought, maybe, would indicate the presence of alternate universes.

Let's talk about the Cold Spot.

Actually, first, let's talk about the cosmic microwave background, which was discovered in the 1960s. It's the remnant of the first light in the universe. Sort of like fossil radiation. It fills the universe and gives us important data on what, exactly, came *before* the Big Bang.

So in 2004, scientists discovered what they called the Cold Spot. A giant region of sky in the constellation Eridanus that was cooler than the surrounding area. The borders of it were hotter than normal. It was massive, and the chances of this happening at random seemed to be pretty nil, statistically, so it raised a lot of questions about why, in the expanse of the cosmic microwave background, there was just this giant void.

Basically, it challenged the standard cosmological model.

One of the theories offered was that it was a scar: some kind of collision between our universe and another. Maybe even a pathway, where the two were touching. So sort of like a wormhole but not really a wormhole, because a wormhole would connect two places in our universe, whereas this would connect our universe with another universe next door.

To be clear, space stuff is very weird and very complicated, and for as much as we understand, there is a lot we barely understand, and even more that we'll never ever be able to understand in a billion years, but those are the things I can remember.

So there are three main theories of how the multiverse could work. There's the Copenhagen interpretation, the many-worlds theory, and Stephen Hawking's inflation theory. I will remind you I'm reciting this stuff from memory, so don't expect anything too hyper-specific here, but . . .

In quantum physics, all possible states in which an object can exist are called the object's coherent superposition, made up of that object's wave function. Quantum mechanics favors a fully deterministic wave function—which means it requires the information that realizes the characteristic of the object while eliminating all others.

Okay, I'm sorry, I can see how that could be confusing . . .

Think of an apple. An apple is not an orange because of the various things we can measure and observe about it. We know it's an apple.

In the Copenhagen interpretation, which was surmised by Bohr and Heisenberg, a particle doesn't have material existence until it's subjected to measurement, which means not until it's observed.

Which means until you measure the apple, it could be an orange.

This is why Schrödinger came up with the thought experiment of the cat in the box. If you don't know that one, a cat is placed in a sealed box with a bit of radioactive material and a Geiger counter. When the Geiger counter detects the radiation, it releases a poison that kills the cat. So until you open the box and observe the cat, you don't know if the cat is alive or dead. Which means the cat is both alive *and* dead.

This whole thought experiment was meant to point out how dumb the Copenhagen interpretation is—the cat can't be alive and dead at the same time.

The many-worlds interpretation, which was formulated by Everett (I don't remember his first name) in the 1950s, said the universal wave function is real, and doesn't collapse, but that every possible outcome of a quantum measurement is realized in another world or universe.

So if you're at an intersection and you turn right, a parallel world is created where you turned left.

Which means there's a very large, infinite number of universes.

Then there was Stephen Hawking, who thought that the rapid expansion of space-time may have happened repeatedly after the Big Bang, making a whole bunch of parallel universes from the jump, which could mean there's a smaller number of them.

My money is on Everett, based on what we're experiencing right now.

Okay, so I just threw a lot of science at you, and I don't even know if it was helpful. I guess the important thing to know here is that the universe is big and confusing and complicated and in some ways unknowable. It's beautiful, in that way, but also completely terrifying.

So I guess what I'm trying to do is piece together some kind of explanation for what happened, which means we have to start with what we know firsthand: the ship was hit by two explosions as we went around Titan. It appears we got knocked into some kind of parallel world where things are slightly different but not incredibly different.

Stitch and Ryan, thank you for sharing your experiences. That's helpful data. It seems to indicate that the other versions of you—because, just to say it out loud, one thing we can safely deduce from this bizarro experience so far is that there are other versions of *all* of us. So we'll call Ryan and Stitch's doppelgängers Ryan-B and Stitch-B. So, those guys were faced with decisions, and they made drastically different choices—they turned left where you turned right (I should have started with the road metaphor, I think it makes more sense than apples and oranges).

Anyway, Stitch, you said your mom is still around. Ryan, your family is still there. Things aren't *so* different. They're just different enough.

Mike, Della, Alonso—you have farther to travel until you get home, and presumably it's going to take you a little longer to get on here. But we need to connect. I need more data. What's different for you?

(Because nothing really major seems to be different for me, other than all my plants are dead, which, I'll explain that later . . .)

Stitch, this is a great start, in terms of information collection. Thank you for setting this up.

One more thing: Before we left, a man named Lerner tried to get in contact with me. He said he had some important information about the trip. Something that would affect our safety. We never got the chance to meet, and Camila told me he was a mentally ill and disgruntled employee of theirs. I believed her—mostly. I poked around for information on him, because there's also supposed to be some kind of redacted report (it came up at the first press conference), but I can't find it.

Either way, we have to assume that Ward knows something about what's going on. Ryan, he gave something to you so you could give it back to him . . . that makes no sense. Unless he thought that something like this might happen?

Which means this goes way deeper than any of us could have expected.

If anyone has any ideas, I'm open to them.

Oh, one last unnerving thought. If we are here, where are the Earth-B astronauts? Back on our Earth? At our homes? With our families? I'm a loner, but for the rest of you, that's pretty effed up.

EMAIL DRAFT
FROM RYAN CRANE

I can't begin to wrap my head around pretty much anything Padma said. Especially the idea of another Ryan playing the role of me with my real kids and my real wife. So I'm gonna stick to logistics. My wife's grandfather left her a cabin. I don't even know if we changed the deed information. I'm willing to bet they could trace it back to us with enough time and effort, but it's still pretty remote. No cellphone signal, nothing. It's in the Shenandoah Valley.

The link to the address is copied below. Let's make that our fallback in case something happens. We all head there in case of emergency. You can't fly. There'll be a record of that. Try to get a car. Rent one, or even better, borrow one. Something that's hard to trace back to you.

Speaking of phones, go somewhere and buy a burner smartphone. Pay in cash. The shittier the electronics store, the better; the less of a chance they'll keep records or have surveillance. Probably not a good idea for us to be calling each other just yet, but at least we can access this thread a little bit easier.

Keep an eye out for someone who's following you. The best way to do that is to pull into gas stations or onto remote roads and see if anyone does the same. You can also make four consecutive right turns, making a square, to see if any car behind you does the same.

And thoroughly check your car, especially if you step away from it and don't have it in eyesight, in case someone puts a tracker on it. In fact, you can go to Walmart and get GPS bug detectors. They're cheap. Again, pay cash. They're not foolproof, but it's better than nothing.

You're all smart. Just use your head and do your best.

And, yeah, I really wish I had opened that envelope . . .

EMAIL DRAFT
FROM STITCH

Hey, so Ryan, this thing with my mom really threw me, like, big-time, but also the explosions were pretty messed up, too. And maybe messed me up a bit. I think I was subconsciously worried that you were going to be mad, and I'll admit that you still have the right to be a little mad about this because it wasn't entirely cool, but I went looking for something to read in your bunk and found the envelope and tucked it away and kinda forgot about it after we nearly died in fucking outer space and anyway I just opened it and there was a thumb drive inside.

More on that later.

JOHN WARD
OVAL OFFICE, WASHINGTON, D.C.

The Treasury secretary was droning on about something, but Ward couldn't focus. All he could think of was the report he'd gotten back from the Secret Service, that the six astronauts had a chance to speak, briefly, and no one was able to make out what they said.

He'd have to have that team reassigned. Fired, if possible. Bunch of goddamn failures.

The *Starblazer* crew had to have noticed by now that things were different.

The best thing he could think to do was to have Camila put the fear of the White House into them, then hire Castle Keep on a permanent basis to follow them. Other than that, he had nothing. He didn't want to face them. How could he answer their questions without telling them the truth?

"Mr. President?"

The entire plan was crumbling, and he had no idea how to control it. He wished he could take the six of them and throw them in a black site prison somewhere, completely separated from one another. But they were currently the six most famous people on the planet, and his press secretary was messaging him every half hour, complaining that the press had climbed so far up his ass they were lodged in his small intestine, wondering when they were going to get an interview.

"Mr. President, are you listening?"

Ward snapped to attention, looking at the Treasury secretary. At the entire room of bureaucrats and assistants who were staring at him. He had no earthly idea what they had just been talking about. And didn't have the time or focus to ask.

"Everyone out," Ward said.

The group exchanged confused, frustrated looks before there was a grand shuffling of papers, people climbing to their feet and exiting the Oval Office. Camila didn't need to be told; she knew to stay behind. She waited until the last person left and then closed the door as Ward put his feet up on the Resolute desk.

"So what's the plan?" she asked.

"The plan is, we keep a close eye on them. As close as we can. We have to control the narrative here."

"Maybe we can convince them that the trip created some kind of brain damage. Something affecting memory . . ."

"No, because then that's the story. And it's not a good one." Ward sighed. "Wish I could just have them all killed . . ."

Camila furrowed her eyebrows, and Ward put up his hands in surrender.

"I'm kidding, I'm kidding. Just, this is getting out of hand. We need time."

"We had a year, and we weren't able to come up with anything other than threatening them to be quiet."

"Until I hear back, that's the best I've got at the moment," Ward said.

Camila sighed and sat in the chair opposite the desk.

"Maybe we just level with them and tell them what's going on?"

"No. This could be a part of his plan."

"Do you really think . . ."

"I think in this moment," Ward said, "anything is possible."

VER1TY
DARK WEB FORUM

Anonymous: Something is going on. Why is Ward hiding from the press? Why was the parade so hasty, and where was the follow-up interview?

Status0verr1de: He's hiding something.

PettyDespot: Definitely hiding something. I think the Vatican is involved. The crew made contact with alien life but it's being covered up by the pope to prevent worldwide unrest over the challenge of his power.

Anonymous: It's not aliens. But there is something going on. I'm hearing a private security firm has been brought in.

NotReallyJohnWard: You're all a bunch of crackpots. I bet the president is just busy.

RealityCheck1: No. Something is happening. Something big.

9

BRETT

BRETT TURNER
NASA HEADQUARTERS, WASHINGTON, D.C.

"Aliens, right?" Kentaro asked. "It has to be aliens."

Brett downed the last of his coffee, placing the empty mug on the break room table. "No, it's not aliens."

Kentaro shuffled in his seat, looking around to see if anyone was listening, keeping his voice low. He brushed his artfully askew hair out of his eyes. "C'mon, man, we've been friends for how long? You really can't tell me what you're up to in there?"

"No can do," Brett said. "You know how it is. I signed a whole bunch of paperwork and, I'm not saying I don't trust you, but if word gets around I'm talking . . ." He leaned back in his seat. "This isn't the kind of job you want to lose."

Kentaro sighed, clearly disappointed. "You suck. Okay. I get it."

"Trust me," Brett said. "Whatever you think it is I'm working on is probably not nearly as interesting as you think."

"Dude, I work in IT," Kentaro said. "Ninety percent of my job is asking literal rocket scientists if they turned the computer off and then on again."

"Well, I'll make you a deal," Brett said. "If something breaks, I'll specifically request you come in and fix it."

Kentaro brightened up. "Deal. A bunch of us are going to that new ax-throwing place later. Over on Larkwood, probably around six. You in?"

Brett checked his watch. It was already three. He still had a lot of work to get through today, but it'd be nice to actually go out and socialize a bit. His entire life for the last year had been inside this damn building.

Much of that time thinking about Padma.

"I'll do my best," he said, before standing, patting Kentaro on the shoulder, and placing his empty coffee mug into the sink.

"First round is on me," Kentaro said.

Brett laughed. "Don't think you're gonna get me drunk to pry information out of me."

Kentaro put his hands up in a surrender gesture and smiled. Brett left the break room and wended his way through the building, passing through hallways, taking the elevator down to the basement, and walking past the armed guard standing outside his office. It was a new guard, one he hadn't met yet. They all looked the same. Shaved head, baby-faced, with the air of all the kids who picked on him in high school. As he keyed in the code to the door, Brett asked, "And what's your name?"

The guard said nothing.

"Fine," Brett said. "Gonna call you Steve. See you in a bit, Steve."

Brett didn't wait for a response—it was unlikely he'd get one anyway—and stepped into his office, which wasn't much more than a desk, a computer, and piles of printouts. He synced his phone to the speaker system on the shelf and put on his EDM playlist—something high-energy, to keep him alert.

And he got to work, at whatever the hell he was supposed to be doing.

After the *Starblazer* explosions, he'd been pulled aside by Henry Owens for this assignment. Previously he'd been a statistician, and Owens described this as a promotion, even though it was just more hours for the same hourly rate. His job was to review data surrounding the entire *Starblazer* mission—ship's logs, satellite imagery, every bit of data imaginable—for anomalies.

What am I looking for? he had asked Owens.

You probably won't know until you find it, the director had responded.

Which was one of the reasons he didn't have much to say to Kentaro. How would he describe this job? He was looking for stuff. The only thing he knew for sure was that the math here was off. There should be an entire team assigned to this. Sticking one person in a secured, guarded room meant they were hiding something.

Which made him just curious enough that he could justify the long hours.

Brett had briefly considered sharing with Owens that Padma was his ex, but his instinct told him that the information might just cost him this supposed promotion.

He logged in to the desktop and checked his email. There was a secured file waiting for him. Images from the James Webb Space Telescope, taken near Titan about a week ago. That was new. He clicked the zip file, then pressed his finger to the thumbprint scanner next to him, to clear the security protocol, and he started clicking through.

Nothing interesting, just huge chunks of empty space. In a few of them, there seemed to be something out there, almost like a smudge, and as he flipped through the images, it got closer and sharper, until finally . . .

No, that can't be right.

He clicked through a dozen more images, getting closer and closer until he realized what he was looking at. Which should have been impossible. Swallowing his panic and bewilderment, he immediately picked up the phone and plucked a Post-it note off the wall.

Owens's cellphone number, which the director had given to him, to call if he found something that required immediate attention.

The phone was answered on the third ring.

Owens's voice was gruff. "Who is this?"

"Sir, this is Brett Turner. From the, uh . . . I don't know what we're calling this. Special research division? Anyway, remember how you said I'd know what you were looking for when I found it? Well, I found it . . ."

"Stay there."

The phone line went dead. Brett returned to the images, wondering what he should do, but before he could decide, he heard Owens's voice from outside. "Who am I? I'm the director of fucking NASA. Step aside." That was followed by the beeps of the numbers on the security panel, and then the door opened. Owens's face was red and puffy; it looked like he'd ran there. He closed the door behind him, leaned down to the computer, and said, "Show me."

Brett slid over a little, and Owens peered at the screen.

"That's . . ."

"Yeah," Brett said.

"But that couldn't . . ."

"I know."

"Did you show anyone?" Owens asked.

Brett shrugged. "Nobody. It's between you, me, and whoever sent me the data."

"The images are compiled and sent to you automatically, which means we're the only two right now," Owens said. Then he leaned down toward Brett, getting nearly nose to nose with him. "And it needs to stay that way. Not a word of this, to anyone. Especially not John Ward. If word gets out, I promise you, you won't be able to get a job at a fucking Arby's by the time I'm done with you."

"Yes, sir," Brett said. "But what does this mean? Because if that's what I think it is, those astronauts—"

"Shut your mouth," Owens snapped. Then he stood and smoothed out his suit. "Not for you to worry about. Remember what I said."

And with that, he turned and left the room.

Brett sat back in his seat and considered his options. Of which there were few. The smartest thing to do would be to just keep doing his job, keep quiet, and carry on with his day. No need to make an enemy of a man like Henry Owens.

But then he thought about Padma.

Didn't she deserve to know? Wasn't she a part of this? He still felt lousy, promising to water her plants and then never following up on it. Granted, she'd done a fantastic job of making him feel like shit before she left.

He picked up his key fob chain and flipped through until he found his USB drive. He inserted it into the computer and copied over the clearest of the photos.

Just in case.

RYAN CRANE
MPD SIXTEENTH PRECINCT, WASHINGTON, D.C.

"Hey, Crane!"

Heading home for the night after catching up on some casework that'd languished while he was gone, Ryan turned to find Wilkinson bounding down the steps of the precinct toward him, discreetly holding a paper bag. Ryan sighed. He had tried to sneak off without being noticed. He was glad that Wilkinson was able to help him with that impromptu photo shoot at the parade, but he'd been doing his best to avoid the detective since, even choosing to leave a couple of minutes early, while the man was in a meeting with the captain.

"Yeah, what's up?" Ryan asked.

The lieutenant glanced around to make sure they were alone. Then: "You forgot your lunch," Wilkinson said, offering him the bag.

"I didn't bring lunch today . . ."

Wilkinson frowned and dropped his voice. "Stop playing games."

Ryan took the bag and held it down at his side. He was pretty sure it didn't contain a tuna sandwich. He nodded, said "thank you," and turned to leave, but then Wilkinson put his hand on Ryan's arm. It wasn't exactly threatening, but it didn't feel friendly either.

"Listen, we got a little OT thing coming up a week from tomorrow," he said. "We could use you in there. Another withdrawal. Easy in and out."

"I'm still on leave. Not even sure if I'm coming back yet."

Wilkinson gripped Ryan's arm. "I'm sure Ward padded your pockets nicely, but this isn't the kind of thing you walk away from, okay?"

Ryan wanted, more than anything, to tell Wilkinson to go fuck himself and then march inside and let the captain know exactly what was going on. But he still had no idea the extent of what *was* going on here. Hell, the captain could be in on it. Better to continue with what he'd been doing: keep his head down, act like everything was normal.

"Week from tomorrow," Ryan said.

Wilkinson loosened his grip, then patted Ryan on the shoulder. "My man. Details soon, okay? Go enjoy your lunch. You seem to have forgotten how good we eat here."

Ryan walked away, trying to get as far from the exchange as quickly as possible. He turned the corner and found his car, and as he was fumbling for his fob, he saw his favorite armory guard and coffee buddy, Simon, coming around the corner.

"Hey, I was looking for you in there," Ryan said, relieved to see a friendly face. "You're a sight for sore eyes."

"Whatever," Simon muttered, quickening his pace.

Ryan sighed. Okay then, guess they weren't friends on this planet. He climbed into the car and put the bag in his lap. He took a breath, made sure there was no one around, then opened the top. As he expected, it was full of thick rolled-up wads of cash. Nickels, really, compared to the Ward windfall, but the very concept of this payout made Ryan sick. He closed the bag and tossed it into the footwell of the passenger side, then started the car.

He hated this. Hated that there was a version of him so willing to go over to the dark side. Did that mean he was, at the root, a bad person? What was it that kept him on the straight and narrow, back on his original Earth?

It didn't take long to get home, and once inside, he found Scarlett sitting in the playroom, having a tea party with her stuffed animals.

"Hey, Daddy," she said, without looking up.

Ryan crossed the room and kissed her on the head, then went into the kitchen, putting the paper bag on the counter. Nina was sautéing something in a pan, her back to him. The kitchen smelled like frying garlic. She glanced at the bag and smiled. "You know, Wilkinson really came through for us while you were away. Not that we really needed it, with Ward's money, but it's nice to know all that time you invested didn't go to waste."

Ryan stopped, staring at Nina.

She knew?

She'd always been so proud of him for refusing to play along, even though it left him stuck on the night shift when he should have been picking up Teddy from football practice . . .

He didn't know what was worse. That there was a version of him who was willing to compromise the morals he had spent years meticulously crafting, or that Nina endorsed it.

Did that mean his Nina back in his right-side-up world secretly resented him?

"Could you hand me the tomatoes?"

Ryan tried to speak and found he couldn't. He didn't know how to process this. His refusal to play ball with Wilkinson had made their lives infinitely harder. And she'd never once held it against him. She told him it made her proud to be married to him, to know he was a man of integrity.

He knew this Nina wasn't his wife, but this wasn't even close to the woman he knew.

She turned. "Ryan? You okay?"

"Yeah," he said.

"The tomatoes?"

Ryan picked up the opened can on the counter and handed it to her. She added it to the pan and went on cooking. Teddy came bounding through the kitchen, grabbed an apple, and exited just as quickly, not even regarding them.

"Love you," Nina called.

The front door slammed in response.

Nina just shook her head. "That kid is turning into a little asshole," she said under her breath. Then she brightened up. "Listen, don't worry about the money. I have to see our accountant this week anyway. I'll have him take care of it, okay? We can finally upgrade—get out of this hellhole and into the suburbs. Maybe even a gated community."

No, this woman was not his wife.

Ryan wanted to ask her what happened, why things were so different, but he didn't know what that would help. He'd turned to leave, to go sit with Scarlett, because at least she was the way he remembered, when Nina said, "Hey."

Ryan turned.

Nina switched off the stove, the sauce sizzling away. "What's going on?"

"Nothing, I'm just . . . getting used to all of this again," he said. "It's hard, being away for two years, then coming back."

"I bet," Nina said, moving toward him and putting her arms around his waist. She pecked him on the lips. He tried not to let on about his revulsion. It was like kissing a stranger.

Clearly she didn't pick up on it, because she stretched up to his ear and said, "I know this has all been a lot, but maybe tonight after Scarlett goes to bed you can finally show me how much you missed me."

Ryan took a step back, and a beat. "This is embarrassing to admit, but I'm having trouble . . . rising to the occasion. Apparently it's a thing for people after being in zero-gravity environments? Blood flow or something. The doctors said it should pass, but I think I just need a little time."

Nina's eyes narrowed. Ryan wondered if she suspected something—like the fact that he'd completely pulled that out of his ass.

Then she went back to the sauce and turned on the burner again. "They do make pills for that, you know."

"Yeah, yeah," Ryan said. "I'll ask the doctors."

"Please do. It's been two years. I have . . ." She craned her neck to make sure Scarlett wasn't in earshot. ". . . needs." Smiling, she stirred the sauce a bit, then said, "By the way. I didn't realize they'd sent someone to keep an eye on you."

"What do you mean?"

"Well, we keep getting reporters stopping by," she said. "But then that guy sitting in the car across the street—he said his name is Carl—keeps shooing them away. He said he works for Ward?"

Ryan kept a straight face. "Yeah, sorry, should have mentioned."

He stepped into the living room, peering through the window at the man sitting in a black SUV across the street. The man—Carl?—glanced at Ryan before going back to whatever was playing on the screen on his phone.

There was a rattling sound next to him. He looked down at Scarlett, who was immersed in her tea party.

"Did you save a seat for me?" Ryan asked.

Scarlett looked up at him, confused. "But you never want to play tea party."

And she went back to what she was doing, both unbothered and uninterested in his participation.

In that moment, Ryan felt his heart fracture, bits of it flaking off like ash.

What kind of father was he in this world?

DELLA JAMESON
CAROL STREAM, CHICAGO, IL

Della sat in the patio chair, watching Mila and Nora playing on the jungle gym—climbing the rock wall, going down the slide, crawling through the bottom of it, pretending they were on a spaceship.

Just like their mom.

Della knew that so deeply it was embedded in her DNA. These were her girls. No one could tell her any different.

Sean had bought and assembled it while she was gone. The first time she noticed it, she went out and checked the connections, all the joints, just to make sure it was stable. Like if Sean did it, he might have half-assed it. It felt sturdy, and the girls loved it, and she hated to admit that having him back was making things easier.

He still had his own apartment, about a half hour away, but he'd agreed to let Della—or, the other Della—enable location tracking on his phone, so she could always see where he was. A way to reestablish trust, he said. It was still active, and she could check it and find that when he wasn't at the house, he was at his apartment, or work, or hanging out with his brother on the other side of town.

It didn't sway how she felt about him: once a cheater, always a cheater. When she discovered that about him, it was like a switch went off in her brain. Once, he had been the most rugged, attractive man she'd ever seen. Learning that truth about Sean made him suddenly look plain, uninteresting.

But she'd indulge him. It wasn't for her. It was for the girls. She and Sean would never be together again, but he was good with them, and she wanted Mila and Nora to grow up with a father.

Whatever this place was, it was a better version of the one she'd left behind. The girls had an easy rapport with their dad, and he doted on them. They even had their own inside jokes, referring to one another with Pokémon names. Mila was Jigglypuff, Nora was Diglett, and Sean was Geodude.

The girls were still deciding on a Pokémon name for her.

Maybe this was her fault. Maybe she was too hard on Sean, shutting him out the way she did. She could hold her boundaries and protect her girls at the same time. This proved it.

She sat back in the chair, watching the girls, and took a sip of her ginger ale. The sun seemed a little brighter. She liked it here.

It was a good life.

The back door cracked open, and Sean's voice came across the yard, strained and a little terse. "Della. Can we talk?"

"Girls, I'll be right inside," Della said, and she stepped into the kitchen, where Sean was leaning against the counter, arms crossed. The look on his face was heavy—not upset, but certainly not encouraging. She closed the glass door in case their voices rose.

After a few moments of silence she asked, "Everything okay?"

"No matter what, I'm still their dad," Sean said, not looking at her.

"I get that," she said. "Where are we going with this?"

"I'm just saying, if you're going to let someone else into their life, I deserve to know. That's something I ought to at least have a say in. Meet the man and look him in the eyes and see if he's good enough to be around my babies."

"Sean, what the hell . . ."

He put his hand up, still looking at the ground. "I get that what I did was wrong, but can't you at least keep me in the loop? Did you have to hide it from me like this?"

Della sighed. "Sean, I have no earthly idea what you're talking about. I've been in goddamn space for two years. And as lovely as Ryan and Alonso and Mike and Stitch are as humans, I can't say that any of them were my type. So why don't you tell me what's going on."

Sean reached into his pocket and put Della's phone on the counter.

Her other phone.

The burner smartphone Ryan suggested she buy on the email thread. She'd traveled into Englewood to get it, paying cash at a cheap electronics store that she was pretty sure didn't have functional cameras. She didn't connect it to the Wi-Fi, and it would be good for another month, at which point she'd have to get a new one.

She felt guilty for how it looked to him. He was trying so hard, and it looked like she was actively hiding something from him.

But then it struck her—where she kept the phone—and her mood suddenly turned dark.

"You went into my room," she said.

"I was just looking for something . . ."

"In my underwear drawer," she said. "What exactly were you looking for, Sean?"

He crossed his arms again. "Doesn't change the fact."

Della crossed the room and picked up the phone. "That doesn't answer my damn question. You went into my room, into my underwear

drawer. There is not a single good reason for you to be in there. And this."
She held up the phone. "This is not a thing you need to concern yourself
with."

Sean finally raised his eyes to meet hers. "Who is he?"

"There is no *he*. And even if there was, it wouldn't be any of your
business."

"Della, you'd better . . ."

Della got closer to him. Her voice exploded out of her, saying all the
things she'd always wanted to say to him. "Better what? What do you
have to say to me right now? Let's talk about the fact that your suspicion
is based in your experience. The experience of keeping a separate cellphone so you could double-time me. And like an asshole, I invited you
back in here. I see that was my mistake."

Sean seemed to shrink as she spoke. He opened his mouth to say
something, but she stopped him.

"You know what?" she asked. "Get the hell out of here. I don't have
the patience for you right now. You're still on probation, as far as I'm
concerned, and you just crossed a very big line."

Sean reared up, his eyes taking on a glint of anger. "Don't you
dare . . ."

Before Della could even register what was happening, her hand
lashed out. She slapped him across the face. The sound reverberated
through the darkened kitchen, and the two of them stood there. Sean
held his face for a moment, more shocked and confused than hurt, before
walking toward the front of the house. He closed the door quietly on the
way out.

Della choked back some tears and took a long breath. Then she
turned and saw Mila and Nora, their faces pressed up against the glass
door. She slid it open and pulled the girls into her, the three of them sob-
bing into one another's shoulders.

"I'm sorry, girls, I'm sorry," she said, running her hands over their
heads.

No. No, this place wasn't better, Della thought.

Because people didn't change.

MIKE SEAVER
ST. DYMPHNA'S CHURCH, CHERRY HILL, NJ

"Hi, I'm Mike, and it's been, uh . . ."

Shit.

He looked out at the circle of chairs—ten men and women who were all part of an Alcoholics Anonymous group that he, or at least a version of him, had been attending.

According to Helen, this was the meeting he went to every week, at the church around the corner. Clearly it was the truth; they were happy to see him, greeting him with hugs and backslaps, like he was some kind of conquering hero. He was able to grab a cup of shitty coffee and some cookies from the folding table in the corner just as the meeting was starting.

And it felt good to be there, even if he still wanted a drink.

And he thought, sure, if this helped, if it kept him sober, then it was worth a shot.

But he didn't know exactly how long the other version of him *had* been sober. Roughly six years. That's the best he had. But he should know his day count, and he didn't.

So he said, "Look, I'm struggling today."

Everyone nodded at him, encouraging him to go on.

"It was tough out there," he said, wringing his hands together, thinking about that moment when he tried to make a distillery to make mouthwash drinkable—as close to rock bottom as he'd ever gotten. "It's been harder being home. Things feel the same, but different. I feel like I've got my family back. But it's all so tenuous, you know? I don't want to let them down. I don't want to let myself down."

Mike thought he should say more but didn't know what.

The man across from him—an older Black man with a thick beard—clapped his hands together once. "Thanks for sharing, Mike. And let me just say, it's great to have you back here. We missed you."

"Thanks, uh . . ." He realized he didn't know the man's name. "Thanks. That means a lot."

The meeting continued, and Mike listened to their stories, feeling a bit like an impostor. Even if he couldn't say exactly what was going on, the meeting helped. Being home with the kids was hard. They were loud, and they needed stuff, and he forgot how much he liked it when he was in his apartment, alone, and no one bothered him. Which made him even more ashamed.

The meeting ended. He didn't linger, not wanting to get caught in a conversation he couldn't finish. He was on his way to the door when the man who addressed him after his share—Terrence was his name, apparently—pulled him aside.

"Hey, man," he said, "you good?"

"I'm great, why?"

"Something about you seems . . . different."

Mike blushed. "Well, I . . ."

Terrence put up his hands. "Look, I'm not going to judge. What you did was extraordinary. You were up there for two years. Maybe you slipped, maybe you didn't. Doesn't matter. What's important is you're here now, and you've got a place to go. You still got my number?"

Mike nodded. Presumably it was in his phone.

Terrence put a hand on his shoulder. "Any time, day or night, you got me? I know we had to put things on pause while you were away, but I'm glad to get back to the business of being your sponsor."

"My . . . right . . ." Mike nodded. "Thanks, man. Yeah, I'm just getting used to things again, you know?"

Terrence nodded. "We're here, brother."

Mike shook his hand and left the church, feeling both hopeful and embarrassed. Hopeful that someone was there in his corner. Embarrassed that there was a version of him, somewhere, who had made better decisions, and why wasn't he capable of doing that?

The past few days had been like seeing what he could do when he committed to himself—and realizing how much time he had wasted.

He stood there, breathing in the evening air on the darkened street, and after a moment realized there was someone across the way, staring at him.

It was a young man, wearing clothes that looked secondhand. He was clean-shaven, his long hair tied back in a loose ponytail. They stared at each other for a moment before the man crossed to him and called out, "Mike. Mike Seaver."

Mike figured it was a reporter and put his hand up. "Not a good time, pal."

"Listen, I know you're confused, and I can help . . ."

Before the man could make it across the street, a car door opened behind them, and another man with a thick neck and a sour disposition made a beeline directly for the ponytail guy—who took off at a run. Mike found himself jogging toward the man in the car, yelling, "What the fuck is going on?"

The man turned and raised an eyebrow. "Nothing you need to worry about."

"Who are you?"

"Here to make sure no one's harassing you."

"Well, I didn't ask for whatever this is."

The man smiled and got close. "I'm going to do my job. And you're going to shut the fuck up. Now, I suggest you head home."

The two of them stared each other down for a moment. The guy looked like he could handle himself, and Mike was a few steps past his prime. And while he wanted a drink—that hypermasculine part of himself thought that throwing a punch or two might be the next best thing, to take the edge off.

"I can see what you're thinking," the man said, with an eerie calm. "Can see it in your eyes. You make that choice, the next thing you see is going to be the inside of an ambulance."

And with that, the man returned to his car. Mike stood there, looking toward where the other man had disappeared. Then he stuck his hands into his pockets and walked home, back to his family that wasn't his family.

To his life that wasn't his life.

ALONSO CARDONA
ALLANDALE, AUSTIN, TX

Alonso hung up the phone and stared into the middle distance. He felt numb. The woman on the other end of the line had been gracious about him rescheduling the event at the LGBT center. He promised to call back, even though he had no intention to do so. He said he'd caught something when he got home and needed to cancel in order to rest.

The reality was, he had no desire to be out right now.

Everything was too strange. But more than that, he didn't want to stand on a stage and discuss his sexuality in front of a group of people he didn't know. That felt like too much.

It should have been easy. Clearly there was an Alonso out there, somewhere, who'd made the decision to live his best bisexual life and not get hung up on what other people thought. But here *he* was, ducking his mom, and Ethan, both of whom loved him dearly, and . . . why?

What was the point?

All he knew was that he wanted to stay inside and not leave.

He picked up his phone and ordered some food, then sat on the couch while he waited for it to arrive. He considered the television but didn't know what he wanted to watch. He considered checking the email thread Stitch had set up. He'd gone and gotten himself a burner phone so he could access it more easily, but he didn't know what else to say.

The thread was helpful, at least, for him to see that he wasn't the only one struggling with the differences, and he hoped Padma was taking all the information they were providing and processing it into . . . something. He had no idea what.

His phone buzzed on the couch next to him. His mom.

Yet, not his mom.

He couldn't duck her forever, whoever she was. He picked up the phone, and all she said, in a voice that was both pointed and frustrated, was: "Mijo."

Alonso struggled with what to say.

"What's wrong?" Liliana asked.

Alonso's throat grew thick, and his vision became blurry. The voice on the other end of the line was both his mother and a stranger. A stranger who knew an intimate part of him that he'd never shared with her.

"I'm sorry," he said, struggling to keep his voice from cracking. "It's just a lot, being home."

"I'm sorry, sweetheart," she said. "But your mami needs to hear her baby's voice. To know you're good. I need a big hug. And I need to know more details about that event we're doing, at the center . . ."

"I just cancel—I mean, I postponed it. For now. I need to rest."

She paused. "That's too bad. I think those kids would get a real kick out of meeting you."

"I just . . . I need . . ." He sighed. "I'm sorry. I don't know what I need, mami. And now I'm letting you down."

"Hey," she said. "I love you. You could never let me down. You are the best son a mother could hope for. Your father, god rest his soul, would be so happy to see you happy. Doing what you love, with a person you love."

"Is that true?" Alonso asked, his voice finally cracking.

"Of course it is, mijo," she said. "Will you please tell me what's wrong?"

There was a knock at the door. Alonso sniffed and wiped his face, then took a deep breath. "I ordered some food, I need to go grab it. But I think I'm going to lie down a bit. Can we talk a little later?"

"You get some rest, okay?" his mother said. "Te amo."

"I love you, too," he said, before hanging up the phone. He took one more deep breath, letting the muscles in his back unfurl, then went to open the door, thrown to find Ethan, holding up a brown paper bag.

"I caught the delivery guy out front."

Alonso was already emotionally spent from the phone call, so rather than object to an uninvited visit, he stepped aside and let Ethan in. Ethan seemed to hover, like he wanted to greet him with something a little more intimate than a nod, but Alonso went into the kitchen and sat at the counter.

Ethan quietly unpacked the food—Styrofoam containers of brisket and bread and pickles and mac and cheese. Then he opened the cupboard and took out some plates. As he placed them down, he said, "So when are you going to tell me what's going on?"

Alonso looked at him and shrugged. "With what?"

"With"—Ethan waved his hand—"all this. You haven't been the same since you got home. You go back and forth between scared and cold. I mean . . ." He put his hands on the counter and dropped his gaze. "What happened to the man who said he wanted to get married when he got home?"

Alonso considered more excuses, more lies. But it was too much.

So he gave up.

"That person didn't come home, Ethan."

Ethan stared, dumbfounded. "What are you saying?"

Alonso knew it was a bad idea. Knew he needed to keep the circle small—him and the other crewmates. But he couldn't help himself. He needed to talk to someone. Needed to get this off his chest. "There's something really, really wrong here. When I left . . . this isn't the world I left, Ethan. When I left, I was still with Maddie, and I wasn't out, and it's almost like I left one Earth and came back to another . . . Actually, it's exactly like that."

Ethan looked up at him, his face twisted in confusion.

"Me and the others, we found a way to communicate, because Ward—well, not Ward, Ward's assistant—threatened us and told us not to. But I can't just keep sitting here like nothing is happening. I'm scared. And I don't understand it, and, I don't know, Padma is talking about some kind of multiverse theory thing with no real answers, and . . ."

Alonso dropped his shoulders and began to sob. Just saying it out loud to another person felt like an incredible weight off his shoulders. He felt a hand on his arm, and he looked up to see Ethan was crying, too.

"I think you need to talk to someone."

That . . . was not the response he expected. It knocked him off-kilter for just long enough that he was able to regain his composure.

"What do you mean?" Alonso asked.

"Do you realize how this sounds?" Ethan asked. "You came back to a different Earth? Alonso, you're the same, I'm the same. The only thing is I think you're starting to regret some of your decisions, and you're try-ing to run from them. I thought you'd finally gotten over that. I guess I was wrong."

"No, this is all real though," Alonso insisted. "You have to believe me . . ."

Ethan shook his head. "I always wondered when this would happen. You want something until you get it, and then you want something else. Or maybe I was just a phase. I'm sure Maddie will take you back."

Alonso thought back to the texts with Maddie. He hadn't responded—he didn't know what to say, or what even happened the last time they spoke—but it still made him feel guilty. There was clearly something he was keeping from Ethan.

"No, please . . ." he started.

"I think I need a little time. Maybe we both do."

He leaned forward, pecked Alonso on the top of his head, lingering in that space for a moment. Then he turned and left.

Alonso sat there for a long time, wondering how many mistakes he'd just made.

And if that's who he was, at his core.

STITCH
PARK SLOPE, BROOKLYN, NY

Stitch hustled up the stairs as his mom called from the kitchen, telling him dinner was ready.

"Not feeling good, I'll be down later," he shouted, before ducking into his room and locking the door.

All he ever wanted in the world was the love of his mother, and now that he had it, it felt so alien that it scared him. Like if he allowed himself to accept it, she might take it away again.

He didn't want to think about that.

He set the package he was carrying onto his desk: a cheap laptop. He didn't need something expensive to do this. He just needed something that would accept a USB-C connection.

Stitch plugged it into the wall and booted it up, going through the various steps necessary, creating an assumed name, and then he got to the screen where it offered to connect to his home Wi-Fi. He skipped that step. He'd already done his research; the computer would be functional enough without doing that.

Once it was set, he plugged in the first USB drive, the one he bought yesterday before heading to the library and disabling the protocols that prevented anyone from downloading things to the computer. After which he ripped a copy of BitCryptBreaker from a site on the dark web.

It took only moments to upload the file to the computer. Then he took out Ward's USB. He didn't know why he took it. He was just curious. If he saw a button that said "don't touch," all he wanted to do was touch it to see what happened.

The mystery of this was just too delicious.

He didn't try to open it on *Starblazer*. His computer was already connected to the ship's network; if the drive had some kind of tracker or alarm on it, it would be tripped. He knew the trick was to come home, download a program to break the potential password, and then get an air-gapped computer: brand-new, out of the box, never connected to the internet. That way any kind of alarm would be neutralized.

And that's why it so easily dropped out of his mind. It was hard for him to focus on things that weren't right in front of him.

But now, at last, here he was. There was a decent chance that BitCryptBreaker wasn't advanced enough to get in, or the data was heavily encrypted, or it would self-destruct, erasing the contents at the first sign of intrusion, but he had to try. He plugged it in and let BitCryptBreaker do its work as he sat back and waited. A spinning wheel popped up. That was a good sign, at least.

Ryan didn't say anything about him sneaking into his stuff and taking it out. He was probably a little annoyed—Stitch shouldn't have gone into his bunk—but they were all probably thankful that they had something to work with here.

There was a knock at the door.

"Honey? Are you okay?"

"Yeah, Ma, I just need to take a nap."

"Do you want some tea, or a plate of food?"

Stitch went to the door and put his hand on it. He wanted more than anything to open the door and let his mom wrap her arms around him and tell him everything was going to be okay.

But this mom had also decided to love and accept Stitch because Stitch did not love and accept himself. He got a grown-up job, he made money—the version of him that was a broke artist wasn't worth this kind of love and attention. It made his stomach turn to think about.

There was a soft ding from the computer.

"Maybe later," he said.

"Okay, honey," she said. He listened to the footsteps recede, and as she descended the stairs, he sat at the computer. The drive was open. That was interesting. It seemed something like that ought to be way more encrypted and much harder to get into, which made Stitch think that maybe Ward just did it himself, thinking he and one other person would see the contents—that he wasn't too worried about the chances of it slipping into the wrong hands.

Well, it did.

Time to find out what it said.

He clicked open the zip file and it unpacked the contents. Stitch picked a spreadsheet and clicked. It was financial and inventory reports. He scrolled up and found it was for a precious metals mining company Ward owned in South Africa. He clicked over to another file, a series of reports about a neural link implant they were developing. Stitch checked the size of the folder, seeing it was several gigs' worth of documents. Thousands of them.

And after an hour of skimming through it, all he found was . . . nothing. No smoking guns, not one thing mysterious. Surely this kind of information was proprietary, and probably worth something to someone, but Stitch couldn't see what the value was.

He picked up the burner phone he'd bought, opened the email folder, and put together a report for the others to see.

PADMA SINGH
FAUST TOWERS, WASHINGTON, D.C.

> It's a whole lot of nothing. The security protocols were lame, and it's just a bunch of data and spreadsheets. I'll keep reading to see if there's something buried in here. But overall, it just feels like he put together the information from all his companies, and that's it. I have no idea what the significance of this is. Will report more later.

Padma slipped the burner phone into her purse, making sure to check that Mei wasn't in the room. She'd gone out to lunch, but the woman seemed to move like an assassin: completely silent, and appearing out of nowhere over her shoulder when she least expected it.

She opened up the latest batch of files and tried to look at them, but she couldn't help but get stuck on her current problem. Which was: Where the hell were they?

She'd been doing some more reading on multiverse theory, and while she was still leaning toward Everett's many-worlds model, it seemed to her that the differences between this world and their world would be greater.

But many of the changes were small—except for the crew.

According to the reports she'd been getting, Mike was sober, and she was able to trace it back to a moment several years ago when he told his wife he was going to an AA meeting, lied, and went to a bar. Apparently, in this world, he went to the meeting.

Ryan joined some other cops in taking dirty money, and Della gave her ex-husband a second chance, versus throwing him out right before their mission. Stitch chose commerce over art. Alonso had been cagey so far but indicated he chose one relationship over another.

One of the problems Padma was having was that these things didn't happen around the same time. She had initially wondered if they did, if all of them had been faced with a choice at some specific point, nudging their world into a branch world, but no—Mike's meeting was six years ago, Ryan's incident was twelve, Della's was right before they left.

It didn't make any sense.

The other thing throwing Padma was that she didn't seem to have a moment in her life where she chose one thing over another. The rest of the crew had them, but everything in her life was the same, except for Brett. The only thing she could surmise was that Brett made a decision, at some point, to not water her plants. Unless he did the same thing back home, which she probably deserved.

The door opened, and Mei came in. She hoisted a plastic carton packed full of salad and sat at her desk. Padma picked up her bag—she didn't like leaving it unattended with Mei in the room—and said, "I'm going to get some air."

"Sure thing," Mei said, looking at her computer, the salad untouched.

Padma walked out of the office and into a stairwell where she was sure there were no video cameras, and she pulled out her burner phone. She had found Brett's work number and had been wanting to give him a call. To ask what happened. To see what she could glean from how things ended between them.

It was for the mission, she told herself. It was to help the others.

Not because she was sad, and she missed him.

She dialed. He answered on the third ring.

"Um . . . yeah?"

"Hey, Brett. It's Padma."

"Padma? How, uh . . . how are you?"

"Look, I was hoping we could meet for a cup of coffee. There's some stuff I wanted to talk about. I totally get if you don't want to, but . . ."

"No, no," Brett said. "Actually, I was thinking of calling you, so your timing is pretty weird." He dropped his voice. "Is anyone around you right now?"

Padma craned her neck to look up and down the stairwell. She was alone.

"I'm good."

"Okay, because . . . I know we have a lot of personal baggage to unpack, but . . . I found something. Something you need to see. I was reassigned, and I've been sequestered in an office going over data from your mission, and there are these photos. I showed Owens and he freaked. Told me not to tell anyone. Not even Ward. But I think you need to see this."

"What is it?"

"Better if I show you. I don't know what I should be saying on the phone."

Padma's breath caught in her chest. She was glad she'd called him on the burner. "Yeah, probably best to not say anything else right now. Where should we meet?"

"Let's get out of D.C. Tomorrow night. There's a restaurant in Alexandria. It's called Elaine's. It's on Queen Street. Meet me there at seven, okay?"

"Okay. Listen, Brett . . . be safe, okay?"

"You, too."

Padma hung up the phone, then walked up and down the stairwell a few times to make sure she was truly alone. As she climbed back up to her office, her regular cellphone rang. She wondered who it could be: Ward asking for an update, Mei looking to see where she went.

But when she pulled it out of her purse, the incoming call read DAD.

The phone fell from her grasp, landing on the concrete with a snap that surely meant the screen had broken. And when she picked it up, she confirmed that the glass was spiderwebbed, but the missed call notification was still visible through the cracks.

JOHN WARD
WHITE HOUSE, WASHINGTON, D.C.

I showed Owens and he freaked. Told me not to tell anyone. Not even Ward. But I think you need to see this.

Camila held out the phone, letting the rest of the conversation play out.

It was just the two of them, sitting in the back of the Beast: the presidential state car. It was Ward's favorite new toy. It was hermetically sealed against chemical attacks. It came with night vision, run-flat tires, and smoke screens. It featured armor plating of ceramic and steel, the windows were five inches thick, and the door handles could be electrified to deter entry. It was the safest he'd ever felt.

Especially since it was just him and Camila.

As soon as he saw the look on Camila's face, he'd dismissed the Secret Service agent in the driver's seat to stand outside so they could talk in private.

They sat in silence after the recording ended until Ward finally asked, "How'd you get this?"

"Castle Keep is thorough. They've tapped the phones at NASA. Which, for the record, you could probably go to jail for, if that ever came to light. This is spiraling out of control in every conceivable way."

"I'm aware."

"Bad enough the thumb drive was lost, or so Crane says."

This got under Ward's skin. "I'm *aware*."

Camila decided to let this outburst go. She took a calming breath, then asked, "What are we going to do?"

"First off, get Owens into the Oval, right now. Make him sit and wait until we get there. Then . . . whoever this kid is? Brett? Pick him up, along with the others. Send Castle Keep. Tell them to take extra care with Crane. He's a cop. He's likely armed, and he's had training."

Camila's eyes went wide. "We can't just disappear people that visible off the street."

Ward's anger flashed. "I'm the president. I can do whatever the fuck I want. If things are spiraling, it's time to get them under control."

"The astronauts are public figures, and heroes."

"Well . . ." Ward said, trailing off, his mind wandering. "We have to change the perception of them, don't we?" Then it hit him, something that would ensure they had no choice but to scatter, with no one they could go to for help. He snapped his fingers. "I got it."

"Got what?" Camila asked.

"A plan."

Camila frowned. "Do you want to share it with me?"

Ward shook his head. "In due time. Don't worry. It's a good one. Just get them, now."

10

RUN

BESTEATS.COM
BLOG UPDATE

Did anyone see this? Apparently McDonald's has discontinued the McPizza. No warning, no nothing. Usually an item has to drop in popularity before it gets pulled from the menu, but there are normally warning signs. It always seemed popular around here (Nashville).
 RIP McPizza!!!!!!!!

EMAIL DRAFT
FROM PADMA SINGH

Okay, here's where things stand:

First up, I want to share my latest working theory. This is rough, and based more on guesses than actual data, because finding the data we need is harder than finding a needle in a haystack. It's like finding one particular unmarked piece of hay in a haystack.

I talked a little bit about multiverse theory—particularly the Everett model, which says that every decision we make creates an offshoot universe. So, if one day you had to decide between having a muffin or bacon for breakfast, and you choose the muffin, there's a reality where you choose the bacon. This is oversimplified, and pretty difficult to comprehend, right? Because think about all the decisions that you make every single day. Then multiply that by the eight billion people who live on this planet, and then take it a step further and consider whether it applies to inanimate objects: Is there a universe where Mt. Vesuvius didn't erupt? Because it erupted here, on schedule: A.D. 79.

That's the thing I've been trying to wrap my head around, right? Because Vesuvius didn't choose to erupt the same way that you choose what to eat. That was a complex series of events, all of which were probably preordained because they lacked an outside influence.

But I was doing some research, and remember that big glacier that was falling apart when we left? The Thwaites? It's fine. In fact, global temperatures in this universe aren't as high as they are in ours.

That's very big, and very complicated, so I'm going to put it aside for a moment.

I keep coming back to the ability of humans to make decisions. And because we *can* make decisions, it seems to influence the universe on an almost subatomic level. I can't say for sure if there are multiverses, but this is definitely a parallel world, one in which things are mostly the same but just a little different.

Many of us seem to have what I'm calling, for right now, a branch point. Let's look at Ryan as an example. Years ago, he had the opportunity to join corrupt police officers in stealing money. He didn't take it and became an outcast in his department.

But the version of Ryan in this universe did take the money, which resulted in changes to his life. The only thing I'm a little stuck on is his wife's appendix operation—why she had it on our version of Earth and not here. Maybe the change in Ryan's life resulted in lifestyle changes that prevented it from happening. Could be a difference in diet, stress levels—I'm not sure.

Again, this is where we get into Vesuvius/Thwaites territory.

It also means that there was a version of Ryan on this world that ended up being drafted into the mission, right?

The problem is, that terrorist attack, where Ryan stopped me and Ward from getting killed? I went back and did some research. It didn't happen on this world. So it seems Ward just up and asked him out of nowhere.

Which is immensely confusing. What happened behind the scenes there? This version of Ward said it was because he wanted to focus on his campaign, and he picked Ryan after doing a national search of likely civilian candidates. But that's just what he told the press.

These worlds are different enough for it to be noticeable, but the mission was still the same, the participants were still the same, the timing was still the same. Everything happened in tandem. Which means both ships followed the same path.

This brings me back to the Cold Spot—that void in the cosmic microwave background—and the theory that it could be where two different universes are touching. What if the two ships—ours and the presumably identical one from Earth-B—just threaded some kind of cosmic needle? A little crack in the walls between worlds, and we traded places? Maybe the explosions had something to do with that.

The only thing that I'm concerned about is . . . whether there might be some kind of cost. We're not supposed to be here. We're not made of the same star stuff as this universe—we're different on an atomic level. I can't even begin to speculate what that might mean. Maybe nothing. Maybe something bad?

In summation, that's what I've got: there may or may not be more universes out there, but we know there are at least two, they might be close enough together that they're touching, and we might have passed through a weak spot between them, and who knows what the consequences are. I don't know how we get back. I don't know anything else.

But here's something else that happened: I talked to my ex-boyfriend, Brett. Don't worry, I did it on my burner, and no one at work knew we were even dating. He found something. He wouldn't share what it was, but he wants to meet. Apparently he's been sequestered away reviewing data from the flight, looking for abnormalities. He wants to meet tonight at a restaurant in Alexandria. He said he can show me what he found but doesn't want to discuss it over the phone.

Ryan, since you live in D.C., do you think you can come with me? This is getting a little too cloak-and-dagger for my taste.

EMAIL DRAFT
FROM RYAN CRANE

I'll do you one better, Padma. Let's go to him right now. In case someone caught on to your dinner plan. Leave your cellphone at home. Meet me at the Union Market Politics and Prose at 2 P.M. I'll make sure we're not being followed.

EMAIL DRAFT
FROM STITCH

Guys! I've got another theory I think we need to talk about. What if we're all suffering from Capgras delusion?

I've been researching it all night, and apparently it's a psychiatric condition where a person believes that a friend or family member or loved one has been replaced by an impostor. Some patients reported they found time or events to be warped. It's a result of brain injury to the parts of the frontal lobe that regulate familiarity, and the right hemisphere, which messes with visual recognition.

We were out in space for like two years, and who knows what that does to a person, plus those explosions, like, what if it messes with the radiation shields, and we've all got brain damage? We have to consider every theory, right?

Because the woman living in this house is *not my mom,* but maybe that's just my brain telling me it's not her . . .

EMAIL DRAFT
FROM DELLA JAMESON

Stitch . . . how long have you been awake?

EMAIL DRAFT
FROM STITCH

Three days? Is it Tuesday? Three days.

EMAIL DRAFT
FROM DELLA JAMESON

Stitch, sweetheart, go get some sleep.

MIKE SEAVER
CHERRY HILL, NJ

Mike sat in the musky basement, reading through the latest emails on his burner phone. He would have suggested the same thing—moving up the meeting and finding Brett on their own. He felt a little itch. He wished he were there to help. But it was a two-and-a-half-hour drive from the house to D.C., and anyway, tonight was movie night with the kids.

They'd agreed to let him pick, so they were going to watch *Raiders of the Lost Ark.* His all-time favorite movie. And the kids actually seemed excited. He was a little worried about the scene at the end where the Nazis get their faces melted. He had always covered his eyes during that part when he was a kid.

But they were tough. He wondered if they would look away.

He turned off the phone to preserve its battery and stashed it at the back of a shelf laden with old paint cans and construction supplies; no one went down here but him, which was why this was where he used to stash most of his booze. Then he climbed the stairs, and a surprising thought hit him.

He couldn't remember the last time he wanted a drink.

That ache had felt constant. Scratching at the back of his brain with a feverish insistence. But it'd been, what, an hour since he felt it? Maybe two. He stopped, his hand on the doorknob, and smiled.

If it was possible to forget for that long, it would be possible to forget for longer. He felt a weight coming off him. And he thought back to what Padma said.

About finding a way back.

Back to his lonely apartment, and his daughter who spent most of the time hating him, and his wife who was eternally disappointed in him, and an endless stream of empty liquor bottles. Here, he had his family. He had his sobriety.

He had everything he could ever want.

Why would he want to go back?

He laughed to himself. He was just fine where he was. He could get used to this kind of life. It was a second chance, and he didn't plan on wasting it.

He stepped into the kitchen. The microwave was buzzing, and Mike could smell the movie-theater butter heating up on the popcorn. Helen was sitting at the table, staring at the laptop, a confused look on her face.

"Everything okay?" he asked.

"Sit," she said, patting the top of the table next to her.

Mike did, and saw she was looking at their banking information. She turned the laptop toward him and asked, "What do you make of that?"

It took Mike a second, staring at the columns and numbers to find out what she was talking about. And when he did notice, his mind went blank, trying to wrap his head around what he was seeing.

The sum of their savings account had increased by more than ten million dollars.

"The hell . . ." Mike started.

"I know you were getting a bonus from Ward for the trip, but I didn't think it was that much," she said.

"It's not," Mike said. "Not nearly that much."

A burning smell filled the kitchen. "Shit," Helen said, getting up to stop the microwave, which had run too long, scorching the popcorn. As she retrieved it and pulled out a fresh bag, Mike scrolled through the recent transactions.

And there it was. A deposit for ten million dollars, earlier today, from China Regents Bank. He ran the name through Google just to be sure and confirmed that it was, indeed, a joint-stock commercial bank with headquarters in Beijing.

"Why would a Chinese company be sending you that much money?" Helen asked.

Mike jumped, not realizing Helen was standing over his shoulder. He didn't know. But he knew it wasn't good.

Emma came wandering out of the living room, drawn by the smell of the burning popcorn, scrunching up her face.

"Is everything okay?" she asked. "Are we starting the movie?"

"Yeah," Mike said. "Just, give me a few minutes, okay?"

EMAIL DRAFT
FROM MIKE SEAVER

Guys, I don't know about you, but I just found $10 mil in my banking account from a Chinese company. This can't be good, right? Is it just me?

EMAIL DRAFT
FROM DELLA JAMESON

I just got it, too. Alonso? Anyone else?

EMAIL DRAFT
FROM ALONSO CARDONA

RUN

ALONSO CARDONA
ALLANDALE, AUSTIN, TX

Alonso hoisted himself over the fence and landed in his neighbor's thorn-bush. It raked his skin as he stumbled and struggled to extricate himself, but his adrenaline was pumping so hard he could barely feel the pain.

He had gotten lucky. He was sitting at the kitchen counter, reading over the latest emails, and he had just pulled up his own bank account to reveal that ten million dollars had been deposited into his account, too. He was responding when he saw a group of men in black suits through the window, coming toward the door of his house.

Nothing about the scene looked good, so rather than wait, he grabbed the go bag he'd packed in case he needed to make a speedy exit to Ryan's cabin, and he ducked through the back patio. As he opened the door, he heard someone shout, "Check around back!"

So he sprinted for the fence and vaulted himself over.

There were no shouts, no sounds of pursuit, so hopefully, they'd just missed him.

From there he sprinted, as far and as fast as he could, thankful he'd spent most of that two years in space on the treadmill.

As he ran, he pieced together the loose thoughts rattling around in his head. He was a U.S. astronaut who'd just gotten a payoff from a Chinese company—a not insignificant sum from a rival nation. The others got it, too.

And there'd be no explaining it away. Not easily, at least.

Someone was setting them up.

There was only one place he could go. He jogged the last few blocks until he made it to Ethan's house. He wondered if they might have him under surveillance, too, so he snuck through the back and crept up to the sliding glass door, where he found Ethan sitting on the couch watching a cooking show on TV, tapping away on his laptop.

Alonso knocked on the glass and waved.

Ethan looked annoyed at first, but then clocked the expression on Alonso's face. Ethan frowned, got up, and slid the door open. "You okay?"

"No," he said. "I need to get to Virginia. Can I borrow your car?"

Ethan breathed in through his nostrils, then out in a long stream. He looked around the apartment, then back at Alonso.

"No, you can't borrow it," Ethan said, straightening his back and offering a sly smirk. "But we can go together."

"I thought . . ." Alonso started.

"I'm still mad at you," Ethan said. "But that's the thing about love, isn't it? Makes us do crazy things. Virginia is a long way off. We'll have plenty of time to talk."

Alonso didn't know what to say.

So he expressed his feelings the only way he could.

He stepped forward and kissed Ethan on the mouth, lingering in the moment for as long as he felt safe.

RYAN CRANE
UNION MARKET POLITICS AND PROSE,
WASHINGTON, D.C.

One thing in this weird universe broke in Ryan's favor—he was still on good terms with his neighbor, Darnell, who was happy to lend Ryan his car. The man had simply tossed him the fob over the backyard fence and asked him to fill the tank.

It was the smart play. First, the car was down the block and around the corner; Ryan was able to climb over the backyard fence without alerting the guy sitting in the SUV outside. He couldn't be sure they hadn't stuck a tracker on either his car or Nina's, so this seemed like the best way to avoid their gaze.

But he still waited five minutes outside the bookstore. The cap and sunglasses helped keep passersby from recognizing him, and he didn't see any more black SUVs, nothing to tip him off that either he or Padma had been followed here.

Once he felt confident, he stepped inside the store, enveloped by the musty smell of all that paper, and walked slowly, browsing the spines of books. The store was crowded enough that he went unnoticed. He wandered for a bit until he found Padma in the U.S. History section at the back of the store.

As soon as he saw her, he had to suppress the urge to dash forward and hug her. She was the only true thing in his proximity, the only thing he was sure that he knew. By the way her face lit up when she saw him, she must have felt the same way.

Ryan stood next to her and took a book off the shelf, looking down at it as he spoke. "You ready to go?"

"Yeah," Padma said.

"You sure you weren't followed?"

"I'm sure. And my phone is at my apartment, so hopefully they think I'm there. Brett doesn't live too far from here. It's a short walk . . ."

"Let's drive, in case we have to get out of there quickly." Ryan clocked the nervous look on her face. "It's okay, I borrowed a car."

Padma nodded, and the two of them exited the store, hustling down to the corner to Darnell's Honda. Ryan shoved the fast-food wrappers on the passenger seat onto the floor, and Padma climbed in. He pulled away from the curb and asked, "Address?"

Padma rattled it off. "Do you need directions?"

"No, I know where that is," he said. "But I'm going to drive around a little, to make sure we aren't followed."

They drove in silence for a few minutes, Ryan taking a series of right turns to make sure no one did the same. So far, they were in the clear.

Finally, Padma said, "This is a lot."

"I don't even know where to start," Ryan said.

"You've been able to follow the stuff I've been putting in the thread?"

Ryan frowned. "I'm a cop, but I'm not dumb."

"No, not like that," Padma said, taking out her burner phone. "I feel like it's all rambling, and it's all theory, and frankly, none of this makes any sense. Like, I feel like I'm trying to solve complex physics equations in the dark, with an abacus."

Ryan nodded. "The only thing I know for sure is that everything is wrong. We have to get back. And fast."

Padma didn't respond.

Ryan wondered if maybe she hadn't heard him, so at the next red light, he glanced at her and saw that she was staring down at the phone, frozen. "Everything okay?"

"No," she said. "No, it's not."

"What's up?"

"Mike and Della both found ten million dollars deposited into their account from a Chinese company," she said. "The next response is from Alonso. It just says 'Run.'"

Ryan's stomach dropped. "Shit."

"I don't have my phone, so I can't check my account," Padma said. "I shouldn't check it on this thing, right?"

"No, absolutely not," Ryan said. "But why . . ."

"The optics of that are pretty bad," Padma said.

"Yeah, they are."

"There's something else, too. My dad . . . he called me."

Ryan didn't want to take his eyes off the road—traffic was heavy—but he threw her a quick glance. Her face was blank, like her emotions hadn't caught up to her words.

"So your dad is alive in this universe," Ryan said.

"I didn't answer."

"Did he leave a message?"

"I don't know," she said. "I didn't check. I dropped my phone. It broke."

"Did you not check because the phone broke, or for other reasons?" Ryan asked.

"Other reasons," Padma said quietly. Ryan wondered if there was more to that, but Padma didn't say anything. He remembered what she had said about them not being on great terms when he passed. If he'd waited this long to call her after she got back, those bad terms might still be in place.

There was a lot to digest. Ryan thought it best to let that one lie.

They turned onto the block of Brett's apartment. Ryan rolled down the street, glancing into the cars parked on either side of the block.

And there it was. Another black SUV, another angry-looking man sitting behind the wheel, like he was waiting for someone. Ryan turned his head away and kept going to the end of the block, hoping he hadn't been noticed. The driver didn't seem to be moving; he was looking for Brett, not them.

He turned the corner and parked the car.

"There's someone outside the apartment," Ryan said.

"How is that possible?" Padma asked.

"I don't know," Ryan said. "Maybe we should go."

"If this is escalating, and Brett has something, we need to know what it is," she said.

Ryan nodded, thinking. "Maybe there's a way we can sneak inside. They might just be waiting for him to come out."

"So what do we do?" Padma asked.

Ryan perked up. "I have an idea."

He stepped out of the car, pulled out his own burner, and dialed the precinct, asking for Wilkinson. After a moment, the detective answered. "Yeah?"

"It's Crane."

"Buddy! How's it hanging?" Then a pause. "This isn't your number."

"I'm on a burner," he said.

"I know how that is. Some things, it's good to keep secret. What can I do for you?"

"I need a favor." He recited the address for Brett's building. "There's a black SUV outside, with someone sitting in it. I need an RMP to go hassle him."

There was a long pause on the other end, to the point where Ryan wondered if he got disconnected. But then Wilkinson said, "You know I'm always willing to do favors for my guys. But you've been acting weird ever since you got back. Level with me, what's going on?"

Ryan swallowed the bile coming up his throat. He hated asking for a favor from this man, but with the way things looked, he was already in for a penny. May as well take advantage of the pound. "You wouldn't believe me if I told you. I'll explain it all later. Can you help me out now?"

"All right, let me see who I've got in the area," Wilkinson said. "But now you owe me one. You know what that means?"

Ryan didn't, but he had no choice but to agree. "I do."

"Five minutes."

And the line went dead.

Ryan sat back in the driver's seat and sighed.

"Everything okay?" Padma asked.

"Not really, no," he said. "But we need to get in there. Because we are currently in a lot of goddamn trouble."

"Right, so the China thing," Padma said. "What do you think that is?"

Ryan turned it over in his head. China was a foreign power, not on the best terms with the United States. Sure, they acted nice for the cameras, but then they went and played dirty pool behind the scenes. The flight crew—they'd had no contact with China, no word from them, nothing. Someone put that money there, and some Chinese government official didn't do it through the kindness of their heart.

The money appeared in their accounts because it made them look bad.

Like they were taking money from a rival. An enemy.

Like maybe they'd been paid to compromise the mission.

"Fuck," Ryan said. "I think we're getting set up."

"How?"

"Because if we got payoffs from China, then maybe we're on the take for them, right? Who has the kind of power and money to just come up with sixty million dollars? Maybe the guy who already had access to our accounts, to wire us money in the first place. Ward knows we're not supposed to be here."

"Why would he do that?"

"No idea."

"We need to find Lerner," Padma said. "He's the key to this."

"We'll add it to the pile," Ryan said, then looked at his watch. "C'mon. Let's go see if the party started."

The two of them got out of the car and crept toward the corner of the apartment building. A squad car was parked next to the SUV. A cop and the driver were standing in the street, arguing, until finally the man in the SUV stormed into his car and slammed the door. He pulled away, and Ryan and Padma turned just in time so he wouldn't see them.

"We have to be quick," Ryan said, hustling around the side of the building. "They'll circle back around in ten minutes, probably."

They got to the front of the building, and Ryan started ringing bells, waiting for someone too lazy to ask who it was to buzz him in. It didn't take long, and then he pulled the door open and ran to the elevator, Padma coming up behind him. They got on, and she tapped the button for the fourth floor.

The elevator seemed to take forever. When it finally got there, Ryan waited for Padma to lead the way; she brought them down the hallway to an apartment at the end, and as they got closer, Ryan's heart sank in his chest.

The door was ajar.

He put up a hand to stop Padma and cursed himself for not taking a gun with him. He hated carrying one outside the job, always thought it would be more trouble than it was worth. In that moment, it would have been nice to have. He got close to the crack in the door and listened. No sound, no movement.

He pushed his way inside, moving the door carefully, so as not to make any noise. Immediately he could see the disarray of the apartment; the couch was on its side, the floor littered with broken dishes. Glass shards and penne pasta were strewn across the floor. He leaned into Padma and whispered, "Stay here."

Ryan swept quickly through the apartment, room to room. Signs of struggle, for sure, but no blood, which was a good sign that Brett might still be alive.

Other than that, it was clear that someone had taken him.

"What now?" Padma asked.

"We have to go," he said. "Get to the cabin."

Padma took a calming breath. "Okay. Let me stop at my apartment real quick . . ."

"Absolutely not," Ryan said. "Whatever's going on is getting serious. We need to disappear. Right now."

Padma shook her head, a determined look on her face. "I need my research. I have a laptop with everything we've collected so far. We're going to need that if we're going to figure this out."

Ryan began to protest. He knew it was a mistake. He knew it.

But there was something about her tone—firm, resolute—a far cry from the anxious scientist he met two years ago. And yeah, the laptop would be helpful.

"Okay," he said. "But we have to be quick."

DELLA JAMESON
CAROL STREAM, CHICAGO, IL

Della tore through the kitchen, grabbing the things she needed: key fob, wallet . . . phone? No, not the phone, that could be tracked. She dragged the stepladder to the refrigerator and climbed to the cabinet over it, hoping the dusty container of oatmeal was there.

And it was, with two thousand dollars in cash crammed inside. Nice to see she and this universe's Della were on the same page. She pocketed the money as Sean came into the kitchen and asked, "What's going on?"

"I have to go," she said.

"Go where?"

The realization she had to leave the girls sank in. A wave of grief hit her so hard, it nearly brought her to her knees. She crossed the kitchen to

Sean and got directly in his face. There was no room for subtlety here. "Call my mom. You and her are going to do everything you can to protect those girls. Get out of town for a little bit. Just take them somewhere. Anywhere. You want to make up for your sins? Then do this for me."

"Della, what—"

A strong, insistent knock at the front door interrupted him. A cop-knock. But she was pretty sure whoever was on the other side wasn't a regular cop.

"Invite them in, let them search the house, tell them I'm not here," she said, taking his key fob off the counter as she moved toward the back of the house.

She left Sean where he was, a look of befuddled confusion on his face, and made it to the sliding glass door. She slipped out quietly, hoping Sean would follow directions. She crept along the side of the house, ready to dash to his car and drive off, but then she turned smack into a short, heavy man wearing a black suit.

Della took a step back. The man looked at her and smiled. "Della Jameson, you're coming—"

Before he could finish the sentence, she drove a hard knee into his stomach. He wasn't expecting it, and it landed true, knocking the air clear out of him. It sent him to the ground, gasping, which was good because if he couldn't breathe, he couldn't call for help. She ran across the neighbor's lawn for Sean's car, which was parked at the end of the street, and yanked the door open.

She got herself situated inside, grabbed the wheel, and took a breath. The front door of the house was open, but the other agents had gone inside. She had seconds to get out of there before they found the guy she attacked.

Yet she couldn't stop thinking about her girls.

Her girls. They were at day camp—a blessing, so they wouldn't witness whatever happened next. But she wished, more than anything, that she could say goodbye to them. To explain what was going on.

As if she could explain this.

She smashed her hand against the steering wheel. Once, twice, then a third time, so hard the impact shot through her arm. Sean and her mom had taken care of those kids for two years. They could do it for a little while longer while this got straightened out.

She started the car and twisted the wheel, driving off down the other end of the block, the road blurring in her vision as she fought back tears.

MIKE SEAVER
LANCASTER, PA

Mike pulled in front of the motel's main office and handed the wad of cash over to Helen. It was the most he could take out of the ATM at once, which he did at the first gas station they saw. After that, he stayed off main roads. It didn't look like they'd been followed.

He got out of the car and stretched his aching back. Jack and Stella were watching something on a tablet, and Emma was playing on her phone. They were mostly unruffled by the whole experience—Mike called in a gas leak, filling the block with fire trucks and ambulances, and in the confusion, they were able to slip away unnoticed.

But while the kids were rolling with it, Helen was not.

She shut the door to the car to make sure they couldn't be heard, then came around the front, her voice a harsh whisper. "Now can you tell me what exactly in the hell is going on?"

"I don't know. Honestly. But I need you to stay here with the kids for a bit. Hold on to the car."

"Where are you going?"

"It's better if you don't know."

"Mike . . ." Helen started.

"What?"

"Are you drinking again?"

Mike felt a storm of emotion in his chest—embarrassment and disappointment, followed by a feeling like he wanted to punch his hand through the car's window. He had finally made good, *finally*, and this was exactly what Helen went back to . . .

No, he told himself. *You earned the lack of trust.*

He took a breath and shook his head. "I'm not. Right now the only priority is keeping you and those kids safe."

"You're scaring me."

He stepped forward and kissed her softly on the lips, then a little harder. He couldn't remember the last time he kissed the other Helen, and he lingered in that moment, doing the best he could to remember every detail.

The softness of them, the fullness, the way she smelled like lavender.

He wondered if it was the last time he would feel it.

"I love you," he said, and then he turned and jogged out of the parking lot, trying to outrace the feeling of his heart breaking behind him.

RYAN CRANE
CAPITOL HILL, WASHINGTON, D.C.

Ryan sat with the car running, waiting for Padma to come out with the laptop so they could hit the road, his body vibrating with anxiety.

It made some sense for them to have her computer, but now he couldn't help but feel like this was not just a mistake, but a huge one. They should be headed to the cabin already.

He checked his watch. She'd been inside for two minutes already. Shouldn't take more than five. Then he'd go in there after her. The back entrance of the building was clear, but he watched every turning car to make sure it wasn't . . . someone. He didn't know who might be after them, what form it would take. Just that they weren't safe.

He considered calling Nina, but they'd have the phones tapped. There was no way to get a message to her and the kids. Hopefully they'd be able to sort this out soon. Though he was again struck by the feeling that they weren't *his* family. Not his Nina, not his Teddy. His Scarlett, sure. They were strangers whom he knew intimately, whom he wanted to save more than anything but wasn't sure if he'd ever see again.

He just wanted his life back, but his life was another universe away. It wasn't a simple thing to just turn around and fix things. He felt like he was drowning, the water barely lapping his nose . . .

And then two things happened at once.

Padma came out of the building, a bag tucked under her arm, just as a white van roared around the corner and screeched to the curb. It blocked his view of her, but nothing about the scene looked good. He considered getting out but realized that by the time he'd make it across the street, they'd already be in motion, and he'd never catch them on foot.

Then a piercing scream and the slam of a door.

He yanked the car into drive and slammed his foot on the gas, just as the van pulled away from the curb.

He considered pulling alongside them and performing a PIT maneuver, smashing the front end of Darnell's car into the vehicle's rear wheel, which would cause it to spin and stop. But it was a van, and it was top-heavy, which meant he ran the risk of the van flipping and Padma being seriously hurt, or worse.

So he stuck to the back of it, and for a moment, it seemed like the driver didn't notice him there.

Then the van lurched ahead. They must have clocked him.

He followed them around the corner. The driver was smart, avoiding the front of the building. Ryan followed, hoping for a red light or a traffic impediment of some kind—something to slow them down.

Whoever this was, it wasn't someone operating in an official capacity.

The van hit a straightaway and picked up speed, and Ryan weaved through traffic, trying to stay on its tail. Ahead of them, a light turned red: exactly the opportunity he needed. He didn't have a gun, but he would do his damnedest to overpower whoever was in there.

But the van showed no signs of stopping as it approached the intersection.

And then it roared through, barely missing a line of cars that spun out to avoid a collision. Ryan practically stood on the brake to halt the momentum of his own car, and it stopped only a few inches from a taxicab.

"Fuck," Ryan yelled, watching the van turn a corner down the block and disappear. He considered trying to follow but knew that by the time he got there, they'd be long gone, and he'd already drawn enough attention.

She'll be okay, Ryan thought, trying to believe it.

He'd just put the car in gear and started to turn the wheel when something exploded.

No, not exploded—another car hit him, sending him careening around the interior of his own car with the sound of screeching tires and groaning metal. His head hit something, he didn't know what, and it spun his vision.

When he came to a stop, he climbed out of the car, instinct pushing him through the pain and the dizziness, to see if someone else had been hurt, but then a body pushed him face-first against the car. He heard the sound of someone spitting out gum, then a harsh voice in his ear: "Stay calm and steady, Crane, and you won't get . . ."

Ryan didn't let the man finish what he was saying. He took advantage of the adrenaline coursing through his system and threw his head back. He heard something crunch, and a yelp, and the hands came off him. He turned to find a hard-looking man with a tangle of dark hair, wearing a black suit and a white T-shirt. He was holding his nose, blood seeping between his fingers.

The man's eyes were full of rage. And something else. Something worse. It was a look Ryan recognized from only a few times in his career, facing down people he was sure would not hesitate to take his life.

So he didn't wait. Didn't give the man a chance to get his bearings. He threw a hard kick into the man's groin—there was no such thing as fighting fair in a situation like this.

The only thing that mattered was surviving.

The man was staggered but then hopped back, putting his hands up in a boxer's stance. He came at Ryan fast. Ryan went to dodge to the left but moved directly into the man's fist. Stunned, he stepped back and absorbed a snappy kick into his midsection, which sent him tumbling to the ground.

His hand came down near a twisted chunk of metal. A piece of one of their cars. He picked it up and spun quick, catching the man on the forearm. The man screamed and stepped back, holding on to his sleeve. More blood. Ryan climbed to his feet and followed it with a quick jab to the man's face and then a hard hook into the side of his head.

The man fell back, and before he hit the ground, Ryan was running. Sirens screamed nearby, and he risked a look over his shoulder; there was another man in a suit, helping his attacker off the ground. There were more behind him, and they were headed his way.

He turned to find a police car, screeching to a halt in front of it. The cops inside scrambled to get out, hands on their guns. The driver looked at him, made a confused face, then asked, "Crane?"

"Yeah." He pointed behind him. "Those guys there. They're trying to kill me."

The other officer drew his gun and pointed it at Ryan's pursuers.

"Freeze!" he shouted.

The cop who was driving pulled out his own gun. "Get clear, and we'll get this sorted out."

"Right, thanks," Ryan said.

He limped toward the sidewalk, listening to the shouts of the men over his shoulders, and as soon as he made it to a safe enough distance, he ran.

JOHN WARD
CNN LIVE FEED, PRESIDENTIAL BRIEFING ROOM

"My fellow Americans, I have a brief statement.

"I know the nation has been waiting to hear from me and the astronauts who traveled to Titan. It has been suspected that the six men and women aboard the *Starblazer* were working with a foreign government to sabotage the mission and funnel important data to an enemy.

"We have now confirmed that this is true. I have asked the FBI to bring the flight crew in for questioning, but they've all fled, and remain at large. If you see them, report them to your local authorities. They are considered dangerous.

"As your president, I will not stand for treason. But it was my mission, and until more facts come to light, I accept full culpability. I'm sorry to say that they tricked me—they tricked all of us. There'll be more information as it becomes available."

DELLA JAMESON
SHENANDOAH VALLEY, VA

Della downed the last of the energy drink and tossed it into the back seat of the car.

After the first five hours of driving, she got nervous about being on the road, so she stopped at a campground and put the seat back, catching a few hours of restless sleep.

Otherwise, she stopped only a few times, for caffeine, or gas, or to switch license plates with cars of similar makes and models as Sean's Nissan. She'd seen that in a movie once, it never occurring to her that she'd someday employ the same move, using a shitty multi-tool in the glove box.

The drive had taken longer than anticipated; she stuck to back roads, avoiding freeways the best she could, and kept the car squarely at the speed limit.

The sun would be rising soon, and all she wanted in this world was to lie down and drift off, but she didn't have a lot of faith that it would happen.

Actually, no, that wasn't true. What she wanted more than anything was to be home—her home, in her bed, with her girls.

Maybe she'd died on Titan—they all did—and this was hell. Some weird afterlife where life just went on, but in the worst way possible. Separated from the ones she loved most, her world spiraling out of control.

The GPS told her to take a turn, and after about a hundred feet, it said she'd arrived at her destination. She climbed out of the car, her eyes struggling to adjust in the darkness, but then she was able to make out a clutch of cars, and beyond that, a cabin. As she approached, a light clicked on in the window, and the door opened.

A silhouette appeared, and then she heard a voice.

"Della?"

Mike. She was flooded with relief at the sound of something familiar.

"It's me," she said.

Mike dashed down the stairs and covered the space quickly, throwing his arms around her, squeezing her so hard she couldn't breathe. The comfort of it broke the floodgates, and she sobbed into his shoulder.

He cried, too, but more quietly. She could just barely feel the shuddering of his body.

They got it out of their system and then looked at each other.

"It's good to see you," Mike said.

"Who else is here?" Della asked.

He paused long enough to make her stomach drop. "You'd better come inside."

She followed him in, up the stairs and into the living room. Ryan was standing at the counter in the kitchen, and Alonso was on the couch, sitting next to a young man she didn't recognize. Alonso smiled and sprung up from the couch, giving her a hug.

"You're here," he said.

"I'm here. That must have been a hell of a drive for you."

Alonso turned and gestured toward the other man. "Della, this is Ethan." He paused, then smiled. "My partner. We drove straight through. Just got in about an hour ago."

Della nodded to Ethan, then accepted a hug from Ryan. Up close, she could see his face: beaten, bruised.

"What happened to you?"

"Got in a car accident, then a fight," he said. "Not sure which one hit me harder. I barely got away."

Then she looked around, hoping to see Stitch and Padma . . .

"This it?" she asked.

"You'd better sit," Ryan said.

Della nodded and collapsed into an easy chair. Ryan put a glass of water on the table in front of her, but she wasn't thirsty, she just wanted to know what was going on, and Ryan didn't make her wait.

"I was in D.C. with Padma. We went to meet her friend, but he was already gone. Looks like someone took him, ransacked his place. We stopped at Padma's to get her laptop, so she'd have her research, and someone grabbed her and pulled her into a van. I tried to pursue them, but . . ." Ryan sighed. "They got away. That's when I was attacked."

Della nodded. Shit. "What about Stitch?"

"We have no idea," Alonso said. "We've been monitoring the email thread, but there's been no update. Ward held a press conference a little while ago and said we're all committing treason. You can still get the death penalty for that. So we're hoping if Stitch isn't here, he's some-where safe, or on the way."

Della leaned back in the seat. "What the fuck is going on?"

"The only thing we know for sure," Mike said, "is that *Ward* knows what's going on. He's doing damage control. It's the only thing that makes sense."

"Agreed," Ryan said. "We know that Padma's ex-boyfriend found something that he wanted us to see. No help there now. But she also said we should try to find that scientist. Stephen Lerner."

"What's the plan then?" Della asked.

Ryan and Mike looked at each other. Clearly this was something they'd already discussed.

"Come morning, we're leaving here," Ryan said. "We have to stay on the move. Sooner or later they'll make the connection to the cabin.

I'm going to call on my contacts in the police department. See if we can't find out more about the white van, and about this Lerner guy. Then me and Mike are going to head out and see what we can find. The rest of you will get somewhere safe and try to find Stitch."

"Fuck that," Alonso said, getting up. "We're not letting you do this solo."

"It's safer if . . ." Ryan started.

"He's right," Della said, leaning forward. "We're all we've got. At this point, we're family. Padma's in trouble, Stitch might be, too, and we're all in this together. End of conversation."

Ryan stared down Della, like he wanted to argue, but then Mike lightly put his hand on Ryan's shoulder. "You'll just be wasting your time," he said.

Then they all turned and looked at Ethan. Alonso nodded and said, "You need to go back."

He shook his head, adamant. "Absolutely not. You're in trouble, and I'm going to help."

"I can't ask you to . . ."

"You're not asking, and neither am I," he said, adding, "besides, having an unrecognizable face along for the ride might be helpful."

Della instinctively nodded in agreement.

Alonso beamed and took Ethan's hand, squeezing it tight.

"All right then," Ryan said. "Let's get to work."

He and Mike broke off, sitting at the table to create a list of supplies and tasks. Alonso and Ethan went to the kitchen, laying out snacks.

And Della took that moment to drift, to rest, knowing, at least, that she wasn't alone.

PADMA SINGH
UNKNOWN LOCATION

Padma paced the confines of the space. It was the basement of a house, but she had no idea where. The windows were so grimy she could barely make anything out, except a vague look at the house next door, which had fallen fallow and was covered in graffiti. She tried screaming through the windows on the first day, but it didn't produce anything. She guessed she was in an abandoned neighborhood.

At least she was comfortable. There was a cot with fresh bedding, plenty of food, and a working bathroom, all of which seemed to have been scrubbed clean before her arrival—she could still smell the bleach. There was a stack of secondhand books and magazines next to the cot, which helped pass the time but didn't exactly blunt the fear and anxiety.

Other than that, the basement was empty. The place had been stripped. She spent the first few hours looking for something to get through the locked door at the top of the stairs, but she came up empty.

So she resolved to wait until her captors returned.

She still had no idea who had taken her. As soon as she was shoved into the van, a hood was pulled over her head. They drove in silence for an hour, maybe two, before she was marched into this place. They stood her at the top of the basement stairs, then the hood was pulled off her head, followed immediately by the door slamming closed.

Sometimes she heard footsteps upstairs, but other than that, it was silence.

Which gave her plenty of headspace—too much, probably—to think about her dad.

He called, but he'd waited to call. He didn't call right when she got back. And Padma hadn't noticed any recent texts from him when she first got her phone, which meant they must be buried farther down the list.

Was he just as disappointed in her here? Could this be related to her branch point? Or was it his?

She pushed the thoughts away. Nothing she could do about it now. She sat on the cot, finished eating the last package of fruit snacks, and reached down to the pile of reading material, selecting an old issue of *National Geographic*. Then she lay down on the cot, ready to read about the journey of the painted lady butterfly.

Just as she was getting absorbed in the article, there was a muffled sound upstairs, like a door opening, and then heavy footfalls across the wood. She didn't think much of it—until the basement door opened.

Padma scrambled into a sitting position as two people—a man and a woman—descended the stairs. They kept their distance, though Padma wasn't sure she could fight them even if she wanted to. She wouldn't know where to start.

They were both young, and a little unkempt—long hair, dirty finger-nails, and looks on their faces like they hadn't slept in days.

"Don't scream," the woman said. "We're not going to hurt you, Padma."

Padma took a deep breath, attempting to soothe her nervous system. Their faces were calm, their body language easy. She didn't feel threat-ened, despite the circumstances.

"What the hell is going on?" Padma asked. "Who are you?"

The two of them looked back and forth, between each other and her. They looked familiar, but she couldn't place it . . .

And then it hit her.

The ecoterrorists. They were the ones who had tried to shoot her and Ward back on their Earth.

She leapt from the cot, moving backward through the space, looking for a place to hide or something to put between them. The woman put her hands up but stayed where she was. "I meant what I said. We're not here to hurt you."

"What do you want?"

"Stephen Lerner," the man said. "You know who he is?"

"Yes," Padma said.

The man nodded. "We're trying to find him. We think you can help."

"Why should I trust you?" she asked.

The woman gave a little smirk and said, "I don't know that you really have a choice right now. But the important thing is, we know you don't belong here. You're not where you're supposed to be, Padma. And we want to help you get back."

"Actually," the man said, "we *need* to help you get back. All of our lives depend on it."

F

BERRYVILLE, VA

"Who did that to your face? Ryan or Mike? I wouldn't put it past Della. I bet she can rumble. And you look like a punk anyway."

The kid had balls. Not that the bluster was helping him much.

F stood at the door of the kid's room—effectively a bare-bones hotel room with a door that locked from the outside. Castle Keep owned the facility, using a network of shell corporations to obscure the connection. It was the first time F had actually been there. This was the kind of work he left to his underlings. But clearly, this required a guiding hand. He had plenty of room for the others here.

Everyone except Crane.

For Crane, he had other things in mind.

"Where are they going?" F asked.

"Where are who going?"

"Your friends, Courtney."

"Stitch," the kid said, pointing a condescending finger in the air.

"Stitch is not a name," F said.

"Neither is F. That's a letter."

F sighed. He wanted to slap the kid.

Really, he wanted to peel off his fingernails to try to extract some answers. No doubt the flight crew was in contact with one another and had probably agreed on some kind of bug-out location. It was the only explanation for how they all got the jump on his men and were able to get away.

"What if I told you that you weren't going to leave this room alive unless you told me what I want to know?" F asked.

Stitch flopped onto the bed, putting his hands behind his head. "Then I would tell you that I haven't slept in days, I am currently suffering from hallucinations and delusions, and whatever information I tell you now would not be useful. Nor am I taking you very seriously because you look like you have three heads. Like Cerberus. I am not a reliable witness."

F's earpiece squawked. "She's here."

"We're going to revisit this," F said, slamming the door and locking it before the kid could make some kind of wiseass comeback. He turned down the hallway and made his way to the lobby, where he found Camila. She had a look on her face so sour, it was clear he would not enjoy a single second of this conversation. F nodded toward the security guard behind the desk. After he'd left the room, Camila said, "I thought you were professionals."

"We are."

"Doesn't look that way."

"We're dealing with a number of individuals who happen to be brilliant. Whatever you did to keep them separated, they figured out a workaround. And Crane . . ."

Camila tilted her head, eyeing F's profound facial bruises. "So Crane did that?"

"What are the next steps?" F asked, ignoring the question.

Camila opened her suit jacket, extracted an envelope, and handed it to F. "Your fee."

"That's not due until we're done."

Camila gave a soft laugh. "We are done. Five people still in the wind. Six, actually, because you didn't bring in that NASA kid, Brett. So now I'm going to find someone who's up to the task."

F winced. This was not good. It didn't matter that what they did was meant to be secretive—word would get around, and then Castle Keep's reputation would be tarnished. Probably beyond repair.

He put his game face on and stepped forward—but didn't reach for the envelope.

"Starting from scratch is going to set you back, and right now, every second counts," he said. "We have eyes on the families. Let us go to them, see what we can find out. As for Brett Turner, I'm working on something."

Camila shook her head. "We're not touching the families. Not yet. We're trying to preserve what little we can of your employer's deniability on this. They'll be questioned through the proper channels."

Then she pushed the envelope forward.

F stepped to the side of it and got even closer to Camila. He didn't want to threaten her—and the reality was, this woman was probably impossible to threaten—but he dropped his voice. "We will do this job. We will get it done. Because I do have something else to share, that I think you might be interested to know."

Camila smirked. "What's that?"

"We knew you were coming up empty here in regard to Lerner, so we expanded our search. We got a hit. He's in France."

"Where in France?"

It was F's turn to smirk. "Wouldn't you like to know."

Camila nodded and put the envelope back inside her jacket.

"Daily updates," she said, then turned on her heel and left the building.

F sighed, thankful it worked out. Because the truth was, it wasn't just Castle Keep's reputation he was worried about.

It was his own.

This whole thing had just become personal, and he was very much looking forward to the next time he saw Ryan Crane.

EMAIL
FROM JOHN WARD

At this point, I may as well let you know that I've got one member of your crew, and the others will be here soon. And I've got evidence that *my* crew never made it to you. Whatever it is you have planned, it's not working out, so I'm giving you one last chance to respond. If you don't—this is war. And I bet the last person you want to fight is an angry version of yourself with the might of the U.S. military behind him. The ball is in your court.

Do the smart thing. It's what I would do.

11

THWAITES

LOUISE DEARBORNE
NEWS1 BREAKING NEWS REPORT

"Scientists have confirmed that a massive piece of Antarctica's Thwaites Glacier has collapsed. The Thwaites has long been referred to as the 'Doomsday Glacier,' because its total collapse could cause a catastrophic rise in sea levels.

"Roughly the size of Florida, scientists first discovered it was losing ice at an accelerating rate in the 1970s. Each year, it contributes to four percent of sea level rise as it sheds billions of tons of ice into the ocean. Its complete collapse could elevate sea levels by two feet, which has the potential to put more than ninety-seven million people in the path of expanding flood areas.

"But the Thwaites also plays a vital role in the stability of the surrounding ice sheets. According to the University of Oregon's Glacier Lab, a complete collapse could destabilize the surrounding sheets, which has the potential to raise sea levels by ten feet, causing catastrophic global flooding.

"The piece that broke off is roughly the size of Rhode Island and is enough to set off alarm bells in the scientific community that a total collapse could happen in our lifetime.

"According to Leslie Dahl, a researcher at the Glacier Lab, her team was shocked at the size of the collapse."

LESLIE DAHL: "We're still struggling to understand how it happened. This is an incredibly troubling thing to see, and we need more data on this immediately. It's as if years of erosion happened overnight."

TO BE CONTINUED . . .

ACKNOWLEDGMENTS

I first want to thank my television agents Ari Greenburg and Ryan Draizin at WME. It never occurred to me that I could somehow write a novel. I pitched *Detour* to them as a TV series—and maybe someday it will be—but they heard the pitch and suggested I first write the book(s).

So I have to thank my WME book agents, Angeline Rodriguez, Jay Mandel, and Mel Berger. They took on a nervous, neophyte author and introduced him to the publishing community. Angeline, in particular, has guided me every step of the way with patience, expertise, and enthusiasm.

Thank you to the very excellent people at Random House Worlds, especially including editors Sarah Peed and Elizabeth Schaefer. I still can't believe you gave me this opportunity. Your thoughtful hand-holding and creative collaboration have been a gift. Thanks as well to production editor Jocelyn Kiker and copy editor Laura Dragonette. Your careful attention to detail—and there were a lot of details—is so appreciated. As is our gorgeous book design by Debbie Glasserman. Additional thanks to managing editor Susan Seeman and production manager Samuel Wetzler.

Thank you to my readers slash note-givers: my parents Sandy and Bill, my in-laws Wendy and Ivan, my brother Gary, and my friends Jake, Ryan, and Nate.

Thank you to my true kitchen cabinet: my wife Paulette and our kids Talia, Evan, Joey, and Becca. For reading, for gently critiquing, for cheerleading, for supporting me night and day.

And of course, thank you to the brilliant, bionic Rob Hart. I have no idea how you do what you do. But I do know that I quite literally couldn't have done this without you.

—JEFF

First and foremost, thanks to Angeline Rodriguez. Angeline was the assistant to my editor on *The Warehouse,* and she was brilliant, bringing an incredible amount of insight and enthusiasm to the project. It was no surprise to watch her climb the publishing ranks to become a superstar agent. One day, out of the blue, she called me about a client who needed a co-writer on a project—and I was thrilled at the chance to work with *her* again.

Then she introduced me to Jeff. You never know how you're going to mesh with someone, but we hit it off like gangbusters. He's a brilliant storyteller and a generous collaborator. I feel lucky to be working on this project, and I'm deeply thankful that he gave me a chance to help him build out this world.

I want to echo Jeff's thanks to our team at Random House Worlds, including our marketing and publicity folks: Annie Lowell, Kay Popple, David Moench, and Lauren Ealy. This was a big, complicated project, and they all did a remarkable job guiding us over the finish line.

Thank you, as always, to my agent, Josh Getzler, for making the trains run on time. And to my daughter Abby, as well as my partner Cyn and her son Auggie, for putting up with the relentless amount of time I spend sitting at the kitchen table with my headphones on.

—ROB

ABOUT THE AUTHORS

JEFF RAKE recently served as creator, executive producer, writer, and showrunner for NBC/Netflix's *Manifest*. He previously developed and executive produced *The Mysteries of Laura*, which aired for multiple seasons on NBC and in more than one hundred countries. His past credits include consulting producer on The CW's *Beauty and the Beast*, TNT's *Franklin & Bash* and *Hawthorne*, and Fox's *Bones*. Rake also executive produced ABC's *Cashmere Mafia* and *Boston Legal*, NBC's *Miss Match*, and Fox's *The $treet*. On the feature side, he has written screenplays for MGM and Disney. He lives in Los Angeles with his wife and their many children.

X: @jeff_rake
Instagram: @reallyjeffrake

ROB HART is the *USA Today* bestselling author of the Assassins Anonymous series, as well as *The Paradox Hotel*, which was nominated for a Lambda Literary Award, and *The Warehouse*, which was translated into more than twenty languages. He also wrote the novella *Scott Free* with James Patterson, the comic book *Blood Oath* with Alex Segura, and the novel *Dark Space*, also with Segura. He lives in Jersey City, New Jersey.

robwhart.com
Instagram: @robwhart1
Bluesky: robwhart.bsky.social

ABOUT THE TYPE

This book was set in Caslon, a typeface first designed in 1722 by William Caslon (1692–1766). Its widespread use by most English printers in the early eighteenth century soon supplanted the Dutch typefaces that had formerly prevailed. The roman is considered a "workhorse" typeface due to its pleasant, open appearance, while the italic is exceedingly decorative.